STAY BACK

Elwood Corbin

Stay Back
Copyright ©2025 Elwood Corbin

ISBN 978-1506-915-04-3 HCJ
ISBN 978-1506-915-05-0 PBK
ISBN 978-1506-915-06-7 EBK

March 2025

Published and Distributed by
First Edition Design Publishing, Inc.
P.O. Box 17646, Sarasota, FL 34276-3217
www.firsteditiondesignpublishing.com

To my sons and daughters,
Each of whom has met each day with grace and courage.

Shakespeare said, "All the world's a stage...."
Yes, but as we watch the players -
some seats are better than others.

PHILADELPHIA
1915

Chapter 1

I can still remember when Mrs. Washington moved on our street. It was a week after I turned thirteen. She had five children; two boys and three girls. The oldest one was a boy about my age. I charged into the house, slamming the screen door behind me yelling, "Momma, guess what! Colored people are moving in down the street where Mr. Kruger used to live!"

She had sent me to Broudy's corner grocery. I stood in the kitchen with the straw market basket on my arm waiting for her reaction. Momma didn't look pleased.

"Keep your voice down," she admonished, taking the basket. "-Colored people?"

"Yes, ma'am, a whole gang of 'em!"

I noticed she didn't scold me for slamming the door.

Momma was tall and thin; she didn't smile a lot. I don't know if I ever heard her laugh out loud. She was lighter than the rest of the family, the color of an Indian. She boasted that her color, straight black hair and piercing black eyes were from Lenape Indian blood.

She set the market basket on the kitchen table and headed for the front door to see the newcomers for herself. I tried to tag along but she shooed me away and closed the door to the vestibule behind her. Since another colored family was moving in on the street, maybe I could play with the boy. I ran to the living room window and looked out.

Momma wasn't the only curious one.

Heads poked out from windows. Housewives stood in doorways silently examining the shabby, horse-drawn wagon piled with shabby furniture in front of Mr. Kruger's vacant house.

It reminded me of that day last winter when we heard a loud noise coming from the sky. People came out of their houses to stare up at the sky. They pointed excited fingers at a strange, noisy thing moving through the clouds.

"It's one of them aero planes!" Mr. Tobin shouted. "There's a man up there flying it."

"- How come it don't fall down?" Mrs. Steinholtz cried, fearful.

"I dunno, but it's an aero plane and a man's up there, too...."

Now they were staring again. No fingers pointing. Curious hostile, eyes searched every inch of the invading horse drawn wagon. To the onlookers' dismay, two black men set about removing one piece of shabby furniture after another and carrying it into the house. Everything was faded and gray. A collection of pots and pans hung from the sides of the wagon.

Five Negro children, shrieking with excitement, raced in and out of the house oblivious to the glare of their new neighbors. The biggest girl wore a dress a size too large; it was pinned at the neck to keep it from falling off.

One of the two horses brazenly lifted its tail and commenced dropping yellow mounds of manure onto the street. It was something that horses were known to do with regularity. But this horse seemed to be doing it on purpose.

Momma seldom voiced anger. She let her beady black eyes and cold silence do it for her. After she witnessed the family moving in, I could tell from the set of her mouth that she wasn't pleased. I think I knew why.

Until that morning, we were the only colored family living on that block. And Momma wanted to keep it that way.

Only recently, Mrs. Steinholtz, our next-door neighbor, was the first white woman on the block who deigned to drop in and have a cup of tea with her. Momma had never been invited into any neighbor's house, so she was delighted for this little show of acceptance from a white neighbor. Momma served tea with her best chinaware.

The entire neighborhood was composed of neat, red brick row houses with limestone steps that were scrubbed regularly to a clean white. Wooden shutters decorated the second-floor bedroom windows. Some people closed them during the night against the "bad night air."

The houses were identical except for a few that had awnings over both the front door and bedroom windows to ward off the summer sun. The sidewalks were paved with brick which were beginning to work loose in places. In winter the streets were quiet and seemed deserted except for a housewife returning from Broudy's corner grocery with her grocery basket in the crook of her arm. There might be a car or two parked by the curb.

Seven colored families were scattered throughout the area. Most of the adults were the parents of my friends - Little Billy Ross, Thomas Jones, Alexander Witherspoon and Steven Purnell. When it was Momma's turn to entertain the other colored ladies, they sat comfortably in the kitchen or living room and agreed with Momma that if more colored people moved into the neighborhood, the white people would get hostile. Especially people like those newcomers. They were marked down as bad news. They didn't look respectable. Their clothing was shabby; they were bound to be loud, ignorant and bring uncouth, countrified ways with them.

Nobody knew that I heard every word because children were always sent from the room when grown folks got together. I was a serious snoop.

My clothes closet was one listening post. There was a hole in the closet floor where a pipe from the kitchen below passed through. I could lie on my stomach next to the hole and hear everything children weren't supposed to hear. Other times I would lie on the floor at the top of the stairs and monitor the living room.

I heard the clatter of tea cups and saucers on the kitchen table. "You mark my words," Momma warned, pouring tea, "it won't be a month before we'll be missing milk from the doorstep and clothes from the clothesline. Then there'll be eight or nine other no-account people moving in with them. Before you know it, there'll be fighting, hooting and hollering and trash all over the street just like it is down there in the Seventh Ward!"

"What I'd like to know," Mrs. Ross protested, "is who in their *right* mind would rent to Negroes like that! When me and Paul moved around here, we had to get Mr. Diebold, the committeeman, to vouch for us, and on top of that, the landlord had the nerve to ask for *three months rent* in advance!"

Mrs. Ross was a stout, tan colored woman with a round face and a small mouth. From the sound of her voice, I knew her plump cheeks were glowing with outrage. I'd heard a dozen times about Mr. Diebold and the security payment. She'd never gotten over the shock.

She went on: "Whoever rented them that house ought to be *whipped!*" There was the *crack* of a whip in her voice. Her plump cheeks must be quivering.

The cast iron lid from a burner of the kitchen coal stove clanged angrily as Momma set it down. I heard a pot placed over the exposed flames. "All you hear from morning 'til night," she complained, "are those children whooping and hollering! They're out there nine o'clock at night! Who ever heard of letting children stay out after dark!"

Mrs. Witherspoon offered her opinion in the quiet way she had of speaking. Like her son, Alexander, she was tall and lanky. "That's 'cause they're no-account, Gert, plain and simple. People like that *always* make it bad for the rest of us. God forgive me for saying it, but if they're going to run colored away, they're the ones who should be run off instead of that dentist over on Seventh Street."

"Lord, I heard about that!" Mrs. Thomas exclaimed. "Wasn't it awful? And the police never did arrest anybody. Wasn't he a doctor or something?"

"I heard he was a dentist - but what's the sense in shooting an educated, respectable man like that and let people like her stay around here? Not that I approve of harming people - Lord, no, I don't approve of that! But still...."

There was a pause. With the sound of cups and saucers and spoons, I could picture the plate of golden brown, soft, sugar cookies being passed around.

Mrs. Purnell broke the silence. Her name was Inez and she was Momma's closest friend. They both liked to read and go to the library together. She was the youngest and prettiest of Momma's friends.

I liked to look at her whenever she came to the house. She had real smooth skin the color of coffee when you put cream in it, and she had sparkling brown eyes and when she walked her shoes didn't clump-

clump-clump on the floor like the other ladies. She seemed to sort of glide across the floor. And she smelled nice, too.

"I don't know how true it is," Miss Inez began, "but I believe Mr. Kruger rented that house to them just to be mean. They say nobody liked him."

"You think he did it on purpose, Inez?" Momma asked." I never got the feeling he liked colored."

"Sure, he'd do it!" Mrs. Ross broke in, leaving no room for doubt as though her size gave extra weight to her words. "He'd do it just for spite. Didn't like colored *or* white for that matter. That house wasn't vacant a month. They don't even look like they can pay the rent."

"No, but somebody must be doing for them," Momma offered. "They have to eat. You think Mr. Broudy lets her keep a book?"

Mrs. Ross snorted, "No indeed! He won't let you keep a book unless you've been buying groceries there a while. Made us wait three months till he let us buy on credit."

"I wouldn't let her have a book," Mrs. Witherspoon agreed. "By the time Friday comes I can hear her now making excuses for why she can't pay what she owes. You can just look at her and tell. Seventh Ward trash!"

*****

All I ever heard was the "Seventh Ward" this and the "Seventh Ward" that, but didn't we used to live there, and everybody we knew? Now they were saying that the people who lived there talked like they had a mouth full of mush. They said "joe juh" for Georgia, "nan" for nine, "moe" for more, "doe" for door, "wretched" for Richard and a lot of other grammar usage that amused Momma and her friends. I heard them say the people there were poor, loud, "trifling" and they cut each other with razors! Most of them drank until they got drunk and these things made white people think all colored people were like that.

But Aunt Tish lived there. We went to church there and some of Momma's friends lived there. It was confusing. I couldn't ask what anything meant without admitting I was snooping.

*****

Granddad defended Mrs. Washington.

He was Daddy's father. Like the rest of the family, he heard what

7

Momma had to say about "that woman." He was a solidly built man with a full moustache and short beard. For years Granddad had worked as a mailman in the Seventh Ward and felt he knew the Ward better than most. That caused a problem one day.

We were having dinner; he was sitting at the head of the table; Daddy was sitting at the other end. When Momma made a passing remark about Mrs. Washington, Granddad wiped his mouth on his napkin and said, "She probably thinks you're 'hincty' – prejudiced – Gert, because you're lighter than she is.'"

Momma's fork was half raised to her mouth. It stayed there for a second. She put it down and stared at Granddad. "'Prejudiced'? - Me? How can you say such a thing, Dad? Nobody's color ever made any difference to me or anybody else who we know. We're not color-crazy. You should know that!"

I was seated across from her and could see the anger on her face.

He shook his head and said quietly, "I don't mean no harm, Gert, but she doesn't know that. Folks like her were raised thinking about their color. Her parents and everybody else she knew were all raised the same way. My friend, Amos'll tell you the same thing. He was a slave a lot longer than I was.

"Slaves know that light-skinned slaves mostly worked in the 'big house' - servants, cooks and what-not. Ate what the white folks ate while the rest of us 'darkies' had hog's guts, hog's head, pig tails and stuff you wouldn't give a dog. They had better clothes - hand-me-downs – but better than the rags we so-called 'field niggers' wore.

"House slaves were treated better and they knew it. You have to understand, Gert, it wasn't just slavers and his family, and overseers, treating us like dirt; you had the house Negroes acting like they didn't want to have anything to do with you. They were half-white because" - he glanced at me and shrugged. "Some owners even sent one or two of them up North with money in their pockets. You don't have to wonder which ones.

"Our people were raised for hundreds of years being told we weren't worth spit from the day we were born. Folks come to believe it. Who was going to tell us different? It was 'nigger this' and 'nigger that'. Never heard the word 'Negro' 'til they come up here. People speak the way they do because everybody they know speaks the same way. When they kidnapped me and took me down South, folks there couldn't half understand me. Poked fun at me."

By that time, Momma's fork was down for good. She glanced at Daddy who kept his eyes on his plate. She turned to Granddad. "That woman wasn't a slave, Dad," she said quietly. Her tone was still angry. "Slavery was over fifty years ago. Fifty. Most of those people down there in the Ward were never slaves.

"What are we supposed to do, Dad? Act like them instead of them acting like people with some sense? Just let people like that bring us down to their level? You have to notice the difference from when you were a boy, before people started crowding in the city after the Civil War.

"We never grinned and scratched our head or danced on the sidewalk for pennies. People weren't color-crazy, they didn't get drunk in public or curse or fight with razors or get arrested. And unmarried women didn't have...." She looked at me and didn't say anything more.

Dessert was apple pie, but Momma did not have any. The rest of the meal was the sound of tableware clicking on china. I was sent to bed early. After Granddad left, Momma and Daddy argued quietly.

I knew what my father would say. He would remind my mother again that his father had been kidnapped off the street when he was twelve, put in chains and taken down South on the pretext that he was an escaped slave. The *Fugitive Slave Act* made that behavior legal. Granddad escaped six years later and was so scared, he never set foot outside of the house until he was twenty.

Daddy said those six years made him far more of an authority on slavery than people like us who had been free for over a hundred years. Then, too, Granddad's friend, Mr. Amos, a slave from birth, could back him up. I knew Momma would say - what any colored person did in front of white people, that wasn't respectable and dignified, reflected on all of us and gave white people an excuse to say we were inferior.

She was tired of seeing cartoons in the newspapers showing Negroes with thick lips, pop-eyes, grinning and acting the fool. And if they wanted to act that way, they should stay in the Seventh Ward or better yet, go back down South and live on a farm.

*****

It took a couple of weeks before Momma finally got to say - *"I told you so!"*

Yesterday Mrs. Steinholtz, our next-door neighbor, was beside herself. Somebody had stolen a bottle of milk and a loaf of bread from her front doorstep! Eyes narrowed with outrage, she charged up to Officer Collins who patrolled our neighborhood. Grabbing him by his sleeve, and pointing to the newcomers' house, she demanded, "I want them arrested!"

"- Who, ma'am?"

"Those negroes who moved in down the street, that's 'who'! I want them arrested!"

Officer Collins was a tall, young man who affected a moustache to make himself look older. He shook his head in blue-eyed sympathy.

"I'd lock 'em up in a minute if I could, ma'am. I know how you feel, but the law won't allow it. You gotta have proof. You know somebody happened to see anything suspicious?"

"- *Proof?*" she hooted, as though he were a dunce. "*Proof?* What more 'proof' do you need for God sake? Who else would do a thing like that? Nobody else around here would steal a bottle of milk. What more 'proof' do you need? *Do your duty!*"

Despite the policeman's offer to take anybody's word that he or she had seen something suspicious and that he would gladly lock them up, Mrs. Steinholtz slammed her door in his face, impatient with the dullard in a blue uniform.

Chapter 2

The newcomer, Mrs. Washington, was a huge, dark, scowling woman who always wore a faded red rag tied around her head. Her kids were often sent outside at daybreak and collected again around dark.

The youngest seemed to be about five or six. The children varied in color from banana yellow to dark chocolate with shades in between. The only play things they had were a beat-up, red wagon and some marbles. The older kids liked to push the younger ones in the wagon and somehow manage to tip it over precipitating loud howls of pained outrage. One or another of them was constantly running home bawling, "Ah'mo tail what you did!"

On rare occasions, Mrs. Washington was moved to bellow down the street to one of them - "You bettuh git chore BEhine in heah!" But it was never clear what was serious enough to set the woman in motion.

"Who's the father, Gert?" Thomas Jones' mother wondered. "Must be more than one with all them shades of color."

I was snooping again. What she said didn't make sense. People only had one father, and what did their color have to do with anything?

"With trash like that you don't have to ask, Callie," Momma said.

"- At least three? maybe four?"

"I saw somebody go in there the other night; probably the latest one. You know what to expect next."

"What color was he?" Callie asked.

"Dark, same as her, maybe a shade lighter."

"Five is bad enough, but six? Who's doing for them anyway?"

"Lord only knows. Can't be what you're thinking because I don't see that much traffic going in there, and even if there was, she can't be worth more than a quarter!"

"Traffic"? What were they talking about? How could anybody be only worth a quarter? Steven would probably know but I couldn't tell him I was spying on people.

Momma, constantly preoccupied with the newcomers, predicted: "Something bad's bound to happen sooner or later." I could picture her tight lips. "Can't steal milk and bread forever and not get caught. It'll just get worse. People like that just make the rest of us look bad."

"They say it's the boy with the funny name who's stealing," Mrs. Jones offered, setting her cup down loud enough for it to be noticed. Momma offered more tea.

"You mean 'Boo Boy'," she spat the name with distaste. She set the tea pot back on the stove. "Sure, it's him but they can't catch him. He's stealing from all over, not just around here. That woman lets those kids roam the streets and go wherever they please. How can you keep an eye on your children if you let them leave the block and you don't know where they are?"

Boo Boy knew Steven and the rest of us were scared of him. Our folks warned us that he was a bad boy who'd make us join a gang, then we'd be locked up in the penitentiary for ten years for breaking the law.

He was already wearing long pants. We still wore knickers and stove pipes. His ragged cloth cap was raked over one eye and he wore a real ring on one of his fingers. We always kept him at a distance. As soon as we saw him, we'd go into the house one by one so it wouldn't look like we were running away.

He knew we didn't want to be friends with him. He never missed a chance to scare us. Standing at the corner, he liked to ball up his fist and grimly touch it to one eye, then to the other eye and last to his lips. Two black eyes and a bloody mouth. We could always see a faint, pleasant smile on his face. Momma said he had mean eyes. - It never once occurred to us that we were five against one.

He ruined everything for me because none of my friends were allowed to come to my house anymore. If I wanted to play I had to go to theirs. Before Boo Boy, we played marbles on the sidewalk, kneeling beside the chalk drawn circle, balling our fist and using our thumb to propel our shooter into the gleaming mass of marbles in the center of the circle. We did not play keepsies. We hoarded our marbles in salvaged tobacco bags and ignored the taunts of those with stronger thumbs and better aim who wanted to keep the marbles they won. They shot with hard accuracy, sometimes cracking the marbles they hit, making them useless.

"You gotta give me a marble!" the owner would cry.

"Don't neither!"

"Do so!"

Other times we'd race down the street on roller skates, coming to a halt, turning with pumping arms and legs back up the street again, straining not to be last.

One time Alexander punched a hole in the bottom of a tin can, threaded a length of string through it and knotted the end. He gave me the other end of the string. I threaded it through the hole in my can, knotted it and we walked away from each other until the string was taut.

"Hello," he said softly into the open end of his can as I held my can up to my ear. "Can you hear me?" He sounded strange and distant and wonderful. Reversing the procedure, I cried into my can, "Yes!" where upon we immediately began a search for more and more string until we could cry out messages almost half a block away to the envy of white boys watching us.

Now and then we got to play with some of the white kids but they were finicky. They might play with us from time to time but never with more than two of us. They played around the corner on the grassy field of the Lutheran church without fear of smashing somebody's window or breaking an arm on hard concrete.

*****

The Washington kids were loud and fond of throwing things. Once one threw a milk bottle that smashed in the street with an arresting noise. When a marble shattered Mrs. Mann's front door window, Momma said it looked like Mrs. Mann exploded out of her front door. Red faced, she marched four furious blocks to the police station. A "Black Maria" drawn by a team of matched horses was dispatched with an avenging Mrs. Mann seated between two police officers. They all dismounted, the officers helping the older woman down. One of the officers confronted Mrs. Washington's front door with the side of his fist. - *Boom-boom-boom!* He waited a few seconds and then BOOM-BOOM-BOOM!

The door opened cautiously. Mrs. Washinton peered out. She found herself confronted by her aggrieved neighbor, two burly men in blue, and a gathering of hostile neighbors drawn by the awesome sight of the black police van, a thing that had never visited our neighborhood before.

It was street theater. The spectators expected to see the black interlopers dragged bodily from their house one by one and hurled with satisfying thuds into the back of the Black Maria. We watched from our door step.

Eyes round with surprise, Mrs. Washington looked from one police officer to the other. She expressed shock that any of her "churren" would be throwing things on the public highway, and fell to questioning the children clustered around her skirt. She soon flushed out the culprit.

After glaring at the frightened six-year-old miscreant, the policemen shifted their attention to the astonished Mrs. Washington.

"You have to go to court and pay for the damages," the shorter of the two curtly informed her.

"Go to coat! But ah ain't break it," she protested reasonably.

"Neither did I, but it's broke and it's got to be fixed or we're going to have to lock you up!"

"Ah's sorry, Mr. Poleese man, but ah ain't got no money. Ah got all these li'l churrens here to feed an'...."

"That ain't no concern of ours, girl!" his taller partner, standing on the sidewalk, broke in. "You let these pickaninnies run wild, destroying respectable people's property then say, 'Ah's sorry.' You better pay for the damage or you'll spend *ten years* in the state penitentiary!"

Thoroughly alarmed the woman addressed Mrs. Mann for the first time. "Ah's deeply, deeply sorry, ma'am, truly ah is, an' ah swears tuh *Gawd* it ain't nev' gone happen agin! Ah pay, if you jus' let me pay ten cents week! Please, lady, Ah pay. Here's my right han' to Gawd!"

With reluctance, Mrs. Mann and the officers put their heads together and estimated a new window pane would cost twenty-five cents. After a considerable amount of grumbling and recriminations against people who let their children "run wild like dogs in the street," Mrs. Mann agreed to the arrangement. The policemen left to the manifest disappointment of the less forgiving spectators who wanted the Washingtons off their street.

Those who were disappointed, included Momma and me.

*****

This depressed her. Lips pressed together in a hard line, she would peep out the front window, as though -miraculously - the Washingtons would be gone. They stayed, as though to annoy her. Why didn't the woman sweep her sidewalk or get one of those kids to do it? Look at her front door-steps! Black with filth; everybody scrubbed theirs at least once a week. Why couldn't she? She wasn't in the Seventh Ward now. Her brats should be playing in their own backyard or confined to their pavement instead of roaming the streets. And she ought to get that rag off her head!

Momma's state of mind got worse when Mr. Stoltz, who lived at the far end of the block, snapped at me. On my way home from Broudy's grocery store, he was sitting on his front door-steps with his dog. I stopped to pet Sparky, like I always did.

"Get your hands off him and keep 'em off!" he flared. Rudy Stoltz was a big bellied man with drooping jowls like a hound dog. But his eyes were a clear hard blue. He offered no reason for this sudden change. Momma said hostility from the white neighbors seemed to spread. The white kids didn't want to play with me anymore.

Daddy shook his head, confident we were over-reacting. I silently wondered how he would know. He was a butler for a rich family and was away most of the time. He hadn't heard what Mr. Stoltz said to me or how it had sounded or anything else.

"Go along like you always do, Gert," he advised quietly. "People know who we are. Things'll be all right - you'll see."

"No, they won't!" she shouted. Her thin face was fierce with anger. "Even if those people move tomorrow, it won't ever be the same! They changed *everything* coming here with all that screaming and hollering and stealing. They're bringing their loud, ignorant habits with them and won't change. That woman won't even so much as sweep her sidewalk! It's what white people expect out of us; it's what they're afraid of! Everything we've worked for all our lives is being wasted because of them. You saw what happened to that dentist. It wouldn't have

15

happened last year or the year before. I'd move tomorrow but there's no place to go! Where can we go?"

Daddy seemed to reel back from the thunderous storm of her anger. His long, dark face was puzzled. For several seconds he stared, speechless.

They'd forgotten I was there.

"- It'll be all right, Gert," he finally said, watching her face. She turned away from him to the comfort of her anger.

I'd never heard her sound like that before. It didn't sound as though anything was ever going to be all right again, and I wondered what that would mean from now on.

That night I wet the bed for the first time since I was real little. Momma, eyes flashing, opened her mouth to yell at me; but she stopped. Several seconds passed.

"Go take a bath," was all she said.

*****

Her dislike for the Washingtons only hardened after a nasty run in with Boo Boy. He urinated in the alley against our fence. Momma saw him from the window of the shed kitchen where she was washing clothes. Her mouth flew open. Storming to the back door she shouted, "What do you think you're doing, you nasty boy! I'm going to tell your mother. Now you get on home where you belong right this minute!"

"You go tuh hail!" he shot back. Looking over the fence, he fixed her with venomous eyes, then deliberately thumbed his nose at her.

Stunned, mouth open, she stared at him. I did, too. It was beyond imagination. A child would never do that! Her black Indian eyes flashed ominously. Galvanized into motion she dashed out the back door and opened the gate to confront him. I don't know what she expected to do. Take him by the ear and lead him home?

He shocked us both. Standing his ground, churning his balled fists in front of his chest, he snarled, like a growling dog baring its teeth - "I dares yuh to lay a han' on me! Gone, I dee-double-dares yuh!"

I hated him from that second on. Suppose he punched Momma in the face and gave her a black eye or a bloody mouth? What would I do? I hated him because I was scared to death of him, and I was not certain I'd have the courage to protect my mother. I hated him for making me feel helpless.

Momma was astounded by defiance from a child, to say nothing of fists balled to offer violence against an adult. They stood there, three were feet apart. They stared at one another. I watched from the kitchen window, uncertain what to do.

Seized with impotent rage, Momma turned and rushed into the house. She paused to remove her apron and straighten her hair. Then she marched out the front door and up the street to the boy's house, without her hat, her coat or her purse.

I dashed out of the house after her, afraid of what might happen to her. Boo Boy had raced ahead to give his mother his version of events before we got there.

Like Boo Boy, Mrs. Washington was well aware of the animosity directed against her and her children. She probably figured it was one thing when hostility came from white folks; it was about what you'd expect. But when black folks started putting on airs and acting hincty, she had an answer for that.

She filled her doorway, arms crossed, eyes narrowed. Her dark face moody and sullen. She listened to Momma's complaint.

"- What chu so concerned about?" she finally rumbled. "Alley ain't yo's. You 'spect him to pee hisself? If you was mindin' y'own biznis 'stead of mindin' hisn, you wouldn't seen nothin'!"

It was too much. From the sidewalk, Momma stared at the woman. Mrs. Washington glared back. Collecting herself Momma snapped, "No, I don't expect him to wet himself, but I do expect him to go home and do his business in private where we have toilets. After all," she said, as a parting shot, "this is a *decent* neighborhood, not the *Seventh Ward!* We aren't accustomed to *our* children cursing grown people, thumbing their nose, to say nothing of balling their fists up and having a filthy mouth!"

Eyes blazing red with pent up rage, nostrils flaring, the big woman rumbled down to the sidewalk. "Nigguh," she roared for all the neighbors to hear, "don't choo dass put on no airs wif me, you heifer you! Don't choo dass low rate mah churren or I sho give you somethin' to complain about! Ah cut yo' half-yella ass long, wide and deep! Tail me I won't, you hincty bitch you!"

Nigger was a word that should never, *ever* be uttered in the presence of white people.

I know Momma felt real bad to be called, not only that, but bitch in front of our white neighbors. She was half the size of Mrs. Washington but a little taller. She stood her ground. Both tried to stare the other down. Mrs. Washington had her hands on her hips, her red eyes and flaring nostrils were thrust in Momma's face. She was pleased at having publicly "told off" her "hincty" neighbor.

Momma, looking down her nose, pretended to be unruffled and dignified. But I think she must have been close to tears. I knew she was burning with shame and humiliation because I was, too. Boo Boy stood next to his mother, eyeing me with dead, brown eyes.

Momma broke off the staring contest. Squaring her shoulders, she said in a quiet, serious tone, "You touch me and you'll find yourself in the penitentiary where you belong. That's not a threat, that's a promise. And the next time you have a minute, stop by the police station and ask *them* what the penalty is for urinating in public. It might surprise you to know that in *this* neighborhood it's against the law!"

"...'Yure' *who*?" Washington roared back, ready to attack.

"It's the *proper* word for 'pee,'" Momma sniffed, and walked away.

Momma's threats didn't make the slightest impression on Mrs. Washington. She lunged after her but Boo Boy pulled on her arm, whispering something that sounded like "People." Mrs. Washington looked around, suddenly aware of neighbors staring and frowning from doorways and windows. They were witnesses. With her recent encounter with Mrs. Mann fresh in her mind, she reluctantly shuffled back to her house.

On the way home I wanted Momma to hold my hand as she usually did when she took me someplace with her. My friends laughed at me and called me "Baby Boy" but I didn't care. This time she didn't.

She walked home swiftly, erect, her long skirt skimming the sidewalk. I struggled to keep up. She swept into the house leaving me to shut the front door, and went directly to her bedroom where she firmly closed the door.

I knew something real bad had happened and I could comprehend the length, depth and breadth of it. I sat at the foot of the steps, looking up now and then, hoping to see her. I felt abandoned and afraid and ashamed. All because of that black bastard Boo Boy.

*****

About an hour later, Momma came downstairs again. She was silent and when I looked at her face, I thought she might have been crying. I wanted to say something to her, and I wanted to do something for her, but I didn't know how to do anything for a grown person who was also my mother. Maybe I should have yelled at Mrs. Washington for talking to my mother that way, but I could still see the huge woman bearing down like a snorting, dray horse and she scared me. And there was Boo Boy beside her. Anyway, children were not supposed to talk back to grown people.

So I shoveled the ashes out of the kitchen coal stove without being told, and helped in the kitchen anyway I could, and went to bed without being told. I was half asleep when I heard her talking to my older brother, Ned, after he came in from work.

Ned sounded angry and even raised his voice. Momma had to shush him. "No, you won't," she said. In my mind's eye, I could see her shaking her head firmly. "That's exactly what people like her do, Ned. Fighting, cursing, using knives and razors. All you'll do is end up in jail and for what? Don't you ever let people like her bring you down – you hear? Your father always said, 'Don't fight a battle and lose the war.'"

The next day was no better. Momma, walking swiftly, with me beside her, visited one friend after another to recount the incident. First, we stopped three blocks away at Mrs. Ross' house.

"Good God Almighty!" Mrs. Ross shouted, eyes wide, hands covering her mouth. Putting her arm around Momma's waist, Mrs. Ross led her back to the kitchen. I stayed in the living room. "Can't you have her arrested?" Mrs. Ross asked. "That woman threatened you, Gert!"

Mrs. Witherspoon was more cautious. "I think you should just let it go, Gert. I know she'll be thumbing her nose at you from now on, but it would just be your word against hers and where colored folks are concerned, you know the police don't care one way or the other."

Inez Purnell was furious. "Send Ned over there, Gert. He's a grown man! Let her see there's a man in the house."

But Mrs. Jones wondered why Momma was surprised by what had happened. "You said yourself, they'd be trouble the minute you laid eyes on them…"

Two days later Daddy had his day off and got an earful as soon as he stepped in the door with a newspaper under his arm. "You wouldn't believe what happened with that woman down the street!" Momma began. Later, they both reluctantly agreed with Mrs. Witherspoon that Momma had to let it go, and it was the first time that I saw him put his arms around Momma, hold her close, and kiss her.

*****

Boo Boy struck.

Little Billy, with blood streaming from his nose and mouth, had to be rescued by a man who held Boo Boy back while Billy ran away screaming. Boo Boy was a muscular pit bull, we were lap poodles. He was used to street fighting; we were punished if we fought because it wasn't "dignified" or "respectable."

Just a week before, my mother had told Mrs. Ross about the awful things "that black hussy" had said to her and how mortified she had been. Now it was Mrs. Ross's turn to pour out her distress at Momma's kitchen table. Naturally I snooped.

" -Why'd he hit Billy?" Momma asked, placing a teacup on the table before her.

"Billy said the boy just walked up to him and said, 'I heard you been messing with my brother!' Before Billy could even open his mouth, that boy hauled off and punched Billy in the mouth and kept on hitting him. That boy liked to killed him if some man hadn't held him and told Billy to run!"

"Now, that's going too far!" Momma cried. "Have him arrested! Let the police handle him. He belongs in jail!"

"I am, as soon as Paul gets home. It was all a lie. Billy never even saw his brother! We knew the minute they moved here we'd have trouble. They get their filthy ways from her. When we moved around here, we had to get the committeeman to vouch for us and the landlord wanted three months rent in advance."

When Steven and I saw Little Billy, he looked awful. I didn't even want to look at him. His lips were swollen and looked like black, gleaming bananas; his left eye was black and swollen shut. All the skin around his eye was black, too. He was lucky he didn't have any teeth knocked out. He hung his head; he didn't want to look at us.

"- Did they lock him up?" I asked, hoping he'd say yes.

He mumbled through numb lips, "Dey didn't do noughfin to 'im."

It was hard to understand him, but he said that at the police station, the police had asked his mother whether or not he had any witnesses because if he didn't, the other boy could claim Little Billy was the one who had started the fight. They wouldn't know whose word to take. The boys should just shake hands and forget it. Boys were always getting into fights; it wasn't anything to get the police involved with. But if either of them showed up at the station house again, they'd really be in for it.

Steven and I mulled this over while sitting on Billy's front doorstep. I was afraid I might be next and Steven was, too. "Suppose he tries to fight you again?" Steven asked, looking at Billy's disfigured face. "He's bigger than we are."

Little Billy shrugged hopelessly.

"If he bothers you again," Steven advised, "pick up a brick or something and hit him in the head with it and knock him out!"

Billy probably figured, like I did, that fighting back was a recipe for ending up in the hospital.

*****

Deliverance came eight weeks after the family moved in.

Mrs. Steinholtz stood on the sidewalk and knocked on the bottom of our front door. She had grown distant since the Washingtons moved in. To Momma's dismay, she no longer stopped in for tea.

"I thought you ought to know, Mrs. Winston," she announced from the sidewalk, "that the police locked up that boy!"

"Thank God Almighty!" Momma exclaimed, and urged her to please come in, but Mrs. Steinholtz held her position on the sidewalk and explained in a pleased voice that, "The Washington Boy" had accosted Timmy, who lived across the street, and tried to take the money Timmy had collected delivering groceries. Sarah, Timmy's mother, told her that Timmy refused. Then "that boy," who was almost twice Timmy's size, grabbed him around the neck and tried to choke the life out of him! Thank God for Rudy Stoltz! Sarah said he happened to be coming home early from work, and well, sir, - the minute Rudy saw what he was doing to Timmy he rushed right over and caught the boy red-handed!"

"Did he try to fight Mr. Stoltz?"

"Oh, I wish to God he had! God, I wish he had! Rudy Stoltz is a stevedore and he would've beat that little sneak to within an inch of his life! No, sir, when Rudy caught him, Rudy slapped him so hard the boy's knees gave way. Meek as a lamb after that. Claimed he was 'just playing.' Started grinning and tried to shake Timmy's hand and make up, but Rudy says, 'Here, here, none of that, you black devil. You're not to touch him!' That boy's lucky Timmy's father wasn't there. He'd be near dead by now!

"Rudy turned him right over to Officer Collins. Just thought you'd like to know. I know you've had trouble enough with him already."

Then she was gone. In the living room, Momma clapped her hands and let out another, "Thank God!" She clasped her hands together over her chest and whirled around the room a few times, a smile creasing her thin face, her eyes bright with pleasure.

I went to bed with something nagging me. Then little by little I realized that while Boo Boy *was* a black devil and worse - I could call him that - but I didn't want Mr. Stoltz to say he was a black devil.

Chapter 3

The new family wasn't the only thing that had been troubling Momma, though truth be told, things had quieted down since the Washington's two brushes with the law. Now her children played more in their own backyard.

But there was Ned, my brother. He was eight years older than I was so he wasn't anybody I could pal around with. He was just Ned, somebody who dragged himself into the house every evening, tired, dirty and smelly.

Momma worried that he was going to get into trouble sooner or later because he spent so much time in the Ward. He lived with us but often stayed over at Aunt Tish's, Momma's older sister. She and her husband owned a catering business; Ned worked for them on weekends even though he didn't like being a waiter. After work, he often stayed with them.

Aunt Tish was tall, gray and laughed a lot; she wore glasses that slid down her nose. Momma made a point of stopping by her house after church even if it was just to say hello. If we stayed for dinner, we helped clean up.

Once, when we were cleaning up, Aunt Tish smiled at Momma and told her quietly, "You worry too much, Gert. Ned's a grown man now. Why in the world wouldn't he spend time around friends he's known all his life? - Besides, where else is he going to meet girls? Not up there where you are."

Momma was stacking the dishes that she had just dried. "-True, but that's not the point, Tish. He's dissatisfied. He graduated back in 1910 and still hasn't really done anything with his life. I'm worried about him.

I think inside he's angry and he's going to say or do something that he's going to regret."

Ned was lean and tall like Momma and when she spoke of him, there was a certain pride in her voice, as though his intelligence was special and beyond comprehension. I knew he was her favorite. He finished high school and had a diploma, something not everyone, white or black could say.

That prompted Momma, from time to time, to shake her head and say, "It's a pity we couldn't send that boy to college."

He'd gotten one scholarship offer, but it was to a Negro college in Alabama. Momma and Daddy, sitting at the kitchen table, mulled the offer over five or six times as though the offer would change if they read it often enough. They always came to the same conclusion –

Ned would be risking his life in the Land of Lynching to go to a college none of them had ever heard of before. The issue was settled when Ned admitted that he was afraid to go down South.

"They still think we're still slaves," I heard Daddy say. "Lynch us for looking cross-eyed. The NAACP said they lynched 56 colored last year. That's like one a week. Killed one man just because he didn't take his hat off to a white lady, and another who didn't say 'sir'!

"Ned'll say the 'wrong thing' and never even know it was the wrong thing to say. Or he'll do something natural that nobody up here would think twice about and have a mob chasing him."

Momma and Daddy couldn't afford the two-hundred-and-fifty-dollar tuition it would take to send him to a local college. I heard her say that he faced a "bleak future" unless somebody opened some doors for him.

"I'll just have to go to work, Harold," she concluded. "Money's got to come from somewhere. He'll just be considered another 'darkie' barely able to count his pay or sign his name. Look what's happened so far."

"Work? - Like hell you will!" Daddy roared.

Hell? Daddy said a bad word!

"A job doing what, Gert? Scrubbing floors on your hands and knees?"

"No, not scrubbing floors, Harold. I finished school. I can do something besides that. Maybe a sales girl or...I don't know. I'll have to look...."

"Look where? The most a colored woman can do is scrub floors or work in a laundry. Besides, there's not a woman on this street or anybody we know who has to leave her house and go out and work. I'm the breadwinner in this family. I'd be ashamed to have people say you have to work because I can't afford to support my own family!"

"But what about Ned, Hon?"

"We've been through this before, Gert. Rich people go to college. We're not rich. Who do we know - white or colored - who's been to college? Nobody. I told him I could get him on with me but no, that's not good enough!"

"Shhh. Keep your voice down. Let's drop it...."

*****

Meanwhile Ned held down one menial job after another while taking civil service exams in hope of getting on with the post office. Everybody said, "Don't worry, he'll do all right. He's industrious." Next to getting an education, a person had to be industrious to get on. Ned had been being industrious since he was twelve. Momma often recounted how he'd taken a bucket of water and some cleanser and gone door to door asking people if they wanted their front door-steps scrubbed. He charged a nickel.

"Those steps were spotless white when he got done," she'd boast. "That boy was earning as much as fifty cents!"

By accident, when he was fifteen, he had a little "business" among people we knew as a rat catcher. A rat got into our kitchen one day. Momma screamed. We both raced to the kitchen to find her standing on a kitchen chair.

"There's a rat over there!" she cried, pointing to the icebox. "It's underneath!"

Ned didn't know what to do. He looked at the incredible sight of Momma standing on the chair, and then he looked at the icebox. Finally, he saw the open cellar door. He grabbed the kitchen stove poker where it sat beside the kitchen coal stove.

"Get the broom!" he said to me. "Hurry!"

The broom was a lot taller than I was but I lugged it over. Snatching it, he handed me the poker.

"Here," he said. "If it comes your way, hit it!"

He commenced pushing the broom around under the icebox.

25

"Close the kitchen door!" shouted my mother. "Don't let it get in the house!"

As I raced to shut the door, the creature dashed from the back of the icebox directly toward me. I dropped the poker and sprang up on the kitchen table. Instantly Ned hurled the broom at the rat before it reached the kitchen door. The beast spun around and scurried for the cellar door. We heard it thump, thump, thump down the cellar stairs.

What happened after that established Ned's reputation. Once the rat was in the cellar and the cellar door locked, I was sent to fetch Mr. Purnell. He was the husband of Inez, Momma's best friend. Mr. Purnell was the only colored man we knew who worked in an office. He was having supper when I arrived with the summons. A portly man with a disgruntled expression, he was reluctant to leave the table after a day's work.

"Rats are dangerous!" Mrs. Purnell reminded him. "Go on before it bites somebody. I'll keep your supper warm. Go on."

He sent Ned to the corner store for a rat trap. It looked like a much bigger mousetrap. Mr. Purnell set the trap with a piece of bread, assuring us that rats would eat anything, not just cheese. After he left, my mother had us drag an armchair into the kitchen. We wedged it against the cellar door which only had a latch. Confident, we waited till the next day to recover the corpse of the intruder.

The rat had ignored the trap.

Rat poison was fetched. Ned laid it down near the foot of the stairs. The rat strode past it. Ned tried the trap again, this time with a piece of fresh cheese. The animal enjoyed the cheese but did not spring the trap. Ned set the trap so that the slightest jar would release the spring. The beast, after thoughtful inspection, ignored it altogether.

That is when Ned saw the light. It was a mistake, he realized, to make things too easy for a rat. He drove a nail into the base of the trap, tied a string to the nail and hung the baited trap from a pipe in the basement ceiling. It seemed impossible for a rat to get to it and - SNAP - he had a rat.

He even placed traps in cardboard boxes and sealed the boxes. The harder he made it for a rat, the more certain he was of killing it. At five cents a rat, he did not make his fortune, but he became confident that one day he was going to be a successful businessman just like the *Prominent Negroes* he read about in the colored paper. No one doubted him.

"My picture's going to be in the paper just like theirs," he promised with the assurance of youth. "Just wait and see. I'm going to be *prominent* just like them!"

Momma smiled encouragement. "You just need a spark," she told him.

The spark eluded him. Years after he graduated from high school, he either got fired from a succession of menial jobs or he quit. What he needed wasn't a threadbare coat of admiration, but a magic flash of something, a spark. And it came from the most unlikely of places, Mr. Amos, Granddad's friend, who could neither read nor write.

*****

Mr. Amos had been born a slave. He was a good friend of my granddad, Levy. They had fought together in the Civil War. Mr. Amos often spoke, with deep satisfaction, about how he'd run away from his slave owner to join the Union Army so he could kill as many "slavers" as possible. After the war Mr. Amos allowed that one place was as good as another and followed Granddad to Philadelphia.

Sometime when Granddad was invited to Sunday dinner, he'd arrive with Mr. Amos. Mr. Amos, tall and skeletal, hobbled along on a wooden cane. He wore the same olive drab sweater, worn brown coat and baggy black trousers.

They were an unlikely pair. They were about the same age and height, but where Mr. Amos was hobbled, Granddad was erect with strong sloping shoulders and a pugnacious air that said, "Here I come - get out of the way!" He didn't need a cane but carried one anyway, holding it in the middle of the shaft as he swung along.

Mr. Amos didn't care how he dressed; Granddad was always neat, his derby hat rakishly tilted a little to one side. He carried a pistol and never left home without it. I wasn't supposed to know this so I couldn't ask what I was dying to ask – can I see it?

Mr. Amos, with much effort and peevishly refusing help, would descend from Granddad's rented carriage. He'd slowly mount our front doorsteps while wheezing, and join Granddad in the living room. In summer they sat in the back yard under the awning.

Granddad, his full mustache giving him an imperious air, would call for the bottle of whiskey that he kept at our house, and with glasses filled, the two old men complained about the weather, folks today, politicians, prices and brazen young hussies who were too fresh for their own good. Things sure had changed, they agreed. Then one or the other would add, "Gotten worse. A lot worse."

I remember that Daddy didn't care for Mr. Amos because Mr. Amos had a habit of referring to colored people as niggers.

Daddy took pains to hide his dislike. After all, he reasoned, the man had suffered slavery where nigger was all they were ever called. He'd escaped and begged to fight in the Union army. The trouble was the Union Army considered escaped slaves as "contraband," the spoils of war and not fit soldier material. Since "contraband" could provide cheap mule labor, they were put to work, enabling the army to put more white soldiers in the field while at the same time depriving the South of its labor force.

Barefoot, Mr. Amos skulked along behind an advancing colored Union regiment waiting for his chance to fight, declaring he was through doing mule labor. Granddad befriended him and they cooked up a scheme to have Mr. Amos take the place of another colored soldier who was missing. They figured he was dead. If he'd been captured, it was the same difference because the Rebs didn't take colored prisoners alive. If he'd run off, they were doing him a favor by pretending he was still with the army and not a deserter.

The two men figured that the white officers couldn't tell one black man from another. After the officers were done squinting at Mr. Amos, and taking second looks, they were either fooled or quietly went along with the scheme. In the end Mr. Amos took the missing man's name, fought in his place and received his pension.

But he didn't have the clear speech of my parents' Northern born friends. They pronounced their "ing's" and "s's" and didn't say things like "he be" or "ain't." Still, he had undeniable intelligence, a storyteller's gift and a sense of humor that was a welcome relief to the sober demeanor of my parents and their friends. A bit impish, he liked to stir things up with conspiracy theories. That also grated on Daddy's nerves.

"You realize," Mr. Amos once declared after dinner, lowering his voice in furtherance of his favorite conspiracy theory, "they got it fixed so niggers can't even make a living 'less we go to them and beg for a job?"

If we had company, a remark like that would start a flood of anecdotes about being chased off jobs, being beaten up, being denied union membership here or an apprenticeship there.

"...You can be bleeding to death," he assured his listeners ominously, "and you can't even go to the hors'pital 'less they let you in. That's 'cause they's plotting to do away with us. They *scared!* Them folks *be scared to death of niggers!* Yes siree!"

This time, goaded beyond endurance, Daddy let himself be drawn into the sort of engagement he always tried to discourage.

" - Scared of what, Mr. Amos?" he challenged, struggling to keep the irritation out of his voice. "With all due respect, nobody can sit here and tell me those people are scared of us. Scared of what? Is that why their snot-nose kids call us nigger to our face? Why they refuse to serve us in restaurants? You can't even go to a theatre downtown to see a colored man on the stage because they won't sell you a seat, and if you say anything, you'll have a cop's billy club to deal with!"

Mr. Amos heard him out, smiling tolerantly, nodding his head and then declaring blandly, "Might be so, young fella, but they scared all the same. That's why they so mean."

He had a way of injecting race into most of his conversations leaving Daddy frustrated and annoyed.

"For the life of me, Gert," I overheard him complain once, "I just don't understand some of our people. They act like they live in the same house with white people, like they're handcuffed to them day and night and can't get away. They see white people the minute they open their eyes in the morning, they think white people when they go to bed at night, then spend all night dreaming about them. White, white, white - that's all you hear! To listen to them tell it, the only thing white people live for is to sit around all day worrying about us and plotting ways to keep us down."

Momma murmured something soothing.

"I told a fellow once," he said, 'Why in the world would they waste time "plotting" against us? We don't have any money. We don't own any property to speak of. We don't have any Congressmen to speak up for us. I never heard of a colored mayor in my life. We've got no senators, no generals. We don't have an army - when you get right down to it, what *do* we have except a lot of poor folks just out of slavery practically begging, and most of them can't read or write? If white people were so all fired worried about us, all they'd have to do is pass a law and make us all slaves again. Who's to stop them? The folks down South?"

But like a mighty river, Mr. Amos flowed along undeterred, year after year, with secret knowledge exposing white conspiracies. Smiling he informed the company that he kept a rifle by his bedside against the day "they" came to try to take him away. That made me wonder about the pistol that Granddad carried.

I liked listening to Mr. Amos. It didn't matter what he talked about, I just liked the way he talked in his slow faintly amused fashion. His bald head and skeletal face used to scare me, especially when he drew his lips back to grin.

Like a lot of constant talkers, he tended to repeat himself which was good because it was how I learned as much as I did about slavery and the years in which they lived. If the conversation were interrupted one day, I could be sure that sooner or later I'd hear the rest another time. I heard so much that inflamed my imagination, that sometimes I felt as though I'd been born in 1845 rather than 1905 and that I'd lived before the Civil War and during all the years after.

Their past became a part of my reality.

"You see," Mr. Amos said one day, "folks, they come here from Europe, can't speak English as good as me, but give 'em ten-fifteen years and they *rich!* Us colored? Naw, suh, you can't take our folks for example. Other folk just naturally hep each other out, but niggers too jealous an' too color-crazy. I seen it even on the plantation.

"Lawd, don't *never* tell nobody you escapin', 'cause them white fokes catch you for sure! Niggers 'fraid somebody gonna do a little better than they do. They grin an' laugh an' say, 'You right,' then run right to massa tellin' him everything.

"I got whipped 'thout mercy 'cause of fokes like that telling on me. I got scars on my back to this day to prove it!"

"Thick as this," Granddad affirmed holding up a finger. "I seen 'em."

Putting aside his conspiracies, other things he said were true. One of them fired Ned's imagination and changed his life. It was by listening to Mr. Amos at the dinner table that Ned got his spark.

"You gotta git up and git!" Mr. Amos preached between mouthfuls. He commanded us to look at foreigners. First, he pointed out, they got themselves a basket to sell goods. Next time you saw them they had a pushcart so they could sell more goods. When they got themselves a horse and wagon, it wasn't long before they had a store! It was all so simple, he pleaded, looking around the table for understanding. It was so simple that he wondered aloud, "- Why can't *we* do that?"

*****

Without wondering why Mr. Amos had never gotten a pushcart himself, Ned's imagination was fired up. A week later he quit his job carrying bricks. He and Momma put their heads together. He'd always brought his pay home and given her most of it, and she always tucked something aside for him. They counted out the money and Ned straightway rented a pushcart and off he went to Dock Street down by the Delaware River to buy produce and make his fortune huckstering in the Seventh Ward. In time he would become a *Prominent Negro*.

To his dismay being a huckster was a lot harder than Mr. Amos had let on. He found simply moving a push cart was mule work. Dock Street was covered with cobblestones so horses could have sure footing, but when trying to push a cart over the stones, the wheels got stuck in between the stones.

He heaved, hauled, slipped and got stuck on the cobblestones until Momma suggested it might be easier if he pushed the cart along the smooth run of the trolley tracks. It worked but it was still hard work. By persevering, he managed to drag himself home in the evening with money in his pocket.

He made enough to put some aside each week against his dream of getting his own horse and wagon. Confident and emboldened by what he had already achieved, he rented the pushcart by the month. He saw a future, clearly within reach, the glowing success that Mr. Amos had promised. A wagon glowing in forest green with red trim and gold highlights, and a splendid chestnut pull it. And then his store. He'd already decided that I was to help him wait on customers. But he wasn't going to give up his wagon; no, he'd hire somebody to run that for him.

Nobody asked me what I thought of all this.

Anyway, once he had the store, he could think about opening up another one next to it or across the street to sell clothes. After that would come the furniture store. And why not? Didn't Alfred Thomas own ten houses? And everybody knew for a fact that Marshall Stone owned the Jewel Theater in South Philadelphia where the colored people went, and Marshall Stone even had *two* automobiles. Then there was that lady, Madam Walker, who had a factory making hair products for colored ladies. They were *Prominent Negroes*.

But right now, Ned's biggest problem was storing the cart overnight. Nobody would let him lock it up in their storage yard at the end of the day like everybody else was allowed to do. Some merchants were rude and dismissive as though he had no business dabbling in the produce business. He took chances and chained the cart wherever he thought it would be safe until morning, expecting each day to find his livelihood gone. It was risky but he couldn't take the cart home at the end of each day; twenty city blocks each way was too far to travel.

He was clattering down Dock Street with his empty cart one morning, heading for the produce markets, when a little old bearded merchant whom he had noticed before waved him over. This was holding him up. Time was money. What did he want, anyway? Hiding his annoyance, he went over to the man.

"You vant, maybe, to lock your cart up at night?" the bearded man asked quietly.

"Gee, yes, sir, I sure would!"

The little man nodded. "I know, so, you come vit me," he said, leading the way around the side of the building.

Leaving the cart by the curb, Ned followed him, trying to contain his relief and gratitude. Sol Wasserman pushed open a door at the back of the building. He showed him where he could store his cart in the backyard of his dry goods store for ten cents a night, "Sundays free."

Ned was elated. He could have hugged the little man but settled for pumping his arm until Sol Wasserman shooed him away.

Now and then at the end of the day, Ned would stop to chat with Wasserman. Sometimes the little man offered him a glass of tea, but Wasserman was always willing to talk and ask questions. Had Ned finished school? Where did he live? What kind of work did his father do? Did Ned read the newspapers? - No?

"You read," he scolded gently. "For two cents you buy the *Pubic Ledger* newspaper. Read. Smart people," he tapped his temple, "they read the paper. And books, too."

Ned liked him and was flattered by Wasserman's appeal to his intellect. Sure, he agreed, he would buy a paper and read it. Then maybe, he thought to himself, maybe they could even discuss the war in Europe, or how General Pershing was making out in Mexico. Still, a part of Ned was on guard. True, Wasserman treated him like a person but Ned could not help steeling himself to hear the inevitable "boy" slip out or worse. With white people it was always what lay beneath the surface that mattered.

A couple of days after the newspaper advice, Wasserman allowed that Ned was not like "the others." Uh, oh, Ned thought, here it comes. Hadn't Mrs. Steinholtz told his mother that she wasn't like "the others", then distanced herself the minute Mrs. Washington moved in down the street? Momma never hid her bitter disappointment about that. Now Mr. Wasserman was telling him he was not like the "others."

"It's here," the old man told him, tapping his temple. "You tink, you vork hard so tell me this, vhat for you wanna buy a horse and vagon?"

Ned bristled. He didn't want this little man telling him to be satisfied with his pushcart. To strive no further because what he had was good enough for the likes of him.

Spreading his arms, Wasserman pointed out, "You gotta horse, you feed it, a stable you need. - So you look. You got nodding left - just horse manure to shovel. You wanna get ahead, better you should *rent* the horse - let odders feed it! *They* should shovel."

For the love of God! The idea had never once occurred to him! He stared at Wasserman. Then he began shaking his head in wonder that so simple an idea had eluded him. He didn't know whether he should feel foolish or not. Of course, it was better to rent the horse! And the wagon, too. He could not suppress a wide grin. Sol stared back, nodding, eyes gleaming with a mirth of his own that said, "You see, I'm right."

That night at the kitchen table Momma - and Dad who was home for his one day off –wondered why they hadn't thought of it. Sol Wasserman was absolutely right. And that wasn't all. "Suppose the horse got sick?" Daddy said – "You wouldn't even be able to go to work…"

"Or," Momma added, "the horse could die." Then she asked, "Did you remember to thank him?"

"Yes, ma'am, I thanked him and I shook his hand, too."

She was pleased and smiled. Ned had his wagon; he was on his way.

But I knew her well enough to know that what pleased her more than anything was that a white man had singled Ned out and had recognized that her son was not "like the others."

Chapter 4

I finally got to see the Seventh Ward.

That's where Ned and I, with the wagon piled high with produce, went to huckster every day. From out of the blue Momma had told me, "I want you in bed early tonight. Ned wants you to help him on the wagon; he said he'll give you a half dollar."

She made it sound as though I were being presented with a splendid opportunity. Her face lit up when she mentioned the half dollar. I guess I was supposed to jump for joy but I was devastated.

Her brow creased. "...Don't you want to help your brother out?"

"Yes, ma'am," I lied. But I didn't want to ride around all day on a horse and wagon in the hot sun selling stuff. I wanted to play with my friends. I didn't want to have to get out of bed in the middle of the night like Ned did, either. The half dollar he offered didn't make any difference because it wasn't really a half dollar. I knew Momma. She'd take the money, fish around in her purse and present me with maybe fifteen cents.

"We'll save the rest for a rainy day," she'd say with great satisfaction. I knew she would but that wasn't the point. I didn't want to help Ned or anybody else. My half-hearted lie didn't fool her.

"...I thought you'd be glad to help your brother," she scolded, standing over me at the kitchen table. "He's offering you a chance to earn some money, and instead of being grateful you have the nerve to look annoyed! There's nothing in this world worse than a lazy person. If you think all you're going to do is spend the rest of your life playing marbles in the street, you've got another thought coming, mister!"

She seemed to go on forever. I was reminded again that only trashy, no-account Negroes were lazy. I was sent to my room with her favorite command - "Get out of my eyesight!"

Huckstering was rude and crude, I fumed to myself. Why would anybody want to go about the streets yelling at the top of his lungs, *"Sweet po tay uhs - corn - waaahder melon!"* First they tell you never to raise your voice in public, then that's all Ned does. And it was supposed to be all right!

Nevertheless, at five o'clock I was routed out of bed, and sent sullenly with Ned. We took the trolley to the Dock Street wholesale markets. There were stables and places to rent horses and wagons. We got ours and were on our way.

Dock Street was a curving cobblestone street down by the Delaware River. The sidewalks and curbs were jammed with crates and barrels and boxes of all kinds of produce. They were stacked so high that the front of warehouses and stores were half hidden. There were the fragrances of oranges and apples and pears and grapes; the odor of cabbage, corn and tomatoes mingled with the smell of poultry, fish and rotting refuse.

Sounds dominated everything. The rumble of heavy wagons grumbling over cobblestones; the coarse oaths of draymen, the crack of their whips, the exclamations and shouts of "Whoa!", "Gittyup!" and "Gang way!"

Trucks wheezed and rattled, and honked their horns. They sputtered, snorted and stalled to the raucous annoyance of draymen who envied the truck drivers. Pushcarts were everywhere. Like everyone else, we jockeyed for position amid shouted sarcasms, curses, threats, whistles and occasional laughter.

It was a marvel anyone could move in any direction. Everyone seemed to be in each other's way. Defying logic, the situation managed to straighten itself out. Ned finally managed to back his wagon up to the curb, get loaded with produce and go on about the day's business.

*****

The moment we turned the wagon off Fifth Street into one of the dirty, narrow side streets, I entered a different world, the Seventh Ward.

This was the place I'd heard so much about. It was where colored people lived crowded together, sometimes eight to a room in foul smelling, ramshackle houses in danger of toppling over. The side streets and sidewalks were open trash heaps. They were never swept. Filth accumulated day after day. Paper, broken glass, bits of rag, garbage, dead cats, puddles of dirty water carpeted the area.

Until Election Day. "Wait 'til Election Day," people grinned with cynicism. Just before then, the sanitation department appeared. Armed with brooms and wagons, they tried to do in one day what they had not done the preceding year. Soon after, white politicians, trailed by Negro henchmen, brazenly materialized. They grinned shamelessly, and shook hands, and handed out gifts of tobacco. They shared bottles of whiskey with their cynical constituents, and they pretended they were Santa Claus.

Everyday we would turn into narrow streets teeming with people who lived more in the streets than in their stifling houses. The noise was astonishing. Nobody talked. People shouted at each other no matter how close they stood. Their laughter took on the tone of jeering. After a few days, I got over the shock of seeing boys my age smoking cigarettes and grown people ignoring it. Grown people cursed in front of kids, and the kids cursed in front of adults. They used curse words like "shit" and "damn" and "ass" and "hell!"

Once in the street, Ned stretched his mouth wide, threw back his head and shamelessly bawled at the top of his voice - "*HICK KEE! HICK KEE! HICK KEE! RED RIPE WAAA DER MELON!*"

I cringed. *Good God Almighty!* Did he actually expect *me* to do that, too?

"*WE GOT 'TAYTERS, 'WE GOT MAYTERS, CORN 'N YAMS - WAAAA DER MELON! GET YA RED RIPE WAAAA DER MELON!*"

People came out of their houses into the crowded street and bought the things they needed. Ned weighed produce on the spring scale on one side of the wagon, while I clumsily did the same on the other.

Once a wizened, sly looking, toothless man asked Ned what one tomato would cost. He had mean looking, red rimmed eyes.

"I'll let you have two for a penny."

He threw his head back and sneered, "Hail, I git a whole pound for a nickel!"

My mouth flew open. An old man cursing! He even had gray hair!

Ned looked at him calmly for a minute. "What do you think it's worth?"

"Nuthin'! Ain't wuth nothin.' You oughta *give* it to me. You see I'm old. You ain't gonna miss one mayta with all them you got piled up there. You oughta be tryna hep your own color 'stead of cheatin' 'em!"

Ned's jaw clenched. His face did not change but his eyes did. He reached into the cart, found three small tomatoes and said, "Gimme a penny."

"Keep it, it mean that much to ya. Gone 'n keep your got damn maytas!"

"Go on, mister," Ned said, eyes flashing. "Go on about your business. I don't want you here cursing in front of children. You're old enough to know better!"

The red eyed man did not leave though. He had a lot more to say, none of it nice. Ned told me to get up on the wagon. We left him standing there, exulting that he had driven us off.

*****

I never got used to the trash and garbage in the streets, or to the narrow alleys and byways of South Philadelphia. The alleys had names. They were really streets with houses fronting on them. Some of the houses went back to colonial days. It wasn't easy to drive a horse and wagon through the narrow pathways. Mangy, stray dogs sniffed the garbage and refused most of it.

People crowded the streets. No one seemed to have anything to do. Women, resembling Mrs. Washington, leaned out of windows on comfortably large arms, watching the street which for them was like watching vaudeville. They might bawl to a child here or shout to a neighbor half a block away. Shabby men in overalls lounged on corners smoking. They sat on the steps of the nearest house. They grinned and stared at the hips and breasts of everyone else's wife, daughter or mother.

They shot dice, expecting to parlay five cents into a dollar, and angrily brandished sharp razors if they didn't win. Barefooted children raced heedlessly in front of our wagon followed by stray dogs. Everyone was loud, shouting as it were - "Look at me! Here, over here!" Life swirled, smelled, exploded.

It was only when I was older that I fully realized why this was what Momma feared and hated. One by one the colored residents, who were fortunate, escaped the narrow streets and filthy alleys to better themselves. They left behind not only filth, squalor and crime, but something far more important and as elusive as smoke - they rid themselves of the *insidious idea* that colored people must forever be damned to the soul diminishing confines of the Seventh Ward.

They escaped. Scattering to West Philadelphia and North Philadelphia and the far reaches of Lamont, Reading and New Jersey. Some bemoaned the loss of Yesterday. Yesterday was the time before the Civil War. The war's end sent floods of poor, ignorant, illiterate field hands - ex-slaves – into canyons of harsh stone walls, unyielding concrete, bare ground, and into the narrow, enclosing confines of cobblestone city streets.

They brought with them the legacy of three hundred years of slavery. Fear, ignorance, drunkenness, illegitimacy, degradation, superstition, self-hatred, and strange ways.

They had a strange way of talking, as though their mouth were full of mush or their lips were numb. They also ate strange food. Things called chit'lins and hog maws. They prayed to strange gods who seized them and made them dance in frantic gyrations as they flung their arms about; they brought with them sloe eyed girls with frank stares and warm smiles and easy, fascinating ways; they brought yellow-skinned boys with reddish hair, and white featured children with blue eyes and light brown hair.

Beyond everything else, they brought a bottled-up exuberance which exploded and expanded into every corner of the city, and over time, with loud laughter and throaty curses -they would one day render the old timers of Philadelphia, like Momma, irrelevant.

*****

Many of the girls were dressed strangely.

"They're poor," Ned explained. "People take flour sacks and cut out places for the arms and neck to make dresses for them."

There were holes in stockings, patches on trousers, and oversized clothing on a lot of the children. They were like Boo Boy and his brother and sisters who wore oversized clothing. And the Washington children's skin had the gray, ashy, unwashed appearance that I saw now. The boys seemed never to comb their hair which presented a million individual tightly rolled kinks, like rows of minuscule black cabbages.

A dark little girl was staring up at me. Our eyes met for just a moment and without the slightest warning my heart beat a little faster. She had a smooth, heart shaped face and for some reason, I think she was the first girl I had ever really noticed. When she put the three pennies in my hand, I watched her fingers count them out one by one. I watched her when she bent her head to count out the pennies and I caught a glimpse of her young, unshielded, budding breasts. It took my breath away.

From then on whenever we came into her street, I no longer cringed. I searched for her, hoping her mother would send her out to the wagon to buy something. Finally, she did. As she waited her turn, once again I saw her openly staring at me. I pretended not to notice. When her turn came, she fixed me with her eyes which were large, clear and almond shaped.

" -You talk funny," she informed me with disconcerting frankness. Then turning to a girl who was with her, "Don't he talk funny, Jessie?" She pronounced it JAY es SEE.

"He sho do," Jessie agreed amiably, "but he do look matty nah's."

Burning with embarrassment and a little frightened, I didn't know what to say. People didn't talk that way; not with you standing right there in front of them.

"What do you want?" I managed to ask, dry mouthed.

"See!" my little dark girl shouted gleefully. "Don't he talk funny? 'Whot dew yew whant!'" she mimicked.

"What chore name, boy?" Jessie demanded. She was much lighter, the color of a banana. She had hazel eyes and she was a little taller and had the same direct stare as my little dark girl.

" - Aaron," I mumbled sheepishly.

My little dark girl cried, "I ain't never heard no name like that before! Don't you wanna know my name?"

"Her name Junie Mae," Jessie volunteered, grinning. "You wanna know my name? My name Jessie Mae Smith. She my cousin an' we live right over there in that house," she said, pointing.

A large lady standing by the wagon bawled, "Yawl little fresh-pots git on in the house! Young as you is, talkin' to boys fresh! I'm moe tell yo mother soons I see 'er!"

"Ain't it a shame," another lady added. "They gittin' to be reg'lar lil hussies!"

"A razor strop on they behines soon fix that!" the first lady glowered.

Obediently the girls quickly scurried away. I was left confused. I was filled with wonder and echoes of how I felt whenever I saw Junie Mae. From then on, I did not mind getting up at five. I lived only to turn into her street, oblivious to the dirt and the smell and the noise, searching only for the sight of her.

She would appear, always with her chatty cousin, yet it was some time before I could bring myself to say hello. Once, I closed my hand around her fingers as though by accident. I felt a thrill run up my arm that I always remembered. It never happened again. Jessie orchestrated the course of our romance.

"Ooh, I believe he lak you, Junie Mae," she cooed one day.

"No, he don't," Junie Mae grinned, squirming.

"Yes, he do. - Don't you lak her, Aaron?"

Squirming with embarrassment but filled with the pangs of young love, I managed to nod my head, not looking at either of them. This caused a shocked, wide-eyed cry of, "Oooooh!" from Jessie. Then covering their mouth, both girls ran off with gales of giggles and animated whispering.

The next day we had hardly turned the corner, when Jessie, face glowing with mischief, ran up to the wagon and cried out in a loud whisper: "She say you got pretty eyes, Aaron!" Off she ran, giggling to join Junie Mae on the sidewalk. I scrunched down in my seat and tried to pretend I did not hear her. I shot a sideway glance at Ned then breathed a sigh of relief; he appeared not to hear.

I wasn't accustomed to girls who stared at you and asked you point blank questions. Yet, it somehow made me feel that I could actually kiss Junie Mae; I could feel it and began to long desperately to kiss her smooth, dark, glowing face. I think I would have, had there been someplace where I could have run later to hide.

Jessie continued a drumbeat of questions and comments that served as dialogue for the two of us. Not that Junie Mae was shy; she seemed more content with giggling secretly with her cousin and whispering strange girl things in Jessie's ear.

"How old you, Aaron?" Jessie asked, a little more serious than usual.

"Thirteen going on fourteen," I told her, while gazing at Junie Mae.

"She 'leben. She kinda big for 'leben, ain't she?"

I think Ned noticed my little romance. Maybe he stayed a little longer in that street though he never let on that he saw my eyes light up whenever Junie Mae appeared. But he did comment mysteriously once - "If you give anybody anything off the wagon, you'll have to pay for it."

His remark was puzzling until a couple of days later. Jessie in her bold way declared, "You should give Junie Mae an apple 'cause she yo girlfriend." Numbly I selected one and gave it to her somehow feeling it was not quite right. It was a "don't" but I could not identify which "don't" it was. Along with my pals, we all knew the do's and don'ts. We got sick of hearing them.

Don't speak loudly in public; it's not dignified; people will think you're common.

Don't dare sass your elders - Children should be seen and not heard.

Don't say "ain't."

Don't chew with your mouth open. Keep your elbows off the table.

Don't laugh loud in public – act dignified.

Don't yell up and down the street; you're not in the country calling hogs.

Don't ever strike a girl; only cowards do that.

Don't give girls money; girls who ask for money are bad.

Don't ever use curse words; you'll have your mouth washed out with soap!

Don't grin or scratch your head or dance in front of white people. They'll think you're common.

Somewhere hidden in there, the apple was a don't; I just didn't know where.

*****

We were robbed near the end of July.

We'd no sooner turned into Junie Mae's street when three boys in knickers charged the wagon. They grabbed handfuls of whatever they could from the bushel baskets hanging from the sides. Without thinking, I sprang from the wagon and charged after them. "Hey, get back here!"

Ned yelled.

Bystanders whooped for joy. "Run, Lil John!" somebody urged. A man in overalls tried to block my path as I chased after them. I no sooner tore around the corner when I was confronted by five boys in long pants. They grabbed me, tore my money apron off, ripped my pockets looking for bills, and furiously punched me in the face and stomach until I staggered drunkenly across the pavement, dripping blood.

Ned galloped up just as they thundered off whooping with glee, dropping coins as they ran. Men and women, girls and boys, cried encouragement to them as though they were watching a street race. In the excitement, several more boys charged the wagon, grabbing what they could and tossing fruit and vegetables back to people behind them. Grinning people in the crowded street picked up the coins that the boys had dropped.

Ned charged down from the wagon, roaring at them, "Get the hell back!"

Reeling, I felt, more than saw, grinning faces staring at my bloody face with eyes filled with pleasure. I was too wobbly to care. Ned helped me back up on the wagon. The feeling of shame would come later.

Ignoring the jeers of the men and women looking on, Ned slashed the horse forward, headed in the direction the boys had run. "Y'ain't gone ketchum!" somebody cried. After two blocks he reined in, realizing the futility of the chase.

"Son-of-a-bitch!" I had never heard Ned curse before. He handed me his handkerchief to stem the bleeding from my mouth. The fire seemed to go out of him. Glumly we clip-clopped back the way we had come.

"Look!" I shouted, "There's a policeman!"

Immediately Ned perked up. Hurrying the horse forward, he pulled up and blurted, "Some plug uglies just robbed us a minute ago and took stuff from the cart!"

The officer stared up at him for a long moment. "Get down from there, boy!" he ordered brusquely.

Startled, Ned hesitated a moment. The officer reached up, grasped his collar, and hauled him from his seat. As Ned stumbled over the sidewalk trying to regain his balance, the officer took out his nightstick. I watched with growing apprehension, my mouth hanging open.

Still grasping Ned by the collar, the officer demanded, "Where's your license!"

Ned told me to look at the ceiling of the wagon over the driver's seat. Fumbling with haste, I found a piece of paper attached to the roof with thumbtacks. The officer snatched the piece of paper from my fingers, glaring at Ned with unconcealed hostility until Ned lowered his eyes. Finally, he read the document. Turning it over, he scrutinized the back, the front, and then the back again.

Again piercing Ned with cold blue eyes, he ordered: "Show me some identification!"

Ned took his wallet from his pocket and the officer snatched it out of his hand and rifled the contents. He examined the license again, stared at Ned a moment or two longer.

"Nigger, you better get this damn thing off the street before I count to ten, and if I *ever* see you around here again - you're going to wish to God Almighty you never saw a horse and wagon, you hear? - Goddammit, boy, *I said YOU HEAR!*"

"Yes sir," Ned mumbled, eyes downcast.

Chapter 5

Grimly, we headed back to the stable. He never uttered a word or looked at me. Numb with shock and shame, I sat beside him running my tongue over my swollen lip from time to time. I stole surreptitious glances at him wishing I could somehow comfort him but lacking the skill to even try.

At the stable Klinger, the proprietor, regarded him with suspicion. Eyeing first his horse then the half-filled wagon, he bent and began examining his horse for any possible damage, running his hands down his legs, pulling his halter to see how the animal walked. Noticing my battered face, he turned to Ned, "What's the matter? You done already?"

Ned looked at the perpetually unshaven stable owner with flat, dead, brown eyes. "You can keep the stuff on the wagon," he said quietly. "Feed your horses. Give me my deposit back."

They stared at each other for a moment. I tensed, suddenly realizing how tall Ned was, how strong he must be to toss crates of produce around the way he had on Dock Street. He could knock Klinger flat on his back and could have wiped that nasty sneer off that cop's face, too, if he'd wanted.

Sensing his hatred and rage, Klinger didn't call him "boy," and for once he didn't grin and tell Ned that the colored girl across the street had some watermelon waiting for him, and something better than that if he'd just go on over there and act nice. After spitting out a brown stream of tobacco juice, Klinger returned Ned's deposit and led the horse and wagon away.

We didn't take the trolley home. Ned walked with anger and I half ran to keep up, feeling my ripped knickers flapping from pocket to knee where the boys had torn them searching for money. I didn't complain. I felt an overwhelming sense of the awesome injustice that had been done to my brother.

For the first time in my life, I felt a conscious closeness to him. He belonged to me and I belonged to him. I understood then that he was my brother and that I cared deeply what happened to him. Reaching out I grasped his belt so I could keep up with his angry strides, and together we strode with purpose the long city blocks to our house.

I knew that he would never huckster again.

*****

No one ever said it, and I didn't formulate the thought until years later, but society had broken faith with Ned. Society had told him -

"Do the things that I command and you will succeed in life. You must rise early and work diligently, wash your face, shine your shoes, look a fellow in the eye; obey the law and love your nation's flag; finish school, choose a star and follow it, then pray to God and I will serve you well."

He'd done all of those things. He'd plunged his hands into the pools of work only to draw them back reeking from excrement and writhing with pain. What he was left with now was his view that the city's promises represented monstrous, empty, fraudulent idols fit only to be thrown down into the dust and smashed into little pieces.

Momma took one look at his grim face and another at me, beaten and torn, and instantly pulled us both to her for a moment. Then she released Ned's angry, impatient body. She knew the shape of anger and when it must explode and when it must bestride the world and when it must smolder like red, pulsing lava. She let Ned's lava swell and subside in the private reaches of his room. Her other arm held my head against her tall, flat body.

I put my arms around her waist, surprised I could reach around her and hugged her, impressing on my mind, for all time, the feel of her firm body that I would search for in other women throughout my life.

"Who did this to you?" she hissed. Without warning I began to cry like the little boy I felt I was. It felt good to cry, to feel her deep mother comfort, to feel safe and warm. I pieced out for her what had happened. She was bewildered and it echoed over and over in her question –

"Couldn't he see you were *respectable?*"

When my anger and hurt subsided days later, I realized that I would never see Junie Mae again. Maybe she would sit on her front doorsteps with Jessie and wonder whether or not our wagon would appear again. But she would never know how much I cared for her and wanted to see her almond shaped eyes and her smooth dark face. She would never know how much I wanted to touch her girl fingers or how my scalp would tingle under her frank stare. And she would never know anything important about me because there had never been a chance to tell her who I was. Nor would I ever know who she was.

*****

By the simple act of trying to earn an honest living, Ned had brought "trouble" into the house. "Trouble" was another name for reality. "Trouble" was anything that forced us to face racial prejudice; "trouble" was the cat bringing a dead mouse into the house and dropping it at your feet, a thing that must be dealt with like it or not.

Ned brought into question who we were as far as white people were concerned. Were we really a proud, respectable, colored family to them, or just another bunch of ignorant, brawling, indistinguishable niggers?

Daddy was home that night and, during dinner, heard the story from Momma.

"Don't let it get you down, Son," he said, quietly. "You're not to worry about it. We're behind you a hundred percent, but why'd you have to go down there almost near the river? That's the worst part of the whole Seventh Ward."

"Go where?" Ned asked. "You got hucksters all over the city. People know them and wait for them. Mom used to do the same thing when we lived down there; she just bought greens and stuff from Mr. Sam."

"- Well, I wish to God you'd started in with Mrs. Woolman like I asked you to. You'd have been a butler in no time for sure. Except for delivery men, a butler only deals with first rate people, the kind cops tip their hat to. People with money. Position. Education. People who can open doors for you, not shut them in your face. When you got them behind you, it makes you stand a whole lot taller." Left unsaid were the magic words - And it's *dignified.*

Ned took his time answering. Chewing deliberately and without bothering to look up he said, "- I'm thinking of doing something else for a living. I don't want to be a *butler!*" Ned made it sound like something ugly. Daddy winced. "Sick and tired of people treating me anyway they want," Ned snarled. His eyes were narrow and mean. He pushed away his dinner plate.

"They see I'm trying to make a decent living, I'm not stealing, I'm not laying around, I'm not staggering around drunk - what else am I supposed to do!" he exploded. "It's been that way every job I ever had since high school. I've taken civil service tests eight times, and I always pass at the top. Do I ever get called? NO! Because that so-called President Wilson put a stop to hiring colored!

"That's why I wanted something of my own, but I'm not climbing up on another wagon as long as I live so help me God! - Don't worry, I'll find something, but when I get a little money together, I'm leaving this country for good!"

"Indeed you're not!" Momma cried, alarmed, fork poised.

"Never heard such a thing!" Daddy exclaimed, staring at him, and wiping his mouth with his napkin.

"You're part of this family!" Momma declared. "Leave for what? We'll see that you get started again. The Seventh Ward's not the only place in the world!" She glanced at Daddy for support.

"Go where?" he growled. " You can't let some dumb cop run you out of the country. Your place is right here in this house with us!"

But Ned stunned them into silence.

"This is not the first time I thought about it. All you can do here is what they let you do. This is 1917, Daddy! We're not in slavery anymore. It's 1917 and you can't even live unless they *let* you live. They tried to lynch a boy downtown right outside of City Hall yesterday and this is Philadelphia, not Georgia! There has to be someplace better than this. There has to be!"

Nobody was used to hot anger in the house. It was almost like an attack. I didn't know what Momma or Daddy were going to do or say, but then I realized that Ned was a grown man.

He glared over the dinner table at Daddy. "You've just been lucky," he told him. "You got a lot of lucky breaks because you met some nice people. But I'm not you. I don't get lucky breaks. I got a high school diploma that I might as well use for toilet paper! If I was white with a diploma, I'd be working in an office somewhere; but a colored man'll never get anyplace in this country unless he gets a break.

"That Steinholtz boy next door didn't even finish high school, now he's an apprentice making four times what I make. Did you ever see a colored apprentice? No. You have to have a white man behind you to even get a job running a damn elevator. What kind of job can I get? I can't even get on as a waiter or Pullman porter because I'm 'too dark.' Ever notice all of those porters are light-skinned? I have.

"You think I'm going to spend the next 40 or 50 years, day after day sweeping up, shining shoes, shoveling manure, digging ditches – then taking insults from crackers who never finished grade school?

"'Boy this,' 'darkie that!' You got the breaks, Daddy and I can't get 'em, and I'm not hanging around till I end up in jail or worse for killing somebody because I didn't grin!"

The grandfather clock in the hall punctuated the silence. *Tick-tock... tick-tock... tick-tock.*

It seemed a long time before Momma found her voice. Leaning forward, she spoke very softly, almost in a whisper: "...Ned, you can't mean you actually want to leave the United States! How can you leave your family? Where would you go, Son? This is your country, where you were born. This is where you belong."

Daddy shook his head as though to clear it. He sputtered, "You...you can't just pick up like that and leave, Ned!" Groping for reasons, he looked around as though the answer were floating just beyond his vision. Then he announced, as though the very idea were preposterous – "People don't do that!"

That settled nothing. There existed vast and subtle differences among the things that my father, my mother, my grandfather and Ned believed about white people, and how each of them thought of themselves as a Negro.

None of them held white people in awe. Each of them could read and write which was more than a lot of white people could say. Ned and Daddy had attended schools that were mostly white, and they believed that they were as smart as anybody else. Some of their classmates had an edge, but they held the same edge over others.

Sure, there was some name calling but you learned to ignore it. The important thing was that everybody read the same books, recited *"To be or not to be,"* believed the same myths, puzzled over geometry, knew that George Washington was a good guy and Benedict Arnold was a traitor; "ain't" was bad English and you didn't lie, cheat, steal or hit a man when he was down.

Out of this mix, Daddy and Momma saw themselves as God-fearing Americans who just happened to be colored. Daddy rejected Grand-father's bitter belief that a Negro would never be a *real* American whether he begged to die in wars, was a university president or a captain of industry.

But then Daddy had an ally - God. If you truly believed in God, he said, you would feel His Presence right here (placing his hand over his heart). You mustn't let others decide for you the shape of your life while you stand in a corner saying, 'I dare not.' Let God decide for you, not mere mortals. For Daddy, the world was a stage; it was just simply that some people had better seats than others did.

Ned didn't mind that white people saw him as different from themselves. He never expected anyone to pretend that he wasn't. But he wanted to be respected the same way that a foreigner who was different was respected. He hungered most for the hearty fellowship and good opinion of other colored men who could invite him to join the Elks or Masons or Odd Fellows lodge. He wanted to move among them with solid money in his pocket, fashionable clothes on his back, and ideas for investment.

He wasn't about to stoop to pretending to be "Ethiopian" or adopt a phony accent as some colored did in order to escape the stigma of being a Negro. He didn't view being black as a stigma. If life were a stage, he wanted to sit anywhere he could afford to sit, even if it were the best seat in the house.

Nevertheless, he was a pragmatist. You had to be a powerful colored person to get that kind of respect. Somebody like Booker T. Washington or Frederick Douglass or maybe a politician. Still, he didn't intend being left to the mercy of any half-educated white man who came along with half-baked superior airs.

Granddad was a well of bitterness. The well was dug from his experiences as a soldier in the Civil War, and from the degradation and cruelties he had lived through as a kidnapped freeman forced into slavery. He was humorless. Only Amos, who had been his comrade in arms, could bait, tease or dispute him. Grandfather refused to even read the newspapers which he dismissed because: "...There's nothing good in there about us."

He wouldn't join the Grand Army of the Republic or any other Civil War veterans' organization, sneering at the idea of marching in his uniform for Loyalty Day parades. "When I feel like I'm a free man, I'll be leading the parade!" he declared.

These drops of bitterness gathered and formed an acid well. The world might be a stage, but they could keep their damn seats; he was content to skip the show.

The three men had in common only that they were related, and each had a sense of his own worth, and fought to get the price.

Now Ned was challenging everything that Daddy and Momma believed. Daddy, after blurting out that Ned could not simply leave the country, realized how foolish it was to say that. He tried reason and a softer tone.

"Son, we can run but we can't hide. This is your country as much as anybody else's. Don't let people run you off the face of the earth. That was just one cracker cop. Sore because he thought you were making too much money, and...."

"He was mad," Ned snapped, "because I was too excited and didn't say 'please,' or 'sir,' or 'boss man' or some other Goddamn Tom foolery and I'M SICK OF IT!" he yelled, knocking over his chair as he stood up. "Every day I go to that stable and that stupid Klinger's grinning and insinuating that all I'm good for is to eat watermelon, drink gin and worse!

"You know what I think?" he cried, leaning over the table and pinning Daddy with wild eyes. "I'll tell you what I think - I think half these people resent us if we work hard and make something out of ourselves because they're scared we'll think we're just as good as they are! That's what I think. Then they turn right around and claim they despise us because we're too lazy and don't want to work!

"You have to take chances, Daddy, you can't be scared! Leaving this country's not 'running away.' It's just common sense! Finding something better. It's trying to be somebody, and if you're colored you can't do it here! Every time you pick up the paper another Negro's been lynched; it's one a week every week. Where else in the *whole world* does that happen, tell me that?"

Daddy wouldn't give up. "You can't just pick up and leave. What would happen if everybody did that?"

Out of patience, Ned blazed: "Where did all these foreigners come from, Daddy? Tell me that! Where'd they come from? I'll tell you where. They got sick and tired of people beating them, kicking them, spitting in their face, spoiling their women and daring them to do something about it so they left! *They left!* And everybody thinks that's so brave and wonderful. So why the hell can't *I* be 'brave and wonderful,' too? I'm only doing the same thing.

"Negroes run up here from the South for the same reason foreigners run from Europe, but what's so good about the North? They hung a fella in Minnesota and you can't get farther north than that! You just believe there's no place better than here because you've never been anyplace else. I'm not going to let people scare me and tell me that if I sail, I'll fall off the side of the earth! You have to take a chance to be somebody, Daddy, and I'm taking that chance!"

In the silence that followed, Momma sent me to my room. I was surprised I'd been allowed to stay this long. I made immediately for my listening post at the top of the stairs.

Ned was on the verge of tears. I was astonished. He was grown, over 21; he was too big to cry! He apologized for cursing, and Momma tried to soothe him. I could tell she was hugging him; I could almost feel it. I couldn't understand what Daddy said but it sounded soft and kind. They mentioned my Aunt Gloria.

*****

Aunt Gloria was my mother's youngest sister.

They urged Ned to wait. Maybe Aunt Gloria could come and tell him about Europe and maybe South America, too. She had a lot of experience, and had been all over the world. She could even speak French. Let her tell you what it's really like before you go.

In the meantime, Daddy allowed that there were two ways of looking at things - either a glass was half full or half empty. "Things take time, Ned. Right this minute we've got colored doctors, dentists, and lawyers. I can remember when we didn't have any. Your mother can, too. Now we got the Frederick Douglass Hospital, savings and loans, teachers, newspapers. When I was a boy there was none of that.

"What if all those people gave up just because things were a little rough? We wouldn't be as far ahead as we are now. Give it a chance, Son, and give God a chance, too. *Please.* I've had my share of hard knocks; your mother has, too. What black person hasn't? I don't know anything about being 'lucky,' but I'll admit - yes, I've met a lot of decent white people and they balance out the nasty ones. If somebody does something nice for me, I figure it's because I've been nice, too. But when I meet up with prejudice, you know what?" he shrugged his shoulders, "I'm not shocked by it...I expect it."

He paused to let that sink in. I could almost see him nodding his head slightly, a faint smile on his lips as though he knew a secret he was about to tell. "Negroes who get upset about the mean things that white people do, don't act shocked or surprised when a Negro robs them or spits in their face or cuts them with a knife. That's what you should be shocked about, or when color-crazy people with lighter skin than you, want to put on airs because you're darker than a brown paper bag!"

Come to think of it, Ned hadn't had much to say about the plug uglies who robbed our wagon and beat me up. Momma had been the one to excoriate and damn them to her private hell where she made skin sizzle and flesh pop.

Daddy flowed on, trying to give Ned reasons for staying. "White people don't even like each other, Son. Look what they're doing in that war over there in Europe. I read in the paper the other day that they even use Zeppelins to drop bombs on people! Can you imagine that? And they treat German citizens here like they're all spies even if they were born and raised here. That's how white people are, Son. The English pick on the Irish, the Russians pick on the Poles, the Germans pick on the French and they all pick on the Jews.

"...Me, I hope for the best, but I'm prepared for the worst. Every time I leave this house, I can see with my own eyes that white people have all the power. And if you don't have God on your side, Son, you can feel mighty lonely."

Later, lying in bed reliving the anguish and anger, I thought - what about me? Would the same thing happen to me that had happened to Ned?

I'd never heard them speak like that before. They made it sound as though white people were a lot different from us and that a lot of them were not even nice. They had all the power. The kids who I went to school with weren't like that. What about our neighbors? I didn't see where they had "power."

Chapter 6

The argument between Ned and my parents made me remember incidents that had happened in the past. One especially took on a different focus. I was ten years old. I had just returned from school, still in my coat, books in hand, waiting to be told something I needed to know. - "What color am I, Momma?"

Color permeated everything in my life. My parents might be reluctant to discuss race, but color was different. Let Mrs. Witherspoon mention a person who my mother didn't know, and the first question my mother would ask would be: "What color is he?"

"He's brown-skinned."

"Light brown?"

"No, dark, about Martha's color, only about two shades lighter."

People adjusted "shades" in their mind until they felt they had an idea what color someone was. A person could be light-skinned or *real* light-skinned or almost white or a little lighter or a shade darker than this or that person. Maybe it would have been easier to say chocolate color or lemon or olive. Still if anyone said chocolate, somebody would be bound to ask: "Dark chocolate or light chocolate?"

Alexander, Steven, Little Billy Ross, Thomas and I got into an argument about our color one time.

"You're dark," Thomas informed me apropos of nothing.

"I am not!" I cried indignantly. "My mother said I'm brown-skinned!"

"You're not brown-skinned," he told me authoritatively. "Brown-skinned means you're kinda light like Alexander."

"Mark's brown-skinned," Steven told him, coming to my aid,

"because he's the same color as my cousin and my mother said he was brown-skinned."

"I'm light-skinned," Thomas boasted. "You can tell by my hair that I'm light-skinned."

"No you're not!" Billy Ross scoffed. "Your hair's no better than mine. You're just a couple shades lighter than me."

"Why don't you all stop fussing about dumb stuff like that?" Alexander protested. "We're all colored. Period."

"But why do people say we're black," Thomas persisted. "I never saw anybody who was black, have you?"

None of us could say that we had. We looked at the asphalt paving in the street, looked at ourselves and concluded that none of us was remotely black. That was the summer just before school started and I found myself sitting next to Teddy Connor.

Momma was at the kitchen table rolling out dough for biscuits when I asked her about my color. Sighing with exasperation, hands white from flour, she put the rolling pin aside. "Don't you know what color you are, Aaron?"

"Teddy Connors called me a 'black tar baby' in class in front of everybody!" I protested. "He keeps on calling me names, and I don't like it. He called me a 'black Sambo' one time and another time he called me a 'coon'!"

With resignation, she wiped the flour from her hands and taking me by the hand led me over to the kitchen coal stove. "What color is the stove?" she asked.

It was obviously black. She held my hand next to it. "What color is your hand?"

"Brown but he said I'm black," I insisted.

"Look at your hand, Son, are you black?"

"...No," I said, unable to refute her logic though I was not at all convinced.

"If somebody calls you an elephant does that make you an elephant? When people say things that aren't true, you just have to ignore them. As long as you know it's not true, that's all that matters; there's nothing to get upset about."

I wasn't the least satisfied with this. "Can't I call him a name, too?"

"Don't you dare!" she scolded. "People like him are just ignorant. You have to learn to ignore them. Did you tell the teacher?"

"Miss Kelly said I shouldn't be a tattle-tale."

What bothered me more than anything was the malicious grin on Teddy Connor's face when he called me names. The rest of the kids were all right, but they sniggered which just egged him on. He was chubby and had freckles and mean little eyes. The torment would just go on and on with no relief in sight. I took off my coat as instructed and sat down to my cup of tea and a bologna sandwich trying to hide my disappointment in my mother.

She could read my face. "'Sticks and stones may break my bones,'" she recited looking at me seriously, "'but names will never harm me.' Remember that, Aaron. It won't be the last time somebody calls you a name."

Steven had a better solution.

He was my best friend and a lot tougher than I was. His mother, Inez Purnell, and Momma were good friends so he was often at my house or I was at his. People used to say that we looked alike but we both scoffed at the notion. I was a lot better looking than he was and he thought he was better looking than me. When he started wearing glasses, nobody said that anymore.

"He can call me lots of things," I pointed out hotly. "How come there's nothing I can call him?"

"- Why don't you call him a shit-head?" he suggested.

I was horrified. "You know I can't say that! It's a bad word."

He regarded me tolerantly for a moment. "So call him fat behind. That's not a curse word."

"But he's not fat."

"You're not black, either, but you still get mad."

*****

Teddy looked uncertain when I called him a fat behind. No one sniggered, but all eyes turned to him for reply.

"You're still a coon," he retorted, thumbing his nose and wagging his head. He wasn't smiling. Then he added for good measure, "A black coon!"

"And you're a...a roly-poly lard behind, "I replied, sticking out my tongue and thumbing my nose in return. There were a few muted sniggers.

"And you're a nigger!"

His listeners stiffened.

I hesitated, then blurted: "–Shit-head!"

"Ohhhhhh!" went the girls while the boys sniggered. Face red, my tormentor hurled himself out of his seat and charged up to Miss Kelly who was seated, glaring at the disorderly room. Leaning over her desk he complained, in a loud whisper, that I had cursed at him. Miss Kelly was youngish with brown hair which she kept in a tight bun. A little plump, her eyes widened for a second before searching me out. She summoned me to her desk monitoring my every step. The class leaned in, delighted to have their day enlivened with a bit of theater.

Her glare swept the room. "Silence!" she commanded. "Since you're acting like children, you're to fold your hands on your desk this minute."

Without hesitation six rows of hands collapsed in the center of each desk.

Free of disturbance, she pinioned me with her eyes. They were blue. "Did you use a curse word in here?" she demanded.

"He called me...."

"That's not what you were asked! Did you use a curse word? Yes or no!"

"He keeps on call...."

"Shut your mouth! You're not to say another word!"

Turning to Teddy, she elicited a whispered confirmation of the damning statement. Lips compressed with indignation, she swiftly wrote a note, called the tallest girl in class, Kate Gallagher, up to her desk and handed the note to her with instructions to escort me down to Mr. Smith's office.

Mr. Smith was the principal. He was a man given to mustard-colored suits, squeaky shoes and a stern demeanor. The threat of being sent to his office was enough to command immediate compliance from the unruliest pupil.

I was solemnly delivered to him together with the note. Kate was told to wait in the outer office. I stood somewhere between his desk and the door, uncertain and afraid. Seated at his desk, framed by the window behind him, he perused the note. He pursed his lips. His office, like the outer office, was silent. He lifted his head. His eyes were gray behind shiny pince-nez glasses.

"You have quite a filthy mouth, boy," he said distastefully, reaching into his top desk drawer. "Is that what they teach you at home?" He extracted a ruler.

"He called me a 'nigger'."

Rising from his desk, ruler in hand, he loomed over me with an air of offended righteousness. "Hold out your hand."

Timidly I proffered my right hand holding it back as much as I dared. Whack! I was ordered to hold out my other hand. I held it back as much as I dared, arm pressed to my side. Whack! Right hand again. Whack! Left - Whack! Five times on each hand and I absolutely refused to cry though I screamed inside with pain, vividly aware of the monstrous injustice that I was suffering. I stared at him with loathing through tear dimmed eyes. He scrawled something on a piece of paper, and called Kate to escort me back to the classroom.

"Get your books and go home. You're not to set foot in this school again until I've spoken to your father. I'm going to have you expelled. We don't want your kind here."

I saw his eyes again through the shining lenses. He thrust the paper at me. I tried to grasp it but it fell to the floor. Stooping to pick it up, my fingers would not work. Bending, Kate retrieved the note, folded it and tucked it in my shirt pocket. She led me back to class, blond curls flouncing with young girl importance. There she helped me button my coat while the class watched. Miss Kelly's face was inscrutable. I gave her a cold look of hatred.

I mumbled thank you to Kate and left.

*****

"That's what you get for being disobedient!" Momma stormed; her hands white from flour. "Haven't you been told never to use foul language? Didn't I tell you to ignore him? Didn't I? Now he's sitting there like Little Jack Horner while you're the one being punished and dismissed from school!"

She seized my hand to examine it. When I cried out in pain, she flinched. Leading me over to the kitchen sink she turned on the faucet and let cold water run over my hands. I cringed, fighting the urge to whimper. I was never sure what happened next but I found myself sitting on a kitchen chair, staring at the dough she had been rolling and the rolling pin. I saw her apron flung over another chair. It was an angry apron which inexplicably made sense to me.

She reappeared in her good button up shoes and best navy-blue dress with the white collar. She put on her coat and hat against the chilly March wind. Taking me by the wrist, she strode purposefully the six blocks to the school.

The school secretary looked up. Her eyes were questioning. She was short, thin and timid looking. Her hair was beginning to gray around the edges.

"Good afternoon," Momma said. "I understand the principal wants to see me about my child. He was sent home an hour ago."

The secretary went into the principal's office. His door was open. There was an inaudible exchange. She seemed to hesitate then came back.

"-I'm sorry, Mrs. Winston," she smiled apologetically, "Mr. Smith said you'll have to come back when he's not busy."

"May I ask when will that be? This is urgent. I'm willing to wait. The note said 'immediately.' I'm here and I'd appreciate the courtesy of being seen."

She was hesitant and didn't seem to know which way to look. Finally, with a sigh she returned to the principal's office only to return almost at once. She smiled weakly, shaking her head in sympathy. "-I'm afraid Mr. Smith can't see anyone today, Mrs. Winston but..."

To her astonishment my mother, who was twice her size, swept past her and charged straight into the principal's office partially closing the door behind her. There was an instant clash of voices.

"How *dare* you barge in here like that!" he roared. "What do you think you're doing? You were specifically instructed by my secretary to go home!"

Momma never shouts when she gets angry. She speaks in a low, menacing voice. Her lips are stiff and barely move. But we could hear every word she said.

"Don't you 'How-dare-me!' How dare *you* brutalize my son then tell me come back at your leisure? What gives you the right to be discourteous?"

"I'm the principal, that's what gives the right! He's got a vile, filthy mouth and needs to be taught a lesson, that's what gives me the right. I'll not have Negroes like that in my school! He's to be expelled. Now get out of here or I'll have you thrown out!"

"Don't you *dare* speak to me of filth! Don't you dare! 'Nigger' is a filthy word and I'd slap anybody in the mouth who called me that. 'Coon' is a filthy word and so is 'Sambo' yet you let that vile mouth white trash get away with insulting my child day-in and day-out and the second my child opens his mouth you try to lynch him! We're not in Georgia!"

"And you're mighty lucky we're not, girl, because you'd be whipped! You're too fresh! You need to be put in your place and taught a lesson!"

"I'm *Mrs.* Winston to you, *boy*, not 'girl!' And I'll tell you what my place is - it's right here in this country. My grandmother was a full-blooded Indian and we were here long before creatures like you sneaked off the boat and don't you forget it!"

The door was violently yanked open. His face was purple with rage, veins stood out on his forehead. "Out!" he bellowed, eyes bulging, "Out!"

She was taller than he was and stood regal and rigid. At first she refused to move, glaring at him and emanating fierce hatred. Her nostrils flared, her black eyes were slits of venom, her mouth a thin, rigid line. Then she swept past him.

"You haven't heard the last of this!" she flung over her shoulder, leading me away by the wrist out into the bleak March day.

*****

Dr. Samuelson dressed my hands with liquids that stung and ointments that smelled. He bound them lightly with gauze. Then we began an odyssey of first one trolley car after another until we ended at a building with a lot of steps. The halls were dim and cold. At the end of one corridor was a door with *Superintendent of Schools* printed on the glass.

Inside, a secretary whose desk was near the door, glanced up as we entered, then resumed typing. I was curious to see how the typewriter operated but kept very still. Pressed close to my mother, I listened to the click, click, click of the machine. We stood before her desk and waited. Finally, she stopped typing, put a fresh sheet of paper in the machine and resumed typing.

Spying another secretary near a window in the large room, we moved in her direction but the woman suddenly got up from her desk and disappeared into another room. There were other doors in the room. My mother began a slow circuit of the room, examining each door. The typing secretary got up and came over to confront her. She was a robust woman with a flat face, a thin line for a mouth and hard eyes that reminded me of marbles.

"Get back where you belong, girl! You've no business back here."

"How do you know what my 'business' is, girl? Get back to your precious typing."

Like the principal an hour before, her face flamed. "Don't you *dare* take that tone with me, girl! Who do you think –!"

Another voice intervened. It was the woman who had disappeared on our approach. "What do you want, lady? Who do you want to see?"

"I came to see the superintendent on a matter of some urgency."

"Dr. Matthews isn't in. All I can do is leave a message."

"...Perhaps I can speak to his assistant or...."

She shook her head, "There's no one here. You'll just have to leave a message."

Looking around, my mother saw only tall, closed, forbidding doors and no sign that anyone was behind any of them.

"- I'm afraid a message won't do. I can't wait a week to settle this. May I have his telephone number?"

The two secretaries looked at each other. The more civil of the two again shook her head. "We're not allowed to do that. Dr. Matthews' telephone is private."

After a moment of the three of them exchanging hostile, knowing stares, she took me by the wrist and we left.

I felt that she was under attack. People were yelling at her and being mean to her. No one had ever yelled at my mother before except that Mrs. Washington. Now Momma was very angry and no one wanted to talk to her and I couldn't understand why. I wanted her to hold my hand and I wanted to be able to hold hers.

We left the building and stood irresolutely on the pavement for a while. A tall man with gray hair and an important air approached. He was about to mount the steps when Momma spoke to him.

"Pardon me, are you by any chance the school superintendent?"

Curious, he stared at her. "- No, I'm afraid not, Madam. Have you been inside?"

She said yes and then our odyssey resumed. We took one trolley car after another but this time our trip was different - we ended at the train station where we boarded a train.

We got off the train and walked a long time. We passed enormous houses that had driveways leading up to them. Horse carriages passed us occasionally and even a car. We reached a house with a gate. We entered and went to the back of the house. Momma knocked on the door. A maid answered. She was dressed in black and her blonde hair was tucked inside a white cap. She stared, inquisitive.

"- May I see Mr. Winston?"

A puzzled look from the maid. Momma said, "I'm his wife."

Her mouth opened in a silent "Ohh!"

We were seated in the kitchen and Daddy appeared almost at once. His anxious eyes dominated his long, dark face. He appeared to be upset and even more so when a realization struck him.

"You mean to say you walked all the way from the train station!"

As he put his arm around Momma, her chin started to crumble. Quickly he led her away from the eyes and ears of the cook and her staff. I stared after her. Scared and alone I stared dully at a kitchen larger than our living room.

"Here, boy," a large woman in a white apron said kindly, "come sit by the stove and warm yourself."

Once settled, she set a glass of milk before me and a jelly sandwich with thick slices of fresh bread.

*****

With enormous satisfaction Momma told everybody, detail by detail, what had happened. Whenever she did, I was summoned. "Hold out your hands, Aaron, so Mrs. Jones can see."

Armed with proof of the outrage, she would once again excoriate Mr. Smith. "You know what that man had the nerve to say to me?" She turned her mouth down, placed her fists on her hips and snarled – "'You're too fresh! I'm going to teach you a lesson!'" She paused to let that sink in, relishing their astonishment, disbelief and cries of "Lord!" Narrowing her eyes and speaking with rigid lips, she drew herself up, and reproduced her indignation: "Don't you *dare* 'How-dare-me!'"

She assured them that the typing secretary at the superintendent's office was an "insufferable, flat-faced hussy," and God bless Mrs. Woolman who was an intelligent, kind, decent, wonderful woman. She was a Quaker and they were known for being fair.

It turned out that when Dad informed Mrs. Woolman what had happened, she called two of her friends on the school board, "...and Harold said she told them in no uncertain terms that we were *respectable people*, not some riff raff! Well, sir, let me tell you, they called the superintendent right away and told him point blank to get hold of that Smith, even if he had to go in *person*, and to make sure nothing like this never happened again!"

Momma embellished the story as time went on, but it was her reward for a hellish day.

We had gone back to school the next day expecting to confront Mr. Smith, but his door, like a fortress, was resolutely sealed against us. The school secretary was very nice and took us up to my classroom to be readmitted. Miss Kelly listened quietly to the secretary but steadfastly refused to look at either Momma or me. I took my old seat. Teddy was moved to a seat in front of Miss Kelly's desk.

So the days were not all that nice before Mrs. Washington moved on our street. She wasn't the first one Momma had done battle with. It was that I was older and everything that happened afterward stood out. I saw that Ned was right. You did need a white person behind you. The only way Momma got anybody to listen to her was because Dad had a white person behind him.

Chapter 7

Steven was my best friend but he was bound to get both of us into trouble. His advice about Teddy Connors was one example. What if Little Billy had taken his advice and tried to hit Boo Boy in the head with a brick? Momma always said Steven was a bit "too grown" for his age. After the trouble he got me in with Teddy Conner, maybe she was right.

Steven moved to the Seventh Ward a couple of months after he told me what to call Teddy Connor. His father had lost his job and then had been injured. They were destitute. Mr. Purnell was crossing Market Street near City Hall one day when he met with a terrible accident. A trolley car came barreling through an intersection without slowing down like it was supposed to and plowed right into him.

No one could say why he hadn't been killed. There was never any question about whose fault it was. The trolley company paid his hospital bill and gave him two hundred dollars to settle all claims and he accepted it. That dumbfounded everybody. They wondered why in the world he settled for a measly two hundred dollars? And he was left with a limp.

Leonard Purnell used to be an important man. Leonard Purnell WORKED FOR THE CITY. He wore a suit and a tie to work. Since he was a colored man, that was akin to walking on water. Nobody WORKED FOR THE CITY just because he was smart or honest and respectable or even white. No, they said it was a clear signal that you had power and influence. If you were colored, it showed you had a white man behind you which amounted to the same thing.

Momma said Mr. Purnell had doors opened for him because his

father, Roscoe Purnell, was one of Mike Dempsey's henchmen. Mike Dempsey was a city councilman. Both Roscoe and Dempsey were tall, big bellied men. Strutting about in bowler hat and tie, Roscoe's job was to see to it that the colored people in the Seventh Ward voted the right way, which was for Dempsey. Roscoe got them out of jail on Saturdays, shot dice with them on street corners (letting them win a half a dollar or two) and frequently passed around a pint of liquor, being careful to take the first drink. Occasionally he got somebody a job.

Henchman or not, Roscoe was no fool. He delivered votes and the day came when he hinted that if Dempsey wanted Negro votes, it might be time a colored face was seen in City Hall. Dempsey wisely agreed and, with a growl here and a grunt there, prevailed against considerable opposition from other ward leaders in seeing to it that Roscoe's son WORKED FOR THE CITY.

With that Mr. Purnell became a *Prominent Negro*. His picture appeared in the colored paper, The *Tribune*, staring forth in dignified calmness, moustache neatly trimmed, under the headline "Prominent Negro Appointed Clerk."

He went to work each day, his hat tilted slightly on his head. Mr. Purnell was proof to our white neighbors that we colored were well capable of doing more than wield a pick and shovel. He elevated all of us.

Before his appointment, it had been a good-natured question as to whether Alexander Witherspoon or Thomas Jones' father was the more Prominent. After all, Thomas's father owned a barbershop in West Philadelphia. He employed two men, and all his customers were white. Mr. Jones let it be known that he could go to some of them to open a door or two if the need ever arose.

Alexander's father was the *de facto* foreman in a large print shop. He was never called foreman because the white men in the shop wouldn't tolerate "working under a nigger." Yet he could do the work of any two of them and everybody knew it. He could set and read type faster backward than most people could read it forward. But he was a practical man. What mattered most was not being called 'foreman,' but the promise that his son, Alexander, would be taken on as a printing apprentice. He would be the only colored one in the city.

Leonard Purnell's preeminence ended when his patron, Mike Dempsey, florid of face and generous of girth, dropped dead from a heart attack scarcely a month after Leonard's own father, also florid of face and generous of girth, passed away. Unprotected, Leonard was raw meat thrown to hungry lions.

Ward bosses fought snarling battles over who would inherit the right to award Mr. Purnell's patronage job to a more deserving favorite of their own. Devastated, Mr. Purnell found himself out of a job. Then the trolley car accident rubbed salt into the wound.

When he settled with the trolley company, everybody called him a fool behind his back. Daddy, who never talked about his friends behind their back, wondered like everybody else, what had "gotten into" Leonard. Why accept a paltry two hundred dollars after having been nearly killed.

The day of reckoning came when Leonard could no longer pay his rent or put food on the table. Inez Purnell might have to go out and scrub floors or work in a laundry like other colored women did. For a respectable, erstwhile prominent colored man, it was like being stripped naked and forced to walk through the streets.

"- Guess they'll just have to stay with us until he gets on his feet," Daddy concluded somberly.

"...I don't know if that's the best idea, Harold," Momma demurred.

His dark long face got longer. "-They need help, Gert. We can't turn our back on them, now. Suppose it was us?"

Momma held her ground. After criticizing "that Washington woman" for bringing "a bunch of trashy people" into the neighborhood to live crowded in one house - how would it look if she turned around and did the same thing? It didn't matter that Mrs. Washington never did that, - but given time -she would. Nor did it matter that Inez was her best friend. Appearance was what mattered.

"But who's to know, Gert?" Daddy pleaded. "People have house guests all the time. She won't be sitting on the front door steps hootin' and hollerin', gaping and gawking. Who's to know?"

As for Steven and me, we were to play in the house or go visit one of our friends. They would be so unobtrusive as to be nearly invisible. Momma finally gave in but it was half hearted. I clamped both hands over my mouth to stifle my shout of excitement.

Insensible to anything except ourselves, Steven and I wrestled, gleefully slid down the banister, sat astride the arm of the sofa and urged our imaginary horses to a gallop; we muffled our shouts and tumbled our days away. There were walks to the corner and back, arm in arm to show we were pals. We waved away clouds of huge green, face-beating flies that rose from mounds of horse manure lying in the street.

It was a splendid time for Steven and me; we flung ourselves into a world of play and were never at a loss for something to do. The house was never too small, never too crowded, days always too short. We were oblivious to growing tension, to dark clouds of insecurity and to fear that permeated the house. His parents' eyes were haunted. They looked to a future delineated by the soul diminishing poverty of the Seventh Ward.

Once Momma and Miss Inez took us to the library with them. Next door to the library was the Wagner Institute. They took us inside. What I saw astounded me and left a glowing imprint on my mind forever. Skeletons of huge things, ten times bigger than a horse, with teeth as long as my arm.

"They're fossils of dinosaurs," Momma said. "They lived millions and millions of years ago. Their bones were in the ground and scientists dug them up."

Steven and I didn't want to leave. I wanted to stay and examine each creature, each bone, each tooth and stare forever at the drawings of what they might have looked like. Momma and Miss Inez let us stay in the Wagner and the attendant promised to keep an eye on us. He was a kindly looking man with white hair who tried to answer the questions that tumbled out of me. He spoke funny, but I understood him. He explained that men called paleontologists and archeologists were the ones who found the fossils.

"You be but a wee lad and a long way from learning everything, but ask a question and you'll have an answer," he said kindly.

Momma came and led us away. I was still asking questions and puzzling over what a million years was like. After that, whenever she went to the library, I tagged along. I never tired of looking at the fossils, and she took out books for me to read. It was then I knew I wanted to be a paleontologist or an archeologist.

*****

When Steven and his parents moved back to the outer edges of the Seventh Ward, we didn't see each other except for an occasional Sunday when they came to dinner or he was allowed to spend the night. I fooled around with the other boys. We played with single minded energy, vying for dominance, making treaties behind each other's back, forming alliances then breaking them, waging little wars, making peace and doing it all over again, quarreling like the nations of Europe. Often we fell to wishing that we had rifles and could dash off and fight in the Great War that was raging across Europe.

We never realized that photographs in the newspapers never showed geysers of blood profaning the earth. Photographs concealed the man-screams, and hid the insane shrieking of shells about to burst. Photographs and headlines lured boys into dreaming of life lived upon another's pain. But then we were but boys who easily slipped into grown men's wishes but always returned to the imagination of immature boys.

Chapter 8

Steven was more mature than the rest of us. He got in serious trouble about eight months after his family moved away. School had just begun. In a dream, woodpeckers tapped at the legs of my bed. I lay unable to move, knowing the bed would soon give way, plunging me into a void. The wooden frame collapsed. I grabbed the sides, frantic, and then woke up, gasping.

I still heard the woodpecker.

Disoriented, I stared about in the darkness. There! A figure crouched outside my window, tapping. Springing from my bed, prepared to dash for the door, something about the figure arrested my flight. I stared, fear crawling over my skin. I made out the frantic gestures of Steven motioning me to open the window. Puzzled, I threw it open.

"I need your help!" he gasped, sobbing, snot running from his nose. His eyes were wild with terror.

"Shhhh!" I warned. "Wait'll I get dressed!" I never questioned why he was there in the first place. "Go back down in the yard. I'll meet you!"

I flung on some clothes and stepped out on the roof of the shed kitchen. From there it was an easy drop to the backyard. He was leaning against the house, arms clasped about his chest, rocking back and forth.

"I need your help," he panted. "I need your help, Aaron. Please help me!"

"Shhhhh! Keep your voice down!" I ordered, glancing at the darkened windows staring at us. I made him squat next to the house, as far in the shadows as possible. He did not have his glasses. He was never without his glasses.

"I... I just killed somebody!" he gasped, close to hysteria, gripping my

70

wrist. "...I'm gonna get locked up!" he blubbered. "I'll get executed! They'll put me in the electric chair!"

"Shhhhh! Keep your voice down!" I hissed, glancing around. "-What happened?"

"Promise you won't tell! You gotta promise," he sobbed quietly. All I saw were the large frightened whites of his eyes.

"I promise."

"You have to cross your heart and hope to die!"

I drew an X across my chest. "Cross my heart and hope to die."

Between half sobbing and half moaning he told me of a girl named Beulah. He'd met her while she was visiting her cousin who lived down the street from him. Whenever he saw her, she was always after him to come and see her. Finally, he said he'd meet her in a park near where she lived. It was a bad part of the Seventh Ward.

She did not sound like a nice girl. He shouldn't have gone. I hesitated to say anything, But I did anyway.

"– What's she look like?"

It was some time before he answered in a shaky voice. "...OK, I guess. Kinda skinny and brown-skinned. Sometimes I can't half understand her. She says 'nat' for night, 'show' for 'sure'...." Beulah was thirteen. She did not wear a brassiere though most girls like her did. He said her tits were big and she let him touch them. She claimed her mother told her it was all right for him to come see her, although only girls much older than her were allowed to keep company.

But she lived in the Seventh Ward. "Why'd you go?" I asked.

" - She...she said she'd give me some."

My mouth flew open. "...For real!" I croaked. "For real?"

No sooner had he shown up to claim his prize, she appeared with a group of boys. Pointing a finger at him, her young face vindictive, she announced in a shrill voice: "Thas him, Stump! Thas the nigguh. Whippis ass, Stump!"

Too shocked to move, Steven was immediately grabbed by two boys. Struggling, he only remembered hands restraining him.

"Whippis ass!" Stump commanded. He was muscular and bigger than the others.

Fists were smashing his face and pummeling his body. Feet were kicking him and his glasses flew off or were knocked off in the struggle. His nose was bleeding; he had been punched in the mouth. He was dizzy and terrified.

"Thas enuf, thas enuf!" Stump ordered. "- No, got dammit, don't turn 'im loose! Hold 'im...This meat mine!" Stump said, reaching into his hip pocket. He drew out a straight razor.

Arms pinioned, Steven watched in tears. He'd seen the horrible, raised, gleaming, thick scars razor cuts caused. Stump advanced like a plantation overseer about to punish an uppity slave.

"You one ov them hincty nigguhs think you bettern ev'body else cause you got straight hair, ain't choo?"

Steven hardly understood him. He said Stump spoke like his mouth was full of mush. Steven shook his head wildly in denial, "Naw, not me, not me ain't like that!"

"He lying!" she flared. Her voice had the ring of truth. "He hincty!"

Casually grasping Steven's collar, Stump turned and asked, "Where mus ah cut 'im, Beulah Mae? Tail me, what mus ah do?"

" - I wont choo mess up his face so he won't be hincty no mo. Cut his face up real bad, Stump!"

Incredulous, Steven said he saw that Stump intended doing just that. "Like he wasn't doing anything bad. Like I wasn't even real! And he wasn't even mad at me or anything. He just said, 'Hold 'im still,' and the ones who was holding me kept saying, 'Don't git no blood on me, Stump, don't git no blood on me - '"

He stopped, trying to compose himself. "I don't know what came over me, 'cause all those boys was bigger than me. Some of them had on long pants, but all I know is I flung those boys this way and that and I took off running.

"I never ran so fast in all my life. I could hear the wind whistling past my ears. I don't even know where I ran. I can't see too good without my glasses and it was dark, but I was out of that park in a second and almost got run down by a horse and wagon.

"I know one time they almost caught up to me, but one of them slipped in horse manure and the rest tripped over him so I ran six or seven more blocks.

"Then I didn't hear anybody in back of me. I was just trying to get away, honest to God! - I was walking down the street out of breath, when suddenly Stump jumped out from around the corner and said: 'Gotcha!' I just felt like crying. Wasn't nobody around to help me. He said, 'I dares you to run; go 'head, I dares you to run!' because he said he'd catch me anyhow.

"He was big, Aaron, and real strong. When he tried to grab me, I ducked out of the way. I was too tired to run anymore. He was grinning and said, 'Why'd you run, nigguh?' He'd swipe at me with the knife then say, 'Why'd you run?'

"He was teasing me. He wanted to scare me before he cut me up. I kept yelling, 'Leave me alone. Don't cut me!' but nobody would come to their door and I know people heard me!"

He broke down in pitiable sobs, shoulders heaving rhythmically. I implored him to hush lest the neighbors hear. Exasperated, I grabbed him and clamped my hand over his mouth, whispering fiercely, "Shut up before somebody gets the cops!"

He stiffened. With effort he composed himself. He said he was constantly dodging Stump's knife until he was backed into a corner next to a doorstep. His back was against the wall.

"Why you run an' make me chase you, huh? - Want me to let you go? Huh?"

On the top step of the house were empty milk bottles left for the milk man. Scared to death, Steven said he seized one and smashed it against his tormentor's head. Blindly seizing the second bottle with a speed fueled by fear he smashed that one against Stump's head, too.

Then he ran and ran and ran.

"...But how...how do you know? I mean - *how do you know?*"

"I just know, that's all," he said dejected, resting his head on his knees. "I just know. And they're going to find my fingerprints on the bottle and lock me up in the *penitentiary*. But it wasn't my fault. None of it was my fault. I don't even know him. I never saw him before!"

He had cried himself out. Dispirited, he sat huddled in the dark. We were both too stunned to think properly. The very idea of actually killing somebody seemed too monstrous to contemplate.

I was surprised that he even knew a girl like Beulah. He'd told me so much about what went on where he lived that I shouldn't have been surprised. Still I couldn't fathom his having the nerve to do it to a girl. I stole surreptitious glances at him.

He showed me blood on his trouser leg and blood on his shirt. Stump's blood had spurted out violently from his neck and that was how Steven knew that he was dead. We sat on the ground for most of the night huddled together. He shivered and shuddered violently and I held him close and told him everything would be all right.

"...How come nobody saw all that blood? Didn't you take the trolley to get here?"

"I couldn't get on the trolley looking like this; I had to hitch on the side."

That was very dangerous. I pictured him hanging from the side of a trolley car, his fingers grasping the window ledge, his feet resting on the top of the wheel truck. They say that once a boy hitched a ride on the side of a trolley. The trolley passed a beer wagon parked by the curb. There was maybe a foot of clearance between the wagon and the trolley. They say his blood and brains were smeared the length of the wagon.

We put our heads together and figured that I if I lent him a shirt and a pair of pants, he would be able to travel in public.

"-What about my glasses?"

I lost patience and told him to think up his own lies.

Chapter 9

"How come they didn't lock me up?" Steven wondered. He stayed at my house as often as he could.

We both worried about this, waiting in fear for the police to pound on the door with heavy fists. Nervous, we urinated frequently, precipitating curious glances from my mother.

"...Maybe they don't know what happened yet," I offered.

The trouble with Beulah started because he often refused her invitation to see her. She lived in the rotten core of the Ward. He was too scared of the gangs who banded together at the street corners like ragged sentries barring the way. They roamed the Seventh Ward like wolf packs, cursing, smoking, staring menacingly at strangers, randomly throwing bottles to hear their arresting smash and pouncing on the stray lamb with foot, fist and fear.

I thought he should've been honest with her. He should have told her why he couldn't see her. Evidently taking his repeated refusal as a slap in the face, she set out to punish him for being "hincty" even after he changed his mind.

An appalling thought occurred to me. "Won't she tell on you? She knows where you live!"

"- Maybe she won't tell because she'll be in trouble, too! All I did was try to save my life. All of them were doing something wrong. They're all in it together. I bet that's why the cops didn't lock me up. They're scared to tell because if they lock me up then I'll tell what they did!"

It made sense. They were as scared as we were. He stared at me waiting for my reaction. When I told him that I thought he was right, he let out a sigh of relief.

*****

Stump's fate was revealed in the weekly Negro paper, the *Philadelphia Tribune*. Steven happened on it by accident. His parents had bought the paper to look at the real estate ads. The article was on page three. *THROAT SLASHED WITH BOTTLE; ASSAILANTS SOUGHT*. The article gave Stump's real name as William Jones. He was fifteen and had been in an altercation with a "group of five or six rowdies." who attempted to molest his young cousin. Noble Stump had sprung forward, routed the molesters, pursued them only to be ambushed and slain some distance away.

Assailants Sought. My heart sank. That meant the police were looking for Steven. And for me, too! I had helped him. I looked at him with stricken eyes.

But he was jubilant. "I told you so! Read it. They want people to think a gang of boys bothered her. They don't want anybody to know what really happened!"

It made sense and once again there was a wave of warm relief. That should have been the end of it. But it wasn't. Steven started changing. His parents noticed. Suspecting he was in some kind of trouble, they questioned him. They threatened that they would put him away in a home for wayward boys if he didn't tell them the truth. They made him turn out his pockets, and ordered him to look them in the eye when he talked to them.

Mr. Purnell, now reduced to being a porter and having to send his wife out to work in a laundry, took his uncle's suggestion and had Steven's address changed to ours so that he could go to my school and escape the noxious school environment that they blamed for their son's behavior. He often came back to my house after school and sometimes spent the night. But he still lived twenty-five blocks away.

A couple of months after the thing with Stump, we were sitting at the top of the fire escape in the school yard, scene of our recent cowboy and Indian encounter. The sides of the fire escape were not enclosed. We sat with our feet dangling dangerously over the side. Steven never did get his glasses replaced because his parents could not afford a new pair. He squinted a lot. It gave him a worried look.

Without warning he blurted, "- I'm going to the police station and tell them what I did."

My head jerked around. "- What'd you say?" I croaked.

"My conscience keeps bothering me. That blood spot never did come out of my shirt and I can still see spots on my pants, and my mother keeps making me wear them! I can still see him," he said, looking miserable.

"Half the time I can't go to sleep and when I do, all I do is dream about what happened. When I hit him with the bottle, he dropped the knife and grabbed his neck to try to stop the blood. It was a whole lot of blood, and when I hit him again, his eyes...it was like he was begging me to help him and... and... I didn't!"

His chin crumpled and he began quietly sobbing, his shoulders heaving.

"Shhhh!" I hissed, glancing around, "People'll hear you!"

I was scared again. I felt the same knot in my stomach. If he tells the cops, I'll get locked up, too, since I knew all about it. Why should I get in trouble about somebody like Stump? I hadn't done anything wrong; I didn't even know him. My parents would find out and say that I had lied to them, and that I had been a bad boy.

I flushed with anger. I had never asked him to tell me about this mess. What right did he have to drag me into it? Looking at his miserable, snotty face, I tried to conceal the anger. I hated him. I fervently wished he were dead. If he were dead that would solve everything.

Maybe if I beat him to the punch and told my parents first, it would not be so bad. I could tell them that *my* conscience was bothering me for lying to them. Then maybe if we went to the police station and told on him, that would solve everything.

I couldn't begin to comprehend why Steven, or anyone else, could feel the way he did. At the very least, Stump was trying to cut his face up and leave ugly, raised, shiny scars on him for life. He might even have killed him, especially after he chased him. Was Steven sitting there with his snotty-ass face saying that *he was sorry that he had escaped from Stump?* That's what it amounted to, didn't it? It was becoming difficult to hide my anger. It was then that a solution occurred to me. - I tried to suppress it but then I embraced it.

- If I pushed him off the fire escape, he might hit his head on the pavement below and die.

I didn't know Stump. I did not care in the least what had happened to him. He didn't exist for me. But I did care very much what happened to me. Stephen was sitting on the step below me, legs dangling over the side, his hands lying limply in his lap. His shoulders were slumped in dejection. I could stand and sort of "accidentally" brush him forcibly with my hip. With his hands in his lap, he wouldn't be able to catch himself.

"...Maybe," I suggested, forcing myself to sound calm, "maybe you ought to tell your mother first and see what she says before you go to the police station."

She and Mr. Leonard would be sure to dissuade him. They would be horrified at the very idea of their son going to prison. There was no greater disgrace for a respectable colored family. It was like a daughter saying she was in a family way.

He barely heard me, sniffling and looking glum. Threatened by his impending confession, and drained by going through alternate sessions of relief and fear, I moved down a step and sat beside him.

"You used to say you want to be a doctor so you can help people," I said. "We hardly have any colored doctors now. You can save a whole lot of people - maybe two or three *thousand* people before you die. That's almost a whole army. You act like you want to let all those people die just because of that boy. I'll bet he never wanted to be a doctor or anything else except be a bum hanging around on the corner carrying a knife!

"What did he have a knife for in the first place? You don't carry one; I don't carry one. What do people need a knife for except to hurt somebody else? Momma said only bad, ignorant people carry knives. All they do is get drunk and fight and cut each other up! I never heard of anybody cutting somebody's face up on purpose, did you?

"You have to think about yourself, Steven. You can be real important when you grow up. If he cut you up and you were laying there in the street, he'd be bragging and laughing about the nigger he scared so bad that he peed his pants; and he'd be showing his friends the place where he cut you to death and he'd be talking about how you hollered and begged and cried. That's why he kept teasing you, to make you beg and holler."

Stung, he swung around and flared, "I didn't holler! And who the hell told you I peed my pants! You make it sound like he won instead of me! I thought you were supposed to be my friend!"

I don't know whether or not his anger was the turning point in his attack of conscience, but I felt relieved even though it was directed at me. I pretended to be contrite while examining every inch of his face. A moment later, still angry, he swung around and clumped down the fire escape without looking back.

That was the end of our friendship.

His burst of anger never quite resolved itself. After a while he stopped coming back to my house after school. Maybe it was my fault. Could he somehow know I was prepared to murder him? Had he felt how deeply I had hated him, if only for that moment?

Maybe my guilt echoed in the days that followed, helping to cool our friendship. Yet I convinced myself that I wasn't a bad boy for planning to push him off the fire escape. It came down to my belief that I was worth infinitely more than Stump, and that I should not have to suffer for the evil he had set in motion. Why should I suffer when Steven had dragged me into his mess, and then grown irrational?

Chapter 10

I didn't really get to know my father until he took me to work with him at Mrs. Woolman's estate.

He was not the sort to play with children, but I didn't know anybody's father who did. Fathers came home too tired to walk in the door. Daddy wasn't tired, but working as a butler for Mrs. Woolman kept him away from home except for a day or two in the middle of the week. I knew he cared for me by the way he looked at me and spoke my name; he would squeeze my shoulder or pat me gently on my head as he passed me in the hall.

I did not know his face as well I knew Momma's because I did not look at him the way I looked at her. I saw the corners of her mouth, and the crease between her brows. I watched her lips form words and saw her eyes grow soft at times and hard at others. She spoke quietly.

His employers were accustomed to having servants appear whenever they rang for them no matter the time or season. Without complaint, he traveled with them when they summered in Bar Harbor; he accompanied them for their season in Florida after Christmas, provided, of course, that they had not been delayed in Europe. When the family was at home, we saw him about twice a week.

There was considerably less pressure on him after Mr. Woolman died in 1910. Mrs. Woolman cut back on her activities and, to the consternation of her friends, she gave up her stables. She had never been fond of riding and her children were out of the house. No longer did she sail to Europe or go to Florida for Christmas. She did what she most wanted to do - stay at home; she enjoyed being there.

When Daddy and I got off the train on the way to the Woolman estate, the same automobile that had carried Momma and me away from the house after that arguement with the principal was waiting for us. I remembered the huge kitchen and discovered that the large lady with the bright blue eyes and white apron who had given me milk and a jelly sandwich was the cook.

I was put to work washing windows with vinegar and water, wiping down white painted surfaces with damp rags, scrubbing linoleum floors and sweeping the long walk curving up to the front door. I stood on a ladder and removed cobwebs from the corners of the ceiling. I dusted the edges of picture frames. Exhausted I fell asleep after dinner only to be awakened the next day to do it all over again in another part of the house.

"Mrs. Woolman's very particular," Daddy advised me with serious brown eyes. "She wants everything neat and the floors clean enough to eat off. Do right and you won't find a more decent lady in the world."

I already believed she was a wonderful person because she had been kind to Momma. And that was the first time I remember Daddy speaking to me as a person. Before, I was just someone to be banished when grown people were talking. Now he looked only at me as he spoke; I felt closer, set apart from the rest of the family. Straining for praise, a glance, or a smile - I redoubled my efforts.

"Daddy, can I ask you something?" I was drying breakfast dishes and he was washing them because one maid was sick and the other had the day off.

He looked dubious. "...About what?"

"Do you like being a butler?"

He chuckled. "Indeed I do. Yes-sir-ree-bob. That's how I met your mother. She was a chambermaid - they make the beds, used to empty the slop jars before they got indoor plumbing. They clean and scrub, but they work upstairs. Back then I was a footman which is like a junior butler. Don't find many footmen anymore. Butlers either.

"Used to be two of us. Me and Evans. That's when people had carriages. We'd answer the door, help wait on the table, and after a while I got promoted to butler the same year Frederick Douglass died. Took me ten years. Started working here when I was 14 back in - let me see...must have been 1884.

"A butler runs a house. He's the boss as far as the rest of the servants go. I'm *Mister* Winston; they take their orders from me, even the housekeeper. Only one who won't is the cook, Margaret. She said right off, 'I'll take the job, Ma'am, but I won't take orders from a Negro, butler or not.'

"She wasn't nasty about it, just spoke up. Mrs. Woolman sort of - well, she didn't know *what* to say. I know it took her a real long time to find a new cook because she has to have her food cooked special or she'll get sick. Anyway, she looked at me - 'What do you wish me to do, Winston?'

"I said, 'Hire her.'"

"You see, Son, don't ever try to win a battle then lose the war. What I did made Mrs. Woolman respect me because I put her welfare first and got her out of a tight spot. She turned to Margaret and said, 'Very well, Mrs. Cornell, you are engaged, but Mr. Winston is still my butler in every respect, and he is *Mr.* Winston to everyone in this household.'

"You can't go into somebody's house, Son, with your cheeks puffed out, full of resentment. Being a servant's hard work, but you have to take pride in what you do. It does my heart good to see a table full of polished silver so bright it lights up a room."

He stopped, glowing with memories recent and far, his eyes seeing rooms long lost to sunshine, hearing distant bells summoning him, feeling vanished courtesy bows, anticipating tomorrow and tomorrow and tomorrow.

I digested this though it did not mean as much to me as Daddy thought it did. It wasn't what I wanted to know. I wanted to know why Ned was so set against being a butler. What was so awful about it? I hadn't seen my father do much of anything. Sometimes he wore a long, white apron that never seemed to get dirty.

I did not ask him anything further. He liked being a butler because he liked being a butler and Ned did not. When I was a lot older, I figured that being a butler, and being addressed as Mister Winston, gave Daddy a dignity he could not have gotten anywhere else. It might have been as simple as that.

Best of all was that first Saturday when he called me over and laid a shiny half-dollar in my open palm. It took my breath away. I stared at the lustrous coin before turning my face up to ask, "Is that for me?"

He laughed, "Your eyes are big as saucers. It's all yours. You worked hard for it, Son."

He put his hand on my shoulder and squeezed affectionately. I still remember the deep flush that coursed through me. At the end of August, he told me I could not work with him any longer.

"You belong in school, young fella. Mrs. Woolman's right - education's the only thing that'll get colored people on their feet." He put his hand around my shoulder and gave me a brief hug. "You've been a big help, little fella. I'm mighty glad I brought you."

I wanted very much to hug him back, but I had never done that before and the fleeting moment escaped me. I spent years waiting for a similar moment but it never came. I know now, that is the way of fathers and sons who do not know how to say I love you.

*****

During that summer, I made an important discovery in Mrs. Woolman's house. I was moving some photographs from a glass top table when I paused over a view of colored soldiers standing at attention in two ranks. They were from the Civil War. Three white officers with whiskers stood in the back rank. A colored sergeant, at the end of the front rank, was holding a huge sword. The photograph nagged at me off and on throughout the day. Several times I crept back into the silent library to stare at it.

"Daddy, who are all those colored soldiers in the picture in the library?"

" - Colored soldiers? I never saw a picture of colored soldiers. 'Course, I don't do the cleaning but it seems like I'd notice."

Later that day I was summoned to the library to see Mrs. Woolman. Had I done something wrong moving the picture? I entered the library. She was seated in a chair by the big bow window. My father stood erect behind her. She was a tall, slender lady with white hair, eyeglasses, and a pleasant face.

"Come over here, Aaron," she smiled. When I drew near, watching her face for some clue as to why I had been summoned, she handed me the picture. "You have sharp eyes, young man. Do you recognize anybody in that picture?"

I stared at the faces in Civil War uniforms. Some faces were darker than others. Some men were clean shaven, others bore mustaches. All of them were young and wore serious expressions.

"No, ma'am."

She looked at my father.

"See the man in the second row," he pointed, "third from the right? Do you recognize him?"

I scrutinized the photograph again and shook my head.

"That's your granddad - my father," he smiled. "He was a lot younger and didn't have his mustache then."

I stared at the picture again, but couldn't recognize the man from fifty years ago as Granddad. But since they said he was, I smiled and said, "So that's how Granddad used to look."

Mrs. Woolman was delighted. To think, she said, her blue eyes twinkling, that her husband, the officer on the left, had been in command of the same regiment in which my grandfather - my father's father - had served.

"Matthew loved his 'boys' as he called them. They went through difficult times together during the war. I sometimes think they had a harder time against the Union Army than they did against the Confederates." She shook her head in wonder as distant conversations unfolded.

" - First, they didn't want Negroes joining the army at all, then when they took them, they were used as stevedores. As if that weren't bad enough, the government refused to pay them a full salary. - Oh, it was a dreadful beginning.

"Mr. Woolman wrote such despairing letters to me. No uniforms, no leave, no this, no that. When they were with the provost marshal, doing guard duty in Virginia with General Grant, some of the Union soldiers shot and killed some of Mr. Woolman's men.

"His men were actually the police - that's what the provost marshal does, but when they told some white soldiers that they were off-limits and had to leave where they were, the white soldiers attacked them.

"Matthew was beside himself with outrage when he saw nothing was going to be done about it. He was on the point of resigning his commission - he already had the letter written - when the regiment was finally sent into battle. Well, of course, he couldn't permit his men to go into battle without him, so he stayed.... And never came back."

While my father stood respectfully behind her chair, she held the photograph clasped to her body, reminiscing about distant battles won and lost, and I stood before her in the sun of an August afternoon.

*****

Grandfather refused to be summoned to Mrs. Woolman's house to see her. Clenching a pipe between his teeth, he stood in our living room, thin, gray, angry and imperious.

"She ain't got no say-so over me," he growled.

Once or twice he glanced at the picture Daddy had brought to show him. His face took on a sneer I had never seen before. It matched the ugly quality of his voice. I had two grandfathers, this ugly, angry man and the other man who came to dinner. As a child I did not realize that being old did not necessarily make a person kind, gentle, or wise. They had had many more years to practice being mean and ugly.

"Yeah, that's him all right," he glowered at the photograph. "We hated him and the rest of 'em. Wasn't a decent officer in the lot. Felt bad being in charge of us, like we weren't in the real army. We were just trash, not soldiers. Got most of the boys you see there killed. Look at them. Count them, and that's just a few of us in the picture. Maybe three you see there came back alive. Didn't I see men's guts laying on the ground? Johnny Mott got his head blowed clean off and hit me right here..." His face contorted and he struggled to say, "...in the chest." He fought to hold back fifty-year old tears. Then he laid the picture on a nearby table.

"Made us charge a *stone wall*," he accused. "A damn stone wall! And we had to do it! Bad enough we had no-count niggers calling us fools for joining up to start with, then the rest of the army calling us niggers, shines, apes - and refusing to serve along side of us. Claimed they got along all right with the Rebels 'til *we* came up to the line.

"Hell, I thought it was a war going on, not a tea party! Way it was, before us colored boys come up, the Rebs and our army would mix and mingle. The officers would act like they didn't see nothing. They'd trade food, liquor, tobacco, drink from the same stream, even send mail to relatives - till we come along. Then the Rebels wouldn't mix with

'Yankee nigger -lovers'. Said it was insulting to see a white man serve alongside us. They'd wait till one of the white soldiers went to the bathroom and shoot him in the hind quarters. The white soldiers got mad at *us*."

No one had expected any of this, and no one remembered to shoo me away. I heard it all. Casting about for something to say, Daddy picked up the picture again. "Did any of the officers get killed, Dad?"

" - Most," he admitted grudgingly. "We had to charge that stone wall and they had to lead us. Army claimed we wasn't real soldiers and wouldn't fight, so we had to go. We charged that Goddamn wall right smart like and died quickern' you can say 'steady, men!'"

Another long pause. I yearned to blurt out - "How many got killed, Granddad!" Finally, Daddy wondered, " - Did you take the wall, Dad?"

" - Reached it. Just reached it. - No, we didn't take it. Rebels wouldn't let us take back the dead, either - You always let the other side get the bodies. Not us."

My father seemed to know just how long to pause. Granddad was not as angry, now; he seemed sad. Daddy asked, "Did the white soldiers act any different after that?"

He was reluctant to answer. He went over to a chair by the window and sat down. Yes, he conceded, there had been some change. After a pause, he admitted that some of the Union soldiers had cheered them, the handful fortunate enough to return through the smoke, the blood, and the hatred.

Momma never injected herself into these kinds of discussions. She usually sat sewing, content to listen to the rumble of voices, the heavy bark of laughter. She would issue a quiet "Shush!" to the occasional curse word. Today she spoke.

" - You think they made you charge that wall on purpose, Dad, so you could earn respect?"

Bristling, he swung his head around glaring: "You don't usually say foolish things, Gert, but just listen to yourself!"

It could be that my mother's "foolish" suggestion had slowly traversed the jagged rocks of bitter memories to make sense, after all, of what had happened at that stone wall. Hadn't three of the four white officers fallen leading the charge? And weren't they as dead as the blue clad black and brown men lying around them? All deaf to the hurrahs of the astonished Union soldiers who had witnessed the charge of Pride and Valor.

Somewhere in time, something took place to convince Granddad to banish the sneer from his face, to muffle the anger in his voice, to put aside that distant stone wall and go to see Mrs. Woolman as her guest.

*****

Sitting in the library in the sun, the big bow window behind them, Granddad and Mrs. Woolman met and talked of ancient pain and anger, of triumph and tragedy. They were about the same age. She showed him an officer and a gentleman that he had never known before nor could have known. It had been Matthew's idea to raise a colored regiment. He had spent his own money to do it. He fervently believed that unless the colored race spilled its blood on the field of battle, they would always be held in contempt.

"Look at the Indians," he wrote to her, "White men murder them because they are inconvenient, some do so because they hate them; but we respect them because they will fight us. The Negro has got to die if he wants to get anything after the war is over."

She shook her head. "I never approved of the war. We Quakers hate war and we hated slavery, too. We were the first to stand up and oppose slavery way back in 1688, and as you know we led the Abolitionist Movement. War is a sin and it was hard on Matthew to break faith with his beliefs. But he did, though he knew how strongly I disapproved. He was barely 25."

Softened, Granddad spoke as though only they two were in the room. He spoke of the taunts, the hatred from Union soldiers, his conviction that the war had only proved that the North could free slaves. It did not care for them any more than it did its own free colored population. If he and the others had been ordered to charge the wall simply to shed blood for all to see, then it was a cruel and futile thing to do.

"If Matthew was ordered to take that wall, I'm convinced in my heart that he hated doing it. Like a lot of things during the war, I'm sure it was reckless and stupid. He always said we'd win the war because we wore the South down, not because we were smarter.

"But, Harold," she said reaching out and taking his hand, "they cheered you when they had not before. I lost my brother Nathan at Fredericksburg. That was another ghastly, stupid mistake. Another stone wall. Regiment after regiment beat itself to death against that wall, and they did not take it either. Didn't come close.

"Nathan and thousands more were murdered. Fredericksburg was the measure of a man for both North and South. You fought your Fredericksburg and it changed you forever, Harold. You've looked every man straight in the eye ever since, haven't you?"

He nodded somberly; his eyes were moist. "...Yes, I reckon I have... but that stone wall's still out there. Everyday."

Chapter 11

Momma had been helping Ned search for a decent job. He didn't have a trade and didn't want to sweep the streets or do 'mule labor' anymore. Without being asked, I threw myself into the search.

To my surprise, the newspaper was full of ads. How come Momma and Ned hadn't seen them? Ads were everywhere - bank teller, mailroom clerk, trolley car operator, hotel clerk, salesman, journalist, dispatcher – jobs all over the place! In triumph I found him a job on my very first try. The best part was, *it paid twelve dollars a week!*

Ned was seated at the kitchen table putting a new wick in the kerosene lamp. Bursting with pride, I wanted to slap the newspaper down in front of him and cry, "There!" Luckily, I didn't. I just handed him the paper. "I found you a job, Ned." He glanced at the ad for a moment and went back to the lamp.

I was puzzled. I expected excitement and a big smile, but he seemed more preoccupied with turning the lamp knob back and forth to test the wick as it moved up and down. Satisfied, and with an amused expression, he gave me his full attention.

"Here, let me show you something, young fella," he said, wiping his oily hands on his work pants. His hands reeking of kerosene left oily smudges on the newspaper. "See this advertisement? - Read it to me."

" 'Negro man wanted for general maintenance at lumber yard. Must be sober and respectable'."

"See the difference?"

I nodded. I offered my opinion that since he had a high school diploma, he should take the one looking for a clerk that I had found. It probably paid more.

He shook his head sadly. "Can't you see the difference in those advertisements, Aaron?"

"I already told you the difference."

He made me read another and yet another until I flung the paper down in exasperation.

"I'm tired of reading that stuff! Why don't you just tell me what you want me to know?"

He stared at my frustrated face. "You really don't see the difference, do you? - Well, I guess that's good in a way and not so good in another. - Here's what I look for when I look for a job." He pointed at the word *Negro*. "If you don't see that word you probably won't get hired. That clerk's job didn't say 'Negro.' I'd have a hard time getting hired because a lot of the people doing the hiring are like that cracker cop who pushed me around.

"They think we're all dumb, ignorant, loud, drunk, thieves and lazy. Sometimes when they hire you - and you show you're not dumb, and you're not ignorant, and that you'll work harder than anybody else – it's O.K until a white man comes along who needs a job. Then you're back on the street.

"If it's not that, it's something else. Even when you show them you're not dumb, they still talk to you like you're stupid – stuff like, 'sho nuf,' 'Ah is' and 'yow, suh.' On top of that – they expect you to grin, just like that jackass Klinger down at the stable. And when you don't grin and scratch your head, you get fired for being a 'trouble maker.'"

I stared at him for a long moment. His lips were tight, his eyes fierce. "Is that why you don't work at the warehouse anymore?" I asked.

" - Partly."

" - And carrying bricks?"

"They're all the same, Aaron. They don't respect colored because we used to be slaves. That's why I want my own business. If I worked for myself, I could act like a normal person and I could feel like a normal person. Daddy says I'm wrong, but I still say a colored man can't just be ordinary and get ahead in this country.

"You need money, you need property. You have to be a successful businessman or a politician. If you don't want people pushing you around like that cracker cop did to me, you have to be somebody like

Booker T. Washington. You can't be an ordinary, colored man if you ever expect to get anywhere in this country."

I frowned. I did not l know what to think. Momma and Daddy never said that.

"...Does that mean me, too?"

"...You won't be ordinary. You're going to get your diploma."

"But you got your diploma. Momma said you're smart enough to go to college. How's it going to be any different for me?"

He turned back to the kerosene lamp and prepared to fill it. "I don't know, little fella. Maybe things will be different for you. You may be lucky like Daddy. Certainly hope so."

*****

October came and Ned was still with us. Momma held her breath praying that his raging fury had spent itself. She decreed the subject of his leaving the country was never to be brought up. In November when he strode into the house just before dinner displaying a rare smile, it seemed he had turned a corner and the worse was over.

"I'm going to sea!" he announced. "I'll be sailing in a couple of weeks."

Momma who was preparing to sit down and have dinner with me, froze in the act of sitting. "Sailing!" she cried. "Sailing where? You didn't tell us you were joining the Navy!"

"I'm not in the Navy; I'm a merchant seaman!" he rejoiced, taking off his navy-blue pea jacket to reveal ordinary street clothes underneath. "Why're you looking so worried, Momma? If the President Wilson decides to declare war, they'll start drafting people. I'm not going in any army just to do mule labor, digging ditches and unloading ships. I'm going to see the world!"

"Won't the Germans sink your ship?" I asked wide-eyed, dinner forgotten. "Don't they have U-Boats?"

"Naw, we're neutral, but I can't worry about that now. Anyway, the war'll probably be over soon. It's already been two years. I'm going to see the world, and as soon as I find a country I like, I'm going to send for everybody and we're all going there to live!"

I could read Momma's face, especially her eyes. She did not like what she was hearing. Her lips tightened. None of what Ned said reassured her.

Motioning to him to sit down to dinner, she got a plate and served him. He hardly waited for her to sit down before - bursting with good news - he plunged on, oblivious to everything except the path down which his story led him. His dark face was alive for the first time in months. He told of scouring the waterfront in search of a ship that would take him on before finally signing on the *S.S. Saxon* as a steward. Their first stop would be Port-of-Spain.

"What's a steward?" I asked.

Tight lipped, Momma said, " – It's like a waiter. Are you going to wait on the other sailors?"

"No, Momma, just the officers," he said, buttering a biscuit. "We're all sailors together. We all work together; everybody has to depend on everybody else."

She had not touched her chicken and dumplings. "...I thought you were trying to save money to go into business for yourself."

He frowned, shaking his head. "It'll take too long, Momma. Even if I don't pay room and board, it'll take too long. Sailors get paid, too," he smiled weakly. "I can save more because money goes farther in other countries."

"But what can you get out of being a steward?" she persisted, color heightening the brown of her face. "You don't have to go to sea to wait on people, Ned. You won't be advancing yourself!"

He grew sullen, his joy gone. He put his fork down and leaned back in his chair. "'Advance' myself?' How am I going to do that? I have a high school diploma; only eight colored kids in the whole city got one when I graduated. Yet I can't even get a job that people can get who can hardly speak English! And when I try to do for myself, I got some God - some lousy, stupid cop! -

"There's nothing wrong with being a steward. A lot of stewards are white. I'll work my way up to able-bodied seaman, but I've got to start somewhere and that means at the bottom. I can advance, but I have to have time."

Momma was not easily put off. I remembered that day when she had stormed into the principal's office like charging calvary to confront him. Now, she picked at her stewed chicken, her black eyes thoughtful. Ships had a peculiar habit of sinking, she reminded him, and even if he were not worried, that did not mean she wasn't. If a ship wasn't lost in a storm, what about those German U-boats?

"Mom, we're not at war with Germany," he explained again patiently. "We may not be at war until sometime next year when the war'll be over."

"No, we're not at war, not at the moment, but soon we will be. They're already talking about sending General Pershing over there with an army. You just said yourself that you joined up to avoid the draft. There wouldn't be a draft if the country wasn't expecting to go to war soon."

His only rejoinder was that he was not in the Navy, he was in the merchant marine.

"What difference does that make?" she flared, head thrust forward. "A ship's a ship to a U-boat!"

To tell the truth, I was disappointed, but for different reasons. He wasn't going to be wearing a real sailor's uniform and climb sails and weigh anchor and stand chained to the steering wheel as waves smashed at his ship. He wasn't a real sailor. I didn't know what he was since I'd never heard of the merchant marine. But I agreed with Momma - what was the sense in going to sea to be a servant when he didn't want to be a butler like my father and meet nice people who spoke good English?

Chapter 12

Mr. Amos died on a cold, wet, November day on the eve of another war. Granddad said he believed Mr. Amos was seventy-four but he didn't know for sure. I'd never known anybody who died. A man died down the street last summer but I didn't know who he was. Staring at the flowing black crepe hanging from his front door, I tipped my cap because Momma told me to. Once, when I was nine, I saw a white crepe tied in a clean, silken bow hanging from a door.

"White crepes look better than black ones," I declared brightly. "I think people should choose white."

"- White is only for children," she said softly. "That makes them very sad."

Mrs. Porter, Mr. Amos' landlady, had come knocking at the door sometime before noon to announce the news to Momma. Later we went with Granddad to Mr. Amos' room down on Hope Street to clean up and sort through his belongings. The small back room was smelly. Granddad had to work to get the window open.

We found no letters or writing of any kind. Mr. Amos had been an ex-slave who never learned to read or write. Neatly hung in his closet was his treasured blue uniform that he had proudly worn in the annual GAR parades down Broad Street. We watched him once, stepping along stiffly, staring rigidly to the front with the mere dozen other surviving colored soldiers.

Momma took the uniform down. "We'll bury him in this," she decided. "He'd like that, don't you think, Dad?"

Granddad's only reply was to snort his disapproval, but not so vociferously as on other occasions. Unlike Granddad, Mr. Amos was one of many veterans who, after the war, joined the Grand Army of the Republic, the Civil War veterans' organization. He'd attended the colored GAR post to fraternize, drink whiskey and play cards. The old veteran never tired of telling about the lone GAR convention he had attended in Ohio in 1880 where he heard General William Sherman give his stirring "War is Hell" speech.

"Everybody used to call Sherman 'Uncle Billy,'" he often recalled with his skeletal smile. "When we heard that he was right there 'mongst us in that very building -well, sir, we all commenced hootin' and hollerin', *'Uncle Billy, Uncle Billy, speech! Speech!'*"

Without fail Granddad would snort, his handlebar mustache quivering, "Sherman wasn't nothin'! Just a poor mouth Rebel in disguise. Hated colored. Quick as slaves ran away thinking his army would protect them, he'd lock em' up, then turn right around and hand them back to the slavers to be whipped and God knows what else!"

His rain of bitter truth never drenched Mr. Amos. A smile would spread across his bony face. His reality was knowing that he had been a part of that overwhelming tide of blue that fought and won the Civil War. Reality for him was being a bona fide veteran of that war, of having shot at his former tormentors, of having that uniform hanging in his closet and seeing his cap with the bullet hole through the brim. Reality for Mr. Amos was his monthly pension check that validated his existence, sustaining him in good days and bad until the day he died.

Smiling at Granddad's frustrations, he would rock contentedly, encased in hallowed memories. Perhaps he had not charged a stone wall, but for him the simple act of defiance was enough.

We searched his room. I didn't say anything but I was looking for the rifle which he said he kept in case "they" came to get him. But there was no rifle. A small wooden box lay under his bed. Momma emptied the contents. There were three photographs of white women, a lock of black hair, a faded pink garter, his army discharge and $76.00 in bills and coins. Momma puzzled over the photographs for some time before putting them back in the box.

"Dad," she suggested, "wouldn't it be nice if you could get the GAR post to come to the funeral?"

"No!" he snapped. "I don't know those people and they don't know me. When's the last time Amos saw any of 'em? Three, four years maybe more. You don't pay your dues, they don't know you."

Momma folded the uniform over her arm and faced an obdurate elder who was obviously intent on getting out the door without further ado.

"He's been sick, Dad - they know that. They'll want to remember Mr. Amos."

"No!" he said like a steel door slamming shut. "Things were said you don't know nothin' about. Long time ago things were said. People don't forget. They'd laugh in my face and I'd spit in theirs."

We all knew his "no" meant forever. His refusals were brave at times, perverse at others but just as inflexible in either case. Though Daddy had not been home for over ten days, Momma, as persistent as ever, handed him the job of going to the colored GAR post and getting a contingent of men to appear at Mr. Amos' funeral. Barely concealing his annoyance at Granddad for not only inconveniencing him, but also for letting Mr. Amos down - Daddy's face seemed longer than usual as he prepared to leave the house rather than sit down to dinner.

"Can I go, too?" I blurted, sensing a great adventure.

Still frowning with irritation, he stopped, hand on the front doorknob. "Get your cap," he snapped.

We bundled up against the cold November drizzle. We rode several trolley cars for what seemed like hours of clickety-clack, clickety-clack, swaying, lurching, stopping and starting. I didn't mind. It was not often that I got a chance to ride on a trolley car.

I gazed out of the window at the red brick row houses with white stone door steps, and the small corner stores displaying merchandise. People hurried along against the cold and children played on sidewalks, oblivious to the weather. I observed that the complexion of the passengers gradually changed as we went along until they were mostly colored.

We got off somewhere on the edge of the Seventh Ward in South Philadelphia. We trudged up one windy, cold street and down another, finally stopping before a barber shop in the middle of the block. By now it was dusk.

We stepped into the welcome warmth of the barber shop. The owner,

Deacon Fortune, was balding with a walrus moustache. He was cutting a customer's hair. Daddy knew him and offered the deacon his hand. The barber paused long enough to shake it.

"Amos Fletcher just passed," Daddy told him.

"- Amos died? Wasn't he your father's friend?"

"You don't mean the tall, thin fella with all the jokes?" asked a grizzled old man with a cane.

My father knew nothing about the jokes, but they established it was Amos who had died. Beyond that no one knew anything helpful. Somebody said the colored GAR post had moved six or seven years ago. Another man was certain the post had been shut down even longer than that.

"Didn't all them fellas die?" asked the barber.

"They was all pretty old to start with," a stout man seated beside a warm, wood stove filled with glowing embers reminded them.

"I think Benjamin Blake still lives over on Chadwick Street," said a hopeful man. He appeared to be about forty and wore glasses.

" - He can't get out of bed," the deacon reminded him, as he carefully trimmed his customer's hair.

"- What were you fixing to do," the man with the cane asked, "tell 'em he's dead?"

"I thought they might come to the funeral in their uniforms - sort of give him a military burial."

Heads shook, mouths turned down, eyes peered over glasses. " - I'll come. I'm a *Son of a Veteran*," the forty-year-old man offered, "but I ain't got no uniform."

When we left, we had one *Son of a Veteran* and two friendly volunteers who promised to be pall bearers, but beyond that, those who knew Amos were also dead.

"Maybe some of the other GAR posts will send somebody," Momma persisted when we returned home. Both Daddy and Granddad rumbled dissent. The other posts were white, they said. It would seem too much like begging. Neither man was in the mood to be met with rejection.

On the day of the funeral, a minister provided by the funeral parlor, and the three pall bearers showed up. They were met with Momma's effusive gratitude. They helped the undertaker load the coffin into his hearse. That done, the undertaker headed the black plumed horses toward Broad Street, en route for the edge of the city.

We rode at a funereal pace in two black carriages behind the hearse. Along the way, men on the sidewalk tipped their hat respectfully; women bowed their head for a moment and children were urged not to gawk at the awesome black clothed-horses. The procession paused at the barren, northern outskirts of Broad Street.

There are distinctions in death as there are in life.

For those who had the means there were funeral trolley cars for hire. The casket would be placed in a storage area beneath the vehicle, and everyone boarded the black draped trolley car for the solemn ride to the cemetery. There they would be met by a carriage that would take the deceased on the final leg of the journey while the mourners trudged silently behind. But we could not afford the luxury of a funeral trolley. Once we reached City Line Road we began the long creaking trip to Fairview Cemetery.

After the eulogy and prayer, the *Son of a Veteran* cried, "Wait!" Taking a pistol from his pocket he pointed it to the sky and discharged it. We heard a clap in the distance. He fired twice more, pausing between each shot.

I had never heard a gun fired before. I can still hear the clapping echoes from those shots. Years later I wondered why we had not draped his casket in a flag. And I think there should have been a sound of music. We should have sung the *Battle Hymn of the Republic*. We needed more, much more, to mark his thousand years of pain offset by one day of sunshine.

Chapter 13

I fell hopelessly in love with Elizabeth.

Her eyes were brown and soft and tinged with the quick sympathy of girls. Her skin was smooth and golden brown. Her hair was silken and braided in two long plaits that framed her face. I saw a gentle smile. We were both at the edge of one age and at the beginning of another, an age filled with strange and wonderful sensations that were new; released from secret, magic places in our body. Sensations suddenly flushed down my spine when I accidentally touched her lovely face.

We both were very young. She was thirteen and I was fifteen.

I first saw her the day I was sent to Shilling's Bakery on the corner to get Momma a slice of cheesecake. Elizabeth entered as I was on my way out. Struck, I stared at her. I heard her ask for a half pint of vanilla ice cream in a voice that was clear and pleasant. I waited outside Schilling's, racking my brain for some reason for lingering. I dropped to my knee and pretended I was tying my shoelace.

I stood up when she came out. Our eyes met. I felt hot, flushed and foolish. "...I live around the corner!" I blurted.

She stared, uncertain what to say. "Hello," she smiled as she walked away. I tingled with a strange emotion. She walked very lightly, almost on tip toe. She crossed the street and went up the steps of 2042. When the door opened, she went in. From that moment, she was my love and all that love could ever be; she was a vermillion streak across the sky. I stared up in wonder. Elizabeth was the sound of a choir in a cathedral. I loved her. From that moment, the corner of Jewel Avenue and Bradley Street held an air of promise.

The next day and the day after and still the next day, I frequently went to the corner of Bradley hoping to catch a glimpse of her. The street remained quiet, drenched in sun. Blue and green awnings cast small shadows on bedroom windows. Quiet lay like a blanket at noon on a summer day in1917. A parked car, gleaming in the sun, was the only witness to my endeavors.

Then one magical day, I saw her on her doorstep playing jacks by herself. Heart pounding, I sidled up to her. She smiled and continued tossing the ball up and swiftly gathering a jack before the ball bounced back down. She let me watch her. I asked her questions about jacks as though I were really curious. I only wanted to hear her voice. She could have recited the alphabet for all I cared. She was Elizabeth, golden and beautiful, and I was a love lost child who wanted nothing so much as to touch her and hear her speak to me.

"– Can I play?" I asked.

She regarded me with surprise, her game suspended. "- Boys don't play jacks," she said quietly. When her soft brown eyes looked at me, I could not tell whether or not she was scolding or advising me nor did it matter. My heart simply thumped in my chest.

"I can learn," I said. "…Can I learn?"

She smiled and said yes, and I stared dumbly and did whatever she told me to do. It was then that I accidentally touched her hand. I remembered the electric thrill all my life. It touched my soul.

A boy a little older than me and taller, appeared in the doorway. He too had light, golden skin and black wavy hair. He was handsome.

"Elizabeth," he said softly, "Mother said you must come in now."

He glanced at me and turned away. They both went into the house. Staring at the closed door, I prayed she would reappear. She did not then nor the days after that.

Finally, I saw Elizabeth on roller skates. Racing home I stormed into the house and dove into the hall closet searching for my skates. They were not there. I could not remember when I'd last worn them. Momma, busy ironing on the kitchen table, watched me scouring the house without questioning me. At the moment, that oddity escaped my fevered efforts. Finally, I cried in frustration, "Momma, I can't find my skates!"

She took her time answering. "They're hanging in the cellar where they belong. If you'd put things where I tell you, you wouldn't have to hunt all over for them."

Plunging halfway down the cellar stairs into the darkness, I stopped. I needed an oil lamp. Bounding back I approached Momma again.

Dreading her reply I mumbled, " - May I have a lamp, please, Momma?"

Ignoring me, she placed one iron on the kitchen coal stove to heat while picking up the second iron that had been heating. "- You know you're not allowed to carry oil lamps. You'll just have to wait until I'm finished."

Sensing that my lovely girl was even now skating beyond my reach, perhaps forever - from desperation I spoke boldly. "This is very, very, *very* important, Momma. Please!"

Setting the iron aside, she gazed at me with black, piercing eyes. "Where are you going?"

"Just down to the corner. I won't cross any streets and I'll look out for cars and horses, Momma. I promise!"

Her lips tightened a little; she fixed me with an expression I had never noticed before. Sighing with something like resignation, she put her iron back on the stove, took down a kerosene lamp from the shelf next to the cellar door, lit it and led me to my skates.

Feverishly hurling myself down the street, I rounded the corner and saw Elizabeth, flushed and glowing, skating towards me. She passed me without a glance. Undaunted I raced after her.

"Can I skate with you?" I cried.

She did not reply. "Elizabeth," I said, more to establish that I knew her name than for any other reason. She said nothing. Because her face was naturally serene and kind, her silence did not appear offensive. I tagged along, glad that she had not driven me away with an annoyed stare or harsh word. We were heading back to the corner.

"Is that your brother I saw the other day?"

"Yes."

Overjoyed that she had spoken, I asked, "What's his name?"

"Pace."

Just then Pace appeared as before. He waited at the curb until we drew up.

"Mother said you must come in," he said.

This time he did not even glance at me. I did not fully appreciate the significance of his slight. Maybe he had that serene appearance that can disguise offensive conduct.

Again I mounted a vigil at the corner. I raced there on any pretext hoping to see Elizabeth. Even when her doorsteps stared back clean, white and empty, they held promise like an empty stage. I awaited the rising of the curtain. One more moment and she would appear. Just wait. Like me, the car that always gleamed in the sun was a silent spectator.

Persistence was rewarded. She was alone again, playing jacks. Eagerly I moved toward her. I stood watching her hand toss the ball up, deftly pick up jacks, catch the ball on one bounce and do it again until all the jacks were gone.

The side of the street that she lived on was shady in the mornings. The sun crept closer as it rose over the houses until sunlight reached her bottom step. It was then that she went into the house without being called.

"Why do you always go in the house when it gets sunny?"

"The sun makes you dark," she explained.

"It doesn't make me dark," I pointed out.

"You're already dark, don't you know that?" she asked in wonder.

*****

"Momma, what color am I?" I blurted that evening as she was preparing dinner at the kitchen stove. Her back was to me. She didn't answer right away. Maybe she remembered the last time I'd asked the question and the ensuing fight with the principal. When she faced me, her lips were tight.

"Didn't we go through this before, Aaron?" she scolded – "You're the same color you were yesterday, the day before and the last time you asked me that! Why is it so hard to understand that?"

"But am I *dark* brown?" I worried. "I'm not black am I?"

"Who said you were dark? You're brown-skinned. -Who have you been talking to this time?"

"Nobody," I lied, relieved. "I just wondered... But am I colored, too?"

"Yes, Aaron, you're colored, we're all colored. Now I want you to stop this foolishness, do you hear? You're the same color your father is. What if you *are* dark-skinned? What's wrong with that?"

I didn't have an answer. I mumbled something, glad Momma didn't press me further.

When I saw Elizabeth again, she told me her last name was Taliaferro and that her father worked for the railroad. Soon they would all be going to Boston for a whole week and then to Washington to visit her aunts and cousins. At that moment her front door opened and a white woman with light brown hair appeared. Her face was puffy; her eyes were a faded blue. I stared at her because she was white, yet she seemed to live there. I scrambled to my feet fumbling for something courteous to say but she did not look at me.

"Elizabeth!" she said curtly.

Elizabeth quickly seized her jacks and scurried into the house past the disgruntled looking woman. The door was shut firmly in my face. It was then that I knew Pace had not liked me just as this woman did not like me. Though she was white, she was their mother. I did not understand how that could be.

*****

"Who do you know around the corner?" Momma demanded the next day as I returned from another vigil. She was setting the lunch table. She paused, holding a soup bowl, waiting for my answer. Her lips were set in that thin line I had come to know.

" - A boy and his sister moved in," I replied evasively.

"I know they did, and I don't think you should be going around there. Do you know them?" I saw the same look on her face that I had noticed the day I needed an oil lamp.

Caught between her question and the fear of lying, I hesitated. She pounced on me with a series of deft questions.

"I don't want you going anyplace where you're not wanted, do you hear? Those people around the corner think they're better than everybody else just because they're light-skinned. - *Look at me when I talk to you!*

"They're color-crazy. They're certainly not better than us. Our family's lived here for over a hundred years. Your grandfather fought in the Civil War and don't you ever forget it! Nobody freed us. We were already free and we fought to help free people like them who were slaves and worse. You understand me, Son? - Don't you *ever, ever* let anyone tell you they're better than you are just because they're light-skinned or half-white like that woman. Do you hear?"

"Yes, ma'am."

"We have enough trouble with white people thinking they're better than us without having to put up with that foolishness from our own race!"

But she didn't understand.

No matter how she or Mrs. Taliaferro or Pace felt, I only cared that Elizabeth didn't feel that way. It began and it ended with Elizabeth. I said, "Yes, ma'am," all the while seeing only my golden girl; remembering and reliving that one magic day when I had touched her hand. I wanted to touch her again and hear her speak to me, and Momma was saying I should not and Elizabeth's mother was saying that I could not.

Momma, never one to abide a heretic, continued her admonitions later over dinner.

"Certain people like to put on airs when all they do is work for the railroad," she sniffed.

"But her father drives a real railroad train and he even went to college!" I exclaimed.

"Whoever told you that nonsense!" she hooted. "Yes, he works for the railroad and calls himself a 'sportsman,' and he may have gone to college, but he's only a common porter so what good did college do him? He makes beds and waits on people!"

"- Doesn't Daddy wait on people, too?"

She was in the act of bending over her dinner plate. Her head snapped up. Her nostrils flared. Thick dark clouds appeared. Lightning flashed; thunder rumbled. Her face was ridged with anger.

I cringed.

"Don't you dare get fresh with me, mister, or I'll slap you away from this table! A butler can have as many as five or ten people working under him - your father's got three; a porter's just an ordinary servant! Your father's *Mister* Winston to the people under him, not *boy* like a common porter.

Your father's probably the only colored butler in the entire state of Pennsylvania, so put that in your pipe and smoke it!"

"Yes, ma'am," I murmured.

Seeing those flaring nostrils, hostile eyes, taut, lean body and hearing the seething anger in her voice, I could well imagine her with a hatchet in her hand. She presented an image that remained with me all my life, an image that helped me to understand that the innate toughness of women was a thing best left undisturbed.

Having touched a very sore point, I was sentenced to sit there, gazing attentively, hardly daring to touch my dinner as she swung her hatchet again and again. But the longer she spoke, the more I wanted to listen.

She began to speak to me the way she did to her friends. She said things that I only expected to hear by snooping. It was an unburdening to a child who might not be expected to fully understand, so in a sense she was talking to herself. What I heard was steam escaping from the engine of her mind and I reveled in it.

"Your Aunt Agatha is going to go to her grave without chick nor child because she was color-crazy. Every man who ever wanted to marry her was 'too dark' unless he was lighter than she was. When I married your father, she just about had a fit because your father was 'too dark.' It didn't matter that he was intelligent and respectable, just how dark he was! I don't know where she got her foolishness from; our family was never raised that way. She was the only one in the family like that.

"She wasted her life chasing Alfred Pease. All you heard was 'Alfred Pease,' 'Alfred Pease.' I'll admit he was good looking. He had wavy hair and had women falling all over themselves chasing after him - your aunt leading the parade. But he was stuck on himself.

"When he got that civil service job at the Customs House, and had a desk and could wear a necktie to work every day, nobody could tell him he wasn't king of the hill. Acted like he was high society. Then he married that Hightower girl from South Carolina and your aunt's been in mourning ever since. Serves her right," she smirked cruelly. "Agatha was black compared to Ernestine Hightower. She was what they called 'high-yellow.' Could almost pass for white."

Momma began to eat her veal stew and seemed to relish Aunt Agatha's long-ago discomfit. As I ate, I watched her face. It was softer;

the anger was gone. She spoke to me not as a child, but as a person the way Daddy had the summer I had worked with him.

"Well, I've got a good husband and wonderful sons, and what does Agatha have? Nothing. Old and living alone in a rented room trying to put on airs, with nobody to do for her. Those people around the corner are just like her. I know who they are. There're a bunch of them and they're all the same."

*****

After that it was with considerable trepidation that I crept to the corner. I hadn't been expressly forbidden to go there so I persuaded myself that I could. Mounting my vigil, I was spinning my top on the hot sidewalk, alert for the sound of Elizabeth's front door opening, when I saw two big, shiny cars pull up in front of her house.

It was unusual to see two cars going to one house. The people who got out surprised me. They all looked like Elizabeth and Pace. They shared the same golden skin and silken hair; some appeared to be white like Elizabeth's mother. As they milled about, there were quick, friendly smiles and gentle laughter. Tall, lean men carried packages wrapped like gifts, and Elizabeth and her family rushed out with squeals of joy to greet them.

Then they all vanished into the house, a medley of silken hair, well-trimmed black moustaches, flashing white teeth, heart-shaped faces and delighted laughter. All in a sea of white and gold and bronze.

Curious, I waited, creeping back out of the hot sun as the day advanced. After an hour, the front door opened. Elizabeth and three golden girls came out, giggling and girly in clean summer frocks. They sat on the scrubbed white marble steps, sipping glasses of lemonade.

I suddenly felt ragged and grimy. I wanted to wash my face and comb my hair and put on clean clothes. Elizabeth gave no sign that she saw me. Pace came out with an almost white boy about his age. They teased the girls before walking away convulsed with laughter.

Quickly I picked up my top and sauntered back up my street. I could not let Pace see me peeping like a peasant through cracks into their lives. But it was too late. He and his friend were at the corner speaking loudly enough so I could hear.

"Many are called, but few are chosen," Pace gibed, laughing.

"You mean some people don't know when they're not wanted?" his friend cried out.

"Especially when they're jigaboos!" Pace chortled.

They marched on, arm in arm, gasping with laughter. Filled with new and conflicting emotions, I watched their retreating figures crossing the intersection of Jewel and Bradley. Then their chant drifted back -

If you're white, you're all right,
If you're brown, stick around,
If you're black, STAY BACK!

I felt a sudden urge to charge after them and smash their sneering faces even if they were two to one. But their insults were too oblique; they were like strangers talking, "unaware" that I existed. Yet I knew as I watched their proud figures, in smart stylish knickers neatly buckled below the knee, I knew that they knew I existed, and I hated them because of the way they made me feel.

Is this how Momma felt? Is this why she was so angry? How could they be better than I was? What made them better? How could being lighter make them better when they were still colored like I was? Why could they slam doors in my face, smirk at me and call Elizabeth into the house the moment I appeared just because they were lighter than I was? What made them feel better than me? Were they smarter? Did they think I was like the Washingtons?

Pace had never really looked at me - he looked *through* me. How do you do that — look through somebody? It was like Teddy Connor raining insults on me while I felt helpless and angry because I couldn't think of anything to call him.

Momma's voice was in my head; I tried to shut it out. I needed to solidify what I knew and what I felt in my own time and in my own way. I tried not to hear her voice though it would echo all the days of my life. It was not the men in my family who set the tone of how we were to live - it was Momma who decreed what we should hate and what we should love, who we should be and who we were.

I once pressed a note into Elizabeth's hand and raced away, burning with embarrassment. *My dearest darling Elizabeth, I love you very, very much. - Aaron.* She never replied, but I do not think she threw it away, either.

I asked her once, "Can I kiss you?" She flushed and shook her head and said no. Undeterred, the next day as she reached for a jack that had fallen to a lower step, I leaned over and kissed her golden face.

She stared at me astonished - and then her eyes flashed. "You didn't have permission to do that!" she scolded. Gathering up her jacks, she went into her house with one last reproachful glance over her shoulder.

She did not appear the next day or the day after that. I began to appreciate the enormity of my crime – I had not had permission. When I saw her again, she was beautiful in a blue middy blouse with her hair lying against a broad white collar. I stood at the corner and watched her fling her rubber ball up in solitary splendor and gather in onesies, twosies, threesies.

Then she looked up and included me in her world again. Timidly, I crept up to her doorstep. I felt contrite but was too young to know how to apologize. I sat in silence, glad to breathe the same air she breathed and to feel the same sun.

Momma called it 'puppy love.' I bristled. My love bestrode the world and spanned the universe. I stood girdled in armor prepared to fight the good fight and wrestle monsters down had they dared look at her.

Each day began when I thought of Elizabeth and ended when I went to sleep at night. The days were never too muggy, the drifting smell from the Delaware River never too noxious. Each day I navigated the stormy seas of Momma's disapproval and Pace's icy insolence. The sun was never too hot, but it was my enemy as it crept across the street and touched the bottom step of her house.

Beyond that I lived in a world without end.

There came that magic day when the sash of her dress came undone. She asked me to tie it for her. With beating heart, I stood close behind her and saw the clean, pure lines of the nape of her neck framed by her silken hair. As I fumbled with the ends of her sash, pulling them together, I felt the weight of her body through the cloth that I held. In making a bow I touched her back and a sudden electric thrill tingled my scalp and coursed down my spine.

Leaning toward her neck I kissed her, reckless and driven, heedless of her flashing eyes and my lack of permission. She turned immediately, lips apart, eyes incredulous. I stood before her, numb, and mumbled - "I love you, Elizabeth, a whole, whole lot!"

She was puzzled and then her brown eyes softened. Turning from me she began to gather up her jacks.

"…Can I have one – just till tomorrow? I'll give it back. I promise."

She did not know what to make of my strange behavior. "…What are you going to do with one jack?"

"I…I want to learn how to spin it. Like a top. But I'll give it back; I promise."

Her calm girl-eyes regarded me for a moment. She slowly shook her head. I wanted the jack simply because it was hers. I wanted to hold it in the palm of my hand and close my hand in a fist and feel its sharp edges; I wanted to keep it forever and look at it and know it was a part of her.

She did not go into the house. We continued to play but mostly I watched until the sun chased the shade to the edge of the bottom step. She had to go. I preferred that she did rather than face her mother's frigid shutting the door on me. Elizabeth gathered her jacks.

Then she held out her hand and offered me a jack. "You promise to give it back?"

"Yes," I breathed. "I cross my heart and hope to die."

She went into the house and closed the door and though the sun had reached the bottom step, my heart soared.

*****

The next day Elizabeth was gone.

The house at 2042 Jewel Avenue stood vacant.

In disbelief, I charged up the front doorsteps. I peered in through the front door window. I saw a few empty cardboard boxes. The silence was loud.

"They moved last night," Momma informed me, as she straightened sofa cushions in the living room. "Not during the day like respectable people do."

I did not like Momma's satisfied tone. The set of her mouth told me that she was glad they had moved. The Taliaferros had resisted overtures of friendship from Mrs. Alexander and Mrs. Jones; as far as Momma was concerned, the Taliaferros were no better than the Washingtons.

" - Do you know where they moved to?" I asked, hopeful.

She was about to leave the living room and glared at me, nostrils flaring again, lips tight. Seeing the expression on my face, her eyes and her mouth softened.

"- No, Son, I don't know where they went...I know you liked that little girl; maybe you'll see her again. Maybe she'll go to your school this fall."

I felt tears well up. I was too big to cry, but not too big to feel hurt.

Momma reached out and pulled me to her. She hugged me against her lean, warm body. I liked being there.

"You'll see her when school starts," she soothed. "You'll see."

I liked that she cared how I felt. Impulsively, I put my arms around her and hugged her as tightly as I would have hugged Elizabeth.

1918

Chapter 14

It seemed as though the world died in 1918.

The Spanish Flu erased the present and smothered the future. Everyday we heard the clip-clop, clip-clop of black festooned horses echoing through the streets, carrying the dead to graves and mausoleums. Often the horses were festooned in white to commemorate the death of a child.

Funeral crepes hung from doors like green holly at Christmas; men wore a black mourning band sewn around the upper arm of their coat sleeve. Motor coaches and funeral trolley cars carried the dead, too, but to me, horses were more somber and majestic; the road to eternity should be somber and slow.

The world cared that Edmond Rostand died. I knew of him because I had to read *Cyrano de Bergerac* in school. No one cared that Aunt Agatha was "carried away" along with cousins I never met. Mr. Purnell died still mourning his lost job, relieved forever from cleaning public toilets. The "Grim Reaper" took Mrs. Woolman, and Mrs. Washington along with all her children except for Boo Boy. He was still incarcerated for trying to rob Timmy back in 1916. Alexander's mother died, too; I saw his tear-streaked face distorted with pain. Mr. Stoltz, who had forbidden me to pet his dog, died as did twelve of my classmates.

Nobody seemed to die, though. They either met the "Grim Reaper" or they "passed away." Some were simply "not with us anymore." The *Philadelphia Tribune* newspaper declared that the deceased had heard the "Dread Summons."

Death by any other name was still death, and I wondered about my golden Elizabeth. Momma might have died, too, had it not been for

Mrs. Portlock. She was another new colored neighbor. There were five colored families on the block now including us. Mrs. Portlock placed thick slices of onion on Momma's wrists to break the fever, and bound them firmly with strips of cloth. She bundled Momma up in blankets, heated bricks on the kitchen stove and wrapped them in cloth, then placed them near Momma's feet under the covers. She gave Momma hot tea and lemon and burned sulfur in the room until we nearly suffocated. There was castor oil as a matter of course. How Momma survived is a mystery, but she did. She was one of the lucky ones.

Daddy swore that God had spared her; but he thanked the portly Mrs. Portlock over and over. He'd been unable to be at Momma's side because of Mrs. Woolman's illness. He said he knelt at any spare moment during the day, and beside his bed at night, and prayed for Momma. I prayed, too, kneeling by my bed. Daddy was convinced God had saved Momma, noting somberly, that people like Mrs. Woolman, with the best doctors and money to spare had died, but not Momma.

During the flu, no one was allowed to spit in public and anybody with a cough was ostracized. There was even talk of closing the schools. We kids waited impatiently for the Grim Reaper to close the doors. For us, death was a holiday.

*****

Steven died along with all the rest.

He'd become a different person since the night he tapped on my window in the middle of the night. He used to be talkative; he became quieter, and ever since the day we sat together on the school fire escape he seemed to avoid me.

He started playing hooky. A rumor went around that he'd gotten suspended for stealing. Somebody said it was money from a teacher's desk, somebody else claimed it was some kids' lunch; then we heard it was worse than that. By the time he died, he'd already been kicked out of school.

I thought I knew why he was acting the way he was. He was probably still feeling guilty, (like Poe's character in *The Tell-Tale Heart)* because he'd killed somebody. But why anybody would feel guilty about saving his own life never made sense to me.

Steven should have died in a time when there would have been a sense of shock and disbelief. With the epidemic, it was too easy to believe death was possible. Before the flu epidemic, every year one or two classmates died from one thing or another. Then, people exclaimed, *"Died! -* How?"

I cornered him one day after school on one of the occasions he bothered to show up. "Hey, Steven, wait up!" I cried, darting after him.

He looked over his shoulder but made no attempt to wait for me. He didn't have any books with him. I caught up to him.

"Didn't you hear me calling!" I demanded.

"Yeah, I heard," he growled, his cap brim pulled to the side to show he was tough. "Wanna make something of it?"

"What's gotten into you anyhow? We're supposed to be pals."

"Pals? I ain't got time for that antique shit!"

Taken aback, I managed to blurt, "- Everybody says you're in a lot of trouble. They say the dicks are after you!"

He slowed. "That's a lie! The detectives aren't after me. Who said the dicks are after me?"

"It's all over the school. They say you stole something."

"That's a goddamn lie!" he flung out, charging off.

My mouth flew open at the word 'Goddamn.' I had to walk fast to keep up with him. "Then why's everybody saying it, and why're you playing hooky all the time?"

He stopped and glared at me, his face close to mine "It's none of your damn business or anybody else's!"

I wasn't scared of him; I'd known him too long. But the cursing and balled fists bewildered me. There was no possible way he could know what I'd been intending to do to him on the fire escape that day. I followed him to an intersection.

"I got some place to go," he said, dismissing me. He wouldn't look at me. It was then I realized how much he had changed though I could not define it.

"- We're still pals, right?" I said.

"I already told you - I ain't got time for that antique shit," he said, stepping into the street.

"You better come back to school! How're you going to be a doctor if you don't finish school."

He paused in the street and looked at me for a second. "Finish school for what, dummy? All you're going to do is dig ditches whether you finish school or not. Just like the rest of the niggers. Look at your brother."

"Not me! I'm going to graduate and get my diploma!"

"Shit!" he flung back, walking off. "You'll just have a bigger shovel, that's all. Wise up, dummy! You'll be lucky to get a job working an elevator. You'll be cleaning toilets like my father."

I never saw him after that. Looking back, I know something real and living had died in him long before the flu took his body; maybe it wasn't guilt.

*****

Mrs. Portlock, who nursed my mother when she had the flu, was a stout, pleasant looking woman. She resembled the lady on boxes of pancake mix. Momma had never met her before she unceremoniously bustled into her sickroom, frowning with concern, crying, "Lawd, have mussy! Ain't nobody takin' care of this chile?"

To Momma's feeble protests, the strange woman simply shouted, "Now don't you worry none, Mis Winston, yo boy done tole me all about it. Aaron, git on downstairs an' start heatin' me up some bricks on the stove."

I knew Mrs. Portlock from the year before when I'd met her ginger-colored daughter, Paige, whose name fascinated me. I used to write it on the cover of my copybook. After staring across the classroom at her for several weeks, I approached her after lunch one day and demanded, "What kind of name is 'Paige' for a girl?"

"I ain't never hear nobody called 'Aaron,'" she shot back, edging away. "That's a funny name an' you talk funny, too!"

"Not as funny as you talk," I retorted, trailing after her. "That's because you're from down South. You say 'doe' for door."

"So what!"

"- Where're you from anyway, Georgia?"

"Ain't none of yo business where I'm from! You too nosy. Ain't nothing wrong with 'Paige.'"

"I didn't mean there was anything wrong with it; I just never heard it before, that's all."

"You was making sport with me," she insisted, not mollified.

I'd never apologized in my life to anyone my own age and didn't know how. I spotted one of the boys I palled around with and, calling to him, raced off.

She reminded me of Junie Mae. There was the same openness, the direct stare, an implied willingness to rough house and yet be gentle. And when not provoked, her full, soft lips formed a natural hint of a smile.

The four other colored girls in her grade considered her "country" and found reasons not to associate with her. I always saw her alone during lunch. Eventually, she told me her "home" was Virginia. Her father worked in the shipyard and her two brothers were still "down home," but they were coming to live with them when the weather got warm. She made it sound like there would be a dozen people crowded into one house. I walked her part of the way home one day, then three quarters of the way, and finally all the way to her house which was on Jewel, the same street Elizabeth had lived on.

The door opened. A large, dark, pleasant looking woman filled the entrance. It Mrs. Portlock.

"Hi, Momma," Paige cried, skipping up the steps. "I'm home."

The woman blocked the entrance, glaring at her, and then she looked at me.

"Where's yo manners, gul?" she barked. "Who that standin' out yonder?"

"Oh, that's Aaron, Momma. He in my class at school."

"An what's my name?" she demanded.

Paige looked flustered.

"You suppose to introduce people when you bring 'em home," her mother informed her in a gentler tone. "You got better manners than that."

Intimidated by her fierce tone and large size, and remembering the pugnacious Mrs. Washington, I did not accept her invitation to come in and have a snack. I didn't walk Paige to her door after that.

"Why you won't walk me home, Aaron?" she asked one day. She grinned, "You scared of Momma, ain'tcha?"

"I'm not scared! I just don't want you to get hollered at again."

She regarded me with sloe eyes and a faint smile. "Why you worried about me gettin' hollered at?"

Flustered, I did not know what to say. We were standing on the corner of her street and mine. She was almost as tall as me and looked me in the eyes.

" - Because I like you," I murmured.

Her eyes lit up. "For real?"

A little taken aback and squirming, I managed to nod, surprised that her face was so alive. It glowed and her eyes were fixed on me with frank, shameless adoration. I felt a flush go through me.

Hooking her arm in mine, she marched me reluctantly down the street to her house. As usual, her mother stood in the front door waiting for her.

"Momma!" she cried. "Aaron say he like me!"

Oh, my God! I groaned, wishing for all the world that I could vanish from the face of the earth. Who ever heard of anybody doing anything like that!

Mrs. Portlock smiled good naturedly. "You churren come on in here an' get you something to eat."

Face burning, and not knowing how to say "No", I slid cautiously past her and entered another world.

Their house was not as neat as ours. There was too much furniture in the living room and too many people in the kitchen. Three women were sitting around a large table. One was stout, one was slender with a distinctive mole on her chin; the third seemed to be the youngest. Two were snapping string beans while the stout woman was peeling potatoes.

Their animated chatter took no notice of us until Mrs. Portlock announced: "This Aaron, an' this Mis Eula Mae, she Mis Nancy and that one Mis Pearl," she said indicating the youngest one. "They all my sisters."

I said hello, shrinking from their curious eyes.

"Who he?" Miss Eula Mae, the slender sister wondered, eyeing me with suspicion. She was several shades lighter than the rest, and not as pleasant looking as Mrs. Portlock.

"He go to school with Paige."

"What she doin' bringing niggers home at her age?" Eula Mae

frowned

I recoiled from the word nigger.

"She ain't 'bringin' no niggers home,' Eula; he a boy live 'round the corner."

We found places at the large table. Mrs. Portlock sat thick, yellow slices of cake before us, together with a bottle of black liquid and a glass of buttermilk. I never liked buttermilk because it tasted like sour milk. Valiantly, I determined to drink it. I picked up the piece of cake hoping it would mask the taste of the buttermilk.

"What!" Mrs. Portlock shouted, standing next to the table. "You don't want moe'lasses?" Picking up the bottle of black liquid, she held it over my plate. "I'll pour you out some," she said. Without further ado, she tilted the bottle. A thick, black fluid slowly oozed from the round opening of the bottle to form a thick black substance on the cake.

I stared first at the black stuff, then at her. "No, ma'am," I murmured, uncertain - "I never had that before."

My confession caused immediate consternation. The sisters stopped snapping beans; a potato was left half peeled; eight amazed eyes swung in my direction. Mrs. Portlock frowned, uncertain of what she had let into her house.

Miss Eula Mae was the first to recover her senses. " - Boy," she frowned, "you mean to set there an' say, you ain't never et moe'lasses before?"

"Where's your home at, boy?" Miss Pearl, the youngest sister demanded. Her eyes were alive with curiosity. She seemed to be about twenty.

" -Philadelphia," I answered quietly.

"She mean where your *real* home at," Mrs. Portlock explained, gently.

"Where was you born at," Miss Nancy, the stout sister demanded in a tone that said she would have the truth out of me or else.

"I was born here," I repeated.

More consternation. Eight pair of eyes pinioned me in the silence that followed. Mrs. Portlock found the solution. "Where your daddy from? Virginia?" she asked hopefully.

"No ma'am, my parents are from here, too. So's my grandfather."

"I told you he talk funny!" Paige interjected with an I-told-you-so tone.

"You hush," her mother, scolded, "he talk different, thas all."

At their urging and aware of their stares, I tentatively tried the molasses and found it not too much different from syrup. They explained that the "cake" was something called cornbread, which when spread with molasses, was tasty enough to make the buttermilk palatable.

*****

There was something about Paige's house that I liked.

There was glowing warmth, easy laughter, and a good deal of kidding disguised as gruffness. Much of life was lived in the kitchen which was always cozy and filled with affection and the warm murmur of conversation. There were new smells, too, of collard greens and ham hocks; cornbread, pigs' feet, potato salad, candied sweet potatoes, sweet potato bread, hog maws and chitterlings and deep-fried chicken.

Mrs. Portlock liked me. She thought I was a "li'l gentlemin." Of her sisters who had come to the city looking for work, only Miss Pearl, the youngest, seemed to share her feelings. The others were suspicious of my origins. I didn't really care as long as Paige and I could share a little time alone in the living room, snuggled together on the sofa.

I had never been that close to a girl before.

Our shoulders touched as I helped her spell out difficult words; I found excuses to touch her hands, to guide her girl finger to difficult passages, to lean ever closer, smelling her, seeing the delicate smoothness of her face and her neck.

Once she shouldered me away. "I can read," she informed me. "You ain't got to git all over me."

Undeterred and bracing myself for I knew not what, I kissed her on her cheek one day. Immediately my entire body tingled. I remembered the sensation I had felt after I kissed the nape of Elizabeth's neck. I saw Paige flush shyly before she pushed me away. I wanted to hold her close to me and kiss her over and over.

Eventually, my kiss on the cheek came to be expected and accepted. It progressed to a hug followed by longer hugs and longer kisses. One day I kissed her on her lips.

She frowned. " - You don't kiss right."

Crushed, I murmured, "I do, too."

"You don't neither. I watched my cousin and J.P. You ain't suppose to kiss nobody with your mouth shut."

Incredulous, I sputtered, - "But if you don't close your mouth, you'll get spit all over you! People don't do that," I assured her. "Maybe where you're from, but not up here. I never heard of such a thing!" I declared, recovering my shattered ego.

Our time alone was up and we parted, both filled with questions that only time could answer.

*****

Mr. Portlock, Paige's father, presented a frightening aspect.

When he first lumbered through the kitchen doorway, he almost filled it. He was bulky, dark, loud and dressed in rough, gray work clothes. Eyes blazing, frowning with anger, he thundered belligerently, "Ah smells food but I sho nuf don't see none!"

"An' you ain't gonna see none, neither, nigger," Mrs. Portlock shouted back at him, "'less you git them smelly ole clothes off and wash yo face an hans!".

Petrified, I gaped, mouth open. Mr. Portlock, wild eyed, suddenly rushed at his wife, roaring, "Come heah, womin!"

Squealing with delight, she nimbly danced around the table despite her large size. "Gone way from heah with them ole clothes, Daniel!"

Grinning, he stopped chasing her.

"You a mighty happy nigger today, Daniel," Miss Eula Mae grinned. It was the first time I had seen her look pleasant. Everybody was pleased to see him. Unaccustomed to such carrying on, I stared, still shocked.

"Ah's a happy nigger every day," he boasted, before his wife pushed him out of the kitchen. "Hurry up, Daniel. We's hungry an I fixed you poke chops, special."

How could anyone call himself that, I wondered, when it meant everything that was bad and despicable? Yet, everybody in Paige's house used the word with cheerful casualness.

And they called me that, too. Momma said only low class, ignorant, bad people were niggers, and it didn't make any difference who said it, white or colored. It was a terrible thing to be called. Like the time Mrs. Washington called Momma that in front of all the neighbors.

Chapter 15

I met Fred. He and his family were one of the new people who had moved into our neighborhood now that white people were moving out. Daddy said the influx was because of the war.

"They brought people in from all over to build ships and make bombs. Had 'em working around the clock; even had women. They tell me a man could get hired on the spot. City's jam-packed with people; they got to live somewhere."

Momma wasn't pleased. "Why do they have to come all the way up here?"

"It's not just here, Gert, it's all over. Trolley cars take you anyplace you want to go. Not like it was when you had to live close by your job. Look at all the cars on the street."

Fred Williams lived in the same house where Elizabeth used to live, 2042, only the house had been divided into apartments. We were the same age, but he was taller and had a loose, mobile mouth that he twisted into funny shapes for the amusement of his friends.

I had begun asking people where they came from; I wanted to know whether or not they were from "down home" or Philadelphia. He had been born here but his parents were from North Carolina so he said, "My home's Carolina."

We only became friends because everybody I knew had quit school and gone to work. Alexander, Billy Ross and Thomas Jones had all started working as soon as they got their first pair of long pants. Nobody had time anymore to hunker down on the sidewalk to shoot marbles with me, or to sit on the front doorsteps as we once had, wishing for dreams to come true.

Thomas Jones worked in his father's barbershop shining shoes and learning how to cut hair. Alexander, working with his father, was the only colored printing apprentice in the city, and Little Billy Ross had been sent to Pottstown to live with relatives since his mother died of the flu and his father had fallen to pieces.

Fred and I became friends because he was the only show in town. Even though his family was poorer than anybody else we knew, they wanted him to stay in school and get a high school diploma. He had a bad habit of calling me nigger.

"Quit calling me that!" I barked.

He was puzzled. " - Calling you what?"

"You know what. You say it all the time and I already told you, don't call me that!"

"What's wrong with it? We all niggers, ain't we?"

"I'm colored! You can be that if you want, but I'm colored. You don't see white people calling each other stupid names, do you? Nigger means you're dumb, stupid, ignorant, loud, that you got no pride. Just calling yourself that proves it!"

"Aw, you just ignorant an' full of shit. Youse a nigger an' just don't wanna admit it. You damn sure ain't white."

Enraged I squared off. "Say that again and I'll knock your block off! Go on - I dee-double-dare you!"

He leaned forward until we were almost nose to nose. "Youse a nigger," he said calmly.

I swung a paralyzing blow to his head. And missed. We went at each other. Both of us thought we were pretty fair boxers, having caught the Jack Johnson fever. Like most boys we tried to emulate the black champion, each boasting that we had developed a devastating knockout punch.

Standing toe to toe, we hurled our paralyzing blows at each other, missing most of them. People stopped to watch, school children urged us on, and more than once a voice pleaded with someone to stop the fight. Finally, a white man stepped between us and ordered us to break it up.

News of the fight beat us home. When I explained why I'd been fighting, Momma was torn between approving my motive but disapproving my means. She fixed her lips in a disapproving line and said nothing.

"What was you all fightin' about, Aaron?" Paige queried.

I was glad she asked. Under cover of being angry with Fred, I told her exactly how I felt about the word and how my mother and everyone we knew felt about it.

She didn't say anything, but I was certain she would take the news home. What her family would do with the revelation was anybody's guess, but if they persisted in calling me that, I'd have to stop going to her house and content myself with talking to her on the way home.

I didn't notice less use of the word in Paige's house, but at least they didn't call me that anymore.

*****

Mr. Portlock was the loudest person in the house, but Mrs. Portlock was the dominant one. He probably stood six feet four and weighed well over two hundred pounds but everyone took their cue from her. He was a giant who roared when he talked, roared when he laughed, glared menacingly, glowered, threatened, and seemed to dominate everybody with his size. But beneath that, Mrs. Portlock and her sisters saw the little boy they had grown up with "down home."

Mrs. Portlock enjoyed his good-natured exuberance. When he roared, she roared right back, glowering and glaring and exchanging good natured threats. She bullied him, smacking him here, and shoving him there because both relished rough edges. I started liking him because I'd never seen anybody so big and strong who at the same time could act as playful as a boy. I think if I'd been his son he would've played marbles with me.

But when he was angry, he was quiet. They said you had to be mighty careful around him when he lowered his voice and spoke soft and polite-like. You better be ready to humbly apologize or run as fast as your legs could take you. I heard a few dark hints that they hadn't moved to Philadelphia just because of the shipyards. Something had happened "down home," - a certain "somebody" had "sure 'nuf let his mouth write a check his behin' couldn't cash."

Armed with steaming heaps of food, Mr. Portlock delighted in ragging his sisters-in-law for still being single.

He claimed he could almost agree with Pearl for not wanting to marry a "geechie" because it was bad enough you couldn't half understand them, but who in their right mind would want to go live with one of them on one of those little islands off the Carolina coast? But Miss Nancy - he would shake his head in mock puzzlement - she ain't had no business turning Solomon Carter away just because the man was fat, especially when she was fat herself.

"He ain't had no money is what it was," he concluded, chuckling.

"Here you come with that ole stuff," Miss Nancy cried, feigning indignation. "Carter was more'n fat. Man musta weighed near three hundred pounds. When a man that big, you got to consider other things, Daniel."

He threw his head back and roared, slapping his huge thighs while Mrs. Portlock gave Nancy a meaningful look, shaking her head slightly. The greatest gibes were reserved for light-skinned Miss Eula Mae who wouldn't marry poor Willie Thomas claiming he was too black.

"He was," she smiled, unrepentant. "Blackest man this side of Kingdom Come. Sun go down, you ain't see nothing but his teeth and the whites of his eyes."

"A nigger *'sposed* to be black," Mr. Portlock protested chewing merrily. "Why you can't see that, Eula? - All the rest of us mixed up with white here, Indian there, mule someplace else, an' here the man done did the right thing and stayed black," he roared in mock indignation - looking around the table in mock puzzlement - "and she won't marry 'im!"

Ignoring the laughter, Eula, who was a light pecan color, declared firmly but good naturedly, "I admit it. I'll tell the world, Eula Mae ain't got time for nobody blacker than she is. I sure God ain't birthin' no tar babies, that's for sure. I know what you gonna say, Daniel, 'The blacker the berry the sweeter the juice,' but Eula Mae ain't never been partial to berries."

Chapter 16

Momma never cared for Fred though he was courteous and well mannered when he came into our house.

A couple of times I had to remind him to pull his stockings up and buckle his knickers at the knee, but he never failed to say, "Yes, Ma'am" and "No, Ma'am." Unmoved she said he was "too grown" and "too fresh" and at bottom "too ignorant." And she never warmed to his mother either. Momma excluded her from her tight circle of friends. Fred's careless "ain'ts" and Seventh Ward attitudes fueled her antipathy toward both of them. "The apple never falls far from the tree," she declared.

Paige didn't pass muster, either, but her mother, Mrs. Portlock did. They probably never would have become friends had not Mrs. Portlock taken it upon herself to nurse Momma the time Momma had the flu. Mrs.Portlock wasn't like any of Momma's other friends. She was too loud and seemed to shout at you rather than talk to you. She called attention to herself by wearing clothes that didn't match. With her hair in plaits under a dull, red head scarf, images of Mrs. Washington sprang to mind.

Her speech was filled with "mo's" and "sho's", "ain'ts", "boss-man", "boss-lady" and other things, but she radiated a kindness that showed in her eyes, and in her good-natured laughter. Their friendship was sealed when she came to Momma for advice; Momma nodded approvingly when she observed her neighbor sweeping her sidewalk, keeping a clean, white doorstep and waiting for her child to return from school.

Momma grew to like her. Mrs. Portlock, with her round, mobile face, would accompany her conversation with frowns of bewilderment, by stretching her eye with astonishment, and with cries of: "Hush yo mouth, Mis Winston!" She was prone to shake her head, roll her eyes, wave her hands, or roar with laughter.

On occasion Mrs. Portlock brought a covered dish when she came to visit, and Momma began preparing food she had never cooked before - collard greens, pig's feet, neck bones, corn bread, grits and deep-fried chicken. For her part, Mrs. Portlock dolefully reported that she couldn't get anyone at her house to eat Momma's lamb stew and nobody liked the ham hocks and sauerkraut or stewed rhubarb.

When I walked Paige home after school, Fred took to joining us, but Mrs. Portlock did not invite him into the house. At first, I didn't mind him accompanying us until he started making it a habit. Everything he said made Paige laugh, but as far as I could see, all he did was make faces or poke fun at people we passed on the street. I told him that it wasn't nice to make fun of people, but neither of them paid any attention to me.

I wanted to tell him that Paige was my friend, not his, but it sounded silly and made it seem as though she was my girlfriend. Still, I thought she was too friendly. There weren't that many colored boys in our school but now that she'd gotten to know all of them, it seemed like every time I looked at her she was grinning in somebody's face or coyly ducking her head. I felt like I should be treated differently. After all, I'd been the only one to pay any attention to her when everybody laughed at her because she came to school with plaits sticking out all over her head like pictures you saw of pickaninnies on plantations.

One day, to avoid Fred, I suggested we take another way home from school.

"Whatcha want to do that for?"

"It's longer," I lied. "We can have more time that way."

"We have to wait for Fred."

"What for?" I said, beginning to walk off.

"'Cause," she said, holding her ground. "Ain't he your friend?"

"Yeah, but I don't need him stuck to me every place I go. -You coming?"

Reluctantly she fell in beside me. I didn't like anything that was happening and my bout with jealousy was slowly turning into anger.

Her face brightened. "Here he come!" she cried joyously as Fred bounded down the street to catch up to us.

I had nothing to say all the way home. I refused to grin, smile, nod or even answer when spoken to. To my chagrin neither seemed to mind. As we neared her house, Fred asked, "Whatchu mad about, Aaron? Somebody insult you again?"

"He mad 'cause I made him wait for you and he didn't want to," Paige chimed in.

"I am not!" I shouted. "You ought to keep your big mouth shut when you don't know what you're talking about!" With this I stalked off.

*****

Fred was the same age that I was, but just as Steve had been, he was years older in terms of experience. Some boys who are old for their age don't want to play anymore; they act too grown and try to make you feel little, but Fred was different; we still walked arm in arm like pals and shot marbles on the sidewalk.

"You ever feel her?" he asked me once, in the school yard.

"Who, Paige? I couldn't do a thing like that! She'd tell."

He expressed surprised. "Girls like for you to feel their titties. You didn't know that? It makes 'em feel good."

"I think she's too young for that," I said, pretending to be experienced.

"They ain't never too young 'cause if they ain't got no titties, then you gotta mess with 'em and it'll make 'em grow, and if they got titties, it'll make em grow even bigger."

"- I don't think I'd like doing that. The first thing you know, she'd be telling her mother and then I'd be in a lot of trouble all for nothing."

"Aw, you too scared for words. Girls don't tell their mother about that stuff; they like it."

I didn't want him talking about Paige like that; she was my friend, not his. He was making her sound like a bad girl. I didn't like it. I cast around for some way to get him off the topic only to have him demand, "How many times you kiss her?"

"I don't know her all that well; I never tried," I said, hoping that was the end of it.

" - What! You ain't never kissed her?" he persisted. "Gee, boy, you slow as moe lasses in January! I kissed I don't know how many girls. It's fun. I even kissed a lady one time."

I tried not to gasp."- A grown lady?"

"Last year. She was twenty-three years old, too! She used to room with us and one day Momma was out and she called me over an' started hugging me and kissing me and she said she was going to teach me how to kiss like grown-ups kiss. You know what she did?" He was wide eyed and lowered his voice. "She put her tongue in my mouth!"

"Ugh!" I groaned.

"You wanna know what else she did!" he cried, basking in my shocked reaction. Leaning over to my ear, he cupped his hands and whispered: "She was a bad lady - she let me do it to her!"

I was aghast! I stared at him. He was only 16 going on 17, the same as me! Seeing the incredulous expression on my face, he doubled over gasping with laughter until tears rolled down his face.

"Boy," he gurgled, shaking his head, "you sho look like somebody stuck you in the backside with an ice pick! Gee, boy, you sure *slow*. You ain't never kissed no girl or felt her titties an' I know you ain't never did it to nobody!"

It took me a week to digest everything he'd told me. I couldn't get it out of my head that the bad lady had put her tongue in his mouth! This bothered me more than that he actually did it to a grown lady. I'd already heard stories about people doing it, but nobody ever said anything about putting your tongue in somebody's mouth. It was so ugly and awful. "Ugh!" I shuddered. It was as bad as what Paige said the time I kissed her with my lips closed.

For all of his "ain'ts," Fred was a fund of information. It was Fred who disabused me of the notion that the stork brought babies. Men gave ladies babies when they "did it" to them and then the ladies' stomachs got real big and they had babies he told me. I turned my mouth down and shook my head in vigorous denial.

I stoutly maintained that he was wrong because I knew in my heart of hearts that my mother would never do anything nasty like "do it."

"Boy, you sure are dumb," he chuckled in amusement.

I squared off nearly in tears. "Put 'em up! You can't talk about my mother that way!"

"Aw, man, go to hell," he strolled away, still amused.

I grabbed his arm and spun him around. "No!" I yelled, eyes blurred with tears. "Put 'em up!"

He wasn't scared of me and I knew it. We'd fought before. He stared at me for a thoughtful moment. His brown eyes were curious, and then he said, "Aw, I didn't mean it. I was just lying. I take it back. C 'mon," he said, hooking his arm in mine, "we're still pals."

Chapter 17

But we weren't still pals.

We strolled arm in arm and shot marbles, but I felt a wall between us because I didn't think of my mother the same way anymore. Once she asked me what was on my mind and I said, "Nothing." I started to ask her where babies came from to see what she would say but I never did. Since there was nothing to say or do, I guess I let a numbness settle in. I was probably dumb just as he kept saying.

But when we finally broke up our friendship it was because of Paige.

At first I figured the only reason she liked him more than me was because he was common. He had a boisterous way of laughing and kidding around just like her parents did. Well, if she wanted somebody common, it was all right with me.

She'd probably get along better with somebody like him who wasn't always correcting her speech or asking: "What did you say?" Like the time she said, 'Wretched toe it' and then got mad because I had to ask her three times to repeat it until I finally figured out she meant 'Richard tore it.'

That wasn't saying she was dumb or anything; she wasn't, but like Momma said, a lot of people from the South didn't take time to learn how to talk right or learn how to act. They probably figured everybody was supposed to adjust to *them* instead of the other way around. They had never heard, "When in Rome do as the Romans do."

Paige didn't appreciate how much I'd tried to help her. She didn't even know what a fossil was until I told her or that stars were really suns. Neither did Fred for that matter.

A refined girl like Elizabeth was the sort I should be thinking about.

She was the kind you married. She wouldn't put up with any foolishness, and she'd never be lovey-dovey with you one minute and then hang all over your best pal the next.

I don't know how long it was before it occurred to me that I hadn't seen Paige in a while. "You and Paige stop speaking or something?" I asked Fred, trying to sound casual. "I don't see you with her anymore."

He didn't answer right away. He was on his hands and knees scrubbing the linoleum on the kitchen floor of their apartment. He crawled along making circular soapy motions, making me move out of his way. "Whatchu care?" he finally managed.

"I don't care; I'm just making conversation." When it seemed he was going to let it go at that, I ventured, "You act like you're jealous or something."

"Don't no girl make me jealous," he scrubbed. "Too many of 'em out there."

"Is that another way of saying she put you down?" I smirked, trying to egg him on.

He raised up on his knees and stared at me for a minute. "Boy, you *really* don't know whatchu talkin' about! If you did, you'd know she went down home and been gone more'n a week."

A week! – Why? Where? For how long? Is she coming back? I didn't ask him anything, but to keep him talking I warned, " She can't miss two weeks from school and still pass. She's going to get left down."

"Shit," he said, wiping the floor with a rag, "she ain't hardly worried 'bout no school. It don't much matter no how. She already quit school."

His tone and manner didn't go along with what he was telling me. He tried to sound unconcerned but I didn't believe him. A lot of kids quit school, but Mrs. Portlock would have mentioned it to my mother. They were always talking about their children or somebody else's. Why hadn't I heard anything?

Come to think of it, Fred wasn't his old self and hadn't been lately. Other things had changed, too. He wasn't allowed out as much, and he'd been given a lot of chores to do. I even saw him scrubbing his front doorsteps. Most of us had to scrub our steps while he laughed at us for having to do "women's work."

*****

"Paige quit school and went back down South," I told Momma, probing for information.

She looked up from her ironing. "Mrs. Portlock's daughter? Who told you that?"

"Fred. He said she's been gone about a week."

Momma was noncommittal but went to see Mrs. Portlock later that week. I tried to read her face when she came back but could tell nothing.

"- When is Paige coming back?" I asked.

"Mind your business," she said, putting on an apron in the kitchen. "What grown people talk about is no concern of yours."

She handed me a rolled-up newspaper and set me to work killing flies buzzing around the kitchen.

'I wanted to ask why I couldn't ask a simple question, but I was afraid of the lightning and roaring thunder it would provoke. Yet I knew there was a reason she wouldn't tell me anything.

Daddy deepened the mystery. "Did Fred tell you he was in trouble?" he asked at dinner that night.

"- Fred? No, Sir. What'd he do, steal something?"

"Worse than that. A whole lot worse. We don't want you hanging around with him anymore. I know friends are supposed to stick together and all that, but when folks get in trouble you have to step back and think. There's an old saying, 'Birds of a feather stick together.' People see you two together, they'll think you're both the same. It won't matter what the truth is; if people think something is true, then it's true."

What in the world had Fred done? He didn't carry a knife so he couldn't have cut anybody; maybe he broke somebody's window or sassed a grown person, but none of it made sense. Stealing was the most likely thing, but Daddy had already said no.

"Did he beat somebody up?" I groped.

He pursed his lips. For a moment I think he was going to tell me and then thought better of it.

"You'll find out one day. Just don't go around there and we don't want him here."

I cornered him at school the next day. "What'd you do? My father said you're in a lot of trouble! I'm not allowed to hang around you anymore. "

"That's a lie!" he shot back, moving past me. I followed him.

"He's got no reason to lie on you and you know it! You did something wrong or he wouldn't have said it, and you wouldn't have to stay in the house all the time!"

I remembered Steven shouting, "It's a lie!" We stopped being friends after that. I didn't say anymore because I still wanted to be Fred's friend. We glared at each other for a moment and then let it rest.

My parents had never cared for Fred. Until now they had stopped short of saying don't associate with him. Truth be told, without him, I had nobody else to pal around with.

He found my sexual naiveté a rich source of mirth, but he basically tolerated my Puritanism and he played marbles with me. He listened as I took him sailing with Ulysses in *The Odyssey* and he let me show him *Leo* springing through the night sky. I deafened my ears to his "ain'ts" and "sho's" and ignored his raucousness. Even his coming between Paige and me was forgivable. Why get sore? She preferred his joking around, his loud, drawling Southern banter and his rough housing. He was a lot like her father, even though Mrs. Portlock never invited him into her house.

*****

I found out that he'd done something nasty with Paige.

She was in a family way. Mortified, Mrs. Portlock had sent her back down South to stay with relatives. Fred was almost seventeen like me. But Paige was just a girl. How could a girl be in a family way? I'd only seen women get that way.

The story spread. Snooping, I heard more bits and pieces. People were saying Paige was "a regular little hussy," always grinning in some boy's face. They wondered why a 14-year-old "fresh pot" like her was alone with a boy in the first place. She was "too fast" for her age. Her mother hadn't raised the child right because any decent girl would know better than to "lift up her skirt." What could you expect from people like that; they think they're still down on some plantation where that's all they did. She and that boy should be made to get married despite their age to at least give the child a name! They should have put a strap on her fresh behind long time ago and beat the devil out of her!

Mrs. Jones was the only one who had anything kind to say about her.

"I'll admit she's too fresh," she allowed, "but why's everybody jumping on her? That boy's the one who got her in trouble. He's just as fresh as she is - more so because he should be out working like other boys his age instead of running the streets.

"I blame his parents. Instead of marching him down to City Hall to get a marriage license, they got the nerve to say he's too young to be burdened with a family! Did you in all your life ever hear such a thing? Wasn't too young to act like a grown man, but now he's too young! Must think they're still in slavery where that's all they did was breed children like pigs for the slave owner to sell. Too young, indeed!

"They tell me her father went over there with a pistol ready to blow his brains out, but his wife dragged him home before he could shoot anybody."

*****

I saw Fred a couple of days later in front of Broudy's grocery store where he did odd jobs. He'd acquired perpetual frown lines between his eyes, and his knickers were smartly buckled just below the knee instead of hanging down casually like the rest of us wore ours when out of our parents' sight. He was standing on a ladder cleaning the store window with balled up newspaper. I was dying to confront him with what I knew. He ignored me.

"When are you going to be done?" I asked.

"I can't talk when I'm workin'," he replied, without looking at me.

I watched in silence as he brought the window to a gleaming shine. As he came off the ladder, Mr. Broudy, a stout man in glasses, wearing a long white apron, handed him two straw market baskets filled with groceries.

"Run these over to Mrs. Bryant's. Her address is written on the bag. Hurry. We're busy."

Fred tried to shoo me away. "Why don't you go home! Can't you see I'm busy?"

That reminded me of Steven dismissing me at the intersection the last time I ever saw him. "I heard all about you and Paige," I accused. I wanted to sound cool and unconcerned.

"So?"

"You called my father a liar."

"So?"

"- I thought we were pals. Pals tell each other their secrets."

"So?"

He wouldn't look at me. Arriving at Mrs. Bryant's house, he mounted the steps, delivered the groceries, received a nickel tip, and was forced to put up with me on the way back to the store.

"I don't understand how you got Paige in trouble."

"I stuck my dick in her pussy an' I came, that's how!" he glared. "You act so dumb I don't see how you even breathe! You don't know *nothing*, dammit. Nothin! I never met nobody like you before. How come you don't know nothing?"

"I don't mean that - I mean how can she get in a family way when she's not a lady yet?"

"You can see she got tits, can't you! Whatchu think they're for? You ain't never seen a baby feeding off a tit before? You can't be that dumb, Aaron!"

"Don't call *me* dumb! You're the one in trouble."

"Oh, shut the hell up! Whatchu know about it? You don't even know how to kiss no girl. I heard all about it."

We arrived back at Broudy's and he stormed into the store. I wanted the last word so I waited to pounce on him when he came back out. Yet the longer I waited the more I realized that compared to him, I really was dumb. He was right - what the hell did I know.

How had he gotten her to lift up her skirts and take her bloomers off? What did he say to her to make her do such a thing? She pushed me away for pressing too close to her. What did he say to make her do that?

I went home filled with questions I couldn't ask because there was never anyone who'd answer them. After that Fred and I still talked to each other in school about little things, keeping the raw edges of our emotions out of sight, but like a ship moving away from a dock, he and I started to part. The movement was so slow that with a start I suddenly saw the distance between us.

He had done something as bad as robbing a store or maybe even killing somebody. It was all anybody talked about. Being friends with a bad person was a hard thing to do. Something had to happen to get rid of the badness. The badness was like an awful stink that made you hold your nose and screw up your face; the stink had to go away before you could do anything else.

Someone had seen us talking, and it wasn't long before Momma knew about it.

"You were seen talking to that boy yesterday," she scolded as soon as I got home from school. "What did we tell you about that? Why are you so hard-headed, Aaron?"

"He just asked me a question, Momma. All I did was answer him."

She looked suspicious. "What did he ask you?"

"- If we were still friends."

"- What did you tell him?"

"I didn't know what to say. You said don't hurt people's feelings - I said I didn't know."

She wasn't satisfied but didn't say anything else, which was a bad sign. She was watching and waiting.

*****

"Whatchu mean, you don't know if we're friends?" Fred objected a few days later. "Either you is or you ain't!" His eyes were unyielding. He was standing too close, breathing in my face. I edged away.

"I already told you what my parents said."

"So? They ain't here now. How come you can't talk to me now? What kinda friend you supposed to be anyway?"

We were standing outside Broudy's grocery store. That is where a lot of us went after school to spend our pennies and nickels on licorice, fudge and all-day suckers. "People talk, you know that. First thing you know my mother'll know I was talking to you, and then I'll catch the dickens when I get home. I can't go through that everyday. Anyway, last I heard, you were the one who didn't want me around; you didn't even want to talk to me. You said I was too dumb!"

"So whatchu saying is we ain't friends no more, right?"

"- I didn't say that exactly - "

"But you saying it anyhow," he shot back.

"I'm not grown, Fred. I have to do what my parents tell me to do, and I don't think you ought to be asking me to sneak around behind their back then lie to them. - I'm not going to lie to them!"

For the first time I realized that his mobile face, so quick to grin and mimic, could show hurt as well as derision. His brown, wounded eyes regarded me for a full moment as though he, too, had reached a realization. With a sneer of contempt, he turned his back and strode into the store.

The ship crept away from the dock. The distance grew wider till one day the ship vanished, leaving a faint smudge on the horizon.

Like Elizabeth's family, and ironically from the same house, Fred and his parents also slipped away, leaving blank windows to stare back at disapproving neighbors.

When would I have another pal?

Chapter 18

I was scared when Daddy was fired after Mrs. Woolman died. I think Momma was, too. I could tell by the worried look on her face when she talked to Daddy.

"Is Daddy going to get another job?" I asked as she did the laundry. We were in the shed kitchen, the small, unheated room attached to the kitchen that was used for storage and laundry. Several times a week she bent over the huge galvanized tub, pumping her arms up and down scrubbing our dirty laundry on the galvanized steel scrubbing board.

"Don't concern yourself with grown people's business," she said without looking up. "...We'll just have to wait and see."

"You know when Ned's coming home, Momma?"

"- I can't answer that."

"Do you know where he is?"

"He's on a ship. Now stop asking so many questions," she said, putting a shirt into the wringer.

"I'm almost seventeen, Momma. I'm going to get a job and help out."

She bent down reaching for another garment to put in the wringer. "You're to stay in school, get your diploma and try to go to college. That's been settled."

"Nobody else is staying in school or going to college. Everybody's working. Alexander and..."

"Now you just hush! How many white boys are quitting school to go to work? Did you ever notice...?"

"A lot of them, Momma," I cut in, "and some even joined the army. "Jimmy Steinholtz next door ..."

She straightened up, rigid with anger, eyes flashing, hands dripping. *"I SAID, HUSH!* - You're getting to be a regular little fresh pot! The nerve of you cutting across me like that! What's gotten into you anyway? I don't care if every white boy in the city quits school, or joins the army - you're to finish and try to go to college, do you hear! Do you want to spend your life sweeping the streets?

"Those boys can quit school any time they want and still get a job in an office - you can't. That boy next door's an apprentice with the steam fitters. His father got him in. You can't get that kind of job *with* a high school diploma! You saw what happened to your brother. You can't ever be just as good as a white person; you always have to be *better*. Not just better, but much, *much* better!"

Upset, she began putting dirty clothes into the rinse water instead of in the wash tub. Braving her wrath, I stepped forward and stopped her. It took a second for her to understand what I was doing and the gathering wrath subsided. Her tone was kinder as she corrected her mistake with the laundry.

" - Only four colored boys finished school last year and six colored girls. How many colored boys are left in your school, Aaron? Just you and Bobby Spears. It was sweet and thoughtful of you to offer to work. I'm not surprised you'd say a thing like that, but your daddy and I want to see you get a good start in life. We're going to try to send you to college and that's that."

Steven's taunt that I would only be an educated ditch digger drifted back. Momma was telling me that even if I finished high school, I could not compete with white boys who were less educated than I was. Ned had said the same things in so many words. Maybe if I hadn't spent so much time playing marbles, I'd have known that she wasn't telling me anything that wasn't as obvious as an elephant in a living room.

Change, like lifting fog, revealed things that had gone unnoticed because they were so common place. Squinting through the fog, I saw with clear focus that colored men lifted the heavy ash cans and hurled them into the trash wagon, but a white man sat and drove the team of horses. In the evening, we children had trailed behind the lamplighter as he illuminated the night, but I never saw a colored lamplighter.

Colored policemen did not patrol the streets twirling nightsticks nor did colored fireman cling to the side of racing fire wagons. Only in a land of fantasy did Negro motormen drive trolley cars. But like three blind mice - Alexander, as a child, was positive that he would be a cop when he grew up; Little Billy adamantly chose the fire wagon where he'd drive the snorting team of horses, and hadn't I chosen to be a general with an army?

The elephant in the living room had gone unnoticed when Ned came home half frozen from shoveling snow all day, clearing the streets and trolley tracks to earn a few dollars. And when he stumbled home grimy and smelling from whatever else he was doing to earn a day's pay. Yet he had a high school diploma, and Steven, who had quit school, mocked his futility.

If I were "much, much better" than a white man, what would I be? More - what *could* I be? College? Was that even a possibility? Would it make a difference?

*****

Before Daddy was finally fired, he came home more frequently, his horse face longer than the day before. When he and Momma talked, they didn't always shoo me away.

"Mister John finally came down," Daddy said quietly after he struggled out of his coat. Seeing me drying dishes at the sink, he gave my shoulder a friendly squeeze before sitting at the kitchen table.

"- Is he going to keep the house?" Momma asked, getting cups and saucers. A hot cup of tea was her way of saying hello. She set the cups side by side on the kitchen table.

Mister John and Miss Emily were Mrs. Woolman's children and heirs. Miss Emily had married and moved to Boston while her brother had settled in New York with his wife. After the funeral, Daddy had been left hanging, pending further arrangements.

"No, they're not keeping the house. Nice as it is, neither one of them wants it. I knew something was up when they let most of the help go, especially the cook. You never fire a cook unless you mean to close up."

They drank their tea with only the sound of their cups on their saucers to disturb the silence. I finished the dishes and quietly sat at the table with them.

"I guess he didn't say anything to you," Momma offered.

He shook his head. " - I asked him a couple of weeks ago if he'd be needing anybody. He wouldn't come right out and say it, but we all more or less figured we'd be let go. I was sort of hoping Miss Emily would need me but now I see I can't depend on her either.

"She used to be the sweetest child, following me everywhere I went, always trying to 'help.' - Remember? I used to tell you about her all the time. But ever since she married that 'Captain' Jack..." he paused, shaking his head, "she just seemed to change. Mr. John was never too friendly. Even as a child. Always too snotty and bossy."

Momma laid her hand over his and patted it gently. "It'll be all right, Ned," she assured him quietly. "- I've got a penny or two put aside...You're too good a man to be let go. You'll see."

Several days later a carriage drew up in front of our door. Two men began carrying in all of Daddy's accumulated belongings spanning twenty-five years. He had been let go without severance pay.

In the days that followed he would shake his head. "I just don't understand. Mrs. Woolman always said I'd be provided for, but at the very least, Gert, you *always* give a person severance pay! I've been there all these years, I've been loyal, never stole a piece of bread. You know that. - Look at all the money I could've made in the shipyard during the war. People were making more money in a week than I made in two, then the minute the war's over - this.

"You couldn't even get servants back then. People took war jobs, but no, I stayed on like...like slaves you hear about staying on plantations after they were freed talking about – 'Ah gotta take care of ole Massa!' Now this!"

For the first time in my life I heard an angry "Shit!" uttered by my father.

Seeing his despair, Momma sat on his lap oblivious to my presence. She cradled his head against her breast and lay her head against his. She seemed to rock him gently. – "I think they're trying to cheat you, Ned." She whispered.

"What's a couple weeks' pay, Gert? They spend that much on dinner."

"They're trying to cheat you," she insisted, a hint of fire in her eyes. " - Aaron, go in the other room."

I didn't want to spy on them. I didn't eavesdrop. His tone and his posture and his face were too disquieting. So were his eyes. To see him worried and puzzled like that was like seeing a huge, solid building tumble down in clouds of dust.

He no longer had a job. That was very, very serious. It could even be worse than when Mr. Purnell lost his job. When Mr. Cramer, across the street, was fired from his job last year, the constable came with some men one day and moved all his furniture out of the house and onto the sidewalk. Mrs. Cramer kept running after them crying, and pleading to let them stay just that night. The men shook their head and said they were sorry, but they had to do what the constable told them to do or they would get fired.

Then there were the Lawrences around the corner. Neighbors took them and their children into their homes but the furniture remained on the sidewalk. There was no place to move it nor could the family afford to store it. Two days later under threatening skies, Momma and other neighbors stored all the things that they could before the rain came and ruined the rest. Everyone took turns feeding them and letting them sleep on the floor in their house. Momma offered to let them sleep in our house, too, but they never came.

If the constable came and put us out, would Momma have to beg neighbors to take us in and feed us? Would anyone even offer? How could so much change so suddenly? Now the days were never soft and smooth and seamless as they once had been. A chasm had already developed between us and our once friendly white neighbors. They resented all the colored people who were moving into the neighborhood, and they behaved as though we were personally responsible for it.

There used to be a time when Daddy would tip his hat to Mrs. Grogan and Mrs. Steinholtz, but he didn't anymore because Mr. Grogan no longer tipped his hat to Momma. Mr. Steinholtz never had. Once some of the white kids in the neighborhood occasionally deigned to play with us; those days had long since vanished.

And if anyone got into a fistfight with one of the white kids, there was no longer any discussion. White parents stormed off to the police station to press charges. Their word was all that counted. Despite apologies and promises of severe punishment, the Rheingolds still had insisted that Jerome Brewster, over on 17th Street, be sent to the House of Detention. Boo Boy had left a legacy that Jerome and all of us were to be taxed with.

Daddy being out of work was serious. People who are out of work are not equal to other people. Not when those with jobs have coal in their basement, a roast in the oven, an extra penny or two for ice cream from Shilling's on the corner, and not when there's a trolley to catch each day for the job that's waiting for them.

Having to go to work every day may be a pain, but being without a job is a worse pain. People out of work are not equal when their furniture is thrown on the sidewalk for all to see, like a hole in your stocking.

Daddy being out of work made the world a harsher place.

*****

I remembered the time Ned was looking for work and I had tried to help with the want ads. Wiser this time and wanting to help Daddy, I looked for "Negro butler" and "colored butler." There was nothing. What sort of job could he get?

"Momma, what's a porter do?"

She was bustling about the kitchen, getting dinner ready. "He's a handy man, sweeping up, putting out ashes and cleaning mostly. That's about all you'll end up doing if you quit school. What made you ask?"

"I was trying to see what kind of job Daddy could get; Ned said if it didn't say 'colored,' you couldn't get the job."

She mulled this over for a few seconds. "…For most jobs that's true, but if you know people who'll open doors for you, it's not true."

"What're 'doors'?"

A rare smile creased her thin face. "The door of opportunity! You have to know the right people. People who like you because you're decent and respectable, a cut above the others. That's how your grandfather got a job with the post office. The man who got him hired knew Granddad from the war, and was glad to help a veteran. Mr. Purnell got on with the city because his father asked somebody he knew to open a door for him. Even Mr. Witherspoon got his job in the print shop because people opened a door for him.

"Now Mr. Witherspoon's the manager in all but name. Those friends of yours who quit school to wash dishes, shine shoes, sweep floors and empty tobacco spit will be doing it for the rest of their lives."

"Couldn't Ned get a job by opening doors?"

She took so long to answer I thought I had said something wrong. She removed a pot from a burner and set it aside.

"- He wouldn't listen," she said, quietly. "He's a little too stubborn that way. Your father could have gotten him on with one of Mrs. Woolman's friends. Opportunity is first cousin to luck, Son. Now you see it, now you don't. It won't wait while you make up your mind."

I was on the verge of reminding her that Ned did not want to be a servant, but caution covered my mouth.

*****

Momma turned to Aunt Gloria for help with Daddy's problem.

Aunt Gloria was the mythical figure in the family. Everybody said she was pretty. A framed picture of a young woman with hair swept up, a narrow face, the hint of a dimpled smile, a direct almost mesmerizing stare, and a slim, boyish figure sat in the living room. She was someone who swooped down on our house amid suitcases and trunks and later departed with exuberance and joy, headed for unspoken adventures in London or Amsterdam, perhaps New York but usually Paris.

Aunt Gloria never seemed to work. When the rest of our family came to see her, they wondered among themselves - "Where's Gloria get so much money? How can she afford to go to Mexico and Europe?" Keeping her counsel, Aunt Gloria simply arrived and departed. Now and then she stayed as long as week, never failing to bring gifts for Momma and a quarter for me and for Ned. It was always wonderful when she stayed because Momma was happy. Her face was creased with rare laughter, her eyes sparkled and the two of them talking incessantly.

Some said Aunt Gloria was married, but others said, no, that man had been a "friend." His name was Calvin, others opted for Frank. She had lots of "friends." Everyone in the family sensed the presence of a man but never saw one. Not even when large motor cars drew up to the door in the evening to whisk her away. No one ever got out to open the door for her.

However, no matter when we saw Aunt Gloria, we were happy because when she came, so did the rest of the family. The house was full.

Over the years I learned that she loved Madrid and Amsterdam, and because of her I wanted to see colorful little gardens and quaint cobblestone streets lined with shops that sold bread, and cheese, and wine and hand-woven fabrics. And I wanted to sit on a bench by the river in the afternoon and lounge in sidewalk cafes in the evening.

She spoke of famous writers and dancers and musicians whose names were just words, like Cocteau, Cole Porter, Josephine Baker and Hemingway. She not only brought gifts but also fire for the imagination, vision for seeing the world. A lavender fragrance clung about her and to the things that she owned and to the things that she touched.

Ned had heard her say that she felt free in Europe, so when Momma asked him to talk to Aunt Gloria before making a decision to leave, he wondered aloud - if she felt freer in other countries, what could she possibly say to dissuade him from leaving America? Maybe Momma thought that Aunt Gloria would paint a different, bleaker picture to prevent Ned from sailing into a raging war.

When she came this time it was different. There were no trunks and suitcases or the festive air of excitement that usually accompanied her. Nor did the rest of the family come to see her. She still pressed a coin in my hand, but her visit was not about Ned.

She held a long conference at the kitchen table with Momma and Daddy. I was banished and did not eavesdrop. The next day Daddy and Aunt Gloria left the house together. I knew if I asked where they were going, Momma would tell me to mind my own business where grown people were concerned so I didn't ask. They left together again later in the week.

When they returned, Daddy was obviously pleased. Aunt Gloria and Daddy had seen a lawyer who Aunt Gloria was friends with. Daddy hugged Momma and grinned a lot. No matter how hard I eavesdropped, nothing made sense. All I could make out was something had happened concerning something called a "will." It involved my father and Mrs. Woolman.

"If it was written down and witnessed, why'd they think they could get away with it?" Daddy wondered.

Aunt Gloria's laugh was short and mirthless. "They almost did get away with it, didn't they? Donald - Mr. Cohen- said people tamper with wills every day."

Momma, with a triumphant air, said to Daddy, "I told you something was wrong. That's why I sent for Gloria. It didn't make sense. Not after all those years."

The next day Aunt Gloria and Momma hugged each other at the front door; they cried a little and then Aunt Gloria was gone again.

A month later, I got the first pair of long pants that I was allowed to choose myself. Momma got the new hat and the matching gloves she had wanted, and Daddy bought a second-hand car. A couple of months later, he came home with a radio. Not only that, he got one of Mrs. Woolman's friends to "open a door" for him. He was given a job as a uniformed elevator operator in a big department store downtown.

It was during that time of fuss and confusion that something else happened - Daddy became a deacon of the Rock of Ages All-Faith Church.

Chapter 19

Momma wasn't pleased when Daddy became a deacon of the Rock of Ages All Faith Church.

How could anybody respectable be anything but Episcopalian? That was part of being respectable. She had quietly established early on that the Episcopal Church was blue blood, and the others simply common; it was a mansion compared to an outhouse. Go ask your Baptist or Methodist what the difference was between them. Neither could tell you. Worse, if you asked what the sermon had been about that Sunday, your holy roller was invariably tongue-tied.

People went to Episcopal Church services for intelligent instruction, not orgies and paroxysms of shouting, screaming, weeping and wailing. Services were meant for praying to an intelligent, philosophical God, not to a theatrical God that had been brought to the city by those people from the South!

No indeed, there was to be none of that for respectable people. Let there be exalted rituals and processions, enhanced by the holy smell of incense. Let there be the sight of candles and robed priests holding the Bible high above their head. Let those who believed, kneel and submit to His Holy Presence.

Anyway, who could deny that St. Mary's sounded so much more refined than the Twenty-Fifth Sanctified Church of Israel? And *Father Nicholas* sounded more exalted than Rev. Williams. More, no one thrust a collection plate at you three and four times a service as though putting money in the plate was the only reason you went to church.

Episcopalians had nuns, just like the Catholics. True, the priests and nuns were all white, but there were vague intimations that someday there might be a few colored clergy. Right now, none of that mattered. White clergy lent a certain prestige to the church that the other denominations, with all their shouting and carrying on, could not begin to claim. Too, when you considered it, all-black anything simply meant exclusion. It was what you had to settle for.

Momma became doubly convinced of her opinions after she quietly announced one Sunday that we were going to visit Daddy's church. The news lent an air of excitement because anything different was something to look forward to.

But Ned was reluctant to go. "Don't we go to St. Mary's?"

This was around the time of the cop incident, and Momma was treating him with kid gloves. "We're just going for a visit," she coaxed. "Your father wants us there."

Loyally we boarded one trolley car after another, then trooped six blocks to Daddy's church near the edge of the Seventh Ward. Rock of Ages was a small, stone-faced building with an obligatory steeple. It stood on a corner next to an empty lot.

We went in and were seated. I looked around for statues of Jesus Christ or Mary or one of the saints. I didn't see any, but there were candles like there were at St. Mary's.

A small, dark man stood at the pulpit scowling as though he had just tasted vinegar. He had not marched down the aisle in majestic procession, preceded by altar boys swinging censers, into the presence of God. He simply got out of a chair behind the pulpit as the choir sang with hand-clapping spirit.

I was surprised to hear people suddenly cry out, "Amen!"

Others added - "Yes, sir, Jesus!"

- "Help him, Lord!" a man in front of us urged.

"Mercy, King Jesus, Mercy!"

Nobody would ever do that at St. Mary's!

To my further astonishment, a heavy-set lady actually had the nerve to stand up in church, raise her arms above her head, and sway with the music!

The choir ended their hymn and without further ado the minister stared out at the congregation, and began to scold them.

"There's a lot of sinners sittin' out yonder this mornin'," he informed

149

them, glaring from the pulpit. "You know who you is an' I do, too!"

A chorus of Amens and people looking sideways at their neighbors.

"You been drinkin', you been gamblin', you been a cussin', you been fightin,' an you been carryin' on with mens and women you got no business being with in the first place!"

A loud roar of "Amens," self-righteous expressions, and women shouting, "Truth befo' God!" with heartfelt conviction.

"Hep him, Lawd!" several more urged.

"Keep on sinnin' an' carryin on,' ya hear?" the minister warned. "Keep it up and you gone wake up some cold mornin' with the Devil starin' you stone dead in yo face just a grinnin'!"

Loud shouts of "Amen" almost shook the building.

"He gone grab holt to you an' say, *'Gotcha!'* Then you git scared enough to mess all over yourself, an' you got the nerve to think," he thundered with righteous indignation, glaring around at all his sinners, "YOU THINK YOU GONNA GIT 'RIGHT' WITH THE LAWD?"

A woman screamed, and others shouted, "Hep me! Jesus, hep me!" Another woman several rows in front of us was flailing her arms about wildly. Her neighbors were trying to restrain her while avoiding the mighty arc of her heavy, black pocketbook.

"You scared now, an' you wanna GIT RIGHT WITH THE LAWD!" he bellowed. "Naw, you ain't gonna git right with the Lawd, he promised, not after you then seen *SATAN*." In a voice suddenly grown stronger and bolder, he demanded: *"WHAT DID JESUS SAY?"*

The question sent several women into paroxysms of ecstasy. Like the other flailing woman several rows in front of us, they too fell to leaping and bucking and shouting and flinging their arms around. Some fell back, rigid, and had to be caught by those seated behind them.

Emboldened, the preacher shouted rhythmically as he stomped his feet, "WHAT DID JESUS SAY? - (stomp) - WHAT DID JESUS SAY? - (stomp) - WHAT DID JESUS SAY?" And like some strange disease leaping from person to person, other women shrieked as though stabbed with a dart. They too leaped up, flinging their huge hips from side to side, shouting hoarsely, "Oh Jesus, ah feels the Spirit!" Others hollered, "Hallelujah!"

Now the preacher took to stomping his feet in a strange circular dance, pounding the pulpit and gasping in cadence, "Wake up some mornin' (gasp); WHAT DID JESUS SAY? Gonna git right with the Lawd (gasp); WHAT DID JESUS SAY? (gasp); Out all night sinnin' (gasp); WHAT DID JESUS SAY? - JeeeeeeSUS! (gasp); Wake up some mornin' (gasp); JeeeeeeeSUS!"

He caused loud, frantic, religious pandemonium.

There was shouting and screaming, twisting and jerking, tears and pleas to, "Have mussy, Jesus, have mussy!" Men danced around in little circles, arms raised, muttering "in tongues" and all the while the preacher, staring balefully, continued to shout and stomp in cadence, sweating and roaring the same awful message, "Out all night sinnin' (gasp); WHAT DID JESUS SAY?" (gasp).

Finally exhausted and drenched in perspiration, he stopped.

Ned seemed faintly amused. I could see from the set of her lips that Momma was in no danger of delivering herself of horrifying screams because the "Spirit" had gotten into her.

The choir began singing *Amazing Grace*. The preacher, composed now, wiped sweat from his brow with a handkerchief and smiled with benevolence. The congregation hummed and swayed to *Amazing Grace*, and beamed and shed unashamed tears of joy.

"I know there's somebody out there, lonely, sick at heart, waitin' to be saved," the preacher said with kindness. "Waitin' to come to Jesus. Jesus said, 'Suffer little children to come unto me,' - and we all little children in the sight of God. - Won't you come?" he pleaded. "Won't you come to Jesus?" he begged as the choir and the congregation hummed.

A young woman in a shabby coat stood and walked slowly to the altar and the preacher came down to meet her. He placed his hands on her bowed head in benediction. Her shoulders began to heave and she broke down in wrenching sobs. A woman screamed, then another. A second woman came forward followed by a man. I saw my father and the other deacons, and some women dressed in white - standing with those who had come, lending them comfort and support as everyone continued to hum "Amazing Grace."

*****

"Why were those ladies yelling like that?" I asked as soon as we were a decent distance from the church.

Momma, grim and exasperated, did not answer. Ned glanced at her quizzically before he said, "They were 'happy.' Some people imagine they can feel God inside them so they get 'happy.'"

I mulled this over with considerable dissatisfaction. "How come people at St. Mary's don't do that? Don't they feel God, too?"

We boarded the street car. Momma wanted no part of the conversation and arranged to have Ned sit by her so that I had to sit alone. I contented myself with looking out of the window at streets that were new to me. A young white lady got on the car and finding no seat except the one next to me, sat with her back to me and her feet in the aisle. I had noticed this maneuver before on other occasions and accepted it for what it was.

We changed cars and again Momma managed to avoid me. On the way home from the trolley stop, Ned offered her his arm like a gentleman. I tagged along on her other side.

"How come people at St. Mary's don't get 'happy'?" I persisted.

"Because only ignorant people act that way!" she snapped. "It's a disgrace! There's no need for all that hollering and screaming. It's got nothing to do with God. Nothing at all! Only common, ignorant people act that way. 'Happy!'" she hooted, fairly racing down the street in her button up shoes, her dress hem almost skimming the pavement.

"'Happy' about what, I'd like to know," she continued. "If they're so close to God, why is there so much devilment going on? Stealing, lying, cutting each other with knives, stabbing people with ice picks, throwing lye in people's faces! Every day, and it just gets worse! 'Happy' my foot! And what did that preacher say, I'd like to know; tell me that," she demanded glaring down at me. "What did he say?" she demanded again.

I thought as hard as I could but only remembered – "What did Jesus say?"

"See!" she cried in triumph, black eyes gleaming. "Those people didn't learn a thing about God, and," she assured me, wagging her finger, "neither did you!"

Truth be told, I couldn't remember having learned anything about God at St. Mary's, either. St. Mary's in my mind was a thing of kneeling and getting up, kneeling and getting up, kneeling and getting up and never knowing why, and dreading having to do it all over again. The St. Mary's that I knew was not the bastion of God that informed Momma's life.

*****

The irony was that when Rev. Mosley, the old preacher who had bellowed, "What did Jesus say?" died from a stroke, Daddy eventually became the pastor of the Rock of Ages All Faith Church. I never wondered how that could happen until several years later. We began going to his church more often, and Momma began to get along with other people there. Ned had left America by then. On the way home, I offered Momma my arm.

Chapter 20

I remember when I finally went to a barbershop to get my hair cut. I was fifteen. Until then, Daddy cut my hair while I sat on a kitchen chair. Everybody I knew eagerly awaited the result so they could fall out laughing, tears streaming from their eyes.

"Daddy, can I get a real haircut?" I asked as respectfully as I could. He lowered his paper and regarded me for a curious moment.

"Everybody keeps teasing me," I added.

"Turn around," he ordered. After a careful inspection, he announced – "I don't see anything wrong with your hair."

"That's because it grew back in. When it first gets cut, everybody laughs and says it looks ragged."

He suppressed a smile, raised his paper, and made a non-committal noise. I waited. Several seconds passed. Then: "I'll let Deacon Fortune cut it, but after that, you'll have to pay for it yourself. You're almost sixteen; time to start looking out after yourself. I was earning my keep before I was nine along with everybody else."

Actually, the first time I was taken to a barbershop I was five so that doesn't count. The barber cut off my plaits and put them in a little blue box that my mother kept. I followed the little box off and on until one day it disappeared. When I asked my mother for my plaits she made them reappear. The ends were still tied with a tiny, blue, silk ribbon. I followed again until one day the box was only a memory.

Deacon Fortune's barber shop was near Daddy's church. Daddy refused to let me take the trolley by myself for fear I'd run into a gang so Granddad took me. From the moment I entered the barber shop, it was a club to which I now belonged. I listened to grown people talk and didn't have to snoop, and what they said helped me learn the reality of being a black boy in America.

The barber shop was a world that had been waiting for me.

There was the heady smell of bay rum, the shaving mugs of blue, green, white and brown lining the shelves, the deep man-sound of laughter, the friendly nudge preceding a joke, the comfort derived from sitting near the stove, the fragrant scent of a pipe or a cigar, and listening to melodious voices remembering stories and other voices telling better ones. There were the cries of greeting for the old men who hobbled in on canes, their cranky faces creasing into smiles and the cheerful call of goodbye.

Sitting in one of the chairs lined up in front of the large front window, I watched a very light-skinned man get in the barber's chair. Deacon Fortune, whose walrus moustache I remembered from when Mr. Amos died, walked over to the shaving mugs on a shelf beside the chair and searched among them until he found the man's blue mug. Mixing a little water in with the soap in the mug, he stirred the shaving brush until he had a lather. He brushed swaths of white foam over the man's chin, stropped his razor, and began the careful job of shaving him.

Seated comfortably between Granddad and a man smoking a pipe, I heard that Jack Johnson lost his heavyweight boxing title to Jess Willard because the fight was fixed. Everybody in the barbershop had an opinion, but they all agreed that what happened was - as Johnson was lying flat on his back on the canvas of the outdoor boxing ring in Havana - after having been "knocked unconscious" by his white opponent - Johnson raised his arm to shade his eyes from the blazing Cuban sun.

"It was in the paper," Deacon Fortune said. "I saw the picture."

"He took a dive," the men rumbled. "All you used to read was 'White Hope, White Hope.' White folks couldn't stand for a black man to be champion. Had to be a white man."

"It wasn't that," another man disagreed. "What it was, was white women. Kept fooling around with white women. Even married one."

"She was just after his money," declared Mr. Carter, a gray bearded man with a cane. He spoke with the air of one who had been there and seen it. He was seated next to the pot-bellied coal stove.

"Which one you talking about?" Poppa John, a stout man with glasses, inquired. He occupied the other side of the stove. I remembered him, too, from before. "Johnson was married to more'n one white woman, and one of them was rich."

A man seated next to us told him it was the second wife. Deacon Fortune paused in shaving his customer. "Didn't I hear she died or something?"

"Killed herself," Granddad rumbled.

"Wasn't she already married?" Poppa John asked.

"Married for years," Granddad said. "When Johnson came along, she didn't have time for her husband anymore. Johnson stole her; spoiled her."

"They say women used to just throw themselves at him," Poppa John said in awe. "Say it was something about him just drove women crazy. If she killed herself, probably 'cause she couldn't keep him and couldn't stand it."

"Wasn't that," the deacon remarked, speaking slowly, making careful strokes with his razor. "- I remember, I read somewhere - they say none of her friends would have anything to do with her."

Granddad backed him up. "Soon's she married a Negro, wouldn't a soul piss on her - just like she was dead. Couldn't take it 'cause she was used to being around people. Blew her brains out."

"I heard it was poison," Mr. Carter objected.

"Don't matter what it was, now," Poppa John declared sensibly. "She dead, that's for sure."

"A colored man won't never get another chance at no title, they'll see to that," the deacon predicted. "They'll kill 'im first."

"You right about that," everyone agreed in chorus.

"Johnson messed his ownself up," the man next to me intoned self-righteously. "Soons a black man get a little money in his pocket, first thing they wants a white woman. They go crazy."

"- Oh, I don't know about all that, Bailey," Deacon Fortune allowed quietly. "If you notice, white fellas more than happy to come after ours. All you got to do is look around to see that. Folks don't get light-skinned just washing their face."

Sarcastic laughter of agreement. "Claim they ain't a man till they get one of ours, but you go after one of theirs," Mr. Carter emphasized, thumping his cane, "she say, 'yeah' one minute an' 'rape' the next. Then you be hanging from a tree. But ours just say 'yeah.'"

"That's 'cause they ain't got no say-so!" Poppa John challenged the old man with the cane. "They trained up that way since slavery days. Fars that goes, what say-so do *you* have down there? They just as hard on women as they is on men."

Despite being outvoted by the rumble in the shop, Mr. Carter insisted with more heat than called for, "Maybe down South, but ain't no 'scuse up here!"

It would take years before I fully understood what they had said that day.

*****

A young dark-skinned man sidled in. Everybody eyed him. He seemed more an intruder than a customer. His grey overcoat had missing buttons. He wore a cap that was frayed around the edges, and his wrists showed below his shirt cuffs. The shirt was dirty; his faded tie shapeless. The whites of his cautious eyes emphasized his dark face. He grinned ingratiatingly whenever anyone said anything slightly amusing. He appeared to give all his attention to whomever was speaking.

During a conversational pause, he grinned, " - Any yawl knows where I can git me a job?"

Everybody stared at him. Nobody said anything. I felt a surge of pity for him, remembering Ned and his angry quest for work. It was a terrible thing when somebody was without a job. People were thrown out into the street with all their belongings piled up on the sidewalk even if it was raining or snowing. I hoped one of the men would say he knew where there was a job.

" - Where you been looking?" stout Poppa John frowned. His tone implied the young man hadn't been looking hard enough.

"All over ever-which way," he replied respectfully. "I then been down where all them ships be at - "

"White folks work them ships," Mr. Carter informed him gruffly. "Lucky they didn't pick you up and throw you in the water. You don't wanna be messing around down there."

"I don't mean to mess with nobody, I jus' want a job," he said quietly.

"What'd they tell you down on the dock?" Granddad asked.

He grinned. "A whole lotta things. Said I was too small, then one boss man said I wasn't in no union, then a real big fat man came out and said - 'We don't hire no niggers.'"

The Cane reiterated unsympathetically: "Lucky they ain't throwed you in."

"Keep looking," the deacon advised kindly. "You'll find something. Job won't jump up and shake your hand, but you'll find something. – Try the stables. Plenty of them around. Somebody's bound to need a stable boy to muck and help out. Work's dirty but it'll feed you."

"...But why they won't hire colored?" he persisted plaintively.

" -Where you from, son?" asked Granddad.

"Nawf Carlina."

"What!" Poppa John exclaimed, eyeglasses flashing. " - You from Carolina where them people lynching us every other day, and you ain't used to white folks yet?" He glared, silently scolding him. Shifting his rotund body, he instructed: "White folks take care of their *own* first, then if there's anything left, you might get *some* of it." He looked around the shop for approval. When he got it, he nodded wisely, "And that's only if they *like* you."

Deacon Fortune disagreed, shaking his head. "- Naw, not when they bring you to this country against your will and make slaves out of you, and..." he glanced in my direction "...and you know about the women." He had finished shaving the customer and was returning the mug to the shelf. "No, sir," he added, slamming the mug down on the shelf, "then they got an *obligation*. It ain't the same. No, sir! Don't start something you can't finish. We ain't asked to be here and now we here, they got an *obligation!*"

The shop nodded in silent Amens.

"You sure right about that, Deacon," the Cane admitted. "Yes sirree."

The jobseeker was silent. A philosophical discussion was not what he wanted to hear. His face grew sullen. "I rather be down home," he finally grumbled, crossing his leg. "Least-wise you knows where you stand."

No one took him up. He grew bolder - "Hell, Nawf ain't no bettern' the Sowf. Food here ain't half fit to eat. Down home you smoke your own ham, got your own chickens - everything taste better. Fokes got nice homes with land... an...an *you knows where you stand!* White folks up here two-faced," he said with a hint of anger. "They jus' pretend they like you, when they don't!"

The light-skinned man, still in the barber's chair, turned his head to face him. He had a luxuriant moustache and straight hair that was spoken of as "good hair." Fearful of the razor while Deacon Fortune shaved him, he had held his peace. Now that the Deacon was trimming his hair, he asked the young man carefully, "How do you mean -'you know where you stand'?"

"You knows where you stand. You knows what you can do and you knows what you can't do! You knows how white folks feels about you, what they be thinking; they don't put on no show. Ain't never no doubt how they feels. White folks up here two-faced!"

Mr. Carter leaned forward on the head of his cane and snorted, "So just 'cause they come and put a rope around your neck makes 'em better?" He leaned back and picked up a newspaper. He shook the folded paper at the young man. "I just finished reading in the paper where they took and lynched two boys just last night down in Charleston. I guess they know where they stand, too!"

The barber chuckled pleasantly as he continued trimming the light-skinned man's hair with scissors. "Now, Mr. Carter, I believe you're putting words in the boy's mouth. I think he means he'd rather have a white man call him nigger to his face, than nigger behind his back."

The young man nodded eagerly, glad for understanding. "But," the deacon, still smiling, dropped the other shoe, "white folks don't change much, son, don't matter where they're from. Some are just more polite, that's all. If you make 'em mad, they'll put a rope around your neck soon as look at you. Hung a boy last month way up in Ohio. Up here they generally give you a trial first, but it's all the same. When they get mad, they'll find a way to kill you."

"...Yes, Jesus! Give me a trial any day," Mr. Carter declared. "I take my chance being locked up than lynched up."

The light-skinned man in the barber chair wasn't finished with the dark young man. "I don't see nothing wrong if a man won't call you nigger to your face. Hell, at least that's showing some respect. Not much, but something. I'd rather have a white man call me Negro any day than have him say nigger. Folks who like the South so much ought to stay down there. There's plenty of rope to go around."

"Amen!" cried Mr. Carter. "Amen," he repeated, thumping the end of his cane on the floor.

The young man fell silent. As soon as the men turned their attention to sports, he quietly rose and slipped out. He had cast his lot with the South and the barbershop had cast him out.

*****

We were waiting for the trolley."- Granddad? - why did that man say he wanted to go back down South?"

"First off," Granddad snapped, "he's not a man, he's a *boy*. Used to being treated like one; can't feel right less you treat him like one. They say you can take the boy out of the country, but you can't take the country out of the boy. Same goes for slavery with some people. You can take a man out of slavery but you can't take the slavery out of the man.

"Soon's some of them get up here, they claim all they're doing is saving up enough money to go back 'down home', but you notice none of them go back down there."

He had an angry gleam in his eye. " Used to see people like that all the time during the war. We'd pass a plantation and call out, 'Come on, folks, you're free!' A lot just dropped what they were doing and ran off with us, but you always had a bunch hanging back talking about, 'Ah cain't leave missy here alone.' Even seen 'em with whip scars thick as my fingers all across their back whining about, 'Ah cain't leave massa.'

"After what I went through being a slave, an' in the war seeing men shot down and blown up - their brains all across my uniform – all to free their sorry asses - I took my rifle one day and blowed one nigger's brains clean out! Woulda killed the whole bunch of sorry bastards but the other men grabbed me and pulled my gun away!"

I stared at his grim, hard face, shocked that he would tell me such a thing. Maybe living as a slave with no right to privacy, decency, or even morality had dulled his senses, and maybe killing people in the war had dulled them even more, but he was a hard man who was still at war.

*****

Three days after the barbershop, Granddad, who only came to our house to visit, suddenly came to stay. The hard bitten, independent Civil War veteran - like the unexpected sound of smashing glass - suffered a stroke. Terrified, he lay for six hours, stunned, blind in one eye, deaf in one ear, his entire side paralyzed, slobbering and unable to utter intelligible speech or even to control his bowels or bladder.

The doctor shook his head and told us what we already knew. There was nothing he could do. With the help of Momma and his own determination, he partly recovered. Hobbled, he was quieter, and spent a lot of time up in his room reading. No one ever came to see him; everyone he had known was dead. The times I went up to his room, a crooked smile would cross his lips. Now he was grizzled, old and gentle where before he had been tall, lean and angry, chasing me away with his eyes because few adults deigned to talk to children. What did a child know that was worth listening to?

He relented over time. I carried up hot cups of tea when the weather was cold, and cold glasses of lemonade when it was hot. Sometimes to keep him company, I would sit on the floor in his room and do my homework. Occasionally Daddy helped him down the stairs where they sat in the living room together. I often wondered what anyone could do for hours at a time in a single room in a rocking chair. Once I asked him, "How old are you, Grandpa? Daddy said seventy-four but I think you must be close to 90."

His faded brown eyes were misty, kind and soft. "Oh, I reckon he's about right give or take."

From time to time he looked into the moving space of long ago, and catching a passing moment here or there, held it up for me to see. Eighteen-fifty, 1860, '70 - years of pain and magic - all once-upon-a-time, long, long ago. I heard the squeal of wagon wheels and the crack of leather whips; caught sight of cavalry and spoke with Indians; I watched the sails of vessels fluff before the wind. Memories caught in the suns of yesterday - the sounds and the shadows of long dusty paths to the pain of plantations, and then the intoxication of freedom.

"-Daddy said some men kidnapped you when you were a little boy."

He nodded, setting his rocking chair in motion, back and forth, back and forth. Because he mused so long, I grew apprehensive, wondering whether or not I had ripped the scab from a wound.

"-I musta been nigh eleven, twelve years old when they came and got me," he remembered finally, peering down a misty street of long ago. "There was five of 'em. Said I was a run-a-way slave, and I told them - I said, 'I'm not a slave; I was born here. You can ask my parents! I'm free - how could I run away?'"

"A real big, strong, white man reached over and slapped me with his bare hand and knocked me flat on my back. Next thing I knew, they were putting chains on me, threw me in a wagon with half a dozen others. Wasn't just me, and off we went just like that. Took an' stole me about 1850, maybe '52- somewhere in there - "

"But didn't your mother say anything!" I blurted.

He looked at me for a moment or two. I could not tell whether he was calling me a fool or trying to remember. "I wasn't near home, young fella. Glad, too, 'cause they woulda taken and put her in chains, too."

"But...but you were in the *North*, Granddad! How could they do that to you?"

"'Cause they had something called the *Fugitive Slave Law*, that's how. Said anybody in the North who had a run-a-way slave had to turn him loose. All a slaver had to do was go to the police and claim you was one, then unless somebody *white* knew you, and spoke up for you, the slavers just took you off. Colored folks didn't have much say - not that they do now – but then it was worse."

He looked again down the dark and filmy road of yesteryear and caught a glimpse of a frightened little boy ripped from his mother and father. "It was a long and painful journey I can tell you that much. My backside got so terrible sore just sitting there feeling each and every bump all the way to Delaware. Put us on a boat there, and on to Virginia –

"Most of the time I was sitting next to a colored lady who never would look up, she felt so bad and ugly inside. Other side of me was a man musta been in his forties. He whispered to me, musta been a dozen times, 'You run off first chance you get, boy, you hear? Run off!'"

Granddad stopped. I had the feeling he was not going to say any more. I knew he had escaped before the Civil War, but he never would speak of how or when or what he had to do to escape. As though it were something he never wanted to remember.

Nor did he speak anymore of war.

Chapter 21

Hortense Simpson gave a tea in the spring of 1920, the year I went to college. Momma insisted I go. Teas were occasional Saturday gatherings held either at the Episcopal Church or someone's house where parents volunteered to chaperone the affairs. Momma said teas gave respectable young people a chance to have fun and socialize. Most of the girls weren't allowed to have company, and boys couldn't even write to some of them. I think the main reason that some people went to teas at all was the fear of not being invited to the next one.

I didn't think teas made any sense. Ned quit going right after high school, and I only went when Momma took me along when it was her turn to help chaperone. As far as I could see, all anybody ever did at teas was make eye contact, or touch someone "accidentally" or maybe say a few words, then wait with for the next tea party to do it all over again.

Crowded into someone's living room or the church social hall, somebody would give a piano recital or sing a song or recite a poem while we boys, with the frustrated eyes of pimply youth, devoured vibrant, healthy, laughing girls. The girls pretended not to notice us, covering their mouths and giggling, secretly communing among themselves.

Everyone prayed that Andrew Stevenson or Reginald Price would show up. Audacious and jolly, they weren't afraid to talk to girls; they could make them laugh. Sometimes they even kidded with the grown ups who acted as chaperones. Reginald would always play "Old Black Joe" on the piano and everybody would laugh and sing along.

We were all self-conscious clods, imagining that nobody had anything better to do than look at us or listen to us. We had the social graces of a rock, and much as we yearned to do so, none of us knew how to keep a conversation going with the opposite sex. The girls made it tough because they always had a girlfriend with them. A fellow had to try to make conversation with both of them when he hardly knew how to talk to one. We sat around the pool, as it were, afraid to stick our toe in the water.

When neither Andrew nor Reginald showed up for Hortense's tea, it was doomed to failure. We had to fend for ourselves. The girls took inordinate interest in one another's earrings or they volunteered to serve lukewarm tea that nobody really wanted.

Aside from Reginald Price and Andrew Stevenson not showing up for an affair, disastrous teas were nothing new. Somebody would promise to sing or play the piano or give a recital and then not show up. It didn't help when some of the other guests failed to come. The young hostess invariably solved her problem by abandoning her guests and fleeing to the kitchen to urgently find something to do.

We were crowded together in Hortense's parlor trying not to stare at one another. Every chair was occupied; the piano bench was full and some of us sat on the floor. Except for whispered conversations among the girls, the room was silent. A tall pleasant looking boy about my age arrived late. He was a diversion.

Every head turned toward him. In the glare of their eyes, the coffee and cream-colored boy smiled uncertainly. I sensed his panic on entering a quiet room to be confronted by a sea of curious faces. There wasn't a place for him to sit. Impulsively I stood up from the floor and went over to him, pretending that I knew him. He clasped my hand gratefully while everyone watched.

"My name's Aaron," I offered in an undertone." What's your?"

"Wesley," he almost whispered, "and thanks. I don't know anybody here except Hortense. Why's everybody staring like that? They never saw anybody before?"

"Ignore them, they've got nothing better to do."

We stood in the hall and talked, there being no place to sit.

"Swell looking girls," he observed. "You know any of them?"

"A couple," I lied, hoping he wouldn't ask me to introduce him to any of them. Against my better judgment, when Ernestine brought him a cup of tea, I said, "Ernestine, this is Wesley, a friend of mine who'd like to meet you."

"Pleased to meet you," she said soberly and promptly left to collapse in gales of giggles among the other girls who had been watching the entire proceeding. Once more, curious faces with renewed interest, turned our way.

"Where're you from?" I blurted, and from there we found a myriad of things to talk about. We discovered we both had been taught the same litany of do's and don'ts that we repeated in derisive unison, "Don't do anything to draw attention to yourself," we chanted; "Always 'act dignified.'"

Our muffled laughter drew a lot of attention but we didn't care. I'd found a pal.

*****

Momma liked Wesley at once.

His stature rose even higher when he let it be known that his father was *the* Wesley Charles, the renowned colored police officer, one of a handful on the police force. She beamed when he announced that he was going to college and then medical school. She offered him tea and cake. For a brief second, I remembered Steven - he too had wanted to be a doctor before the sea of life smashed him on the rocks.

Wesley reminded me a little of Elizabeth's brother, Pace. Both were tall, lean, good looking with a calm, intelligent expression. Wesley spoke quietly but firmly. I felt we shared a lot in common. Sitting on his front doorsteps or mine, we talked about a lot of things that seemed ordinary enough, but nobody else was interested in hearing about them.

We linked arms and strolled about the neighborhood, glad for the other's company. We examined parked cars with the expert eyes of youth. This one was a Chalmers, that across the street was a Maxwell and oh, look – there's a Pullman Roadster! Are you sure? Looks like a Detroiter to me.

We tipped our caps to older ladies, fell silent upon passing a black funeral wreath on a door, we waved away clouds of large green flies that rose from mounds of horse manure as they beat against our face, and stopped in candy stores for penny blocks of fudge and in little ways told who we were.

He described how he felt when he finally got his first pair of long pants. He had been fourteen. I rattled on about astronomy and fossils while he would tell how a coroner extracted a dead person's liver and carefully sliced it. But best of all we could discuss serious boy stuff.

"I knew a girl once," I confided, "who got in a family way."

His eyes widened. "No stuff! You mean she had a *baby*?"

"I didn't actually see it because they sent her back down South, but everybody was talking about it. I didn't know a girl could have a baby, did you?"

Gravely, the young doctor assured me that it was quite possible and went on to describe exactly how it was done. "When you do it to a girl," he said glancing around to assure privacy, "you can't come the same time that she does. You have to let her come first. If you both come the same time-" He let the dire consequences dangle.

"- Gee, I thought it only happened if she put her legs up!"

He snorted scornfully," That's how people get girls in trouble, believing junk like that!"

Eventually I got around to what I really wanted to know." - Did you ever do it to a girl?"

"Did you?" he countered.

"No fair - I asked you first."

"Why're you asking?" he dodged. "That's personal."

"I know you must have kissed a girl," I said, "I don't mean just kissing kissing -"

"You mean French kissing? – No, but I heard about it."

"I heard about it, too. How can you put your tongue in somebody else's mouth! It sounds nasty."

"It is! I just like kissing kissing."

"Me, too - I never felt a girl, either," I confessed. "I never saw any sense in it."

"My cousin did once, and the girl ran right in the house and told her mother. After the whipping he got, you can forget it!"

"I had a friend who said girls like it and won't tell. He said if you feel their titties, it'll make them get bigger."

"Well, I don't know what kind of girls your friend knows, but he'd better not try that with any of the girls I know because they'll run straight home. I know a girl who told just because a boy looked up her dress and saw her bloomers."

"But does feeling them make their titties get bigger?" I persisted.

He considered this for a long moment before nodding wisely, and giving it as his medical opinion that, "It won't happen right away, though, and you have to really get your hands on her good."

"You know, just talking about stuff like that can give you a hard on."

"I know, and it won't take much to give me a hard on. You ever just stand close to a girl and get a hard on?"

"Yeah, and it's embarrassing as hell!"

" - Sometimes, though, at night I have real nasty dreams about feeling girls and...and doing nasty things to them and something happens - "

"You, too? Where you come all over yourself? Me, too! I wonder why. I never think about stuff like that in the day time."

We explored the world of sex as we knew it, exchanging one bit of monumental ignorance for another, giving knowledgeable reasons for preferring one type of girl to another, comparing the merits of big titties to small ones, guessing what size legs lay hidden beneath long skirts and deducing that if a girl had a big behind she was likely to have big legs.

But Wesley had the greatest bit of information of anything we had ever discussed. We were sitting on his front doorsteps one afternoon. He leaned toward me, his head almost touching mine, and whispered, "I heard that the way you could tell if a girl had a big pussy or a small one was by her mouth. If she had a big, wide mouth - "

"No stuff!" I exclaimed, "And a small mouth means it's small?"

He nodded as though afraid to speak. "And guess what else?" he whispered. "You can tell what size private a man has by looking at his feet. If he's got big feet he going to have a big one and if he's got small feet it's small"

Instinctively I had an urge to look down at my feet, but resisted. "You think it's true?" I breathed, wide-eyed.

He looked skeptical. "Well, I don't know, but I bet the one about the mouth is true, though."

Chapter 22

Mom liked Wesley and I liked Wesley, but our new found friendship ended a month before we went to college.

He was treating me to an ice cream soda at the soda fountain of the drugstore on his corner. His parents gave him an allowance every week. I didn't know anybody who received an allowance. He got more for an allowance than I did working with Aunt Tish all day Saturday. By now, I was beginning to wonder whether or not I was making a pest of myself with my questions about race.

"What's it matter?" he asked, a little impatiently. "Colored or Negro? What do you want to be?"

I was a little irritated by his tone. "I'm just asking - what's wrong with the word 'Negro.' If we're all supposed to be colored, does that mean that nobody's a Negro? I looked up 'Negro' in the dictionary and it said somebody from Africa or with African blood - "

" - Keep your voice down.".

"What about you -what do *you* call yourself?"

He finished the last of his ice cream soda and motioned to me to leave. Once outside he said, "I'm an American. You don't see white people running around worrying about whether they're white or not. Everybody came here from someplace else except the Indians. I'm American."

"That's not a race, smarty," I jeered. "That's a nationality."

He dismissed me with a go-to-hell wave of his hand. Just then somebody shouted, "Hey, you!"

Four tough looking boys were bearing down on us. Where had they come from? This wasn't the Seventh Ward. I remembered what happened to Steven because of Beulah and the raid on Ned's wagon. We knew that they meant trouble.

"Keep walking!" Wesley urged. We were about a block and a half from his house.

They caught up to us and barred the way. Three of them wore their cap brims pulled to the side to show that they were tough. The smallest boy carried a stick which once might have been the handle of a shovel. Two were still in knickers which hung down their calves. There were holes in the knees and dirty looking stockings lay bunched around their ankles.

"Dammit, you ain't hear me call you!" demanded the leader. He was burly, and wore an old, dusty derby raked over one eye. He wasn't as tall as we were but he looked thicker.

"Why you ain't stop when I called you?" he persisted, staring at us with hard, brown eyes.

Memories of how Stump had tormented Steven flashed through my mind.

"They ain't got no respect, Stomp," one of the knickers grinned. "You gotta twist your foot up they ass to git respect." Reaching up he seized Wesley by his neck tie.

"Hurt 'im!" Stomp ordered. "Teach 'im some respect."

Twisting to free himself, Wesley warned: "You'd better leave us alone if you don't want to get in trouble! My father's a policeman. He's *Wesley Charles!*"

"Shit! Ah moe really whup yo ass then!" the boy shouted to his struggling victim and rearing back, punched Wesley squarely in the face. Wesley leaped in the air howling, then doubled over grabbing his bloody nose with both hands crying in pain and alarm, "OWWWW! YOU BROKE MY NOSE! YOU BROKE MY NOSE!"

His assailant, still gripping Wesley, looked to Stomp for instructions.

He nodded - "Whippis ass."

I suddenly tore into Stomp with hot, wild, blinding rage. I pummeled his eyes and his nose and punched him in his throat, all in a frenzy of flailing hatred. It was immediate.

The others, not accustomed to being attacked, stared. When Stomp stumbled, dazed, I turned on them. The one with the stick bolted. I sprang after him. They might have been the ones who'd beaten-up Steven, stolen from Ned's wagon, beaten me up and sent Ned to a humiliating encounter with a cop. They reminded me of Boo Boy smashing Little Billy and scaring me to death by threatening to punch my mother.

I didn't think any of this. I felt a raging, blind, unfamiliar hatred. When the boy with the stick took to his heels, I caught him near the drugstore. Grabbing the back of his collar, I swung him around. He staggered and dropped his stick, trying to regain his balance. I drove my fist in his belly driving the air from him, and then I smashed at his puzzled face again and again and again. Before leaving him bloody and writhing on the ground, I kicked his head once then again and again.

By now, Wesley was surrounded by sympathetic adults who had raised an alarm. I ran back. Near the far corner, one of the gang thumbed his nose. Worried about Wesley, I checked the urge to charge after him. A dusty old derby lay on the ground. Leaping up, I came down on it stomping it flat and then held it aloft to taunt them. Filled with anger, I sailed it high, like a platter, into the sky where it disappeared over a rooftop across the street.

*****

I was disappointed in Wesley.

A fellow needed a pal who could stand with him shoulder to shoulder when things got rough. I already knew he was not much of a fighter, but he should have at least tried to duck or something, not just stand there and let somebody punch him in the face. Suppose they had all jumped us at once.

It was stupid to say your parents had forbidden you to fight because it was "uncouth" when other people were throwing punches at your head. That was one "don't" that my friends and I quietly ignored. Especially after Boo Boy had scared the hell out of us by beating up Billy Ross.

A little bewildered by the sudden, deep, unfamiliar hatred I had felt, I was even more astonished at what I had done. Strange, too, how Stomp had not looked burly, but just like a boy who I meant to beat. I think the one with the stick hit me, but I hadn't felt it. Charging after him had felt good and catching him was strangely enjoyable.

Driving my fist into his body had felt so sensual that I wished I had kept on doing it until my arms were too weary to go on. I remember I had to resist the urge to kick him more than I had because I knew it wasn't fair, but I had wanted to kick him in his face and in his privates over and over. I had never felt that kind of searing, consuming hatred before. - Was that how people felt when they killed people?

That's when I knew that I really would have murdered Steven on that fire escape back during the war.

I put my arm around Wesley's shoulder and helped escort him home. He felt humiliated, his hands covering his bloody face. Anybody would. It was the way I had felt when Ned's wagon was robbed and the gang beat me up. Now, though, no one jeered at us like they had in the Seventh Ward. Wesley's neighbors, white and Black, rushed out of their houses, alarmed and several had shouted, "Police!" in hopes of summoning the neighborhood police officer.

That's why I wasn't prepared for Wesley's mother's reaction.

Momma would have reached out to me with a warm hug and asked questions later, but Mrs. Charles just covered her face and screamed in horror when she saw Wesley's blood smeared face and bloody shirt front. Neighbors had to lay her on the sofa and comfort her. She was a light-skinned, thin, nervous woman who always managed to look disgruntled. I never really liked her, and I am sure she never liked me.

She probably felt the kind of antipathy toward me that Momma had felt towards Fred but for different reasons. Once, after probing around, she asked just who my parents were. Somehow, she made it sound accusatory.

"Are they related to the *Maryland* Winstons?" she inquired, knowing full well they were not.

"Oh, no, ma'am!" I exclaimed with feigned, wide-eyed innocence, "We're not from *down South*. We're from *here*. My grandfather fought in the Civil War to help us free the slaves! Are you from Maryland, Mrs. Charles?"

I don't remember what she mumbled, I just felt exultant because I knew she hated me, and I knew that there was something wrong with everything we said to each other just as there was something wrong with our dislike for each other.

Mr. Charles happened to come home just then. Forewarned of the disaster by neighbors, he rushed into the house. He was a tall, handsome man on the beefy side. Dressed in his policeman's uniform he was imposing. But both he and his wife possessed the same disgruntled mouth. Like her, he was only as civil to me as he had to be.

Seeing the blood and bruises on his son, he stormed about wildly, demanding to know whether or not Wesley had fought back, and he did not give a damn whether it was four boys or four hundred! "You have to fight back, *goddamn it!*" he thundered. Then turning to me - "And what'd you do," he roared, nostrils flaring, "- Run away and leave my son there all by himself?"

"Oh, no!" the neighbors cried out. "He chased them all by himself and there were four or five of them! He chased them all the way down the street!"

Faced with this onslaught of testimony, the disgruntled man was doubly dissatisfied. He insinuated that I'd instigated the mess in the first place since Wesley had never in his life had any trouble like this before.

I defended myself. "It was four against us, Mr. Charles. Wesley wouldn't start trouble and neither would I, but I won't run either."

Since everybody supported me, he could do nothing but glare, eyes dead and dangerous, probably wishing he could lock me up. He never thanked me. I left wishing I could call him a son-of-a-bitch.

A young woman followed me to the door. She was pretty and reminded me of Elizabeth even though she was a grown lady. She seemed more like a girl because I was as tall as she was and I could look her in the eye and I liked her right away.

"Are you sure you're going to be all right? she said in a voice that was gentle and concerned. "Those boys might be waiting to get even. You wait here; I'll get somebody to walk you to the trolley."

"Thanks, ma'am, but I'll be all right."

Nevertheless, she trailed me at a distance and waited until I was on the trolley. She smiled and waved to me when I got on. She was a grown lady but I felt a stirring in my body.

I never told anyone about the fight.

I was living that subterranean life that children keep concealed from their parents for obscure reasons. When Momma asked why I was not palling around with Wesley as much as before, I said we'd had an argument. I do not know what I would have said had she pressed me for details. I wasn't sure myself why we weren't as close as before. Maybe he was ashamed that I had witnessed him get beaten up and that he hadn't fought back. I tried to see him a couple of times but his sour-faced mother always answered the door. She would say that he wasn't home and close the door. It reminded me of Elizabeth's mother closing the door in my face. I sent a letter once but never received a reply.

Chapter 23

As our friendship slipped away, I felt a sense of loss.

Steven was dead and Fred was gone. The rest of the guys had slipped into the world of work. Wesley and I had seen a lot of each other. We'd take turns with the long trolley ride to see each other. I lived in North Philadelphia and he was in West Philadelphia amid a scattering of colored families. All we talked about were the girls we knew or wished we knew.

So the long trolley ride was not always to see Wesley. He was an excuse. I went to see someone else who was a part of my subterranean life.

It had happened by accident. One day on the way to see Wesley, as the trolley passed a street corner, I caught a fleeting glimpse of a familiar face. I turned and stared as the trolley hurtled past. A handsome boy, a corner grocery store, a market basket.

The trolley was rushing me away from Pace, Elizabeth's brother.

I sat stupid with indecision. Regaining my senses, I dashed to the center doors and asked the conductor to let me off at the next stop. Racing two blocks back to the corner grocery store, I found the streets empty. I began walking, turning one street corner after another, staring down long city blocks of silent row houses, willing Elizabeth to appear in a doorway, on a doorstep, on the pavement. But the streets stared back quiet and empty. Yet she was near, within walking distance of the grocery store.

She would be 16, glowing and beautiful.

In the weeks that followed, I would get off at the grocery store and search the streets leading from the store, trying to imagine the route that

Pace must have taken the day I had caught a glimpse of him. At the end of the fourth week, as I prepared to get off from the center door of the trolley, I saw her holding a violin case, waiting to board at the front.

I stepped back instantly. Was that really Elizabeth searching for a seat, holding on as the trolley lurched and swayed? Now a tall, slender girl with a smile at the corner of her lips? Our eyes met. She was as lovely as I had fantasized about her over the years. For a moment she stared, then she flushed with recognition and tried to suppress a smile. I approached her, feeling triumphant and shy all at once.

"Hello, Elizabeth."

"…Hello, Aaron."

"There're two seats in the back," I offered.

She hesitated for a second and then she came with me and sat by the window while I took the aisle seat. I offered to hold her violin case, yearning to press against her but daring not to. Having captured a genie in a bottle, I had no idea what to do with it. I sat dumb, growing more desperate as the trolley swayed along.

"…Do you play the violin?"

She nodded. "A group of us play together."

Another long, desperate pause. I did not want this to end with *nice-to-see-you-goodbye*.

"…I've missed you," I blurted. "I've been searching all over the world for you."

"I doubt that," she smiled and I felt emboldened.

"Well, I guess the part of the world that I know about," I said, and I told her I had been looking up and down her neighborhood hoping to see her come out of her house just as I had once waited on her corner, as a little boy, hoping to play jacks with her.

She smiled, examining my face. "You never did learn how to play. You never got past the twosies."

"I only wanted an excuse to look at you. Remember what I told you the day I tied your sash for you?"

She shook her head no, and looked out of the window, but I knew she remembered.

"…I still have the jack you gave me."

She flushed, hiding her face in her hands, and whispered, "- Stop it,

Aaron, you're embarrassing me...."

I looked at her slim fingers and wanted to touch her hands and feel their texture, and I wanted to kiss her hands, and uncover her lovely face and kiss that, too.

I followed her off the trolley at her stop. We stood indecisive for a moment before we began to walk. I carried her violin case for her, and we talked of the little things people talk about who feel comfortable with each other. Our eyes met frequently; a smile always hovered at the corner of her mouth. I stared at her lips as they formed words until she became self-conscious and looked away.

She said she was headed for Mrs. Dubois' house where the Orange met twice a week. I asked her what the Orange was. She said it was a social group, a "set" of boys and girls her age who met at Mrs. Dubois' house and other places.

"What do you do there?"

"Oh, lots of things. We play tennis sometimes, and sometimes croquet...."

"-What's croquet? How do you play it?"

"...It's too complicated to explain. I'd have to show you."

"Will you?"

She nodded. "And we have our music group. We practice at the Episcopal Church and visit other Orange sets in Washington and New York. We do lots of things."

She told me she had aunts and uncles in New York who were in show business; they got to travel all over Europe. She wanted to live in New York, too, and some day travel to Paris.

"Can I join Orange?"

She didn't answer and reaching for her case said, "I think I'm going to be late for practice. I have to go. I have to go by myself. You can't come with me."

"When can I see you again? It's been so long, but I never forgot you. I think about you all the time. Can I come to your house sometime?"

She shook her head, edging away. "I'm not allowed to keep company, Aaron, and," she added, "even if I could, I couldn't invite you to my house. I don't think my mother would let you in."

I wasn't shocked or offended. Deep down I knew this. I'd never for a moment forgotten Pace's jibe '...*if you're black, stay back!*' Nor his icy insolence, nor her mother's nearly white, hostile face. Elizabeth could tell me I was too dark too enter her house, but I knew she did not say it to hurt me but to warn me. That she was here beside me spoke all the truth I needed to know.

"...Can I write to you?"

Her eyes met mine and held them. Slowly she shook her head. "I'm not old enough to write to boys...We can still meet on the trolley, though, if you like."

When my face lit up, she suppressed a giggle and looked away. She told me I was to get off the trolley at the stop after the grocery store. I was to wait there. When I saw her board the trolley at the grocery store, I was to board the same trolley when it came to my stop. We could be together until she got off at her destination. But I must never get off with her again because someone was frequently waiting for her. Then she waved goodbye and went on to Mrs. Dubois' alone.

Once I surprised her. I pulled a blue jack from my pocket and gave it to her. "I promised I'd give it back, remember?"

She was delighted, fingering its points, remembering. "- You kept it all this time? Why'd you keep it?"

"Because it's yours...You know, like a picture or something. It reminded me of you. – Can I keep it?"

She closed her fingers around the jack. "Yes, but I want to keep it for a while. Is that all right?"

"If you promise to give it back," I smiled, "and I'm still wondering, Elizabeth – can I join Orange?"

She grew somber and looked out of the window. I knew without her saying anything that I couldn't. I was too dark. "- You have to be invited, Aaron. All the mothers got together a long time ago and...It's complicated. There are a lot of sets. They go by age. You go from one set to another. From Cricket to Junior Deb to...It's complicated, but everybody knows everybody else and you have to be invited by one of the parents. But I wish you could, Aaron. I really do."

"...Does Pace belong to a set?"

"He's president of Regents."

*****

I needed more than our trolley rides. I wanted to see her for hours and days and forever. I wanted to hold her, to dance with her, to walk with her, to bring her home to Momma. Taking a chance, I began to wait for her after she left Mrs. DuBois's house.

I watched her walk toward me, marveling at her girl beauty; she seemed to walk on tip toe, barely touching the ground. I adored every step that she took.

She reached me, flushed, glowing and embarrassed. Boldly I kissed her on the cheek. She jerked away looking around for witnesses and seeing none, let me hold her gently and I kissed her face and touched her lips with mine, suppressing the urge to squeeze her and melt into her.

"I do love you, Elizabeth, very much. I've been stuck on you from the first time I saw you in Schilling's buying ice cream. I remember all those days playing jacks and I couldn't wait for the next day so I could see you again. – Do you like me, too?"

"Yes," she nodded.

We boarded the trolley and sat together on her ride back to the grocery store. I held her violin, and pressed as close to her as I dared. I timidly touched her hand. When she let me hold her hand, the joy that suffused through my body was a thing of exquisite colors and subtle, splendid sounds.

She didn't appear for our next "date." Nor did she appear the time after. Three puzzling weeks passed, but I didn't see her again. Gradually, I began to understand. There was truth in the old ditty: "Don't make love by the garden gate; Love is blind, but the neighbors ain't."

I had overreached by kissing her in public and by virtually strolling with her all over the neighborhood. I had been stupid and reckless. The loudest sound for all the world to hear is, "I love you." Even when only our eyes say so. I didn't know what to do. I hadn't the faintest idea where she lived; and if I had, I wouldn't have dared show my face at her door. When I left for college, how would I ever see her again?

Desperate, one day I said to hell with it. I got off at the grocery store with no plan in mind. I walked up one street and down the next until I noticed the neighborhood policeman eyeing me. He would know I was a stranger; I was courting trouble. I retraced my steps, reliving Jewel Street and the futility of staring at her empty house. I damned and triple

damned her mother and Pace.
    And myself for my own stupidity.

Chapter 24

I always liked Deacon Fortune's barber shop. I would have gotten my hair cut every week just to be there. Once I left for college, I wouldn't be going there except during summer breaks. Evidently, I wasn't the only ones who liked the shop. Some men came just to be sociable.

Poppa John, a stout, opinionated man always sat in the same chair next to the coal stove; Mr. Carter, the dark-skinned man with a sour face who hobbled along on a cane, possessed a surprisingly merry laugh. The last of the regulars, Mr. Robinette, seldom spoke. Head buried in his paper, he seemed to read the same news over and over, yet he grunted agreement to almost everything that was said, adding a word here and there. Everybody who came into the shop knew them.

A huge dark man, who completely filled the barber's chair, was getting his hair cut one day when I walked in; Mr. Carter must have said something about "colored."

The massive man glared at him. "Who you consider *colored*?"

Noting the stranger's bulk, Mr. Carter paused for a second. " - Everybody, all of us; we're all colored."

"How come we ain't Negroes?" he wanted to know. "That's what the newspapers call us. You fill out any kind of application, what do it say for race? - *Negro*. But certain hincty people feel like if you light-skinned, you 'colored,' but if you dark like me, you a Negro and not as good!"

After a pause Poppa John, from his seat next to the coal stove, ventured "- What makes you say that?"

The big man turned his glare at him, forcing Deacon Fortune to hold off cutting his hair. Poppa John quailed. I did not think the man was angry, but he was like Mr. Portlock – loud, belligerent, and frightening.

"You got ears and you got eyes just like I have," he instructed Poppa John. Settling back in the barber's chair, he continued, "You ain't noticed no difference? When I was young, coming along - people was glad if white people called them Negro 'cause it was better than nigger, almost like calling you 'mister.'"

Several of the customers chuckled, nodding remembrance.

Relishing their agreement, he rumbled on: "Folks, like my Daddy, didn't know the word Negro even existed…" More chuckles and nods of agreement – "… now all a sudden we 'colored' and people wanna get mad if you call 'em Negro. Gettin' so bad you got women out there using bleach on their skin to get lighter!"

"– Say what?" cried Mr. Carter, eyes wide in disbelief. "I ain't never in my whole life heard nothing about no bleach!" He looked around the room for agreement. Most of the men seemed doubtful.

Deacon Fortune, holding his clippers back, shook his head. "– Where'd you hear that, Mister, if you don't mind me asking?"

The man glared around the room, and shook his head in disgust. "Don't you all read the colored paper?" he demanded. "They got ads each and every week, *'Bleach your face, hands, arms, have beautiful skin'*…."

The minute the door closed on his back, Poppa John snorted, "Good God a'mighty! You ever in your whole life hear such ignorance? *Bleach!*"

"Can't be the stuff you wash clothes with," Mr. Carter frowned. "Stuff'll burn your skin off."

"Man's crazy," somebody else said.

Mr. Robinette held up his issue of the *Tribune*. "It's in here," he said quietly. "Just like the man said."

Those who had agreed with the big man only moments before about race, and then threw their allegiance to Poppa John about bleach, were now perplexed. Their eyes pinioned Mr. Robinette who began reading aloud: "*'Madam Murray Stewart - Lighten your skin - golden brown beauty skin bleach and beautifier.'*" He held the paper up for anyone to see for himself. When no one did he turned several pages and announced: "Here's another one: *'Dr. Fred Palmer's skin whitener preparations.'*"

I didn't know what to think. It seemed nobody else did either. I was more confused than ever. Before the man's news about skin bleach, I thought the only questions were whether you called yourself colored or Negro, and what was wrong with Negro?

*****

The name thing was almost like a merry-go-round. I knew better then to ask Momma anything about race, so as soon as I got home I asked Daddy.

"What do white people call themselves?"

A newspaper was spread on the kitchen table where he was filling kerosene lamps. "What do you mean, 'What do they call themselves?'"

"Don't they just say they're white? What are we supposed to be, Negro or colored or black or what?"

It took him a little while to get his thoughts together. "You look at white people, they're all white. You look at our race and you see black, you see light brown, dark brown, chocolate brown, yellow, cream colored, just-about-white. We have all these different shades, all these different colors. We started out saying we were 'people of color,' then just 'colored.'"

This sounded plausible. He went back to his lamps, pleased with his answer.

" - Why do people still say, 'Negro'?"

He cobbled some more thoughts together, rubbing his chin with fingers that reeked of kerosene. "I guess," he said at last, "they figure if you're not white you're Negro. Negro is a race, like Chinese."

"Is colored a race?"

"...I don't think so, no."

"Then what's colored? Am I colored or Negro?"

He sighed. "Son, you can call yourself colored if you want, or you can say you're a Negro. People know what you mean."

Chapter 25

Ned came back.

I was still moping over losing both Wesley and Elizabeth when the doorbell rang one morning. There was Ned. With a scream of joy, Momma flew into his arms. Wearing shiny black boots, he was resplendent in a strange military uniform trimmed in red, green and black. He seemed taller and bigger than I remembered.

Where've you been, my parents shouted; why didn't you write, why didn't you tell us you were coming?

"What kind of uniform is that?" I asked?

"African Legion!" he grinned, punching me lightly on the shoulder. "I'm with Garvey."

"Oh!" Momma and Daddy both intoned. It was hard to tell whether they were surprised or disappointed.

"Who's Garvey?" I piped up.

"You'll find out, young fella," Ned promised. "You'll find out everything you need to know."

I could tell this did not sit well with Momma and Daddy. Their faces were eloquent, but nothing was said. For the time being, the wanderer was welcomed home. His appearance, striding down the street in full uniform and shiny boots, had attracted attention. Within the hour various people "just happened" to drop by.

Momma had acquired a much larger circle of friends from new colored people moving into the neighborhood. A lot of that was due to Mrs. Portlock praising her as a refined lady who was not stuck up. Daddy's position as a minister, even though he operated an elevator during the week, gave him more status with people than he'd had as a butler.

Soon close to ten neighbors filled the house. Momma set about boiling coffee and tea and slicing up pound cake. Ned found himself being invited to dinner by everybody who had a spare daughter, niece, cousin, sister or granddaughter. But his uniform was the main interest.

" - African Legion?" one man rumbled. "Mind me asking - what kind of army is that?"

– "Marcus *who*?" a woman frowned. "Don't think I ever heard of anybody named Marcus Garvey."

"I heard of him," Mrs. Portlock said, looking worried. "Folks say he crazy, son."

A thin woman with an anxious expression, leaned forward - "Is he the one tryna send us all back to Africa?"

"Folks can go where they want," a stout man named Arnold laughed, "ain't *nobody* sending my black behind back to no Africa!"

After the laughter subsided, Mrs. Portlock, still worried declared, "They say he sure God hate white folks. Can't nobody fault him for that!"

Amid general agreement, the thin, anxious woman said. "Well, no need in him starting no foolishness. Next thing you know, they be trying to send us *all* back to Africa! You better think what you doing, son. - Tell him, Reverend Winston!"

Reverend Winston and Mrs. Winston were as dumbfounded as everyone else.

" - Where's Granddad?" Ned broke in from his circle of interrogators.

Without further ado, he and Daddy trooped up to Granddad's room and carried him back downstairs. He had mellowed considerably. His handlebar moustache had grown scraggly and his fierce eyes dim. Seated among us, he was content just to listen.

Seated on a kitchen chair brought into the living room, Ned smiled at Momma's friends and asked, "Who's heard Marcus Garvey speak?"

After a pause a youthful voice admitted, "I didn't hear him, but my cousin Zuber did." She was a young lady with a smooth dark face; her eyes devoured Ned. "From what Zuber said, it didn't sound like he was crazy or anything."

"What'd he talk about, Lottie Mae?" Arnold, the laughing man, grinned, ready to break into laughter again.

"I can't remember. It was around the time Esther birthed Alfreda, but I remember Zuber said he wasn't never going to be ashamed of being dark-skinned no more. He said Marcus Garvey was the only one in the world made him feel real proud of being black and from Africa!"

"- Why would anybody *wanna* be black?" the laughing man grinned.

"But you *are* black," Ned reminded him, gently. "We, all of us, are black. We're brown and yellow and in between but we're from Africa. That's our home. It must be like this: Europe for the Europeans, Asia for the Asians - Africa for the Africans.

"We were once a very powerful people. Now we're down, and it's the white man's turn to be great, but that doesn't mean we have anything to be ashamed of.

"In Africa do you know how they greet their kings? They say, 'Hail, to you who are the *blackest of black!* If you notice, the white man's not ashamed he's white. The yellow man's proud of his skin. But we've been taught – listen to me now – *Taught... To be ashamed... Of our own skin color!*

"- Marcus Garvey is just saying - black is beautiful! Be proud of it. Nothing more." Here he smiled, spreading his arms, and said reasonably - "It's what God intended. Who of you will quarrel with God?

"And Marcus never said *everybody* must go back to Africa. No. He's saying Africa is our homeland. If we *want* to visit our homeland, it should be a place we can feel proud of. A place that's safe, where men are not lynched and burned alive as they are here. Just last year, 1919, there was plenty of that in both North and South. That's why it's called *The Red Summer*. Did you know that?"

He searched their attentive faces. "- Is it unreasonable to want to feel safe? Isn't it our right? And we don't have an 'army.' We don't even have real guns. But when we do go to Liberia, then, and only then, we'll need guns to defend ourselves in Africa, not to attack the white man here."

He paused. No one said anything. Even stout Arnold found no cause for amusement. Ned continued. He shook his head slowly; his tone was more firm than friendly.

"Marcus Garvey's not crazy. - None of us are. We are all in love. We are in love with the black man and the black woman wherever they may be found. He's our blood brother, and she's our blood sister. Is it wrong to want to protect them, to help them, to see them smile, to believe that black is beautiful?"

He wanted to allay their fears while instilling in them a new spirit. Maybe it was because he spoke with such passion, or maybe he simply represented what was new, but he held their attention and seemed to have gained their respect.

I looked at my brother and I loved him as I had learned to love him that day on the wagon. Once our house was clear of company, we sat in the kitchen catching up on Ned's life. I pulled my chair as close to his as I could. He told us of his experiences at sea.

"At first, we mostly sailed between the States and South America, and later to France when the French needed ships to transport troops from Africa - "

"Africa?" Daddy was puzzled.

"Africans soldiers. All you hear about are the French who were killed in the war, but let me tell you – an awful lot of them were black, and they got no credit for it. We sailed back and forth, back and forth hauling them over. It's funny to see people your own race, but hear them speaking another language. I couldn't understand them, and they couldn't understand me until I picked up a little French.

"But I left the ship the first chance I got. The captain told me to my face I was hired on as a steward and that's all I'd ever be. Said he'd never had a 'darky' seaman before and wouldn't now. But I got a chance on the next ship.

"I sailed on three ships, a steward here, a seaman there - but I learned a valuable lesson. Right this minute, the black man's nothing more than a slave in most parts of Africa because people from England, France, Belgium, Germany - control our homeland.

"They send Africans to fight and die for them in other countries, and when they come back to Africa, they still have to kneel just like they did before they left. I saw it. When a man like Garvey comes along and says, 'That's not right, I'm going to change it!' - I'm with him one hundred percent!

"It's already starting. Garvey's getting ready to move some of us into Liberia. Then watch! Once that happens the sky'll open up. Just give us the chance and we'll open the sky!"

He talked passionately until a little past twelve. Everything he said seemed so possible and reasonable that I felt I could reach out and touch the things he spoke about. When he said they would open the sky, I knew he meant unimaginable opportunities for anyone who wanted to stand on tip toe and reach for the sky; or look beneath the surface of the earth for shards and bones of yesterday.

But Momma and Daddy weren't impressed. They saw great, monstrous walls stretching up and away shutting out the sky forever. I couldn't tell what Granddad was thinking. He sat at the head of the table immobile; his eyes once again bright, staring at Ned's face.

*****

"How long you been back, Son?" Daddy asked at breakfast the next morning.

"- I guess about a year."

Ned had been living in New York not far from Marcus Garvey's headquarters.

The silence that followed was its own reprimand. For a while there was only the sound of knives and forks on breakfast plates.

"- You've been in New York the whole time?" Momma murmured with a hint of reprimand in her voice.

"Just about, but I've been to lots of other places, too, helping organize - Baltimore, Chicago, a lot of places. That's how I got to be an officer. In a year or so I might be knighted."

"- *Knighted!*" Daddy sputtered, his fork in mid-air. "You don't really think those 'titles' he gives out mean anything, do you?"

"Sure they do," Ned assured him. "Everybody likes titles. We have the Earl of Lagos, the Duke of Somaliland, the Bishop of Nigeria - they'll be in charge of their provinces in Africa."

Daddy shook his head in disgust and put his fork down. "White countries control Africa, son. You just said so yourself! You can bet your life, they'll have a whole lot to say about who's running things there. Where're you getting the money for all this?"

"From selling bonds, from our newspaper, the *Negro World*, from our businesses – things like grocery stores, laundries, tailor shops. - We even have our own ship, the *Black Star Line*, and we get something from the speeches that His Excellency gives - "

"'His Excellency!'" Daddy cut him off. "Humph. Is that what he calls himself?"

Ned bristled and snapped back - "Yes, '*His Excellency!*' just like the King of England calls himself *His Royal Highness*. How did all those people come to be Duke of this, Prince that, and Baron so and so? They were just a bunch of thugs riding around on horses killing people and taking their land and women. Who decided all that! And what gave them the right? - God? I'll tell you what right - the same right His Excellency has.

"That just goes to show how slick white people are and how dumb we are. They can make everybody else believe that they're the only ones who have any right to any honor or distinction. Anybody who's not white is some sort of joke. An African king is just a monkey with a crown when the truth is Ethiopia is the oldest monarchy in the world! That means Haile Selassie outranks everybody, but does anybody ever tell you that? No. The white man got the idea of kings from us, not the other way around!"

To calm the impending storm, Momma started clearing the breakfast dishes and asked: "Are you working anywhere, Ned?"

"Yes, ma'am, but nothing to brag about. I work on one of our ice wagons carrying ice up three and four flights of stairs."

"You're more than welcome here, Son. Living away's not cheap."

"I'm not worried about a job, Momma. I'm just here temporary. Nothing's changed since I left the first time. I'm going to Liberia with Garvey. We're buying land there and he's going to need people there who don't have families to worry about. In nine or ten years when we get things built up, say around 1929, we'll really be raring to go. You'll see."

He repeated this to anyone who would listen. He was always being invited to places. Sometimes he took me. He never raised his voice when he spoke. He smiled often and took care to listen, so when he spoke, people were prepared to hear what he had to say. He was an excellent ambassador, unruffled, genial, with a ready answer for everything.

We were at the Elks Lodge. Ten or twelve men sat around the empty lodge sharing a friendly bottle of bootleg whiskey. Ned had everyone's attention until Rufus, a large man, trembling with rage, interrupted. He had large, protruding, accusatory eyes. In a loud voice, he denounced Garvey for being a hypocrite. Thrusting his head toward Ned and shaking his finger, he demanded, "How's this man gonna stand with the *Ku Klux Klan* one day, then have the damn *nerve* to send you here the next day to tell us he's with us. - Tell me that!"

The men had been in a jovial mood, but the Ku Klux Klan accusation jolted them. A few laughed nervously. They looked at each other and at Rufus and Ned.

"...But Rufus," a gray-haired man sputtered, "that don't make no kinda sense. You realize what you just said?"

"Gone - ask him!" Rufus challenged, eyes gleaming. He settled back in his chair, hands folded across his ample stomach.

The room grew silent.

Ned nodded. "...It's true. His Excellency did consult with the Grand Cyclops of the Ku Klux Klan. Know why? *Because only the Klan offered to protect him if he went into the South to speak!*"

Still silent, they waited for more.

"Uncle Sam refused to protect him. The states he had to pass through had cops waiting to beat his brains out the minute he crossed their border. The Klan put the word out - 'Leave him alone! Let him speak to all the black people he wants to.' And if anybody bothered him, they would have the Klan to deal with. Half the cops and everybody else was in the Klan so that was that. Who else could have done that? "His Excellency told the Klan that they both wanted the same things. No racial mixing. No politics. No talk about equality. And they wanted to hear us say that this is a white man's country and not for us; that *Africa* is our country.

"So, yes, they've given us donations, and they'll help all they can to see that we get back to Africa. It's where they want us, and it's where we want to be. After all," he smiled, "what's it matter who pulls you out of the river, so long as you don't drown?"

Some of the men nodded; they could see the logic in the arrangement. But Rufus was not mollified. Shifting his big body around in his chair, he crossed his leg, and boomed - "Africa might be *your* country, but it sure as hell ain't mine. And anybody lynching and burning our folks each and every day can kiss me where the sun don't shine! You was born here, you belongs here, not just white folks."

Chapter 26

I was strictly forbidden to go with Ned on any more of his visits.

"Why can't I go with him?" I had the temerity to ask Momma. "He's my brother," I pointed out as though that made all the difference in the world.

"Who's there your age?" Momma countered. "Ned's grown, so are his friends. You stay in your place."

The next day, Daddy was sitting in the living room with a portable desk over his knees framing the next Sunday's sermon. I appealed to him to let me go with Ned.

"We said *no!*" he exploded, his longish face ridged in a rare display of anger. "How many times do we have to say it? Only low class, trashy *niggers* bother with that man and his crazy ideas! Educated people wouldn't give him the time of day. The handful who do are just a bunch of preachers who can't make a living, and ragtag lawyers who don't know what the inside of a courtroom looks like. They're just living off him, that's all. They'd follow Satan if he promised them a meal! I'm ashamed a son of mine wouldn't know better.

"If that man thinks a country like England or France is going to let him walk into Africa and call himself a king, it just shows how stupid he is. The white man controls Africa just like he controls this country, South America, China, India and everywhere else in the world! That man's going to find himself in jail or dead. God only knows how much harm he'll do before he's through. And it's people like Ned who'll get hurt the most!

"Even the NAACPs against him; nobody's more for the colored man than they are. They're the only ones we have looking out for us. I thought you knew that!"

Momma appeared, wiping her hands on a dish towel, looking concerned. Emboldened by her presence I spoke up - "They're only concerned about light-skinned people, Daddy, not for dark people."

"What's that supposed to mean?" he snapped.

" - Ned said he went to their headquarters one day to carry a letter from Mr. Garvey to Mr. W.E.B. Du Bois, who's in charge of the NAACP. He said that everybody in the office was white or so light-skinned you couldn't tell the difference, just like Mr. DuBois. Ned said the NAACP magazine, *Crisis*, never has a picture of anybody dark in it."

He dismissed this with an impatient wave of his hand. "Is that why the NAACP puts out a black flag every time a Negro's lynched? Because they don't care? They're the only ones telling us to stand up and fight for our rights here, where we were born!

"Except for Garvey, I don't know a soul in the world who ever thought of going back to live in some God forsaken jungle with cock roaches as big as rats."

I said nothing but from then on, I no longer believed my father's view of the world; I believed in Ned's. If that meant sneaking around behind my father's back, so be it.

Ned disagreed. He shook his head. "Don't start lying, Aaron. Do as he says. Daddy feels like a lot of people do. Maybe most. They laugh at us for wanting to go back to Africa. All you hear is dumb stuff about jungles, or half-naked people running around with spears.

"That's not Africa. I've been there. They have cities just like you find everywhere else. I guess you can't blame people if they don't know; a lot of our folks still can't read or write. All they know is they were born here so that's all they care about no matter how people treat them. It's something to feel sad about, not mad.

"Marcus Garvey's not dumb. The man's been the editor of newspapers. He's been to places like Costa Rica, Panama, London - places most folks haven't. And he's seen things they haven't."

The seeds of rebellion continued to grow each time I saw Ned. We would whisper far into the night in his room. He told me about his days at sea and about Marcus Garvey and the Universal Negro Improvement Association. We never talked about why he was still living with us; I hoped we never would because I wanted him to stay with us forever.

"You'll never see stars," he once said, "until you've been to sea. Then you see a thick, real bright crust of jewels. Every color in the rainbow - red, blue, yellow and they move and shoot through the sky. You can understand why people long ago spent so much time looking at the sky. You said you like astronomy; we're going to need astronomers just like everybody else does -"

"Are you really going to Africa, Ned?"

"No doubt about it. We even have our own ships, the *Black Star Line*. I wanted to be an officer on it. I was a seaman for a little while but His Excellency sort of took a shine to me, and said he'd rather have me ashore."

"Are you his bodyguard?"

"What for? Who's going to bother him?"

"What do you do?"

"Lots of things. It's kind of complicated. I'm not with him all the time, but if he needs me he knows where to find me."

"-Why'd he take a shine to you?"

"I told him the ship I was on wasn't being run right. Things were so bad I came right out and said I thought somebody was out to sabotage the *Black Star Line*. I was only a sailor, and if *I* knew that a ship should never leave port without a cargo, how come the people in charge didn't know a simple thing like that?"

"That's what you told Mr. Garvey?"

"Word for word and a lot more than that. He looked kind of surprised; said he was going to look into it right away."

"How'd you come to meet him?"

"Saw him on the street. He's not God or anything, he's just like everybody else. People are always stopping him to say something."

"What's he look like?"

"- Kind of short, stocky, real dark, flat nose. When you see him, you might think he's not too smart, but the minute he opens his mouth and speaks you forget all that. When I saw him I just said, 'Excuse me, Your Excellency, may I have a word with you?' He said, 'You are one of my people?' I told him I was one of his sailors and he grinned and asked how things were at sea. That's when I told him.

"Even when you had sailing ships, if you dropped off cargo at a port, you had to load up with a cargo for the trip home, otherwise you'd lose your profit. Ships wouldn't come back until they got a load.

"Sometimes sailors would be away for over a year until they finally got a cargo that would bring them back home again. Nowadays you can arrange it before you even leave port; it's as simple as that.

"I noticed a lot of stupid stuff. The people running things weren't putting things in their contracts to guard against damages. Suppose you run into a storm or the ship sinks? Who's supposed to pay for the ship or the cargo? You have to guard against stuff like that. You could get delayed in port because of a strike. The way these guys were fooling around, instead of a man paying you to haul his goods, you'd end up paying *him* because you were late or something else happened to the cargo. It was a lot of dumb stuff. Like not even charging enough in the first place to haul a cargo.

"After His Excellency looked into it, I heard he got rid of a few people. I don't know whether he actually did or not, but he told me he wanted me close by. Said he needs people he can rely on because too many others come up a day late and a dollar short."

*****

Six weeks passed and Ned showed no signs of leaving.

This made Momma happy and Daddy was pleased, too. No one was more contented than Granddad who got to be with the family more now that Ned could help carry him up and down the stairs.

Yet something didn't seem right. Maybe I wasn't used to a man having nothing to do, and he rarely left the house during the day.

Once or twice Momma stopped talking or changed the subject when I came into the kitchen. If somebody knocked on the front door, only she answered it. All of this aroused my curiosity. There was even quiet talk of sending him to stay with Aunt Gloria for a few days.

It came to me that the thing that didn't ring right was this: If Ned had a job in New York, how could he stay with us indefinitely with no sign of leaving? People always needed ice. It wasn't a job you could just leave.

"- When are you going back?" I asked one night.

He was lying on his back fully clothed. I was lying beside him.

"Soon," he said in the darkness.

"Do you think Mr. Garvey misses you?"

"Probably."

"Will you still have your old job on the ice wagon when you go back?"

"- Not the same one."

There was a long silence. I knew he was going to say something important. All I could do was wait until he said it. Maybe he wouldn't tonight; maybe he would tomorrow. I felt it. I knew it.

"- I'm a wanted man," he said quietly. "The police are after me."

I sprang up, staring into the darkness at him lying on the bed with his hands behind his head. Why in the world would the police be after him? He wasn't bad. He was respectable and had a high school diploma.

"What'd you do?" I breathed. "Does Momma know about it?"

"They both know. You'll be in college soon; you may as well know, too. But not right now."

*****

"You're to keep your mouth shut!" Momma admonished me needlessly at the dinner table. "Your brother struck a police officer in New York. That's as bad as killing somebody. If he's ever arrested, if they don't beat him to death first, they'll send him to the penitentiary for fifty years!"

He struck a *police officer?* How could anyone even *think* of doing a thing like that? It was impossible to picture.

"Your brother was giving a speech, on a street corner, for Mr. Garvey and the officer walked up and struck him on his legs with his night stick instead of telling him to move."

Ned took up the narrative. "People are always giving speeches in New York, but somebody started a rumor that we were collecting guns and hiding them. On top of that, people were claiming we hate all white people. That's a bare-faced lie.

"This cop came up and whacked me as hard as he could on the legs. He ordered me to shut up and move on. I looked at him. - I guess I kinda stared, but I got down off the box and started to walk away. I was sorta limping from where he hit me. He started yelling stuff like, 'Move, when I tell you, boy!'

"That's when I got mad because I was already leaving when, all of a sudden, he whacked me again, across the shoulder. You should've seen the hate on that man's face. I don't know what came over me but I just exploded. It was like lightning flashed all through my head. He had the nerve to be mad at *me* when he was the one doing the dirt just like that bastard..."

"Ned!"

"...in South Philadelphia who stopped me on my wagon!"

"Well, when he raised his stick again, I just went crazy. I don't remember anything after that. All I know is a man came running up yelling, "Run, man, run!" A woman grabbed me by the collar and pulled me down the street. We ran first one way and then another until we ended up in somebody's apartment."

"And you don't remember anything about it?" I asked, breathless.

He shook his head. "The lady told me I'd knocked the cop out cold. I was just standing there looking down at him when they dragged me away. I didn't want to involve the UNIA so I just left word I had a family emergency. I got somebody to take me to Jersey City where I caught a bus."

No one said anything. After a long pause, Dad spoke.

"- Guess they have the whole force out looking for you. They'll arrest somebody else to make it look good."

" They did," Ned confirmed, "but I think they're still looking for me. New York's a big place; so much goes on.... It'll all die down one day."

*****

Like that time when Ned said he was leaving the country, any mention of him leaving was forbidden. Despite tip-toeing around the subject, he left that fall for New York a week before I went to college. I sat on the bed and watched him pack his things, especially his splendid uniform.

"Can I come to New York to see you on the weekend?"

Amusement softened his face. "You have a chance to go to college. Not many people get that chance. Take it, you hear? The United Negro Improvement Association can always get hands – people who can barely read or write; but we need heads. A lot of them."

"I can still see you on weekends," I insisted.

"Not right away. I don't even know where I'll be staying. Maybe this summer. I'll see that you meet Marcus Garvey in person. OK?"

I wanted to hug him but did not know how; it seemed too awkward to show my brother that I loved him.

Daddy drove the whole family to the bus station. Momma mentioned to Daddy that it might be the last time Ned would ever see Granddad. Maybe Granddad sensed this, too. At the train station, he insisted on hobbling along on his cane to the boarding area. He had shrunken and was now the shortest of us all. He glared into Ned's eyes and declared in a weak voice, "I'm leaving my uniform to you, Son. Put it on once in a while if it'll fit."

Ned stared for a moment. "- Be mighty proud to, Granddad. Thank you." He gave Granddad a brief hug.

The bus came and crept away, leaving me and maybe Daddy too, aware that Granddad had chosen to leave his Civil War uniform to Ned and not to either of us. After everything was said and done, his uniform had meant something to him after all.

COLLEGE
1920

Chapter 27

September. College. Alone for the first time in my life.

With the bequest Dad received from Mrs. Woolman, my parents were able to send me to college. There were only ten colored high school graduates that year. Our pictures were in the colored newspaper. Two of us were going to college. We appeared on page one.

Bursting with pride - anticipating cries of surprise and delight - Mom and Dad thrust the paper into the hands of everyone who came into the house. It was taken for granted that anyone who went to college was destined for wonderful things in a magical world where they would strut about in an elevated world, their picture in the society columns of the colored newspaper.

All ten of us, together with our parents and selected guests, received prized invitations to *The Graduation Tea* given by one of the local churches. Momma fussed over my appearance. She wet her thumb and brushed my eye brows down; made me shine my shoes again; brushed lint from my suit again; ordered me to stand up straight and again admonished me to mind my manners. Tonight would "open doors" for me, she promised. Ned was probably told the same thing.

The colored press arrived with cameras. Recitals were given by grownups who knew what they were doing. I was uncomfortable. I didn't know anybody. All I did was stand there. I had no idea what to do with my hands. It reminded me of the teas I'd been forced to attend. A lady handed me a cup of tea that was actually hot.

Later, we graduates were gathered together and each given a certificate of achievement by a group of beaming, gray-haired ladies. One lady stood at a podium and praised us for demonstrating that, "We as a people can succeed!"

Everyone clapped. A priest, who was white, took the podium. Speaking in a solemn voice, he assured everyone that "henceforth" all eyes would be upon us. He let it be known that what we graduates achieved, we achieved not just for ourselves, but "for the entire colored race." He received the longest applause.

Wesley was one of the graduates.

He was a little taller than I remembered. As we milled around, our eyes met. He avoided looking my way and I studiously ignored him. But we were thwarted in our effort to cold-shoulder the other. Mom nudged me to go over and speak to him. I resisted but a chesty woman with a relentless smile seized the two of us. It was her responsibility to make certain the college bound graduates met each other.

"We already know each other," we protested feebly, trying to squirm away. Nevertheless, she propelled us to a balding reporter. Not wanting to admit we'd had a falling out, we lied about what great friends we were and where we were going to college and anything else he wanted to know.

Left together and having remembered some pleasant incidents we had shared, Wesley mumbled, "Sorry I didn't answer your letters."

I already guessed he hadn't been allowed to. "- I thought your nose was broken," I said, staring at his face.

"So did I," he grinned, looking sheepish.

"You're really going to an Ivy League college?" I asked.

He nodded. "My father's cousin lives in Mexico and we got him to apply for me. I got in because the application came from Mexico. Colleges like to have students from around the world."

" - Are you pretending you're Mexican?"

"Well, not exactly, but *from* Mexico. Colored can get in white colleges, but you stand a better chance if nobody knows you're colored. You know – real, real light. Daddy said they don't want Jews, either."

"Aren't they white?"

"Yeah, but that's what my dad said."

I remembered one day coming home and blurting out that Benjamin Cohen had gotten beaten up by some boys because he was a Jew. Momma was outraged because I had sounded like it was all right. Daddy preached a sermon that Sunday saying if you let evil happen, you're evil, too, because by keeping your mouth shut, you're saying it's all right."

So I knew it was wrong that Jews could not go to college just as I could not. But it still didn't make sense.

Wesley and I weren't the pals we'd been, but I knew he meant it when he said he'd write and we'd catch up on things during the winter break. After the Graduation Tea was over, I watched him walk down the street, realizing that he'd been the only one I'd ever been able to talk to about my dreams and fantasies. I'd taken him with me among the stars and he'd gone, curious to see what I saw.

*****

I didn't like Prickly State College.

Prickly State was an all-male Negro college. Momma always said all-black anything simply meant exclusion; a testament to segregation and bias. You'd never see anyone from China or Japan, England or France going to Prickly, but it was the best she could afford. To me, college was a place that everybody knew about, like Harvard, Princeton and Yale. Wesley had gone to college, I had not.

Those places were great castles, hoarding the world's golden stores of knowledge; they were where renowned astronomers probed the skies and paleontologists reconstructed ancient monsters from shards of bone; it was where mathematicians strolled neat, flowered paths mumbling equations that proved nonexistence; it was where the great physicists nodded to even greater physicists, philosophers and doctors.

They were all Gods of Knowledge. They validated each other and together fashioned the shape of the world. The Gods of Knowledge willed what would be and they casually created toys for the populace to play with. They were those we could not understand because they spoke in tongues we could not comprehend.

Wesley was in a castle. I was in a humble bungalow. Any thought of becoming an astronomer or paleontologist or archeologist at Prickly was fantasy; I'd have as much chance of becoming king of England. What difference would it make that I knew the names of famous astronomers or the location of the great observatories - Herschel, Hale, Copernicus, Brahe, Cassegrain? - Then there was the Lick, Yerkes, Mt. Wilson, the Harvard College Observatory. So what if I knew them all. I would never step my black foot into any one of them. I knew the names of all the stars and where they lay. But they would never, ever appear in monstrous telescopes before my inquisitive eye.

And just as swiftly, my eyes fell from the moons of Jupiter to the La Brea tar pits. I wanted to see insects captured in million years-old drops of amber. I wanted to dig into the bowels of the earth for shards and remnants of pre-history; track the path of Roman armies and Ethiopian calvary; find adventures in Tasmania; mysteries in Panama....

Prickly State offered nothing remotely associated with them. I majored in science, just in case, without the least idea how I would put it to use after I graduated. But truth be told, Prickly could and did boast that it had nurtured a number of men who had gone forth and made a difference; men who had gained sustenance from barren tables; men who had grown greater than the segregating walls to become men of genius, of vision, of strength.

I think Richard would become one of them.

He was my dormmate. A chunky boy no happier than I, but he accepted Prickly State better than I did. We shared a small room into which someone had ingeniously squeezed two beds and two desks. Richard said his father was a musician who lived somewhere in New York; Richard was from Detroit and lived with his grandmother. He never mentioned his mother so I assumed she was dead.

He was a lot smarter than I was or anybody else I knew. His steel rimmed glasses gave his chubby face a friendly, owlish look, yet for some puzzling reason, within a matter of weeks, nobody wanted to associate with him. If I didn't sit with him in the cafeteria, he sat alone.

In the beginning, we clung to each other for fear of having no friends at all in the dorm. We got along well enough, but he wasn't a pal like Wesley or Fred. He spent a lot of time in our cramped room lying on his bed reading difficult books, or wedged at his desk scribbling in the notebooks he kept. To humor him I took his suggestion and delved into Karl Marx and Adam Smith. I didn't like them and laid them aside; there was too much "suppose this" and "what if that" for my taste; it was all gristle and no meat.

What Isaac Newton said mattered because he explained why we didn't all go flying off the surface of earth into space; Thomas Edison gave us light bulbs. These were men of substance and science. Even Napoleon mattered because people were always fighting each other just like they did in the war we just had. "If those other guys never lived," I brayed loudly from my desk one day, "what difference would it make?"

He was lying on his bed. He raised up on his elbow and stared at me for a moment or two as though I had grown two heads. He didn't know what to make of me. Puzzled, I stared back.

" - You know what you just did?" he asked, sitting up. "Just like that," he snapped his fingers, "you've dismissed the reason some men are poor while others throw food away; why desperate girls become whores, why some men rob and kill, why we invaded Russia after the war was over and the armistice was declared, why we were slaves for 300 years and are still slaves in all but name - you dismissed all of that, Aaron, just like that."

I wasn't aware I'd committed so many sins in so short a time. His reprimand sounded pleasant enough; it was almost as though I were his errant son caught with cookie crumbs around my mouth. But he aroused my curiosity.

"We have two worlds," he said, holding up two fingers. "The world of Karl Marx and the world of Adam Smith. And they hate each other. One day you'll have to choose which one of those worlds you want to live in. - Haven't you ever heard of communism?"

"- Maybe," I shrugged. "What difference does it make?"

He shook his head as though to clear it. "...That's almost like saying you never heard of Jesus Christ, Aaron. Don't you realize that?"

He made it sound like I was stupid. "It can't be all that important," I snapped or everybody would be talking about it!"

"Just because you've never heard of something, Aaron, doesn't mean you're dumb, and it doesn't mean it doesn't exist, either. The world's been turned up side down since the Russian revolution. You're probably not the only one here who doesn't know what's been happening. Maybe I can help – Some people might call me a Communist. I'd say I'm more a Socialist if that means anything to you."

None of it meant anything to me. Since coming to Prickly State I'd been made aware, on more than one occasion, that I was basically ignorant. I discovered that people subscribed to monthly magazines, went to lectures, and read the newspapers every day, not just when something bad happened.

Common sense told me I had a lot of catching up to do. I put the best face on it that I could, and agreed to let Richard teach me all about communism and socialism and capitalism.

He seemed pleased, his chubby face smiling from ear to ear.

Chapter 28

A lot of the men on campus were light-skinned. A few of them were related to one another; others had met in the summer camps and the exclusive youth social clubs that Elizabeth had told me about. They brought their social networks to Prickly State. They tended to look down, over, around and past us dark-skinned Negroes.

We dark men might edge over to one group or another in Kinsey Hall - the social hub - standing pleasantly by like mannequins, smiling appropriately, laughing on cue and waiting for an opportunity to make a comment. We wanted to be friends, but there were too many casual jokes about people we didn't know, and tales of incidents we had not witnessed at youth clubs to which we did not belong. They used code words that were alien to us. They spoke casually of friends they knew from one "set" or another, and of cotillions and travels to New York and Boston, Washington and Florida.

It was as though we were invisible. If seeing us were unavoidable because one of us had injected a comment, they would pause awkwardly for a second, and then plunge on as though no one had spoken a word. Soon after, the cry would go up: "Hey, let's go shoot some pool," whereupon they would all troop off.

Some of the dark guys sniffed in turn and attempted to dismiss the light guys as "color- crazy." Color-crazy or not, some of us envied them. They would never stand about awkwardly at teas or parties, wondering what to do with their hands. Two of them had even brought a radio to college that they played in Kinsey Hall or in their dorm room for their friends.

Yet economic status had nothing to do with anything. Everybody at

Grizzley State was there because that was where their parents had the means to send them. True, there were some -regardless of color – who were on scholarship, but Benjamin Turner, as dark as any of us, was being groomed to take over his family's real estate business, and Jasper Evans boasted that his family employed three men on their eighty-acre farm in North Carolina.

We were a race separated by color.

More, a guy who was color-crazy wasn't simply named Jones - he was *one of the Charleston Joneses*; another was *a Ralston*. No matter how much we tried to ridicule and mimic them for aping white people, in the end, we crept away wounded and hurt. They were a world apart just as Elizabeth was a world apart from me. The only difference between white people and them was the color-crazies were darker.

We tried to dismiss them. We couldn't. They ran the fraternities and everybody wanted to belong to one. Fraternities were the epitome of color snobbery. Somehow it depressed me that they were also intelligent because that seemed like an oxymoron.

It wasn't a surprise to me that color snobbery was a fact of life at Prickly State - it was the brutal intensity of it. Alarmed at being quartered with a dark-skinned roommate, the lighter skinned fellow would invent ingenious excuses to escape the demoralizing situation.

Kinsey Hall was a large room with two fireplaces, magazines scattered around and polished wooden panels. It was comfortably furnished with overstuffed chairs. Kinsey was invariably crowded with men, homesick and eager for companionship. Cliques abounded. Sometimes a card game was suspended while a photograph was passed among friends, accompanied by dutiful noises of admiration. There were the smirking boasts of upper classmen intimating that they had some "catching up to do with the ladies" during Christmas break. Occasionally we heard brave admissions of homesickness.

The Hall was tantamount to a stage. Various upper classmen like Ames Touisant, Randolph Purvis and Boonie Carter strutted their hour accompanied by a chorus of freshmen and sophomore sycophants. One sanctuary was the athletic teams. Anyone who was outstanding and vital to a team, was permitted to appear in the presence of The Mighty regardless of the shade of skin.

I didn't know this when I went out for football.

The first time I ran the length of the football field, the coach called me over. Boonie Carter and several others were standing with him. They all looked at me strangely.

"Where'd you go to school, son?" the coach asked. He looked out of shape. He had a red face, a veiny nose and a pot belly, but his voice had a certain warmth. "Did you run track?"

"No, Sir. They wouldn't let me on any of the teams at first and when they did I wouldn't join."

They stared. "- Did I do something wrong?" I asked.

"Do me a favor, son," the coach said. "– When you catch your breath, run the field again for me."

I wasn't sure what it was about. Without waiting, I ran the field again and jogged back to where the coach and the others were standing. His face was animated; he wagged his head up and down several times.

"You'll do!" he said emphatically. "You'll do just fine. You just made the team, son! I'll teach you how to play. If you can run like that when the season starts, no telling how far you might go."

Clutching my new uniform, I hurried to the dorm, filled with a sudden sense of power. I was surprised anyone thought I ran especially fast. Stephen ran faster than me, so could Alexander. Yet by the time I got back to my room, the elation was gone. I wasn't sure anymore that I wanted to run track or play football or do anything other than study.

"Don't worry about it, Aaron," Richard counseled from his desk "You're probably a little scared."

I looked around for someplace in the little room to store my equipment. "Scared of what? Getting hurt? When you're used to playing in the street and on sidewalks, what're you going to be scared of?"

"Maybe, not scared – nervous."

I pushed everything under my bed and plopped down, groping for an explanation.

"- I don't think I'm nervous. I don't know…I'm just not all that motivated. I don't feel like pounding my chest at somebody else's expense."

He didn't say anything at first. That meant he thought I was full of hot air or as he put it, shit. Later, he quietly convinced me to give the

209

team a try. I did. Being on the team made a difference. It happened when Hardy Daniels approached me in the dining hall where I had set my dinner tray. He was the best man on cross country.

"Aren't you going to eat with us, Winston?"

"-With who?"

"With us. Guys on teams eat over there. Come on. Bring your tray."

Presto – just like that I was part of a clique. I had scored more touchdowns in two games than they had all last year when the team went 0-6. I accepted my new status while at the same time it bothered me. I had to leave Richard sitting by himself.

"Go on," he urged. "You're part of the team now. Act like it."

I went but wasn't about to "act like it" if it meant looking down my nose at anybody. Having my picture appear, more than once, in the sports section of the local paper took some pressure off to "act like it." I could just act regular.

*****

I received a jolt a few weeks after I joined the football team.

One of the guys on campus always looked familiar. It puzzled me until one day somebody called his name. - Pace. Elizabeth's brother. There was no way of telling whether or not he would recognize me. If he did, would he still have that way of looking through me - with a faint, condescending smile on his lips.

I loathed the bastard. I'd never forget him marching along years ago with his friend, in their neat knickers, jeering:

"*...If you're white, you're alright,*
If you're brown, stick around
*If you're black, **stay back!***

He epitomized the color-crazy attitudes that smothered the campus. But he was my only access to Elizabeth. That might mean kissing his stinking ass. - What would he say if I asked, "How's Elizabeth?"

He was usually around a bunch of guys, their faces wreathed in good humored laughter.

He might make some snide remark in front of them to embarrass me. I wasn't sure what I'd do. He was Elizabeth's brother. Maybe I could ask when he was alone. I was desperate to know where Elizabeth was.

By chance, I found him alone in the nearly empty library.

Surreptitiously I watched him. His books were laid out neatly on the table. His pencils lay side by side. With beating heart, I approached the table. At the last minute I changed my mind. I walked behind him. His sweater was threadbare; the shirt he wore was a size too large. How could he be poor? I knew some of the fellows were poor, but I never imagined that Pace or anyone in his crowd was.

Then I remembered Momma's scornful words when I told her that Elizabeth's father drove a train. "Who ever told you such nonsense! He's a common porter. He makes beds and waits on people!"

She said other scornful things, too. She said porters like him had free passes on trains so they could take their families all over the country for free. They pretended they were well-to-do.

Scolding myself for feeling intimidated, and for feeling anything except resentment, I marched up to his table. I sat down across from him. He eyed me for a second, probably wondering why I had chosen to sit at his table in the nearly deserted room. He had a cleft chin. His clear brown eyes were bold and steady. Like Elizabeth, a natural, pleasant smile hovered on his lips.

Praying I sounded friendly, I ventured, "- Isn't your name, Pace?"

He offered a brief, negligent glance. "- Am I supposed to know you?" he replied quietly, before looking down.

"You used to live around the corner from me. Don't you remember? You lived on Jewel, I lived on Bradley."

"- No, my friend," he replied, head still down, continuing to write. "You may have heard my name somewhere but that doesn't mean that I know yours."

He began gathering his things and stood up. I followed suit. Controlling an impulse to grab his shirt collar and slam him into the bookcases, I blocked his way, forcing him to look at me. I was a little taller and heavier.

"It doesn't hurt to be courteous, 'my friend,'" I smiled through my hatred. "You used to live on Jewel Avenue and I used to play with your sister. Her name's Elizabeth. Am I right?"

Finally, his eyes found mine. They were steady and hard. "I have absolutely no intention of discussing my family with people I don't know. Now if you don't mind, you're blocking my way!"

I wanted to haul off and smash him squarely in his cleft chin. I wanted to smash his nose. I wanted to see blood and pain and fear, and if he showed fear and pain, I knew I would pummel him and smash him the way I had that gang boy who had attacked Wesley and me. Maybe I'd kill the son-of-a-bitch.

But his dignified, calm, cool, unruffled demeanor won out. It was the way I had always been taught to behave. I had to somehow be as dignified, and as aloof and as snotty as he or he would leave with the advantage. Only common people engaged in fist fights.

I kept a small fixed smile on my face and bowed from the waist. "Oh, please, Suh, fo' give me fo' fo'gettin' mah place, mistuh, Boss man. I ain't ree'lize you was white, Suh."

He flushed, disconcerted for a moment. After a slight hesitation he stepped past me, making certain not to brush against me or to look at me. He took the secret of Elizabeth with him.

Chapter 29

It was no good fuming and calling Pace a son-of-a-bitch. It didn't get me any closer to Elizabeth. As much as I yearned to kick the shit out of him, that would have been stupid. Elizabeth would hate me for it.

Maybe she'd come up with her folks on Parents' Day. Probably not. Upper classman sniffed at the thought of having parents visit them. By now dozens of guys were probably chasing after her. I wondered – did she still have the jack? In the midst of my angst, a solution rose before me like Excalibur out of the lake.

The registrar had everybody's address. I'd simply pretend that the bastard was my pal. I'd pretend we'd made plans for the Christmas break but, darn it, I'd misplaced his address, and he'd already left campus. Was it possible to get his address for me? - I was sure it'd work. I'd have to wait months, though, for the holiday break. But it was something to look forward to. The prospect of thwarting Pace was sweet icing on the cake.

*****

"You going to pledge?" Richard asked as we strolled along a path to the dorm.

I shook my head.

"- Anybody ask?"

"Alpha Ohmy Beta and Alpha Light Pi; they both asked me."

Behind his glasses his eyes glowed with owlish surprise. "*Light Pi?*

I smiled. "You mean I'm not light-skinned?"

He gave an embarrassed laugh. He was much lighter than I was. "…. Well, since you put it that way…yes."

I shrugged. "Frats compete. Who has the most money, the best athletes, the most cars; the most this, the most that. Bragging rights. I'm supposed to be a halfway football star like that guy at Rutgers, Paul Robeson."

"Cut the crap, man. -You're *really* not pledging?"

I shook my head.

"- Why? It's all everybody talks about! It's what everybody wants. You have it and you're saying –" Suddenly his eyes brightened. "Oh, I get it! You can't afford it! O.K, that explains it."

I should have dropped the subject. -"It's not money, but I don't care if that's what people think. I just think it's stupid."

We walked in silence for a few moments, passing the bench where Frederick Douglass was said to have sat. Richard wanted a more common-sense answer. Everybody was either in a fraternity or some rinky-dink club.

" -First," I explained, "after kissing everybody's ass, they make you go through all this agony of hoping and praying that you'll get invited to join their frat. And if you're not invited, you feel like shit. But if you do get invited, you get the privilege of having your butt whipped with paddles, or being blindfolded while the 'brothers' take turns beating the crap out of you. Then they make you scrub the dormitory floor with a toothbrush or go out and steal other people's property in the middle of the night; the weird stuff just goes on and on! I heard that in some frats, they even pee on you! And some frats even *brand* you with a red-hot iron! The whole thing's perverse and illogical and plain stupid! Especially for people who're supposed to be the best and the brightest!"

Richard was silent as we trudged toward the dorm. My words were beginning to sound empty because my communist friend, who favored equality and the brotherhood of man, uttered no ringing cry of endorsement.

"- What about you?" I asked. "You pledging?"

With a flick of his wrist, he dismissed the very thought. "I can't be bothered with that reactionary, bourgeois garbage!"

He was lying. He desperately wanted to have his backside spanked. If he had been invited, he would gladly have suffered his head to be pummeled by a bunch of adolescent miscreants, and he would have cheerfully offered his arm to be branded with a red-hot iron. So much for his towering intelligence and disdain for "bourgeoisie conventions."

He took a shot at me as we reached our dormitory. "Why don't you come out and admit you don't like them instead of giving me all that bullshit?"

"Do you hear yourself?" I shot back, tossing my hat on my bed. - I'm listening to the pot calling the kettle black! You spend too much time alone in the library or dorm reading books and magazines. You'll never get invited to anything if nobody knows who you are. You ought to relax once in a while,"

He sat in his chair with his coat on. He propped his feet on his bed and glared at me. "I didn't come here to 'relax,' Winston. Keep on 'relaxing' with those clowns in Kinsey Hall and you're going to find yourself flunking out right along with the rest of them."

"I don't need any advice from you about relaxing," I growled, searching my desk for an apple I'd left there. "I do my work."

"'Work!'" he hooted. "You just *think* you do any work. You may do enough to get by here or at some of the better high schools, but you'd never make it at a real college!"

Flushed with anger, I bit my tongue. Didn't I envy Wesley because he was at an Ivy League college which even had their own law and medical schools? Some of the colleges even had a real telescope. Deep down, I knew that Richard was right. Again. I never felt as though I were a real college student even though some important black men had gone to Grizzley. Richard finally hung up his coat and picked up a book.

"Don't think," he continued to scold, "that you're ever going to get an education just by sitting on your butt listening to some fool like Lewis ramble on. People like him and the rest of these so-called 'professors' don't realize that *why* is where learning starts. To them *why* means you're dumb!

"You'll only learn as much as they know, not as much as you need to know or want to know, and if you don't want more than you can get from Lewis or any of the rest of them, stop wasting your father's money; go home and get a job with the streets department hauling trash. If they'll have you!"

I didn't bother to argue with him. Somewhere along the line, I'd have to admit he was always more right than wrong. It was he who taught me that to appreciate Shakespeare one had to read Marlowe; that music was mathematics; that all wars were a matter of money, and that the day would come when I'd see that communism was the greatest force since Christianity and would be as invasive.

Maybe he was right because I'd began to wonder why one man held a thousand acres while another slept under a bridge, and why a woman should ever have to sell her body and her soul in order to survive. Richard could be exasperating at times but he inflamed me by pointing out that somewhere in the scheme of things, I would have to fight the things that were wrong and not let my life be one of smothered silence.

Only not just yet.

*****

I discovered why Richard had not been invited by any of the fraternities to pledge.

People thought he was 'funny.' Richard and I were lounging in Kinsey Hall waiting our turn at bid whist when Andre Dumois, the captain of the football team, armed with a serious look, pulled me aside.

"Let me ask you something, Winston – Why do you keep hanging around with King?"

I don't believe Dumois had ever said more than ten words to me that were not related to football. His presence was liked a wall - tall, muscular with a bull neck. He stared, waiting for an answer.

"- He's my roommate. Why do you 'hang around' with Hawley, Forbes and Dorney?"

"You want to know why I hang around with them? – Because they're not *funny*,' that's why!"

Seeing the confused look on my face, he lowered his voice. "I kind of figured you didn't know. Everybody else does, though. Gee, but…well, we know *you're* all right…."

I said nothing. I wanted to say, "I don't care," but that would've meant I believed him. I wanted to ask how he knew, but that meant I wanted to be convinced when I didn't really want to know. I started to say, "I don't believe that," but the other thoughts got in the way. I managed to look non-committal and left.

I'd never heard anything about people being 'funny' until I met Fred.

"You don't know what 'funny' means?" he hooted, eyeing me, with moist, delighted eyes. More evidence of my monumental stupidity. "Boy, you don't know *nothin*! I ain't never in my life met nobody dumb as you is!"

After assuring me that every man, woman and child in the civilized world knew what 'funny' meant, he declared he would not tell me. I would just have to find out for myself. But almost immediately, unwilling to deprive himself of the wonderful opportunity to see yet another dumbfounded look on my face, he declared - "If you ever see a man acting like a girl, that's 'funny!'"

"- You're lying!" I cried. "How can a man act like a girl?"

"Easy. - They walk like this," he said, taking several steps and switching his hips in an exaggerated way, "and they talk real high like girls do, and they always do this with their hands," he said flipping his up and down at the wrist.

"How come I never saw anything like that? I challenged. "You ever see anybody like that?"

He hesitated and I knew a lie was coming. "– Sure, plenty of times on South Street. That's where they be at. Anybody'll tell you that."

I didn't tell him that I had been on South Street in the Seventh Ward with Ned on the wagon, and never saw anything like what he was describing. But it didn't pay to argue with Fred because he had proven too many times that he knew lots more than I did. However, this was one thing I was not going to take his word for. Having no one else to ask, all I could do was suspend belief.

Later, when I met Wesley he said sure, people were 'funny.' Everybody knew that, but well no, he finally admitted, he had never actually seen anyone like that. So, why had Andre Dumois said such awful things about Richard? How could he be so positive? Richard was no different from anybody else as far as I could see and I saw him everyday. I kept my mouth shut. For some reason Richard broached the subject to me less than a week later.

We were on our way toward the warm, welcoming lights of the library, hurrying through a stinging wind that blew dead leaves along the ground, when he turned his chubby face to me.

"- Do me a favor, Aaron. I want you to tell me the truth no matter how hard it is and no matter what it is. - Promise?"

"– Sure."

"What do people say about me?"

A week ago I'd have been puzzled by the question. I stalled for time, avoiding his worried face. "- What do you mean, 'What do people say about you?'"

"Just what I said. What do people say about me that they don't say to my face? You can tell me. I promise I won't be upset; I just want to know, that's all."

We trudged along a few more steps through the chill of November. "- Well, some of the guys say you're 'funny.'"

His silence intensified the cold. He faced me, his face ridged with anger. "They're a bunch of *goddamned fucking liars!* Who said it? Foster? Pierce? Who? Who was it? I'll kick their goddamn ass so help me God!"

"Look, Richard - you asked me a question and I answered it, but I'm not about to be in the middle of this. You said you wouldn't be upset; I took your word for it. I'm not telling you anything else from now on!"

We reached the library in silence. He balked at going in. "How about you?" he stared. "What do you think?"

Under his anxious eyes, I shrugged. "- Hell, I don't care one way or the other."

"I said I'm *NOT, GODDAMN IT!* Do you believe me or don't you, Aaron? I've got to know!"

"Just so you can get mad? What the hell's it matter what I think –"

"Goddamn it -, yes or no! I want to know, *now* – yes or no!"

"- Sure, I believe you. I only meant that even if you were, we'd still be friends."

Not the least mollified, he badgered me until I said without equivocation or reservation, no, no, no, I did not think he was 'funny.' "But from now on," I shot back with quiet anger, "like I said - don't you ever ask me to tell you a damn thing again – not even the time of day - because you're a liar!"

From that moment on, I was convinced that what I'd been told was true although Richard didn't fit the descriptions I'd had from Fred or Wesley. But now I wondered - how did Richard feel inside? Was he vulnerable like a girl? Did he really want to be hugged and kissed? People would always shy away from him like they were doing now, so what would that mean for him tomorrow and the days after tomorrow? I felt a little protective of him while at the same time I felt self-conscious being seen with him. I briefly wondered – *can I get undressed in front of him?* Why not? Everything had been all right until Dumois started mouthing off a lot of garbage.

The best thing, I decided, was to use the past as a guide; there was no reason not to. I used to suggest going to Kinsey Hall as partners and wait for a crack at one of the card tables. He'd smile and put me off. Now his refusal would be awkward and my failure to invite him even worse. But he solved the problem himself. He marched down to Kinsey Hall and stormed in with a huge chip on his shoulder, eyeglasses glistening, looking for a fight.

"If anybody wants to say anything," he told me in quiet anger, "they're going to have to say it to my face and they're going to have to prove it or somebody's going to get his ass whipped!"

There was a swagger to him as we waited our turn at the card tables. Normally when partners were beaten, another pair took their place to challenge the winners. When it was Richard and my turn, both winners and losers got up leaving an empty table. Unruffled, he went to the next table and waited. When the same thing happened, he went to the next. I never waited with him. As the room grew silent, I lurked in the background wishing I could steal away. I watched his dogged quest until somebody finally said, "What the hell, it's just a card game."

Richard sat down impassively.

"– Where's your partner?"

He looked around the room until he found me. "You playing?"

The room leaned in on me. My mouth was dry. "– Sure," I said, feeling eyes on my every step. Burning with embarrassment I sat and tried to sound casual. "Deal the cards."

Over time Richard found people who would talk to him and play cards with him. He was not as soft spoken now as he had been when I first met him, and he was leaner. There was a shadow of hardness around his mouth that had not been there before.

*****

Families were invited for Family Day.

Prickly State looked like most colleges. There were ivy covered

Gothic buildings, silent playing fields, professors in academic robes, vast expanses of well-kept lawns lending an air of majestic gentility. My parents came with proud eyes. Dad clapped me on the shoulder with masculine camaraderie, and Mom took us each by an arm and walked proudly between us. I prayed I would I see Elizabeth. She would be sixteen, glowing and beautiful.

Family Day was a time of dignified laughter, erect posture and conservative manners. Everyone jostled for social position on the sunny, undulating lawns of Prickly State.

In the swirl of conversation, we overheard: "…May I present Doctor and Mrs. Lewis-Brown; they're from Charleston, yas…"

"- Look, ain't that Laddie Cawtuh and Sissie – His uncle is *the* Gateway Cawtuh who owns Cawtuh Catering…"

"…Oh, are you one of the *Delafontes* from Washington? You know Ah had the pleasure of taking tea with …"

"We're thinking of sending Boonie to Howard next fall now that he's gotten used to being away, yas – He simply couldn't make up his mind. He wanted to go to Harvard, then Princeton, then Yale so finally I said, 'I'm going to settle it for you.'"

"Yas, we've all heard so much about you. You're *the* Reverend Shiloh Abernathy of Rock of Edam Baptist Church! This is my husband, Ralph Gates; he's a teacher, you know, yas."

"Oh, do call us, we have a telephone you know, yas. So few people have them; it almost seems a waste to keep it…"

During the sun-swept day, no one jostled harder for social position than Mom. Tall and lean, as an 'Old Philadelphian,' she kept apart from individuals she guessed had not been born and reared in Philadelphia. She looked beyond them and they in turn looked beyond her. Noses in the air, they found kindred souls with whom they could laugh and Dad found those to whom he could tip his hat.

I wished Richard's grandmother had been there. From what he told me, she had made a difference in her time, resisting those who would diminish her and assisting those stuck in the mud. She had been a prohibitionist, a suffragette, a revolutionary and anything else that required demonstrating, parading, and shouting in public places for the rights of women. But neither she nor anyone came to see Richard.

The day came to an end. Seeing the pleased glow emanating from my parents' faces, I knew that I would have to stick it out at Prickly State. But I hoped to God the day would never come when I would hear my mother bleat, "Yas, my sister Gloria's just returned from the Continent. She speaks French so beautifully you know…yas."

I had looked for Pace. By tracking him I could locate Elizabeth, but neither appeared. Nothing was left but to wait until Christmas break. Then if my plan worked, I would see her.

Chapter 30

Christmas break, and I knew where to find Elizabeth.

I was determined to see her despite all the stinking garbage about being too dark. I was a Negro. I was *supposed* to be dark, damn it. I approached her house. I was greeted by a large, welcoming Christmas wreath. Marshalling my courage, I fought my apprehension of facing the bastard Pace or his snotty mother.

The day was overcast and cold. I had no gloves and clenched my fists to keep my fingers warm. I only wore my college sweater because it was emblazoned with *Prickly State College*, and I wore my college beanie – both ragged credentials of respectability. Arranging my lips into a smile, I rang the doorbell.

Several seconds passed. Finally, the curtains on the door moved. Another second or two crept by. The door inched opened part way revealing a white, hostile face. Watery blue eyes regarded me without expression.

"Good afternoon, Mrs. Taliaferro," I mumbled through lips numbed by the cold, "My name is Aaron Winston and I'm just back from college and I wondered whether I might please speak to Elizabeth."

Breathless, I waited. Her eyes narrowed. Her mouth was sunken because her upper teeth were missing. It made her look old. When she spoke, her cheeks flushed pink.

"No, you can't speak to Elizabeth," she said with a Southern drawl. "Certainly not. She's in New York and for your information, mister, you're not welcome in this house. You're just a *sneak!* We know all about you. You're a sneak! My daughter's already committed, and she's got no interest in you whatsoever so stop making a fool nuisance of yourself and learn to take no for an answer!"

The door closed firmly in my face.

New York?

Stupidly, I stood there for a moment feeling the cold through my sweater. What did she mean, Elizabeth was "committed?" Was she engaged or married? What did it mean? And where in New York was Elizabeth? I stood on the doorstep a moment longer and then stormed away, filled with mounting contempt, and a deep sense of resentment for this woman.

As my anger rose, I longed to ask her who the hell did she think she was to treat me as though my skin were a badge of shame? But I knew I could never or would ever say that. Yet - why not; didn't I have the right?

The damn woman was practically glorifying slavery! Listening to Granddad and Mr. Amos tell stories about their days as slaves was reason enough to hate slavery and all it stood for. Yet this woman was proud that slavery had made her almost white from generations of rape, and she condemned me because it had not made me so. Hooray!

I stormed into the wind, steaming with anger, not feeling the cold anymore, remembering the things I'd overheard years ago; things I hadn't fully understood at the time. But now they gleamed clear and shouted at me and made me hate her.

I remembered - when I had just turned fourteen - Mr. Amos regaling Daddy and some of his friends with stories from long ago. They relaxed in the parlor smoking cigars and drinking beer from tall, sudsy, glass mugs. They laughed a lot in deep voices, slapping their thighs and urging Mr. Amos on. His voice, waxing and waning in his rich Southern dialect, made the room a warm, friendly cocoon where I sat next to Daddy, happy just to listen and to feel and to smell the fragrant aromas of cigar and pipe tobacco.

There was a pause, and in that silent moment someone hinted: "Little pigeons have big ears."

All eyes turned to me as though I had been secretly spying on them. Concealing my fury at being ejected from my cozy surroundings of grownups, I slunk to my listening post at the top of the stairs. But eavesdropping wasn't the triumph it had once been.

It was frustrating listening to muffled voices instead of being there. The real pleasure was watching Mr. Amos' eyes sparkle and seeing a grin crease his bony face; it was watching Mr. Morgan lean forward, lower his voice to tell the party something; the real pleasure was listening to the chorus of agreement and hearing the warmth of their voices and the richness of their laughter.

The real pleasure was feeling that I could sit snuggled there forever and never grow tired of them or of the fragrance of tobacco. At times there would be periods of quiet reflection before one of them would begin again in a soft man-rumble.,

I remembered that from my listening post, I detected the conversation suddenly turned somber after I was banished from the room. Mr. Amos still held the floor. "...an' Massa Joe brung his nigger dogs. *Big* dogs about that high."

"That's mighty big," someone chuckled. "You sure they was dogs?"

I heard Granddad explain, "Slave breakers used what they called nigger dogs to break slaves who had too much spirit. You have to remember, Otis, they made slaves of people who used to be warriors back in Africa; some of them even fought lions. – I know a slaver came close to setting a dog on me when I first got down there."

"...Massa Patrick," Mr. Amos continued, "brung one, too, and I don't know the other man's name, but there was three dogs and they set 'em on Booby. First thing they did, they made 'im take his clothes off. 'Take them rags off, nigger!' an' fore he could do that one of 'em reached over, took hold to his shirt an' jus' tore it off him. Wasn't nothing but rags no how.

"Told us men to git the rest off him, an' we took all his clothes off like they said. Then Massa Joe pointed his gun at Booby and said, 'Git!' But Booby, he jus stood there. He knowed he couldn't outrun them dogs - He jus got down on his knees crying somethin' awful, pleading with Massa Joe.

"'Please, Massa, please beat me ever day hards you want, Massa, please beat me! I'muh work day an' night, Massa. Oh, Lawdy, have mussy, Massa. I done wrong, I knows it. Please beat me, Massa. Don't turn 'em loose on me!'

"Now the rest of us knew beggin' wouldn't do no good. Jus' make some people go wild. An' after those massas took time off and brung them dogs, they wouldn't be satisfied jus' beatin' him. More'n that, they had us all lined up to watch, women, too. They always make us watch to teach us a lesson; same as saying, 'Your turn gonna be next!'

"Well, suh, one of them - think it was Massa Patrick - got mad, an' took an' hit Booby upside his head with his rifle. Drew blood. Then they hauled him up to his feet and Booby just collapsed, hollering and screamin', beggin' and pleadin' till finally one of em got a rope, tied his feet and they all moved back. Then Massa Joe hollered, "'Sic im!'"

"At first I closed my eyes real tight. Heard him screaming and calling out for mercy, but dogs is mean. Like to tear you apart, and big as them dogs was, it was like grown men pulling on him. Then I opened my eyes and saw one dog had one leg, one the other, an' the other had his arm - all pulling hard's they could. That's why Booby didn't wanna try to run. We all seen what dogs'll do when they sic 'em on you. They was all over 'im. Had him by the face, trying to get his throat.

"The biggest one went after his privates. You never heard such screaming in your life. Then they tore open his stomach and that set them crazy. All them trying to slobber his guts an' all the time him just a screamin' an a-screamin,' rolling this way an' that an' them pulling him every which way. He roll on his stomach, they got after his behind. - There just ain't no where to go a pack of dogs gits after you.

"- That's what slavers want. Scare you so bad, all they got to say is 'kneel, nigger,' an' you pee all over yourself. I seen it happen. Women, too. Don't make no difference. They say kneel and you git down in a hurry. They get you so, if they knock you to the ground, you glad that's all they do to you. You practically thank 'em. Even if a little chile say, 'Kneel nigger,' if he white, you do it. "

There was a long thoughtful pause. I could picture them sitting there, glasses of beer forgotten, looking a little depressed. "I know they did what they wanted with the women," a voice said.

"Yeah, an' tell the truth, that's a reason why a lot of us was glad what happened to Boobie."

"*What!*" thundered a voice seething with indignation. "*Glad?* What chu mean you was *glad* that happen to one of us, Amos?"

Granddad pounced in a quiet, determined voice. "Don't you be jumping to conclusions, Hunter! 'Less you been a slave like us! You got slavers would be in a crazy house if they lived up here or anyplace else. Some like to see pain 'cause it makes 'em feel good. I seen fathers damn near kill their own children because the 'master' said whup 'em, an' if he told you to bring your daughter up to the house so the men could drink and sport with her, you'd do it. - So you just be quiet an' listen to what Amos got to say!"

Admonished into silence, Hunter was quiet. After a long pause, Amos, miffed, continued. " - First off, Booby was a pure-dee nigger, an' most of us wasn't. Wanted to be the Massa's main man so's he could carry a whip in his hand an' come amongst us like a white man.

"Boobie was the strongest man I ever seen in my life. Tall as that there doorway an' have to turn sideways to come through. All muscle. Couldn't nobody beat 'im. Black Bob tried that when Booby throwed Bob's woman down, pulled her legs open an' had his way with her in broad daylight for everybody to see.

"Black Bob hauled off an' kicked Booby in the head hard as he could. Booby jumped up an' hit Bob so hard, it laid him out flat; liked to killed him. Took two days 'fore Bob could even stand up. Wasn't never the same no more. Couldn't never call his own name to mind. Had to lead him to the field and set him to work like a chile. After that, Booby come to his cabin whenever he take a mind, an' take his woman. Black Bob jus' sit there an' grin.

"Booby wanted to be the main man, and he wanted the pick of the women - the ones the massa or his friends or the overseer didn't want. An' he wanted extra food, a whip an' the 'thority to go with it.

"He got it, too. - Know how? 'Cause Old Ezra – he was the main man at the time – Old Ezra had to go git Sally, his granddaughter, and beat her 'cause Mr. Rudy, the overseer, claimed she sassed him. Everybody knowed he was lyin' 'cause when his son – he was 'bout sixteen, seventeen – when he told Sally to go to the barn with him, she musta didn't 'act right.' Girl wasn't moren' twelve, thirteen, but they used to say if they can bleed, they can be butchered. So Mr. Rudy, he gonna teach her a lesson an' all the rest of the women.

"But like I said, Sally was kin to Ezra. He didn't wanna have to do it. But Mr.Rudy shout, 'You hear me, nigger! git 'er and *whup her!* so Ezra got his whip an' soons he went to get her, he just started tremblin' real bad. Fell down, eyes jumpin' out his head, tongue chokin' 'im. He was bad off. Died 'fore sundown.

"Soons Ezra fell out, Booby run up hollering, "I git 'er, Mr. Rudy, I whup 'er!"

"Git the whip," was all Mr. Rudy said. He was a fat sour face man, always spittin' tobacco. Well, Booby grabbed the whip outta Ezra's hand. They laid this board on the ground an' Booby dragged the girl up, threw her on it face down, tied her thumbs to the top and her feet to the bottom, then he tuk and tied her around the waist and bared her from there on down. They called us all to see it.

"A whip'll cut an at the same time peel a strip of skin right off you. Well, suh, that whip sound like a shot each an' every time he hit her with it, and every time you see a strip of skin clinging to the whip or falling on the ground. That girl screamed so bad it make you wanna kill all them slavers, but you too scared to even move.

"Booby was out to hurt 'er. He was strong to start with but he damn near cut that chile in two. Massa, he just stood there, wouldn't say stop, an' Booby just reared back with all his might and all you hear was 'crack! crack! crack!'

"You seen hamburger? Well, you see her backside and legs down to her feets. Girl died that night 'bout the same time Ezra did. Every time she faint, Mr. Rudy say throw water on her and beat 'er some more 'cause - I can see now - looking back - he *meant* for Booby to kill 'er. Usually they don't kill you 'cause you cost money, but he meant to stand there and watch Booby beat that chile to death cause she didn't 'act right' for his son."

I think those words drenched their minds, and like me, I think they tried to picture the tortured girl. What had she looked like? What sort of person was she? And Sally was resurrected after sixty years of dust to live again in the memories and conscience and compassion of the men who listened to Amos. And for me, I listened, too, and though I did not understand at the time why a barn had anything to do with what happened to Sally, I was glad to hear them praise Amos for saying he was glad for what he had happened to Boobie.

*****

There was a period of silence. I thought the conversation was over when the man named Hunter asked "…But what'd Boobie do, Amos? Can't be what I'm thinking."

"You thinking right. Only thing it could be. A lot of us knew that's what'd take to cause them to bring all them dogs. Ain't never had no proof, but, them dogs tole you right off they was gonna kill Boobie - make example of 'im - Massa coulda sold Boobie for enuf to buy two, three more in his place. All I know is after that, Massa's niece, Miss Sue Ellen, was all-a-sudden sent to go live with one of Massa's people some place in Texas."

I remembered the death of Sally as I stormed through the cold that December day. Who did Elizabeth's bitch of a mother think she was to indict me for being black rather than the slave masters who had made her white?

Chapter 31

Dear Aaron-

Sorry I missed you over the Christmas break. College has been quite an experience, but I'll tell you all about it when I see you because you've <u>got</u> to come to Harlem!! Everybody's here. Painters, poets, writers, actors, sculptors, musicians and man you should see the girls! Very fine browns and one finer than the other, and they all wear dresses so you can see their legs. When I first got here, I walked around for days with a hard on. Honest. And everything's interracial. It's nothing to see a colored man with a white woman.

There's hardly any prejudice. It's like we have our own world in Harlem. There're lots of night clubs with dancing girls. You never saw such beautiful girls in your life. All light- skinned and nearly white. Next summer I'm staying here with relatives and you can stay, too. We'll have lots of fun. just give a date. I promise, once you get here you won't want to leave.

Yours,
Wesley

Elizabeth was in New York, too - probably Harlem.

Despite her misbegotten mother and brother, fate was bringing us together because we were meant to be together. I noticed that no matter what happened, I always found her again. And when I did, she was as glad to see me as I was to see her. She must think of me now and then as I thought of her.

The funny thing was, after I received Wesley's letter, "Harlem Fever" seemed to sweep Grizzly State, or maybe I had just never paid attention. To hear the guys talk, Harlem was the center of the universe. I knew Ned was there but he never made it seem that way. True, I wanted to go too, but only to find Elizabeth and to see Ned and Marcus Garvey.

Guys in Kinsey Hall knotted around the latest Harlem adventurer to listen to exotic tales of a city whose streets must surely be paved with gold. Stories were repeated at second and third hand based on what someone from "The Circle" had related.

The Circle was a clique of upper classmen. They'd been to New York a dozen times and came back with joyful tales of "Wonderland." They'd seen Claude McKay here, sat at a table next to Langston Hughes or Jesse Fauset or Zora Neale Hurston; they'd gotten drunk on 125th Street, found whores on Lenox Avenue and the Cotton Club; then there were tales of 135th Street and the night clubs like Small's Café and Connie's, with super beautiful light-skinned dancing girls, and don't even talk about 7th Avenue - Lybia and Connor's! The tales of Nirvana never ended. One need not die to go to Heaven.

Two of The Circle - Boonie Carter and Ames Toussaint who'd known each other since childhood - had second-hand automobiles. Only hand-picked fraternity brothers from among the throng who panted, "Take me! Please, take me!" were blessed with permission to accompany them, and others in The Circle, on their jaunts to New York.

Richard was one of those who probably would have panted.

Though he was the brightest guy on campus, deep down he wanted to be invited to join a club or fraternity but it would never happen. It was fear of rejection that had kept him penned up in our dorm room pretending the rest of us were dunces for "wasting our time" playing cards and socializing.

Once freed from his self-imposed prison, he was in Kinsey Hall more than I was. Even so, he was the last person I would have expected to catch "Harlem Fever" but he did. For a fellow on a bare scholarship, bus fare to New York, to say nothing of food and a place to stay was tantamount to taking a European cruise.

Thrusting reality aside, he announced his intention of making the pilgrimage to Harlem, the Holy Land. And in the dead of winter. More, as we left the warmth of Kinsey Hall, our faces whipped by the sharp wind cutting across the campus, he announced with steaming breath and eager eyes - "We'll go together. We can hitchhike!"

"Like hell we will!" I objected, walking fast to stay warm. "Freeze to death is more like it. You should know you can get locked up for hitchhiking, especially if you're colored. My parents would just about die of shame if I got locked up. And suppose nobody picks us up and we're in the middle of nowhere freezing our butts off?"

For once, he had no answer. He looked deflated. I'd let the air out of his balloon. I felt a little guilty as we trudged toward the dorm. Unless Richard went alone, there was nobody else he could turn to. I was still his only real friend on campus.

"Anyway," I blurted, "what's so great about Harlem? Just a bunch of trashy people shining shoes and living ten to a room. All I ever hear is people giving parties all night to raise rent money, or stuff about 135th Street, Lenox Avenue, Conner's, the Cotton Club, Small's - just a bunch of speakeasies. There has to be more to life than going to parties, screwing, fighting and drinking bath-tub gin!"

He was astonished. It was like the time I said Marx and Adam Smith were irrelevant.

His jaw actually dropped while his bespectacled face took on a glow. He stopped walking to stare at me, steam rising before his face. With the wind numbing my chin, I quickened my step dreading the cloud of arrows that were sure to come. God only knew what he would accuse me of this time.

"Well, well, well!" he cried after me, in the tone of a cop catching a thief red-handed. "Look at Mr. Hypocrite! Yeah, *hypocrite*, that's right. Why didn't you say all that stuff in Kinsey Hall where everybody else could hear you? Why didn't you tell them that? Because you're a hypocrite! You sneak off to the middle of nowhere so nobody else can hear, then start running your mouth!"

Stung, I flung back, "I don't give a good Goddamn who hears me, Richard! What can anybody do to me? Nobody ever asked me what I thought, and nobody ever invited me to hitch- hike or I'd have told them the same thing. You're supposed to be so smart - common sense tells you Harlem can't be that great!"

"To hell with common sense! Common sense has nothing to do with it, Aaron, and I hate to say this, but that's the dumbest, most ignorant thing I've ever heard anybody say in all my life! 'Trashy people.' You ever been there? No! Too scared of getting locked up. Too Goddamn 'respectable!' Yeah, you don't fool me. I know you and your 'respectable' bullshit!

"God, how bourgeois can you be? Sure, maybe there's nothing but 'trashy people' if all you're looking to do is see how late you can stay up, how drunk you can get and how many whores you can screw!"

"That's all anybody does as far as I can tell," I rejoined, hurrying into the welcome warmth of the dorm.

"Don't you know that everybody who's intelligent and educated is in New York? What do you think happens when the best minds get together in New York or Paris or any other place? If you'd read something once in a while, you wouldn't be saying things like that. Haven't you ever heard of Alain Locke's book, *The New Negro*? or of the Talented Tenth?

"This is a new day, these are the *Twenties!* Negroes have suddenly realized that we have talent. We can paint, we can sculpt, we can write, act, teach, create - we have wonderful, wonderful talent and it's been just lying there, under a mountain of slavery, discrimination and distortion!"

He was like the Mississippi River - there was no stopping him. In our room, I'd taken off my coat, but he still stood in his jacket berating me, not even bothering to close the door behind him which I was finally obliged to do. I felt compelled to look at him and give him all of my attention because he sounded so desperately earnest.

It had the strange effect of not only making him sound right in everything he said, but also making me feel wrong and stupid. I let him go on lecturing me as he finally began removing his coat.

"We can be anything we want to be, Aaron. We don't have to settle for a pick and shovel anymore; we have a voice now and it's being heard! That's what's going on today, not parties and playing the fool. We're New Negroes - yes, Goddamn it, *Negroes*, get used to the word.

"Men like Randolph, Locke, DuBois are showing the way. Sure, some of them are wrong headed, screwed up bourgeois capitalists, but they're all saying, *'We're not slaves anymore!'* Things of the mind," he cried, tapping his forehead, "that's our future, not serving dinner, picking cotton, shoveling shit and letting people convince us we're just dirt under their feet!

"There're *always* going to be people shining shoes, grinning and kissing ass, but not us. Each of us here is part of the elite of our race; *we're the Talented Tenth!* We can either party the future away or put our shoulder to the wheel.

"We're fortunate, Aaron. We're in college, we have the brains," he shouted, tapping his forehead again, eyes glowing through his eyeglass lenses, "and we have to use them to write our own history, to dispel lies and myths about lazy, ignorant Sambos and jigaboos!"

I finally managed to sit on the edge of my bed. Still he hovered over me, verbally lashing and slashing.

"Jesus Christ, man, this is *1920!* You realize what that means? - You should be wondering what things'll be like ten or fifteen years from now and whether you'll be able to say you played a part in it! Right now, from where I sit, you belong at a work bench someplace, not here with the rest of us! We're facing a hell of a great future while you're still wallowing around in 1910!"

Had he said that in front of other people, I might have punched his face. Now, nose to nose, he stared down my anger. His uncharacteristic passion made me hesitate. I had never heard of *The New Negro* or that anyone except Garvey thought the word "Negro" respectable enough to brag about it, nor had I heard of the "Talented Tenth."

I'd find out, but I'd be damned if I would ask him what they meant.

Why hadn't Wesley, who was actually in New York, said anything like this? He'd spoken only of "fine women" and sex, and like everybody else, babbled on about parties. It had been disappointing to hear that from him, as though physical pleasures were all that mattered.

But despite what Wesley and Richard said, Harlem was no Mecca as far as I was concerned. Not enough to make me take a chance hitchhiking and facing the awful shame of being locked up like a common thief. What Wesley wrote in his letter and what the guys said in Kinsey Hall was probably closer to the truth than the pie in the sky Richard was spouting.

Maybe he did believe he would find some sort of intellectual feast - a gathering of Gods there, and I hoped he would because he deserved to, but he would have to do it by himself. No one else seemed to see what he saw or hear what he heard.

Swallowing my anger, I turned away from him.

Chapter 32

After our fight about Harlem, we didn't have much to say to each other for the rest of the school term. It's hard living that long cheek to jowl with somebody you're not speaking to. Every move and sound was magnified; we wasted a lot of time trying to interpret every move the other made. When he left a book on my bed, *The New Negro*, by Alain Locke, I didn't know whether to take it as sarcasm or a peace offering.

But that argument wasn't the real reason we weren't speaking to each other. We'd had plenty of those. It went deeper. This argument had simply been a last straw. He had said something earlier one day in Kinsey Hall that I felt was a stab in the back.

A bunch of us were lounging around during finals when I mentioned Mrs. Washington. I probably shouldn't have said anything. At least not the way that I did. Even as I spoke, I didn't feel right because I knew I was saying that my family was "upper class" - like theirs - and the Washingtons were lower class, the sort that we "upper class types" avoided. When I said it, I felt a little slimy. And Richard rubbed the slime in.

" -Why are you blaming the woman for trying to better herself?" he asked from the floor where he was sitting.

We all looked at him. Was he joking? Unperturbed, he stared back, glasses gleaming on his chubby face.

"How the hell can she 'better herself,'" I sniped, "when she doesn't even know what 'better' is?"

I welcomed their laughter, but I should have known better. I was waving a red flag and Richard relished argument. For him, argument was to be alive - an opportunity to pound and shape ignorant minds into his view of the world. Now offered a bountiful feast, he leaned back against the sofa, crossed his outstretched legs and let loose his hounds of war.

"And, may I ask, whose fault is it if she 'doesn't know what better is?' It damn sure isn't hers. See, Winston, you're always taking the bourgeois view. You automatically blame the victim while *you're* the one with your foot up her butt!

"Say you have a dog - no, listen to me for a second - say you have a puppy and you train it to growl and bite people. Why blame the dog when it bites somebody? That lady was trained to be the way she is. It goes back to slavery. She never learned how to be *somebody* because she had *nobody* to teach her to be somebody. Don't blame her. Blame the people who made her that way!"

I felt betrayed. He should never have scolded me in front of other people. He had come a long way since the day I had stood by him at the Battle of the Card Tables. I had helped. If I, a football star, could stand by him, others could, too. Slowly a lot of the fellows had come to recognize that he had the only real head among us and they accepted him; he began to set a collegiate, inquiring, skeptical tone for a lot of us.

Before - barely any of us on campus had ever heard a full explanation of capitalism or communism. And even if we had, we could not have cared less because the implications of those things were crowded out by the everyday stench of racial discrimination, prejudice, police brutality and lynchings. Under the daily threat of the rope, such knowledge was a luxury. It was also from Richard that we heard of Kant, Hegel, Goethe. He breathed life into ideas, concepts and philosophies that were virtually clichés to the educated. Even his sarcasm about the quality of the teaching at Prickly State was being taken up by others. People listened to him now. The laughter I had elicited at first gave way to solemn, attentive faces. I was being pushed into a corner. I fought back.

"So let me get this straight - what you're saying is - if her son beats us up and threatens to punch my mother, you're saying we're supposed to say, 'Oh, it's not his fault; it's all because of slavery!' and just take it? And when his bitch of a mother tries to beat my mother up in the street, I'm supposed to stand there and say, 'Oh, it's not her fault,' – it's slavery - *that was over fifty damn years ago* – is at fault! - Is that what you're saying?"

He shot back, "That's not what I'm saying, damn it, and you know it! I'm saying kick his butt, but once you do, you've got his attention. Then you have to *teach* him. If you hate him because he's black and ignorant, and white people hate him because he's black and ignorant, where the hell is he supposed to go?

"You're in college and you're still saying the same thing you said when you were a snot nose kid. - Let me tell you something - until people like that family get out of the mud, we'll all be in the mud because white people only see people like that and not people like us!"

With that he won the day. One plus one equaled two. But for me, one plus one didn't always equal two. Since neither I nor any of my friends could have whipped Boo Boy, and even if we could, he'd just find another way to get even - probably with a knife - where did that leave us?

Still, all I could do was stand tongue-tied while he called my mother intolerant, snobbish, blind and cruel while Mrs. Washington was a victim of history, an example of man's inhumanity to man. More, Richard took the opportunity to point out that everything I had said further validated his belief in communism. Communist didn't persecute people instead of helping them. No Negro we could think of - not Marcus Garvey or W.E.B. Dubois - offered Negroes real hope.

"Because they're all *bourgeois*. They just want to be part of the system. They don't want to change it. They're perpetuating the *status quo*. Let everybody have all the damn kings and queens and wealth and poverty you please. They don't care so long as they think they're equal. Any dunce can see that. What do they care if one man can eat provided another goes hungry? That clown Garvey is still going around appointing "dukes" and "barons" and shit like that while our people are being lynched day and night!"

My anger in our room, later on, came from that day in Kinsey Hall, not the merits of Harlem.

Why the hell hadn't I said more? Everybody smirked that Richard had wiped the floor up with me, but I didn't see for one second how Mrs. Washington and her thuggish son were victims. We were the victims.

Everything Momma had cobbled together, in the hope of being

viewed as respectable by white people, had been smashed by the Washingtons in less than a week. I didn't give a damn about "history," or communism and less about the Washingtons of the world.

I believed Richard was wrongheaded, but I was too stupid and too ignorant to find a sword big enough to pierce his armor. Neither did anyone else. Because, like me, they wanted to be part of the system; they wanted to be better than the next guy.

*****

It was the end of term and final exams were over.

Everyone was packing for the journey home. Richard was in no hurry, lying on his bed as usual with a book. I'd decided days ago that the angry silence had to be broken.

" - You coming back next semester?" I ventured.

He put his book down and sat up. "– Depends on my scholarship. I think my grandmother found a summer job for me. I'll see what I can save. What I'd really like to do is go to New York, look up my father so I can see what a real bastard looks like."

I knew Richard was dead broke. "How are you going to get home? You have the fare?"

He smiled, "Don't worry, I'll get there."

"But do you have the fare - yes or no?"

"- What if I don't?"

"I'll give it to you."

He studied my face. "Why? You don't have that much yourself."

I couldn't bring myself to tell him that he had been right about a lot of things. Even things that had made me angry, and that I had learned a lot from him; we all had. I felt I owed him.

"- What's it matter?" I said, laying some money on his desk. "If the object is to get home to earn some money, what's the point of getting locked up and spending the summer in jail for hitchhiking?"

Ours eyes met for the first time in a long time.

"…Thanks. - I didn't forget what you did…sticking up for me with all that stuff. I'm not about to forget it. - How about you? You coming back next fall?"

I shrugged. "I don't know. I think my father wants me to be a minister. I don't have to go to college to do that."

"What do you want to be anyway?"

I told him.

"...You want to dig up stuff from the past?"

"Something like that, but I'd have a better chance being elected president than being an archeologist or astronomer. I've no idea what I'll end up doing."

"That shut door may not always be there, Aaron. You can't just quit. I even heard about a colored guy flying an *airplane!* You can look at a glass of water..."

"Yeah, I know - half full, half empty. I've heard all that stuff - 'Don't whine,' 'If you can't go through them, then go around.' I'm sick of hearing it when the only way anybody colored can ever be a bank teller is to have your own bank, and the only way to be a captain is to have your own army. There's no way I can get to be what I want, and if that's all I want, what the hell's the use?"

"You think you're the only colored person interested in astronomy? Find people like yourself and start from there. I'll bet a *group* of you could get an observatory. Think about it. And if I were you, I'd keep my mouth shut about that preacher business. You've got three more years and a lot can happen. Keep your mouth shut and go for the telescope!"

We went to lunch together for the first time in a while. "- How about you? What're you going to do?"

"I want to be a professor. I'll go anywhere so long as I can teach... even down South for a few cents a day and a rope around my neck. Then, too, I was thinking I might try to get into a law school, but I hear that if you pass the bar exam, they'll say you didn't."

"You can't quit either; you keep saying times have changed."

"- Yeah, I guess you're right. The New Negro's definitely going to make a difference by the time we graduate. It's something to look forward to."

On the bus home, it occurred to me that the great irony about Richard was that for all his talk about communism and revolution, he had more faith in the future of America than I did.

NEW YORK

Chapter 33

At home I felt like a grown-up. I no longer waited to be told to help around the house. Getting down on my hands and knees, I reached under the ice box, extracted, and emptied the pan that caught the water from the melting ice. When a new cake of ice was needed, I put the sign in the window for the ice man. If anything was needed from the corner grocery store, I took the store book and shopping basket and fetched it. I was the one who brought the milk in from the doorstep, I carried the buckets of hot water from the kitchen stove to the laundry tubs in the shed kitchen so that Mom could scrub the clothes.

Since Dad's used car did not have an automatic starter, it needed to be cranked. Dad showed me the crank. One end had two prongs. "These fit inside the motor," he said. "Make sure the prongs are in the slots. Then," he said giving the crank a vigorous, circular turn - "you can start it," he said over the roar of the motor

It took a couple of days to get the hang of it. I cranked the car in the morning to get it started before he left to go to work. In the meantime, I trimmed the wicks of the kerosene lamps, cleaned the soot off the lamp globes, and set the lamps on the kitchen counter ready for use. After I lugged coal up from the cellar for the kitchen stove, like Little Jack Horner, I felt splendid about myself.

"We won't have to clean lamps much longer or worry about gas light," Momma said, one day over breakfast. "They've finally gotten around to running wires for electricity up this way. Should be finished before summer's out."

"Gee, electricity and a telephone, too. Guess we're moving up in the world," I teased.

"That telephone's more of a nuisance than a help," she complained, pouring cups of tea for the two of us. "You can't even call people who have a telephone unless they're with the same company you are. People on the Keystone system can't call people with a Bell phone. Then every time you try to use the phone, somebody else is already on the line."

"Somebody else? I thought it was your telephone."

"It is, but it's a party line. There're at least three of us sharing this line. You have to wait until the other party's finished using it before you can dial. When you pick up the receiver to make a call, the other party's supposed to have the courtesy to hang up if they've already been talking a while, or they should at least tell you how long they'll be. I've picked that phone up I don't know how many times and the same woman's still talking. I don't want to be rude, but sooner or later I'm going to have to just break in and ask for the line. After all, we're paying for service just like they are."

"Do you know who she is?"

She shook her head, sipping her tea. "Parties don't know each other"

"But how do you know when somebody's calling you and not calling the other person?"

"Our phone rings three times. The other party's phone rings once or twice. Even so, I know somebody else picks up the telephone when the call's for me and listens in on my conversations. You can tell, but you don't know who's doing it. We'd get a private line but we don't have that kind of money. Anyway, most people we know can't even afford a party line."

*****

I took the bus to New York a month later.

Ned was expecting me by late afternoon, but I arrived in the morning because I wanted to taste and feel the city on my own. As soon as I met Ned, there'd be a litany of do's and don'ts that I didn't want to hear anymore. I wanted to breathe on my own; I was becoming accustomed to feeling free – let there just be me.

I crept off the bus and tried to get my bearings. I didn't want to carry a suitcase around and be spotted for a newcomer. I stored my things in a locker, though truth be told, I was awed by the city. I'd never dreamed of seeing or being in a city so vast and vivid. The streets were wider, the buildings taller, the air crisper, the cars faster, the people more determined. It was a sea of swirling movement.

I knew how to get to Harlem, everybody at Prickly did. With trepidation, I descended the stairs to the subway. When the train rushed in and stopped, I pushed through the doors along with the other passengers. With a lurch, the train gathered speed, roared, shook and shivered, taking me to Harlem.

When my station appeared, I got out and was carried along and up the stairs by a crowd of fellow passengers. I emerged into the sunlight of Harlem, instantly aware that I was in a new world. Here the buildings were also tall, the streets wide, the shop windows gleaming. Everyone bustled along, but now they were accompanied by laughter and music from open windows.

I'd never seen so many colored people in one place before in my life. I was enthralled. It was nothing like the summer I'd helped Ned huckster vegetables in the Seventh Ward. There, entire streets were also filled with Negroes, but the side streets were narrow and crowded, lined with old, decrepit, two and three-story row houses which seemed to diminish the people who crept about in them.

There was none of the vastness that I saw now with soaring buildings and wide avenues rich with humanity. Nowhere had I ever seen street after street filled with nothing but colored people in all directions as far as the eye could see.

The faces I saw were the faces of everyone I'd ever known. I saw Mom and Elizabeth, Paige and Junie Mae; There was Dad's face and Ned's, I saw Fred, Wesley and Richard; Boo Boy sauntered by with his cap pulled to the side, knickers hanging down his calf..

Just as Wesley had written, women wore short dresses with their stockings rolled down to their knees. But it was not erotic to me as it had been for him. It was all a part of a new world where one should expect things to be different and wonderful and strange.

I found myself nodding to people who smiled and nodded back. Once a man grinned over his shoulder, "I see you new here!" he shouted, and I wanted to laugh because he made me feel that I belonged there. I walked aimlessly, feeling the people and the city and loving how I felt and what I felt, and remembering Wesley's letter *"...It's like we have our own world in Harlem."* I don't know how long I wandered around; I was in no hurry, but eventually I'd have to return to the bus station, retrieve my belongings and pretend I'd been waiting there for Ned.

*****

He came neatly dressed in a blue, pin-striped suit. His fedora was tilted rakishly to the side. Two men were with him; each carried a uniform folded over one arm. Ned started to shake my hand, but abandoned that and hugged me. He smelled of masculine bay rum the way my father always did.

"Welcome to New York," the younger man with him said, shaking my hand. He seemed about Ned's age. "I'm Jake. This here's Chester," he said indicating the shorter, stouter man.

"We're all with Garvey," Ned explained. "These are two of my men."

I viewed them with renewed interest. *His* men. I was led to a car. Jake, the tallest, got behind the wheel.

"I could tell you two was brothers right off," Chester grinned.

"They do favor each other," Jake agreed. Chester turned around in the passenger seat and wanted to know what I had learned at college. I was tempted to tell him nothing, but I knew Ned would be disappointed. I just smiled and spoke in generalities. Their talk drifted to other things and I became a boy in the mist of men.

"This is 138th Street," Ned announced. "We call it *The Street.*"

"Everybody know where this is," Chester rumbled. "This the heart of Harlem; this where Marcus live."

Jake parked the car in front of a four-story brownstone. A large green, black and red banner hung from the third-floor windows proclaiming, *Universal Negro Improvement Association.* We got out of the car. A line of people waited along the sidewalk outside the building.

" -Who're they?" I asked.

"Looking for jobs mostly," Ned explained. "Some come to buy bonds. Bonds are how we raise money to buy ships and land in Africa,".

Two uniformed men guarded the entrance to the building. As we neared the steps they snapped to attention and saluted. Ned returned their salutes. Once inside, his companions headed for the basement to change into their uniforms.

"They don't want us parading around the street in uniforms, Ned explained. "It'll just give white people another excuse to start trouble."

"Where's yours?"

"Home. I'll get it when I drop you off."

We climbed to the third floor and went along a corridor. The doors to a few rooms were open. I marveled to see men behind desks speaking on telephones or busy doing other things. I'd never seen a Negro behind a desk before. I even saw a secretary taking dictation on a note pad. They all looked important.

Finally, we stood in line outside of Marcus Garvey's office along with others who had come to pay homage or beg a favor. When it was our turn to enter, I saw a dark man sitting behind a large desk that was crowded with books, pamphlets and papers. The room was sparsely furnished. Two middle-aged secretaries sat on either side of the desk. Sunlight flowed through the window behind the man. Was this Marcus Garvey, the man whom Ned had described to me? He looked a bit dull, and he was stouter than I expected. A smile lit his face when he saw Ned; he stood and extended his hand.

Ned shook it and spoke respectfully. "Your Excellency, permit me to present my brother, Aaron Winston."

I quickly ducked my head in an awkward bow, staring at this dark, heavy-set man whose eyes were quick and alive.

Once at Prickly, Richard had thrust a NAACP *Crisis* magazine under my nose with a page turned down. "Read it," he said with a self-satisfied smirk. The article excoriated Garvey and his Back to Africa movement. He was described as a short, black, ugly man with intelligent eyes. Other than that, he had no redeeming qualities. Seeing the man in person, I didn't find him to be any darker or uglier than anybody else I'd ever seen. He was so unremarkable that he'd be lost in a crowd in Harlem.

Noticing my awkward bow, Garvey shook his head from side to side, and spoke in a quiet voice, " You must never bow, young man; I am only one of you. - So, you are Ned's brother. A college man I am told. All the better. Come, tell me," he continued in the same quiet manner, stepping from behind his desk. "What do you know of Marcus Garvey? You have heard of me?" His eyes were alive and fixed on me.

Remembering Richard's cynical accusations, I nodded, dumb for the moment as he stood before me. He was a little shorter, but not remarkably so.

He smiled. "Yes - Ned would see to that, but what else do you hear? - Come, you must be frank with me. We are all one here; Ned will teach you that."

Remembering Richard asking me the same question, promising not to be upset, and then breaking his promise, I hesitated. Mistaking my reluctance for shyness, Ned tried to speak for me.

Garvey raised a silencing hand. "He must speak for himself. He is intelligent. Go on - what things do your college friends say about Marcus Garvey?"

I'd heard things connecting him with scandals but couldn't think of a single one. I burned with embarrassment. Cornered, I blurted, "Some of the fellows say… you're just using people so you can live on easy street and nothing'll ever change –"

Ned was mortified. The two secretaries gasped aloud, eyes wide, hands to their mouth. Total silence for a careful count of three. Ned stared, bewildered. Then yelled -*"YOU SHOULD KNOW BETTER THAN TO SAY A THING LIKE THAT!* Who do you think you're talking to, some bum in the street! You're talking to a man like Booker T. Washington or Frederick Douglass! That's the kind of man His Excellency is. His Excellency is not a thief - he's for our people!"

Garvey's expression remained unchanged. In an even, clear voice - holding me with his eyes he assured me, "Your brother is telling you right."

I was sorry I'd come. I felt under attack as well as a rising resentment.

Though Garvey was shorter than Ned or me, his erect posture and supreme sense of self-assurance made him seem taller. Clasping his hands behind his back, he paced slowly about the room, keeping his eyes on us.

"You see, young man - and Ned knows this - all of my people understand that the best way for the white man to destroy a black man or a yellow man or a brown man is to get another man of his own kind to destroy him. It looks better that way and he can hold up his hands and say, 'See? They are clean!'

"The white man loves clean hands. And above all else - *God must always be on his side.* You must understand this, young man. He wants to believe that the evil he does was forced upon him."

Half sitting on the window sill, surrounded by light, with a slow shake of his head, he assured me, "You must not believe the lies you hear about me, young man. I depend on you and men like you to go out and tell the truth about me, about us – about our movement.

"But," he shook a finger from side to side, "you must understand practical things and the first is - do not waste time preaching hatred against the white man. I never do that. It is foolish beyond words. Do you hate the tiger? No. The tiger bites, so either you avoid him or you must understand him. If you understand him you can avoid being bitten.

"The white man engaged American Indians to track down and betray other Indians who were defending their own land and families. Slave owners used slaves as overseers to whip other slaves and keep order; the British trained Gurkhas and Sepoys to fight their battles for them, to kill and torture their own kind. The French used the Senegalese. No one knows that a million of those African men died in the Great War fighting for the French.

"And why is that, may I ask? *Because there is no one to write their history.* Is it not enormous that so many died for a thing from which they derived no benefit? The French are right to keep it quiet. It is never the other way around; we can never arm white men to fight for us against other white men.

"Though all of that is true," he stood up, "it still does no good to call the white man vile names and criticize him for his evil ways. He will only say *'Sticks and stones may break my bones but words will never harm me.'*

"When he says this, the people who have been subjugated become angry: 'Then stones it shall be!' they shout." Garvey stood up and paced a little, hands clasped behind his back, smiling sadly, shaking his head. "They soon discover that the white man always has a bigger stone than they have.

"No, we will not throw stones. We do not challenge the white man. We make no threats even though the newspapers claim we have guns and munitions hidden away, and men from the government repeatedly search our premises looking for something that does not exist except as a fantasy."

He went over to the window and stood for a moment, looking out, his back to us. He turned. "I have been to other countries; most men have not, so they see only their own condition. There are things in this world that are horrible beyond belief. The day may come when the white man will no longer offer logic or excuses for what he has done in Asia and Africa.

"But for the present, I tell you it does no good to shout, 'You took our people as slaves.' They will only reply with logic: 'We captured no slaves; we purchased them. We bought them from Africans who sold them to us instead of to the Arabs. We paid better. Go complain to the Africans who captured and sold us their people!"

He smiled ruefully. "In Africa one can also hear: 'You came and took our gold and stole our diamonds!' You can guess how the white man will respond to that: 'What did we take? We took nothing. We traded with you; is it our fault that you made a foolish bargain by trading a pound of gold for a pound of salt? You needed the salt and we wanted the gold.'

"See," he said with quiet urgency, "you must always know the white man's logic. Study him as I have. You are foolish to fight him with hatchets and stones. *You cannot win.*

"He will always have a sharper hatchet. Even when you use logic he will say it is illogical; if you appeal to your own God he will call you a heathen, yet when you appeal to *his* God," here he laughed as at a good joke, "you will soon discover that he does not really believe in Him, either!"

I liked him and what he said. The words sounded intelligent and rational and irrefutable. There was no emotion. Garvey simply made what he said ring true. Here was a man who saw through smoke and sound and fury to make sense of the ensuing chaos. I saw a man who raised a star that I could follow. He did not offer inchoate anger that beats itself against unyielding walls; his was no call to arms and bloodshed that Richard's call to communism subsumed. Garvey was no rag-tag preacher stealing from his congregation.

I also began to understand the nature of those mighty walls of NO that had barred my grandfather and my father, destroyed Steven, daunted Ned, Richard, my mother, me and everyone I knew or ever would know who called himself black or brown or colored or Negro.

He gave Ned a slight nod. The interview was over. It was over too soon; I wanted to hear what else he had to say and I wanted to hear new ideas hurled at me the way Richard used to hurl them. Garvey made me feel alive and special. Reluctant to leave, I had no choice.

Chapter 34

We trudged up four flights of dimly lit stairs to Ned's apartment.

Jake waited in the car. In one of the second-floor apartments, a Victrola was playing and the record was dragging. A woman bellowed, "...Hussy, if you too damn lazy to crank up that machine, keep yo damn hans off it! You know you gotta crank it up; it ain't gonna play by itself!"

I stiffened. I'd never heard a female curse before. Ned never missed a stride.

His "apartment" was a single room with a single window. A bed took up most of the space. A naked light bulb hung from the ceiling. I struggled to keep a straight face.

He busied himself changing out of his clothes and into his uniform. I sat on the lone wooden chair wondering why Ned said he had an apartment.

Maybe people did live ten to a room in Harlem and maybe this was an apartment compared to other accommodations. He seemed perfectly content as he buttoned his tunic.

"Jake's waiting for me. I have to leave you on your own for a while, but you'll be all right. There're some magazines under the bed and you can get a paper at the corner. If you get hungry, go down to the first floor and see Mrs. Price; she'll see you get something to eat. A lot of people go there, mostly Jamaicans. You'll get used to their accent. You'll be all right," he assured me.

Then he was gone, tall, lean and glorious like all young men who have ever strutted off to war in gleaming boots and colorful tunics - the peacocks of death.

I lay on the bed taking stock. My first day in New York had been eventful. The cautious ride on the subway to the glorious explosion of people, places and things in Harlem. Imagine meeting Marcus Garvey himself! He had spoken directly to me; told *me* the politics of the world as though it were important to him that I understood and approved.

I finally dozed off. The room was dark when I awoke. I splashed water on my face in the bathroom down the hall, and then headed down to Mrs. Price's apartment. On my way down, the Victrola was still playing, but I heard laughter now and male voices.

A man was lumbering up the stairs. He was drunk, stumbling and holding on to the bannister. He stopped and stared at me with suspicious and bleary eyes. I squeezed past him and on the first floor knocked on a door where I heard voices. There was sudden silence. Finally, a woman called hoarsely, "Who dat?"

I wasn't about to shout back. I heard Momma's - *"Never raise your voice in public; don't do anything to draw attention to yourself!"*

"I say who dat!" the voice demanded.

"...Ned's brother," I replied in a normal tone.

"Who?"

"Ned's brother."

There was whispering. Finally, a man growled: "...You betta carry yo' ass 'way from here, you know what's good for you!"

There was another apartment on the first floor in the back. A curious head peeped out. "-You Ned's brother?" a heavy-set woman demanded.

"Yes, ma'am."

She motioned me back, staring at me curiously. "I'm Mrs. Price. You must speak up when you go to people's doors," she scolded mildly in a West Indian dialect. "You could be a scoundrel. Who would know?"

There were other people in the smoke-filled apartment. They sat on two couches facing each other across the room. All eyes turned to examine who had knocked at the wrong door. I felt exposed. An electric phonograph was playing.

A tall, young girl was in the middle of the floor shaking her hips and singing along with the record. A man was sleeping at one end of a sofa, leaning his head against a woman who held a glass of gin and a cigarette in one hand. She shook the man with her other hand.

The dancing girl grinned at me. "Why you stare so, mon?" She was dark and had sloe eyes and long black eyelashes. "Come donce with me."

I was captivated by her soft West Indian dialect. She was about my age.

"Leave the boy alone, Melissa," Mrs. Price said. " He is Ned's brother come to see the convention. He is already confused by those foolish people next door. He is smart and attends college."

Melissa stopped dancing. The woman on the sofa with the gin jerked her head around to stare at me anew. "He is from a college?" she asked, frowning to focus her eyes.

" - Who is from college?" a man's voice rumbled from the bedroom that led into the kitchen.

"Come and see for yourself," Mrs. Price answered, ushering me to a sofa opposite the one with the lady with the gin.

"'Pon my word," an elfin-like figure said. He wore a faded plaid bathrobe and appeared to be about fifty. He approached me, peering curiously down at my face. His eyes were puffy and he had a gold tooth in the front of his mouth.

"This is incredible," he declared. "To see with mine own eyes a block mon who goes to college. Whot your name, young mon? You are not from the islands," he stated with certainty.

I told him my name and they still stared. I told Mrs. Price that Ned had told me she would see to my dinner.

"Do you like island food?" she asked.

"He know nothing about island food," the elfin man declared with assurance. "Give him pig's feet and greens."

"Give 'im somethin' to drink," the woman from the sofa urged. "The cat got 'is tongue."

"Go fix him a platter, Melissa," Mrs. Price said, as someone knocked on the door.

Two women with long, shapely legs encased in black stockings entered. One of them was plump and had a gold tooth in the front of her mouth which spoiled her appearance. People who had gold teeth swore it improved their looks. The other woman was taller and wore a red dress that fit her tightly across the hips. Her eyes lingered on me before she turned to Mrs. Price.

"Whatcha got to drink, Christine?" she asked in a West Indian accent.

"Just got gin, Alice. The man ain't come yet, but he will bring whiskey if you can wait."

"I dunno, that last stuff you sold us -.”

"Everybody get sick from that mess," the elfin man broke in. "We no deal with him no more."

"This stuff's all right," the woman on the sofa assured her. "I been drinkin' since ten this mornin' an' it ain't bothered me none - or him," she said, indicating the sleeping man beside her.

Melissa came back into the room and beckoned to me. "Come in the kitchen."

I followed her. The woman in red stared at me as I passed her. In the kitchen an old woman in an apron, with a red kerchief around her head, sat dozing by the kitchen stove. A large table held pans of crisp, golden brown fried chicken, pots of collard greens, bowls of potato salad, sweet potato pies and other covered dishes sitting in the oven and on the kitchen table. She looked up for a moment with bleary eyes then nodded off again.

Melissa cleared a little space for me at the table, and then set a plate of pig's feet and collard greens before me. I was not too fond of pig's feet. Mrs. Portlock had introduced them to my mother and we had them occasionally, but none of us ever acquired a taste for them. Melissa noticed the look on my face though I tried to hide it.

"You must tell me what bothers you," she said. "My gran's food is the best in Harlem," she said, indicating the dozing woman. “People come from all over to buy dinner here. You are new here, but soon you will hear, 'Mamma Alexis, Mamma Alexis.' Everywhere you go people know my gran."

"...Does the chicken...?"

"Oh, you want chicken? Why didn't you say so? Why are you so afraid to speak?" she admonished gently. “You must not whisper you must speak. It is all for sale."

She reminded me of Junie Mae whom I had not thought of for several years. She had the same heart-shaped, open face but Melissa was no child. There was little about her that was demure. She was a young woman who seemed very competent and assertive. As I ate she peppered me with questions, eyes ablaze with curiosity.

What was my name and what did I learn at college; was it hard; were there other colored fellows there; were there any girls at college; how old was I; where did I live; did I visit a special girl?

From time to time someone would come into the kitchen and ask Mamma Alexis for a platter. She had been awake for some time, and was on her feet filling platters which she served with heaping side portions of collard greens, potato salad and golden, brown biscuits. Sometimes a customer would say, "I don't want that, give me something from the islands."

Melissa would get up, whenever needed, to help her grandmother, but she always came back with questions, staring in my eyes, and perhaps, without meaning to, creating an aura of intimacy.

I found myself watching her clean, white teeth and noticing how her firm, expressive lips formed words. When she noticed me watching her lips, she flushed.

The bootleg liquor was dispensed in the living room by the elfin man, now fully dressed. He was cracking jokes and leading the laughter with a loud, strange chuckle. I heard a steady stream of arrivals who transformed the rooms into a place of friendly laughter, gibes, music and dancing.

Often, Melissa had to leave me sitting in the kitchen, and I reluctantly decided there was no point in staying. She was the only one my age, and the more crowded the apartment became the more isolated I felt. Even the bedroom was crowded with people sitting on the sides of the two beds. Some were holding drinks, others platters. As I squeezed through the bedroom on my way to the living room, a firm hand grabbed my wrist. Surprised, I almost jerked my hand away. It was the lady in red; she pulled me down beside her.

"Let him go, Alice," admonished her friend with the gold tooth. She spoke just above a whisper. "He is only a boy; you will be doing rudeness!"

"He is a college boy," Alice grinned. "He is older."

"How you talking?" Gold Tooth replied, with worried eyes. "Buster Matthew is older, too...an' jealous. How old you be, College Boy?"

"Phew! Buster Matthew," Alice scoffed. "Let he go to the devil. Tell her nothing, College Boy. Do you like gin? Here, drink some of mine."

"...Alice!" her friend hissed, her gold tooth gleaming in her worried face, "You must be mad. That is only a boy you messin' with. He can do nothing for you. You are doing rudeness!"

Ignoring her, Alice asked: "So you are Ned's brother?" Her smile was wide, accentuated by her bright, red lipstick.

I told her yes and she asked how long I was staying and whether or not I had a girlfriend and when I said no, she seemed surprised.

"He has no time for foolishness," Alice's friend explained. "He must study. There is plenty of time for foolishness. Ned is the one you want, not this boy."

Alice casually slid her hand over my crotch. Her hand shocked and excited me. Smiling gently, she offered me her glass. I had tried drinking once but had not liked the taste or the smell or the burning sensation. I liked Alice, though.

I was urgently attracted to her long, shapely legs. She was older than I was, but I hardly thought about that. I took the glass and sipped quickly, trying to keep a straight face even as the gin burned my throat.

"It is no foolishness," Alice said, pulling me to my feet and in the tiny space between the bed and the wall, she told me to dance with her. It was awkward at first because she was unsteady on her feet. I didn't know how to dance but gradually we managed to keep time with the music, pressed close together, dancing cheek to cheek. The flesh of her face against mine was intoxicating. It was a new experience for me; I was very much aware that she was a grown woman, bigger than anyone I had ever known.

I had hoped it would not happen but I felt my penis swelling. Once aware of it, Alice pressed closer, rubbing herself against my swollen organ. By the second dance I was holding her close, aware of her full woman's body, feeling masterful, casting about for ways to get her alone.

"Where do you live?" I ventured softly.

"Why you want to know that?" she asked coyly. "I live too far from here. Can you stay out late at night? Will anyone be cross with you if you do?"

"I can go with you," I breathed.

"You may be too young," she teased.

Just then I felt a firm hand on my shoulder. It was Ned. "I have to talk to you," he said quietly.

Alice asked him with mock indignation, "You can't speak to nobody?"

Ned stared at her coldly for a moment. Without replying he led me through the thronged living room. I was breathing hard and beginning to feel resentment at him for interrupting what I felt was my first opportunity to have sex with somebody.

I followed him, my organ swollen to the point of bursting. Without a word, he guided me out of the apartment and out onto the sidewalk. He confronted me, his eyes locked onto mine.

"You're not going to last long in Harlem at the rate you're going," he began grimly.

"First of all, I don't want to catch you drinking again; your breath stinks awful. People die each and every day from drinking that bootleg shit; just read the papers. These people don't care what they sell as long as they get the money.

"Second of all, that woman's a whore! She expects to get paid for you-know-what, and on top of that she's got a crazy boyfriend who goes around cutting people in the face for just looking at her. Last of all you got no business even *thinking* of doing anything like that until you're married. Next thing you know, you're going to have to marry somebody and be stuck with her for the rest of your life!

"Stay with people your own age, you hear me? You're nineteen and acting like you think you're twenty-one. You're not grown. Mom expects me to look after you, but I can't be here all the time so the least you can do is use some common sense. If you can't do that, go back home! And you'd better ask yourself how I knew to come get you when I did."

He paused, standing like a wall in front of me, waiting for me to say something. For the first time I was aware that the gin had gone to my head. I had to make an effort to speak clearly.

"- How'd you know?"

"Somebody came and told me, that's how. They said I'd better come quick before you got your throat cut, that's how. People know all about Alice. She may look good but she's a whore, and you can get disease from a whore. Serious disease."

I was trying to focus. "- What disease?"

He glared, trying to gauge the extent of my innocence. "Blue balls.... Your balls swell up like this." He made a fist in front of my face. "Then they turn black and blue and when you pee it feels like you're peeing red-hot fire. It gets so bad you want to scream out loud. And it won't go away, either. You spend half your time in the bathroom crying with pain."

He made me walk around the block with him several times. Somewhat sobered and feeling chastened, I followed him to the apartment and I fell asleep trying to imagine what blue balls really looked like.

He slipped out of bed the next day and left money for my breakfast on top of the clothes I'd taken off the night before.

Chapter 35

There was soft knocking on the door. Ned must have forgotten something. But why was he knocking when he had a key? Curious, I got out of bed and opened the door. It was Alice.

"Can I come in?" she smiled, brushing past me.

Nonplused, I stood there feeling stupid and exposed. I only had on my drawers. There was no place to go. I tried to reach for my shirt but she put a restraining hand on my wrist and pushed the door shut.

"Whot Ned tell you 'bout me?" she demanded in quiet Jamaican, holding me with her eyes. "He say I a bad woman, that I do rudeness? - Tell me the truth, did he?"

She dominated me standing close like that, my wrist in her strong grip, her eyes boring into mine. She was grown. I felt like a little boy. I refused to answer, not wanting to look at her and not wanting to look away, as though I were afraid of her.

"Let me instruct you; I am not a bad woman, Aaron - *look at me* - I am not a bad woman. I do not sell myself to men - *look at me, I say!* - Do you listening to me? Just because I live with a man does not make me a bad woman; many women live with men. It was the way I was raised. You are a clean, young boy and I naw leggo of you, you hear? You are irresistible to me; does that make me 'bad' because you are a clean, young boy? Does it?"

I turned to look at her. She seemed sincere. She was in a blue dress today. It, too, fit her tightly across the hips and revealed her long, shapely legs.

I wanted her. I knew what Ned had told me and I believed him, but blue balls or not, I let her guide me over to the bed "so we may talk".

We sat there and I held her hand as she earnestly explained why she was not a bad woman. She was "free" but that did not make her bad. I must let my feelings, not other people, tell me what to do even though I might love them.

At that moment she seemed vulnerable. I believed it was important to her what I thought of her. Impulsively I reached over and hugged her. We sat in silence for a little while, then impulsively I kissed her on her cheek and she smiled. She let me push her back on the bed and without the least resistance she let me kiss her on the mouth and undress her and she opened her legs and she let me have her.

I exploded in her almost immediately and she laughed, hugging me close to her, pressing me with her thighs. "You are virgin I can tell," she murmured joyfully. "All my life I have wanted a fresh, clean, virgin man, someone brand new just like you. A *virgin man!*"

She allowed me have her again and again and each time I was astounded and immensely proud at the sounds she made; I felt as though she were an orchestra, my organ a baton and I the conductor; I conducted and she made the most wonderful music.

I explored her body, her great breasts and navel, the abundant soft hair of her crotch, her firm pumping thighs, her strong, heaving torso that tossed me about. Again, the warm, wet inside of her gripped me.

I had her for all of the years I had yearned and masturbated and fantasized and dreamed of making love. I had her for all of the little cartoon books that we boys furtively passed around portraying women with plump thighs spread wide revealing wonderful masses of pubic hair, and men with huge penises splashing into them. I had her for all the taunts I had suffered from Fred and most of all, I had her so that now I could feel I was a man and I could boast and talk and laugh with the best of them in Kinsey Hall and all the barbershops I would ever know.

And I had her for Paige and for Elizabeth and maybe even Junie Mae.

I lay in her arms and she held me against her as a mother would a child and I snuggled against her full, warm breasts. We went to sleep and we awoke and made love again and when we finally arose, I was in love with her.

"When can I see you again?" I asked, breathlessly.

"I will let you know. There are certain people in this world who are a tribulation and easily excited. The man I know is such a one."

We got up and started dressing. "He is angry when I go astray and I must avoid him for a while. He knows I come to this house. He is sure to come here looking for me. I will let you know when we will be together again. Is that agreeable?"

"- He could be here now," I warned, feeling protective. "What's he look like?"

She shook her head, applying lipstick. "I will worry about Buster Matthew, and we will be together many times again. He is shorter than me, with thick shoulders and a hat that is too big on his head."

Then she left, her heels clicking down the three flights of stairs.

*****

Ned was quietly outraged.

We'd had a quiet supper at a nondescript restaurant. He'd seemed preoccupied during the meal. He hurried through his food as though it were something to have done with rather than enjoyed. I couldn't read the expression on his face. On the walk back to his apartment he took pains not to look at me.

"You have to leave," he said quietly, closing the door behind us once we got back to his apartment.

He'd found out about Alice. Though he did not raise his voice, I could tell by his eyes and tight lips that he was furious.

"You can't stay here! You're nothing but trouble. Everybody knows you were with that whore and after all I told you. Now her crazy boyfriend's looking to cut your throat!"

"Looking for me! Says who?"

"None of your business, 'who!'" he shouted. "Let me tell you something, little man - these are West Indians you're fooling around with. You've got no idea what the hell you're doing! They don't take stuff when it comes to their women and the women are just as bad when it comes to their men!

"You're not in Philly now. You find people dead in alleys with their throat cut each and every day and the cops don't give a damn. There're a lot of things you don't know and you won't learn them in college and at the rate you're going you'll never live to find out!

"You're almost grown but almost's not enough. I can't waste time chasing behind you to wipe your backside. Momma didn't send you here to get yourself killed."

"...I don't want to go home, yet. You said you'd get me into the convention. That's the reason I came. I want to see Marcus Garvey."

We went back and forth. I said I wasn't going back home and he said yes I was. I said I was old enough to decide for myself and he said maybe so, but I wasn't staying with him since Buster would come there looking for me. What Ned didn't realize was the world of possibilities that Alice had opened for me. Or maybe he did because he relented a little.

"You can't stay here by yourself with nothing to do, Aaron. The UNIA convention's going to last a week and I have to be there. I can't be there and here, too. How about that boy you know from college? Call him and see if you can stay with him for a few days. If you can't, I'm putting you on the bus and that's all there is to it."

I did not know anyone except my parents who had a telephone and I had never used one. He led me to a phone booth, put money in the mysterious machine and instructed me how to dial the number and what to say.

*****

I came out of the subway in Brooklyn with a change of clothing in a shopping bag. Wesley was there to meet me. We gave each other the once over. He seemed manlier and more confident than when I had seen him at the graduation celebration. We walked in awkward silence for half a block. Something was wrong. I turned to question him, but he'd already decided to speak.

"I don't know how to tell you this, man, but you can't stay at my aunt's house. There was no way I could tell you so you'd know not to come."

I didn't know what to say. We walked a little way further in silence. "- What happened? I thought your aunt was anxious to meet me."

We drew stares from white people who passed. " -We had an argument about something. - I'm not even sure *I* can stay there any-more."

Ned had kicked me out; where could I go? I didn't want to leave New York. Not after Alice. And what about Elizabeth? Dispirited, we trudged back to the subway. Wesley suggested we go to Harlem and at least have a little fun. I didn't know what else to do.

"- Sure," I shrugged. "What the hell."

*****

We stopped by the bus station. I put my packages into the same locker I'd used when I first arrived. We sat on a bench at the station. Neither of us had much to say. I told him that Ned had put me out, but I wasn't going back home. He looked away.

" - What's your aunt like?" I asked. "I mean is she like your mother in some ways?"

"People say they're like two peas in a pod."

If his aunt were anything like his mother, she wouldn't be too pleased to see me. I could hear his aunt telling him not to bring anybody darker than a brown paper bag into her house. But wouldn't Wesley have known this, and not invited me?

"Did you ever invite anybody else to your aunt's house?"

He sighed." - You want to know the truth? Everything was all right until my mother and Aunt Lillian started talking on the telephone. Mom mentioned you. I don't know what Aunt Lillian told her, but Mom said she didn't want anybody on her block seeing a black person staying at her house.

"I never knew she felt that way. Maybe she wasn't all that crazy about *me* staying with her, either, but I'm *almost* light-skinned, and I go to college."

I could see he was dejected. I told him not to worry about it. He had no control over anything. He had invited me in good faith and that was good enough.

"Come on," he said, standing up. "We might as well have a good time. I know some good night clubs. Treats on me."

Chapter 36

Wesley said everybody went to the Carnival Club. They had the prettiest colored chorus girls in Harlem and maybe the prettiest colored girls in the world. They were all light-skinned. After the last show (there were three a night), men lined up outside the club waiting to meet them. We were not going there for that, he assured me; we didn't begin to have the kind of money it took to fool around with chorus girls.

The Carnival Club didn't look that spectacular after all of the exaggerated tales I'd heard in Kinsey Hall. I was surprised to see that over half the patrons were white. Three sides of the room had a raised floor enclosed by a railing. There was a stage on the main floor where most of the white patrons were seated. A band sat to one side of the stage. We were seated on the raised portion of the room.

Wesley smirked and said the white patrons were 'slumming.' "They come here to mix with the 'natives,' only there's so many of them, they squeeze the 'natives' out."

A Negro waiter approached. He wore glasses and looked dubious. "You know," he advised, as though we would be discouraged to hear it, "we got a cover charge here. That'll be a dollar apiece."

"We're aware of that," Wesley said in a my-dear-man tone. He gave the waiter a five-dollar bill and ordered gin for the both of us.

"I know you don't drink, but we can't just sit here taking up space."

The drummer played a riff. The stage was bathed with a spotlight. The master of ceremonies stepped onto the stage. He was a tall, smiling, light-skinned man with slick, straight hair, a trim mustache and a very loud voice.

After bellowing out several bad jokes that were greeted by feeble

263

clapping and weak chuckles, he announced: "… and NOW, ladies and gentlemen, …. those lovely ladies of lusciousness - the *CARNIVALS!*"

The band struck up a tune and six chorus girls pranced on stage.

My eyes popped. My mouth flew open. *My God! - There was Elizabeth!* She was on the stage. There could be no mistake. That was her silken, black hair and golden skin, and those were her brown eyes and her beautiful, intelligent face and the smile that hovered around her mouth. Jesus Christ Almighty, *Elizabeth!*

I said urgently to the colored waiter when he brought our drinks, "You see that girl dancing on the end? I pointed. Tell her Aaron's here!" I pressed a half dollar into his hand. "I'm from her hometown. She knows who I am!"

He tilted his head back in order to stare down his nose. He snorted derisively, flinging the coin on the table. "I ain't doing shit!" Turning on his heel, he stalked off.

Wesley didn't know that I knew Elizabeth and that I loved her. He grinned in admiration.

"- You should have offered him a dollar," he laughed.

Filled with chagrin, I watched Elizabeth dancing with other girls who also had long, lovely legs, golden skin, black silken hair and pretty smiles. But my eyes saw only her gentle slender figure, her constant, friendly smile and her firm breasts.

Before the dance number was over, I received another shock.

The little girl I had played jacks with; about whom I had cried when she moved away; the girl I had met on the trolley and had finally kissed - was blocked from my view by a tall, portly Negro in a tuxedo. He had scar tissue over his left eye and a cigar in his mouth. He stared down at me.

"I have to ask you gentlemen to leave," he said. He was courteous but there was a hint of menace in his voice. Two other waiters hovered near him, staring at us with poker faces.

We were perplexed. " - Why?" Wesley asked. "We're not bothering anybody."

Bending down so that only we could hear, he growled: "You know who Moose Schlitz is?"

"- The gangster?" Wesley asked.

"You can call him what you want," the big man replied. "Just so happen he own this place, and he own that girl your friend so bug-eyed about. I guarantee you one thing, mister; all you gonna get outta messing with his meat is your balls cut off. And I mean *real* balls. You want that? Now I advise you to carry your butt on outta here and don't give me no trouble."

I stared, dumbfounded. "- What...?"

Without another word, the big man seized my arm in a powerful grip and lifted me bodily out of my seat. "Here's your money," he growled stuffing something in my coat pocket. "Drinks on the house. I'm really doing you a favor," he assured me, propelling me down the short flight of steps, past a few startled customers, to the front entrance.

Outside I turned to Wesley, open mouthed. " - What the hell happened!" I sputtered. "What's he saying about Elizabeth? Can he put us out just like that?"

Wesley spread his arms. "-You mean you never heard of *Moose Schlitz?*"

"Hell no, why should I?"

"- And I guess you never heard of Al Capone, either, or Dutch Schultz?"

"Yeah, a bunch of bootleggers."

"Well, this guy and them all do the same thing. They kill people or break their legs or beat the hell out of them. And they get away with it, too. That's with *white* people. People like us don't even make the newspapers. C'mon. I know someplace else we can go."

I balked, furious about the waiter's attitude; the manager's smugness, about being thrown out of a Negro club, in Harlem - in front of a roomful of white people - by Negro employees for no reason at all.

What he said about Elizabeth was even more infuriating.

"They don't own the Goddamned street! I'm staying here. I'm going to see her when she comes out and find out what the hell's going on!"

"You're crazy!" he said. He grabbed my arm and tried to propel me down the street. "You want to get yourself killed over nothing, do it on your own time. I brought you here and I'm taking you away. What you do after that's on you!"

We struggled for a moment or two. He grabbed my coat lapels and pushed me against the wall. I stopped struggling, and still angry, gave him a sketchy account of who Elizabeth was. When he realized how serious I was, he stared at me for a long moment, then let go of me.

" – Damn, it's not like she's your girlfriend, Aaron. When was the last time you saw her? You're talking about puppy love. She's a woman, now; a chorus girl. Men make passes at them all the time, and a lot of girls have somebody keeping them.

"You don't want to get mixed up where a man's spending money on a woman, Aaron. These guys are buying mink coats, taking them to Europe, renting apartments - c'mon, for God sake, use your head!"

"I just want to say hello. I have a right to say hello. She can tell me to go to hell, but nobody's telling me I can't say hello. - You go ahead. I'll catch up with you later."

He refused to leave. He said I had stuck by him the time the gang got after us, and he wasn't leaving. We hung around for the better part of an hour. I gave him a longer account of my relationship with Elizabeth.

In telling it, I was surprised at how little there really was to tell.

What had happened, really, to establish a relationship? A boy playing at jacks, a stolen kiss, a few secret meetings on a trolley car and nothing else. No love letters, no exchanges of I-love-you's, no pledges or promises, we'd only held hands once, and we shared a jack.

All brief glimpses of sunshine on a cloudy day.

Over time Elizabeth had grown, in my mind, into a promise that one day would be fulfilled. I believed it was inevitable. We would and we must meet again, and gaze at each other in wonder. Then together, we would reach up and gently touch the sky.

I cast about for other forgotten memories - a tender touch here, a hug there, a song that was "ours" - but there were none. Only blank spaces where words should be. Did she even have the jack that we shared?

"Here they come!" Wesley whispered.

Two girls were clicking out of a side door, laughing and talking. At the curb a uniformed chauffeur held a car door open and they clambered into a huge, black sedan. The other girls trickled out, one got into a car, another walked away and upon seeing us, turned her nose up, and hurried past. Suddenly, I saw Elizabeth. I pressed forward.

"Elizabeth!" I cried, fascinated by her nearness. Yes. Those were her soft glowing eyes and the lips that once told me that boys don't play jacks.

She stopped short on hearing her name, lips slightly parted, curious. She searched my face, puzzled for a moment, and then recognition lit her eyes. She began to smile and took several steps in my direction. She stopped abruptly. Stepping quickly away – she turned and strode quickly to a waiting sedan.

We watched the car vanish into the night. I stared into the darkness for several moments transfixed, remembering her face brighten and the step she took toward me. The scent of her perfume lingered faintly.

Wesley receded into the background to cushion my humiliation. I started walking. My eyes burned under the lids. I did not feel sadness. I felt anger, an overriding anger that grew and grew, driving me swiftly over the pavement the way it had driven me the day Elizabeth's mother had shut her door against me,

I remembered Ned striding over the sidewalks of Philadelphia the day the cop had pulled him off his wagon. I had struggled to keep up with him, but I did. I had understood and shared his hurt and anger. Now Wesley struggled to keep up with me. "Go home!" I flung at him. He ignored me, dogging me every step of the way.

The things I had heard Mr. Amos and my father and my grandfather say had extended my life. Their memories became my memories; they made me an extension of themselves. I was a freeman, and I was a slave, and I had seen slave dogs rip brave men, and women lashed into submission.

I was old, very old. And very angry.

Elizabeth was Moose Schlitz's slave girl. His "fancy girl." He would have "dogs" sicked on me if I so much as spoke her name. She who had been a precious, pure memory; a glimmering promise, an ethereal part of me - was but a whore to him. And I must be punished for speaking to his whore who had been, in some ways, the reason for my being. I flung these bitter words at Wesley one after another, and I cried at times and cursed at others, and he listened to it all, urging me to keep my voice down, to please stop cursing like that, to walk slower so he could keep up.

My anger would have been a lot different had I not slept with Alice.

Having bitten the apple, I now knew the incoherent cries a man can invoke from a woman and she from him.

How could Elizabeth accept being a whore to Moose Schlitz, I stormed at Wesley.

Why was she showing her ass off on a dingy stage in a Harlem bar, and squirming in the filth of a gangster when she was so much more?

"- Man, for God sake, calm down – *Please!* Just listen, Aaron, *listen!* There's not much a colored girl can do, Aaron. We're both lucky as hell we're going to college or where do you think we'd be? Shoveling shit in some stable or shining shoes or.... Even after college it won't be easy! Guys end up as Pullman porters or working in the post office. What chance does she have?"

"Why does she have to show her ass on a stage!" I demanded, ignoring him. "That's cheap enough without letting some white man do it to her!"

"For *money,* Goddammit*! Money.* She can make more money in *one night* doing what she's doing than she could make in six months scrubbing somebody's Goddamn floors on her hands and knees or working all day in a laundry! Come on, add it up. She can make her money, save what she can, then do what she wants. It's as simple as that.

"You think this is the only club in Harlem or anywhere else with colored dancing girls? Clubs everywhere have them. Nice legs and light-skinned. You think she's the only one? They're a dime a dozen, Aaron! Didn't you see the rest of them? They all look like that, and there're plenty more lined up begging for a chance to do what they're doing."

"IT'S JUST A GODDAMN, FUCKING SLAVE AUCTION!" I yelled back. Use your brains. How come you hardly see any colored in there? We were about the only ones as far as I could see because they charge a dollar just to get in. And all of this is taking place in the heart of Harlem! You call this progress? That waiter practically spit in my face. It's just a plantation full of darkies and fancy girls! If we had any pride, we'd blow the goddamn place up and everybody in it!"

Nothing would mollify my murderous rage.

I walked blindly up one street and down the next, vowing to get one of Ned's ice picks and stab the bastard in the brain. Somehow, I ended up in front of Ned's apartment and Wesley was finally trudging away.

I slumped on the doorstep exhausted. I had no place to go and didn't give a damn. Every sight, every sound echoed and re-echoed in my mind, growing blacker and blacker as I relived the evening over and over. I swore I would get an ice pick and kill that bastard slave master. I could feel it strike the bone of his skull and drive through.

And then I gave up the ice pick.

Unspoken, almost suppressed, was the cold realization that Elizabeth was doing just what it pleased Elizabeth to do. And she was doing it of her own free will. She was no more a slave girl than Alice was. Elizabeth was "committed" and her mother was proud. The bitch! So yes, I had to admit, my dreams had been a one-sided fantasy from the moment I had tied Elizabeth's sash that long ago summer day. Had Elizabeth come up to Grizzly State to visit Pace last fall, I would simply have known a little sooner that in her world, I counted for nothing.

Chapter 37

Ned nudged me awake. Disoriented, I wondered where I was and why he was standing over me.

"Get dressed," he ordered. "Don't make a racket; people are still sleeping."

He was still disgusted with me from last night. "I got to drag you round with me every place I go just to keep you from getting your stupid throat cut!" he had stormed the night before.

He, Chester and Jake found me asleep on the front doorsteps where Wesley had left me. Ned had shaken me awake. Chester and Jake peered down, curious.

"Whatcha doin' here?" Ned whispered fiercely. "Why're you so damn hard-headed, Aaron? Why'd you come back here after what I told you?"

I told him Wesley's aunt wouldn't let me stay there, but that didn't seem to matter to him. If there had been time, he told me later, "I'd have put your backside on the first damn bus to Philly!"

I think he would have found the time, too, had not Chester rumbled proudly, "Whatcha worried about, man? Ain't nobody gonna mess with 'im. They know you his kin an' they know you in the Legion. Hell, man, don't *nobody* mess with the Legion!"

"Not if they know what's good for 'em," Jake added ominously.

To validate that premise, even if it were wrong, Ned grumbled and led me back into the apartment. Now in the early morning I stumbled to the bathroom, splashed water on my face and struggled into some of his work clothes.

I wondered whether I should just say to hell with it and go home. With my fantasies about Elizabeth exposed for what they were, what was the use? Somehow, irrational or not, it seemed that if I did go home, I'd be leaving with my tail between my legs. Ned and I left the house and walked to the trolley stop. There was a wall of silence between us along the way and during the fifteen-minute trolley ride.

We left the trolley car and walked three blocks to a long, ramshackle building that took up most of the block. Horses were kept in one part of the building and wagons in another. Ned said the Universal Negro Improvement Association owned and stowed their wagons there, but rented the horses. Men were leading horses out of the building to hitch them to rented wagons that they had parked along the curb. Some of the men grunted greetings to Ned.

The manager was seated at a worn looking table by the door. He accepted payment for a horse and a wagon. I helped Ned pull the wagon out to the street and we parked it by the curb. Ned walked further down the block to get a horse. I helped him hitch it to the ice wagon. We left for the UNIA icehouse several blocks away.

The streets surrounding the icehouse were clogged with wagons. It reminded me a little of the hustle of Dock Street when Ned was huckstering. Wagons backed up to the platform of the ice house. Colored men dragged three-hundred-pound cakes of ice from the cold interior. They slid the rectangular cakes into the waiting wagons and with a quick upward lift with the ice tongs, while the ice was still moving, stood the cakes on end. Other cakes were wedged in and when the wagon was loaded, the owner secured the back, and left to make his rounds. Once our wagon was loaded, we were on our way.

"Gee, they must be awful strong to lift that ice like that," I marveled.

He ignored me. After we had gone half a block he replied gruffly, "Anybody can do it. You have to let the ice slide, get it going, then grab it real quick at the bottom and lift. You have to let it slide."

Nothing more was said until we reached his route. "Here," he instructed, handing me a thick newspaper. "Put this under your shirt on your shoulder."

I stuffed the paper under my shirt. He handed me a worn, leather contraption which turned out to be a pad. I tied it over the same shoulder. I was to carry the ice on my shoulder, holding it in place with ice tongs. The pad and paper would keep the cold from penetrating to my skin.

"Paper's good for keeping out the cold. Guys get careless about that and next thing you know they got rheumatism so bad they can hardly lift their arm."

Customers left signs in their window if they wanted ice. Ned cut the blocks of ice into smaller pieces with his ice pick. He made a straight line of small stabs that split the ice cleanly. The splits were divided into smaller pieces. I carried the five cent pieces up the stairs to various apartments on my shoulder, holding them in place with my hands, too afraid to trust the ice tongs. He carried the heavier pieces.

He gave me heavier, fifteen cent pieces. They were too heavy to use my frozen hands to steady the ice. In desperation, I relied on the tongs and discovered with relief that they held the ice perfectly well. I knocked on one door and heard, "Who is it?"

"Ice."

The door opened a crack and a pair of woman's suspicious eyes examined me. "- Where's Ned?"

"Outside, I'm just helping."

The lady did not believe me. "- He didn't quit, did he?"

"No ma'am," I said.

She was young and attractive. My eyes were drawn to her slightly parted lips. She sensed my interest and returned a blank stare. Abruptly she held out eight cents. I took it and put the ice in the refrigerator for her. I left wondering whether or not Ned was more than her iceman.

Other women came to the door in bathrobes or hastily thrown on dresses that invited disrobing. I thought of Alice and how she had let me undress her. I yearned for anyone who would let me feel her breasts and enter the moist place of her body. I needed a lot of Alices to extinguish the remnants of Elizabeth, and to prove that I did not need her and that I had value.

When the ice was gone, we headed back to the stable, leaving scraps and shards on the wagon to melt.

*****

"Does Mr. Garvey own the ice house?" I asked.

He took a while to answer. "– "It's not something we advertise. We sell ice to anybody who wants it." He let it go at that and we went along in silence for several more blocks.

"- I used to know a fella," Ned began quietly as we clip-clopped along, "who knew this girl who was kind of "fast," but she liked him a lot. She was about nineteen, twenty. Problem was she was married. Claimed she was separated and wasn't going back to him.

"Fella figured she was lying, but it didn't make any difference to him. Just wanted to do it to her. He'd go see her a couple times a week, bold as could be. One night she was letting him out of the front door when some big guy jumped up in the doorway and hollered – 'GOTCHA!'

"Fella almost died. All he could see was people with their faces slashed open or their guts bubbling out of their shirt and blood on the ground turning purple. Didn't even have time to run. But the man rushed right on by him, grabbed her, slung her up over his shoulder like she was a child and started back up the steps with her.

"She screamed to the guy to help her, and grabbed his sleeve."

Ned stopped speaking for a moment. It seemed as though he had forgotten what he was saying. After taking a deep breath, he continued, "...She was scared to death, hanging on his sleeve, but he pried her fingers loose and almost ran. Just wanted to get away as fast as he could. He was scared. Like a coward."

For a minute or two there was the clip-clop, clip-clop of the horse.

"...Fella learned one thing, though. You don't have the guts to protect a girl all the way, you better keep your private in your pants because once you feel like a stinking coward, you always feel that way...."

Clip-clop, clip-clop. Somewhere between 'coward' and the stable, it dawned on me that Ned was the "fella." I think he was warning me about Alice and Matthew. It felt good having him talk to me like this, revealing sights and sounds that were personal to him and that hurt. I didn't think he could ever be a coward. Because he had shared a little of his soul, I probably would never see Alice again.

*****

When we got back to the apartment, I sat in the tub and let the warm water soak the dirt and weariness from my body. It was a good weariness. I went over everything Ned had said to me. We were brothers again like the time with the cop. When he was dressed, smelling of bay rum, he took his hat from the table, placed it at a jaunty angle and said,

"Let's get something to eat."

We walked the three blocks to 138th Street. I looked in the faces of girls and at the bodies of women and saw them differently now that I had made love to Alice. We settled on Sally's because it had a professional sign instead of a crude, hand lettered one. It did not follow that the food would be any better, but Ned said everybody knew Sally's was clean. There were samples of fried fish, chicken, pork chops and ham displayed in the window.

"First thing you look for is roaches and flies," he said picking up the menu. "You see flies in the window, they'll be buzzing around your table. Uncle Bob's got good food and it's cheap, but he's got roaches. You tell him about it and all he says is 'Roaches got to eat, too.'"

"I thought Mamma Alexis had the best food."

"Yeah, but there's no place to sit. You have to take the food home unless you want to stay and party. A lot of people don't want to be eating dinner hanging around somebody else's house."

A young waitress came to take our order. Her eyes devoured Ned; I think she wanted him to flirt with her but he didn't. For several moments after she left, we were cloaked in silence.

" - How'd you like the Navy?" I ventured.

"Merchant Marine," he corrected. "O.K., I guess. Wasn't what I was looking for. Expected to be a real able-bodied seaman but ended up being a mess boy."

"Where'd you go?"

"Lots of places. Didn't stay in any one place long, though. We went all along South America, then over to Africa. Didn't get to Europe till near the end of the war"

"What was the best place?"

"...Probably France. Worst was North Africa. Whites own it, Arabs run it and Africans just live there."

Our food came and we occupied ourselves with that for a while. I cast about for something sensible to say. I didn't want him to think I was just a little boy who had to be dragged from the arms of a woman and sheltered from harm's way.

"You still want to be a businessman, Ned?"

He smiled ruefully. "You still remember that...I don't know. Not like before, but we're going to need businessmen in Africa. Something might pop up, but that's not why I'm going. I'm going because of white people. I'm going before I end up killing one of them or they kill me, so why wait around.

"I've lived around them all my life, so have you. Went to school with them. Some I liked and some I didn't. But I understand them. It's like they're dogs and we're cats so what do you expect? Like Marcus says, they treat everybody bad, not just us. They don't like Jews, they don't like Catholics, they call Italians, Polish people, Puerto Ricans names, and they murdered all the Indians."

He looked at me, his fork poised over his plate. "- But you know something? All those people had each other. They stuck together, stood shoulder to shoulder. We don't. The white man kicks you in the ass, and niggers come along and kick you in the balls. Maybe the color-crazy ones are the worst. Marcus is going to change all that. In Liberia we'll be one for all and all for one.

"Right now, I have to keep looking over my shoulder ever since I hit that cop. I know half a dozen niggers - and that's what they are, *niggers* - I know they ran to the cops and told them who I was. Know how many times I've moved just in the last month? Three times, and getting ready to move again.

"All we want is to get the hell away from here. We want to be together with people we can trust and love and respect. Just let us get away from here; that's all we ask! You'd think white people would pay us to go instead of trying to bring Marcus down."

We ate in silence for a while. Several flies did find their way into the restaurant, droning around the room and around my head. Impatiently I brushed them away. The waitress came over with a fly swatter, a smile in Ned's direction, and loudly dispatched one.

"...I left here once," Ned remembered, "but you see I came back. A lot of guys stayed in France after the war, but a lot of us eventually came back for one reason or another. That's knowing full well that nothing was going to be any different here. Sounds stupid, like we wanted to be mistreated.

"Me, I came back because I was worried about who'd take care of me if I ever got sick or died. Might sound funny but that's what worried me the most. I never wanted to die and have Mom not know I was dead. I didn't want to be anonymous.

"Won't be any coming back this time, though. Things'll be a whole lot different. We'll all be there together depending on each other, caring about each other. It'll be different. The last time I left I was mad; you'll never know how mad I was. I'd have blown up the whole world if I could have.

"When I was in France, I felt like a stranger in somebody else's house wondering where the bathroom was. Everywhere I looked all I saw were white people. Every place I went I'd look around hoping to see another colored face. Sometimes I did and we'd nod or smile.

"The French were nice enough, but things always felt temporary. Like I was a guest and knew I'd have to leave soon. Now we'll be moving to where we belong and everybody knows everybody, like we're all related."

He spoke as though I were grown and could understand the hidden corners of his life. I held his eye and nodded to let him see that I understood and that I cared and that he could speak to me of things that were important to him.

"Aunt Gloria wrote to me about going to Europe a couple of years ago when everybody was so upset. She never said, don't go - just make sure I had plenty of money. She said people who talk about places like Paris and London and Spain were all on vacation. She said no matter where I went to live, I'd have to earn a living. Finding a job in Europe would be no better than finding one here. Maybe worse. I'd be a foreigner. She was right, too."

" - You ever meet any girls?"

"A few, but I never really felt comfortable with them. I kept asking myself, 'Why's she being nice to me? What would her mother say if she saw me? Is this for real?' In this country if you're colored, white people act like you're an ugly monster. Maybe you start to believe you're an ugly monster since people keep acting like it's true. Maybe that's why I was always wondering, 'Does she really like me?'

"I could never get deep enough to really know any of them. You want to know what's really behind that smile; what does the look in her eyes really mean. Everything was just on the surface - it's hard to explain...."

We finished eating but neither of us made a move to leave. He asked if I wanted dessert and I said yes so we wouldn't have to leave; I wanted him to keep talking to me. We skirted the edges of conversation until our pie and coffee came. He slowly stirred his coffee, then caught me off guard.

"Nobody should be going to Africa just because they're mad," he said. "That's something I learned the hard way. You'll just be running away from yourself. You can't because you carry yourself everywhere you go."

I stalled for time, sipping coffee. "- You think I'm just mad about something?"

"I didn't ask you about last night and I won't. Some things you want to keep to yourself. But something bad happened. I'm not asking, but you're mad."

He had been frank with me so I said yes, I was angry. Angry because it seemed to me that any rejection of me because I was dark-skinned was boasting that light skin was better and white skin was best of all. And wasn't that validating the white man's claim that Negroes were inferior? How could you fight such insidious poison unless you burned it away with towering anger? Either that or supinely believe that you were indeed an "ugly monster" fit only to hide, even from the face of God.

Elizabeth had been the final straw of a mountain of straws. He heard about Elizabeth from the moment I had seen her golden face until the moment she clicked across the sidewalk to go to the embrace of Moose Schlitz. We both knew that if I stayed in the restaurant any longer, I would embarrass myself. I was beginning to bray my outrage for the entire world to hear. We left and linked arms and retraced our steps.

" - I guess Mom and Dad will be disappointed and say we got discouraged," I said.

His lips tightened. "There's a hell of a lot to be discouraged about. Granddad knows it."

"They do, too, but they're still going to say if something gets in your way just go around it. But isn't that why we're talking about Africa - to get around it?"

He took his time answering as we paced along the pavement. "They don't mean leaving the country; they mean staying here, getting humiliated every day. What you don't know is Dad always had the Woolmans to look out for him. When she died, she left Dad some money in her will."

I didn't bother to tell him that I already knew this, but Ned had more to tell me.

"I always said Dad was lucky," he went on, but he always claimed it wasn't luck. For some reason white people liked him. They were good to him. How do you think he got the house? They bought it, and then deducted a certain amount out of his pay each month - like rent. How do you think he got to be pastor of that church? He used some of the money that Mrs. Woolman left him to take over the mortgage when they fell behind and couldn't pay it. He all but *owns* the church.

"Dad can afford to talk about 'going around' obstacles. I don't think he ever had any obstacles to speak of. It sure didn't hurt when Mrs. Woolman found out Granddad and her husband fought together in the Civil War. Dad's been one lucky man. I'm glad for him, but this crap about going around obstacles is just his imagination!"

I'd already begun to wonder how Dad could remain pastor of the church since half the people left when the other guy died. Dad wasn't able to yell and froth at the mouth and drive women into a frenzy like the other guy could. And he damn sure couldn't make enough from collections to pay himself a salary. But what did it matter if he had money from the will and had a job?

Later, mounting the front steps of his apartment building, Ned said causally, "I have to get my uniform. I can get you into the convention tonight."

Chapter 38

Liberty Hall was a squat building that had once been an open foundation dug for some other purpose. Garvey had erected a building on the site, but it never managed to look complete. The building was rather plain inside except for the ornate, great meeting hall with Garvey's throne at the far end.

On the streets surrounding Liberty Hall, red, black and green bunting and streamers decorated store front windows and wound around telephone poles; red, black and green flags fluttered from apartment windows. The street outside Liberty Hall was crowded with throngs of people impatient to enter. Somebody complained that it was worse than trying to see Jack Johnson fight Jeffries.

Police formed people into lines. A semi-circle of Garvey's officers guarded the entrance to Liberty Hall. They examined credentials of delegates, passed some people through, denied admittance to others. Several uniformed men of the African Legion moved through the crowd plucking invited guests from the crowd hoping for admittance. Once we had shouldered our way inside Ned said, "I can't get you a seat out front, but I can get you a seat backstage. You can't see anything, but you can hear. You have to be quiet."

In the dimness backstage, ten or fifteen others were seated on folding chairs. Self-conscious, I inserted myself among them. Ned went back outside to help manage the crowd.

A woman in front of me fanned herself against the heat. When the convention began, I never felt the need to see anything, but it was an elevating experience to hear Negroes speak, one after another, in quiet, cultured, reasoning tones, with British, German, French and Italian accents. Eventually, four men were summoned to stand before the convention: a surveyor, an agriculturist, a pharmacist and a builder.

"These are our brains," a voice explained. "Soon, they sail for LIBERIA. They are the first of many who will go to prepare a place for those of us who shall follow!"

The roar of applause was a force that moved the stage curtain, revealing small beams of light along the curtain edges. Into the maelstrom of applause, the voice bellowed, "THIS IS NO 'DREAM,' this is REAL!" precipitating another storm of approval.

"Thank the Lord Jesus!" moaned the lady with the fan, shaking her head with tearful emotion.

"Jesus and Marcus Garvey!" said the lady sitting beside her. "Jesus set one foot free and Marcus freed the other!"

"Amen!" nodded the man next to me. He was solemn and appeared to be in his fifties.

It felt awkward being the youngest one there, but impulsively I reached over to the solemn man and clasped his hand. He seized mine with both of his and we vigorously pumped our clasped hands up and down.

"We're on our way, now, son!" he murmured in a husky voice. "They can't stop us now. We got the ships, we got the land, we got the people. I know I'm going to be on the first ship that sails!"

Suddenly, shouts of *"Marcus!"* followed by a loud commotion of chairs scraping the floor and bodies moving, accompanied by shouts of, "Marcus!" Instantly others took it up, crying - *"Marcus! Marcus!"* Unable to contain himself, the solemn man leapt from his seat. By the time he reached the curtain, the rest of us had left our seat, too. Pulling back the edge of the heavy curtain, we saw Marcus Garvey standing alone in the center of the stage. He was dressed in an academic gown. His head was thrown back, his arms stretched out and up. He stood motionless. Wave after wave of *"Marcus! Marcus! Marcus! Marcus"* washed over him.

Slowly he lowered his arms. He stood motionless for several moments.

"Why," he asked quietly, as though to a child, "are you shouting?" He surveyed the audience for a moment. "Haven't you heard? - 'You will never get to Africa,' he mimicked. 'You are foolish Negroes of the lowest kind; ignorant Negroes fresh from the cotton fields!'"

There was a roar of laughter.

"Why are you here? Haven't you heard how foolish you are? You should go home. You are wasting your money. 'Marcus Garvey is a *thief!* Marcus Garvey is a fat *ugly ape*; intelligent people will have nothing to do with Marcus Garvey. Your ships will never sail; you will never buy land in Liberia.'

"Why have you delegates come here from as far away as East Africa, Liberia, Nigeria, South Africa, Haiti, Brazil, Ethiopia! - *Why have you come to listen to an ugly fat man who is a thief?*

"Well, I tell you now, and I will tell you true," he cried with fire in his voice. "It is you, all of you, and all of us who have the wisdom. It is we who will prevail in this. We will win! Europe for the Europeans; Asia for the Asians, AFRICA FOR THE AFRICANS!"

The throng took it up, chanting ever louder: "AFRICA FOR THE AFRICANS! - AFRICA FOR THE AFRICANS! - AFRICA FOR THE AFRICANS!"

Nothing could hold back the rush of cheering men and women; nothing could withstand the wave of hope, the sense of triumph. The African Legion lining the front of the stage was swept aside, unable to hold back the wild surge of uncontrollable love.

Those of us behind the curtain gave up all pretense of decorum. We rushed to stand in the wings, staring unabashedly at the sea of people who crowded the stage and the aisles, all hoping to touch this man, to speak to him face to face - this Moses who had come to offer each man unconditional manhood and each woman dignity, pride and respect.

Now I knew for certain - before the night was over - that I would go to Liberia with Ned and Marcus Garvey. Tomorrow was truly ours; we needed only to reach out and touch it. It was there, almost a visible, palpable thing.

*****

The next morning as he dressed, Ned said I could stay for the parade if I wanted, but after that he was putting me on the bus. I opened my mouth to protest but he shook his head.

"I kept my end of the bargain. There's nothing for you to do here. You can't live in a room all day or just walk the streets. And I have to worry about the cops breaking in."

There was no getting around it. I knew he was right. Unspoken was his fear that I would see Alice again and meet Buster Matthew face to face. Then I would have to decide whether to protect her or sacrifice her - and run for my life as he had done. Yesterday it seemed as though that would never happen, but the prospect of entering her again and washing away the reality of Elizabeth was a powerful narcotic. That she was a grown woman only intensified her allure.

After Ned left, there were hours to kill before the UNIA parade began. I left the airless room to roam the streets and take in the sights and sounds of Harlem. Several blocks from the apartment, a slender girl approached taking long rapid strides that spoke self-assurance. I measured the width of her hips and tried to guess what her legs would look like beneath her skirt.

She was dark with sloe eyes and long, black eyelashes. Catching my eye, she paused for a brief second. With a start I recognized Melissa. I immediately removed my hat, words of greeting on my lips, but she swept past me. I hurried after her.

"Melissa, wait up! Don't you recognize me?"

"Yes, I recognize you!" she flung over her shoulder. "Everyone recognizes you. You do rudeness. You are not right for a respectable girl, not even to be seen with. You must go away."

Puzzled, I caught up to her and fell in beside her. "What are you talking about? I never did anything to you. I only saw you once."

She stopped in the middle of the sidewalk, eyes blazing. "It's stupidness you talking. You were disgraceful in my mother's house! Yes, you were, you cannot deny it. Alice is too old for you. She has done lived a lifetime. She's a grown lady! And she's not respectable. She gave you evil things to drink when I gave you food. *It was a bacchanal!* You were disgraceful. That is why I got your brother," She stormed. "- Oh, do not look so surprised. It was I who instructed your brother on what he must do! Yes, *I*. I am not ashamed of it!"

She whirled away abruptly. I chased after her. "And who," she flung over her shoulder, "left the house like a sneak the next day? And what of her? - *The woman is in hiding now!* Afraid for her very life because her man means to kill her and he is known to do so! She is a terrible woman, that Alice. She does rudeness everywhere she goes and her man is insane and chases after her trying to kill every fool who looks at her. She will be dead. You will be next. You will be mighty dead, you can be certain of that!"

Alice in hiding? My God! Was it only yesterday that she had come to the room and left so full of confidence? Buster Matthew must really be angry, maybe enough to throw caution to the winds and come after me despite what Ned's friends said.

I didn't try to defend myself to Melissa. I had very conflicting and mingled emotions because I suddenly realized that Melissa liked me. It was Alice that she was angry about. She probably thought I should have stayed in the kitchen with her and waited until she was done her chores instead of wandering off with someone else a lot older than I was. At the same time I wondered what Buster Matthew would do to Alice if he found her.

I trailed along keeping pace with Melissa's long, purposeful strides. She refused to speak to me. When we reached the house, she went inside, nose in the air, leaving me standing on the sidewalk. Having nothing better to do, I waited outside and sure enough, fifteen minutes later she came out again, sweeping by me on yet another errand. Undaunted I walked beside her. The third time she came out of the house she deigned to notice me.

"Some people don't know when they're not wanted," she sniffed.

"Some people don't know when other people admire them."

"Some people should think before they do rash things."

"Some people are very sorry they made such a fool of themselves. Some people humbly apologize."

Little by little she relented, shooting sidelong glances in my direction. It took a while before we were able to piece together a conversation between her coming and going.

"I was at the convention last night," I offered. "They're having the parade today; are you going?"

She brightened. "- Yes! And you were truly *there*? Oh, you are such a lucky boy! My father is so angry he could not get a ticket. He said those who buy bonds in the Universal Negro Improvement Association should be considered before anyone else. He was one of the first to buy bonds.

Now he refuses to see the parade though it is a wonder to behold."

"- Are you going alone?"

"...And tell me why do you ask such a question?"

"Maybe we could go together."

She looked at me sideways. "...My mother would oppose that. She is very disappointed in you. She expected higher things from Ned's brother and from a boy who is being educated in college."

"...Would it help if I went to her and apologized for my behavior?"

She thought about it for a while, not breaking her stride. "My mother is a strange woman who loves to hold a grudge if you give her tribulation. She says it gives her warmth and strength."

" - She would rather hate me than forgive me?"

"A grudge is not hate. It gives my mother warmth. I will go with you, but I will meet you there."

"I'd rather apologize. Really, I don't mind."

"...I will tell my mother that you wanted me to go with you but were too afraid of her to ask. And if for truth it could be true that you were foolish, I will bring you back to apologize and she must forgive you for your negligence."

I did not fully understand what she said, but I liked how it sounded. I said yes, I would meet her there.

*****

We waited for the parade on a warm summer day, munching peanuts and scattering the shells at our feet.

The sidewalks were crowded with people either gawking at Garvey's administrators on the reviewing stand across from us, or peering expectantly down 138th Street for sight or sign of the parade. Parents cautioned children to stay out of the street, to quit squirming. Others found things to laugh about, jostling each other, pointing and making little jokes to pass the time.

Melissa stood in front of me and when I pressed too close to her firm body, she pushed me back with her elbows but there was no reproach in her movement. We leaned forward peering down the street, waiting for the parade, glad of our nearness that spoke of things we could not say.

Boom-boom-boom drifted on the wind, mingled with the distant summons of bugles. Those milling about on the reviewing stand, in front of UNIA headquarters, scurried to their places. Self-conscious, they squared their shoulders, standing rigid and unsmiling in uniforms with white plumed hats, with swords at their side. One man affected a flaming red cloak. He was stocky and stood with one fist resting on his hip.

"That is Sir Mosley," Melissa said a little awed, "and see her? She is Lady Sarah."

Lady Sarah was a tall light-skinned woman who wore a green and purple academic cap and gown. Melissa eagerly pointed out others on the stand. She seemed to know them all.

" - Here they come!" a boy yelled. "I see 'em!"

In the distance, swinging around a corner, came line after line of uniformed figures with flags fluttering. The figures paced to the steady boom-boom-boom of the drums. Spectators leaned forward in anticipation. Boys in knickers hanging loosely down their legs, and cap brims pulled to the side, noisily shouldered their way to the front so they could strut in the street beside the marching men. They reminded me of Boo Boy.

With dark scowls, policemen stationed at intervals along the parade route sent them scurrying back. All along the parade route, those who were more fortunate simply flung up their bedroom windows and leaned out, or stood on their front doorsteps where they could easily see over the heads of the crowd.

On came the marchers in red, black and green, the colors of the soon-to-be new African Nation. *Stomp-stomp-stomp, boom-boom-boom.* With knees pumping high, they grew larger than life with each step they took. Heralded by trumpets, trombones and bugles - high stepping, stern looking dark men with gleaming black boots, the Royal African Guard strutted into view.

"Dress - left - Huh!" their captain shouted, pointing his gleaming sword. "Dress right - Huh! - To the rear - *Huh!*"

To and fro they stomped before the reviewing stand, drawing loud applause and shouts from the crowd. Finally, they moved on, staring rigidly and fiercely ahead - conscious that all eyes were on them - *stomp-stomp-stomp, boom-boom-boom.*

Now came other fierce looking Negro men with flags flowing and bugles blowing. They were the African Legion. Their captains, too, brandished, shiny swords and bellowed, "Forward - *Huh!*"

"There's Ned!" I blurted, pointing to his tall, handsome and noble figure high stepping and stomping along. Staring fiercely ahead and brandishing a shiny sword, he cried, "Dress right -Huh!" Glorious pride swept through me.

Melissa clapped her hands with pure joy. "They're *our* people!" she cried, brown eyes gleaming. "They're ours, Aaron, they're ours, they belong to *us!*"

Caught up in the panoply of proud figures, shining swords, gleaming rifles, and uniforms splashed with red, green and black, I felt a wonderful thrill course down my spine.

"...That's what I'm going to be!" I promised her fervently.

She took my hand firmly in hers.

The Universal Negro Improvement Association meant to display its full strength for all the world and Harlem to see. The parade was long and wonderful. There were the Black Cross nurses, resembling Catholic nuns in white habits.

"Ohh, do you see them?" Melissa whispered. "Don't they look so lovely and so competent."

The Black Star Line Band passed the stand and after them a large troop of juveniles. The girls wore white middy blouses and sailor caps while the boys were dressed in white sailor uniforms. Close behind them, proudly strutted the women of the African Motor Corps in military uniforms and boots.

After a long pause, a loud cheer erupted far down the flag draped street. It quickly grew into a roar.

"Marcus!" the cry went up, "It's Marcus!"

Everyone pressed forward, a huge mob that had to be held back.

"Marcus! Marcus!"

Presently a large open sedan surrounded by a proud honor guard slowly rolled into view. We saw Marcus Garvey seated in the back of the sedan. People standing behind us, eager for a glimpse of him, pushed forward, thrusting us further into the street. Garvey's splendid uniform was fashioned after that worn by the French Marshall Joffre during the Great War. The gold, curved hat was topped with white plumes, his thick shoulders bore gold epaulets. Gold and red piping finished the sleeves of his uniform and he waved white gloved hands at the crowds of smiling admirers who waved back. There were those who craned their neck to catch a glimpse of his legendary gold sword, but in his seated position it was not visible so it remained for all time just a legend.

This was the man who had spoken to me so openly not so long ago! He willed the best of us and the worst of us to rise up from the dust. He looked directly at me as he passed and I burst with pride though I know he only saw a sea of eyes and heard thousands of voices of love chanting - "Marcus! Marcus! Marcus!"

The walls of prejudice were gone. Those unforgiving, relentless walls that my grandfather charged, the walls that threw Ned back, that squelched my mother's ambitions, the unassailable racial walls that my father only imagined he crept around. And, too, the walls of light skin versus dark skin. Like the walls of Jericho, Marcus Garvey would make them crumble before me and Ned, and all of us who believed in him and chose to follow him back to Africa.

Intoxicated with emotion and abandoning all thought of home, of family, of college of yesterday or tomorrow, I spoke to Melissa who still stood in front of me, in terms of forever. I encircled her with my arms. Our heads were touching.

"-Would you go to Africa with me?" I asked her quietly.

I do not know why I asked her that; I think it somehow made the day seem more real, something permanent. The day had to be more than just a parade. It had to be a way of life. A promise. A thing that extended emotion into reality.

What I asked her was impulsive and emotional, yet it was also an affirmation of who I was now - a person in my own right who could beat back "No!" and say "I will" and go to Africa if I wished to do so.

And with that affirmation I could believe that one day I really would have my telescope, and I would dig for shards in the ancient meeting places of my ancestors. It was a glowing possibility that magic summer day.

What could go wrong?

She turned her head and examined my face for a moment, her clear eyes were searching for an answer. Then she nodded.

"Perhaps," she said quietly. "Perhaps."

END

AUTHOR'S NOTES

Unfortunately, the ships never sailed.

Marcus M. Garvey, a Jamaican, founded the Universal Negro Improvement Association (UNIA) with the purpose of giving Negroes, worldwide, a sense of pride in their race, and a belief in their personal worth. By1920, the organization claimed a membership of over 6 million. Over time, the UNIA established educational and economic opportunities for their followers. The Negro Factories Corporation provided employment through its grocery stores, restaurants, tailor shops, laundries, hotel and doll factory. Their Universal Printing House published the highly successful, *The Negro World* which agitated for Negro rights.

The *World* - also printed in French and Spanish - circulated not only in the United States, but also throughout the Caribbean, Central and South America and parts of Africa. European colonial powers, fearful that *The Negro World's* influence would destroy their authority, banned the paper in Cuba, Trinidad, Guyana, Jamaica, and Ghana among others colonies. Nevertheless, by 1926 the UNIA had grown to a membership of eleven million worldwide.

Despite their growth, the Universal Negro Improvement Association always met with strong, continuous opposition. Surprisingly, it was not only from colonial powers. In America, they were opposed by a variety of politicians and Black leaders. The most prominent and influential Black leader was W.E.B. Dubois.

Dubois vociferously disapproved of Garvey personally, as well as his goal of repatriating Negroes back to Africa. Black leaders in general sided with DuBois. They equated Garvey's goals with condoning and surrendering to racist segregation, instead of fighting for racial equality. More, the UNIA came to the attention of J. Edgar Hoover, director of the FBI.

Undeterred, Garvey founded the Black Star Line, a shipping and passenger line. In addition to shipping merchandise throughout the Black global economy, it would also be used to repatriate Blacks back to their ancestral home beginning with settlements in Liberia.

That would never happen for a number of reasons.

A major reason was the ships that were foisted on the UNIA. They were not only hugely overpriced but also in need of major renovation. The *SS Shady Side,* for instance, was a *paddle ship* that sprang a leak and sank a year later. The *Maceo Calso* blew a boiler, killing a crewman. *SS Yarmouth*, a coal ship used during WWI, was in service sporadically but eventually had to be sold for scrap.

As for the FBI involvement, J. Edgar Hoover, convinced that the racial unifying aims of the Universal Negro Improvement Association, posed an imminent threat to the nation, determined to thwart Garvey. Hoover used his first Black agent, James Wormley Jones, to infiltrate the UNIA. Another spy, Herbert Boulin, managed to inveigle his way to becoming a close confidant of Garvey. Another agent was suspected of throwing foreign material into a ship's fuel tank.

Finally, the Back-to-Africa movement collapsed when the mismanaged Black Star Line went bankrupt. Marcus Garvey was subsequently accused by the government of fraud for selling stocks and bonds in a ship before the UNIA formally took ownership of it.

The charges were widely viewed by many as a technicality that was racially and politically orchestrated by those opposed to the UNIA. Nevertheless, Hoover seized the opportunity to have Garvey prosecuted. Garvey was found guilty and sentenced to five years in prison.

After serving two years of his sentence, Garvey's term was commuted by President Calvin Coolidge. Garvey was deported back to Jamaica where he was, and is now, widely regarded as a national hero. His statue was erected in his birthplace, Saint Ann's Bay.

Marcus Garvey's push for racial equality is credited with influencing later political leaders of Nigeria, Kenya, Ghana, South Africa, Republic of Congo and Tanzania in addition to Americans such as Martin Luther King, Jr., Elijah Muhammad and Malcolm X.

There is a supreme irony of the Garvey/DuBois conflict.

Marcus Garvey never set foot in Africa while W.E.B. DuBois did. He not only went to Africa in the sixties, but he became a citizen of the African nation of Ghana and is buried there.